A Sudden Country

A SUDDEN COUNTRY

A NOVEL

Karen Fisher

RANDOM HOUSE

NEW YORK

Copyright © 2005 by Karen Fisher

All rights reserved. Published in the United States by Random House, an imprint of The Random House Publishing Group, a division of Random House, Inc., New York.

RANDOM HOUSE and colophon are registered trademarks of Random House, Inc.

LIBRARY OF CONGRESS CATALOGING-IN-PUBLICATION DATA
Fisher, Karen.
    A sudden country : a novel / Karen Fisher.
        p.   cm.
    ISBN 1-4000-6322-1
    1. Overland journeys to the Pacific—Fiction.   2. Oregon National
Historic Trail—Fiction.   3. Hudson's Bay Company—Fiction.
4. Women pioneers—Fiction.   5. Whitman Massacre—Fiction.
6. Wagon trains—Fiction.   7. Oregon—Fiction.   I. Title.

PS3606.I776S83 2005
813'.6—dc22

                                                                    2004054179

Printed in the United States of America on acid-free paper

www.atrandom.com

9 8 7 6 5 4 3 2 1

FIRST EDITION

Book design by Lisa Sloane
Map illustration by George W. Ward

For Dave

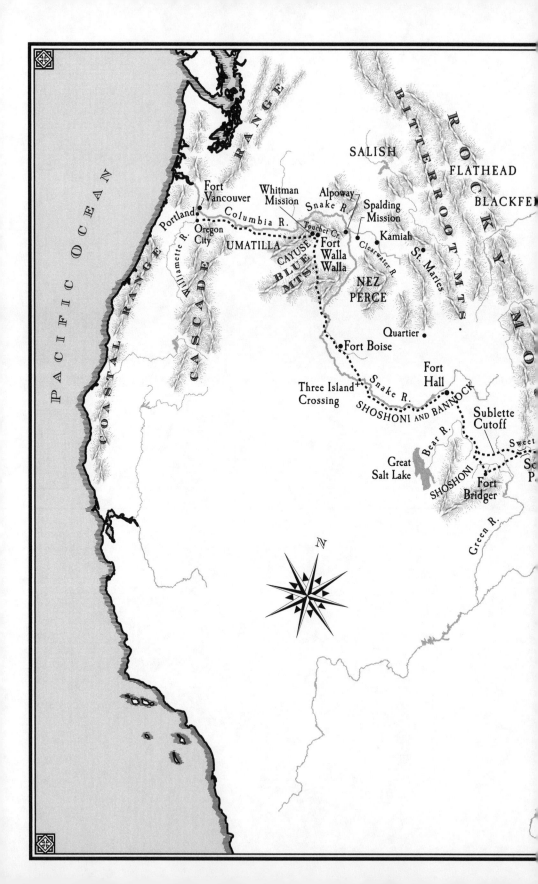

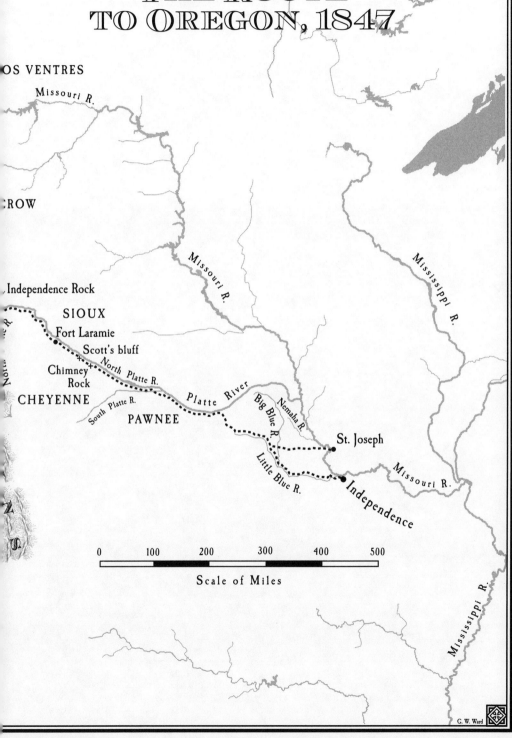

THE ROUTE
TO OREGON, 1847

OS VENTRES

Missouri R.

CROW

Missouri R.

Mississippi R.

Independence Rock

SIOUX

Fort Laramie

Scott's bluff

Chimney Rock

North Platte R.

CHEYENNE

South Platte R.

PAWNEE

Platte River

Big Blue R.

Nemaha R.

St. Joseph

Little Blue R.

Independence

Missouri R.

Mississippi R.

| 0 | 100 | 200 | 300 | 400 | 500 |

Scale of Miles

G. W. Ward

Part One

❧

So we see that sorrow may be good or bad according to the several results it produces in us. And indeed there are more bad than good results arising from it, for the only good ones are mercy and repentence; whereas there are six evil results, namely anguish, sloth, indignation, jealousy, envy, and impatience. The Wise Man says that "sorrow hath killed many and there is no profit therein," and that because for the two good streams which flow from the spring of sadness, there are these six which are downright evil.

—St. Francis de Sales,
"On Sadness and Sorrow"

THERE ALONE

⟋⟍⟍⟋

$\mathcal{H}$E CARRIED HIS GIRL tied to his front, the trapsack on his back, the
rifle balanced like a yoke along his shoulders. He walked all day on snowshoes, lost in effort, in steady breathing. The snow drove thick and clotted
on his eyebrows, filled his beard. It cluttered his drawing breath.

He'd left the cabin, his valley with its knoll of pines. In the barn, the
wind had pulled the uneaten hay and scattered it. He'd left the saddles, stiff
with frost. The horses had run off.

There had been a pass to climb. A north wind to bear against. He'd
thought to catch the clearing weather, though each night the moon grew
smaller.

"Are you there, June?"

He made halt with his back to the wind. Took off his mittens, blew on
his hands to thaw them. She stirred in the bundled blanket.

"Let me see."

Her hands emerged. MacLaren tried to feel them, but his own hands
were too cold.

"All right?"

She nodded. She'd cried the night before, a sad thin wail against him in
the stinging wind. He kept looking at her fingers, held them balled inside his
hand. He squinted at the sky. In all the world now was nothing but the two
of them, and white.

AT MIDDAY, he unlaced his snowshoes, stood them on their tails. Knocked the ice out of his beard, lit a fire, stripped balsam boughs for tea. The snow had quit.

When water boiled, she took the blanket from him, held it tented as he'd shown her, so she could breathe the clearing steam. Her hair was damp, eyes murky gray like his. He watched her fingers curl around coarse wool. He put the steaming pot beside her.

All his life, he'd only gone from one thing to the next, only done what needed doing. His world had all been wood and water, fire, food; it had all been journeys needing made, traplines to set, a world of things to mend and mind with never time enough. But these past few weeks had taught a different kind of seeing. It was as though such endless diligence had muffled him somehow. But here now were the curled edges of his daughter's ermine scarf, and he could see the hairs stir in the wind, and could see each crack and split in her small lips. He had learned, in these past weeks, the shapes of her knees, her feet, had seen her secret skin. He knew the hard black scabs of scars she would come to live with. If he could command it.

She looked at him.

You are mine, he thought. With his eyes, again, he saved her.

She began to cough. He waited. Fed the fire. The wind came up and sprang the pines, and showered them with snow.

HE CAME OFF the forest slopes into the river valley in a waning daylight moon. It took less strength to plod along than to see what shelter he could find, what fuel to make a fire. Everything was frozen. And he'd worked like this, in winter, his whole life, but always in the company of men. It was terrible to stop, to see how small she lay without him, waiting for some warmth.

At last, in a cove of pines, he trod the snow and floored the camp in boughs. Made rough shelter. Hacked down limbs and shook them.

He put the meat to boil, and listened to her breathing. He closed his eyes and waited.

One morning after he had made the graves, he'd stood and watched the wind blow down the snow, watched it spill off the laden pines, drift glittering through the blue. Each joint and twig of aspen lined in snow, a faery openwork of black and white. It hardly seemed the world should be so beautiful. He'd walked out past the barn and seen, on all the stumps and posts and rails, a dazzling crest. A herd of elk was feeding off his snowy hay, yarded up content as horses. He'd shot a cow, cut the meat to carry.

He woke to the stink of his blanket burning.

She was curled against him, her hand inside his coat. Until these recent weeks, it was always Lise she'd clung to. He'd never known this kind of flattery, or what it was to be a source of comfort. Now he heard the rattle in her lungs, like glue.

He'd come to think he could refuse to sleep. That a man could stay awake.

When Lispat went, he'd been sleeping. Lispat—Elizabeth—her lanky legs, sly eyes, the cheekbones like her mother's. She'd raged at the last for scissors, as though she might still cut some figure out of paper. She was ten. He'd had the fever himself by then, and was tired. Go to sleep, he'd said, and left her. Not believing any child of his could die so easily.

He remembered the dry grief cracking out. He'd stood in the doorway's glare, panic-stripped and heaving.

The ground was hard, he'd had no strength to bury her. He kept her for two days inside, then hauled her onto the ridgepole for fear of wolves. He came to fear his own sleep after that as well, for the losing of his other two. He stayed awake. He talked to them. Tried to cool their faces, keep the chill away. The fire he would keep alive.

Five days of fever turned to chill. Engorgement of the flesh. Suppuration. All his life he'd worked with men who had survived, seen women scarred, seen children blinded or made deaf, but now they owned that horror: variola. Agony, exact and inevasible, every surface real, remembered, the eyes, the tongue, the palms that closed around the cup, the soles on which he walked. His lungs shot through as though he had breathed lye. And no one in a hundred miles to know it.

"*Tota?*" June would call as he was dozing.

Alexander suffered it ten days. His golden child of two. Blessed release. He remembered carrying him outside, how the bright cold hit them. In the snow against the cabin wall, his legs had given out. He remembered sinking with his boy in his arms, waking sometime later. Remembered the horror of the snow, which had fallen while they slept, and lay unmelted in those curling palms.

So he and June, his middle child, were left. Still burning. Each breath disturbed what only begged for peace, each effort broke what little surface might be healing, but he tried to answer when she called. He lay festering in his robes, and moaned and would have been glad for death but for the night-mare fear that she'd be left alone. He would not die and leave her there alone. So he stayed, insensible of days and nights or that the horses had run off, until the sores began to melt together and stiffen into solid sheets like bark that split and stank, and he thought the two of them might live. And, for a silent fortnight, they had.

He pulled June's head against him. Smelled her hair. Six days, he thought. Six more, if he could do it. Then there would be rest.

———

THE SUN ROSE in a yellow band below the gray. By midday the sky was clearing. He'd reached the plain along the river, now followed that valley north. Blackfeet, Gros Ventres—he saw no villages, no sign, but they were there. He was making for the mission, St. Marie's. The Jesuits had come out two years before. They had built a crude hall and a palisade against the Blackfeet, who resented them. Their work was with the better tribes: Flat-head, Salish. To bring them God and learning. To heal their sick.

"I'll take you there," he'd promised, when her lungs began to fail. "They'll help you. They'll have something."

At noon he stopped for longer than he meant to rest, and by dusk he was all but ruined. An ache had lodged in the backs of his legs since the fever, and would turn to knives, but the land here afforded nothing. He kept on, though his eyes were falling shut, his course wavering. The plain was too ex-posed. At last he made a camp above the river. It took two hours to find some wood and light it.

He boiled the meat by starlight. They heard voices in the silence, swells of laughter, a distant gathering in happy conversation.

"*Tota?*"

"Hey."

She lay watching him. The whites of her eyes shone in the faint light.

"Can all people fly? After they be dead?"

He said, "Did your mother teach you that?"

"She said some go in the water."

"It's the river you hear," he said. "The river's moving under ice, that's all."

"Tota."

He woke. The sky was filled with stars.

"Tota. I'm cold. Tota."

She fevered, spooned against him, almost touching the last coals.

He reached for the wood behind him, put a few small pieces on.

"*Tota*, when will Sally come back?"

He closed his eyes, saw their horses homing through the snow—against the dark, he dreamed them flying, spinning through the heavy drifts, the spray of ice, steam roiling from their nostrils. The branches, in their wake, freed and springing.

"I don't know," he said. "I'll go out after thaw and find her."

None of them had asked about their mother. They hadn't seen Lise go. He'd told them that first lie and never told another, and wondered since if they'd known more than he. But hadn't found the strength to ask.

"The fire wants more."

She said this—as though she'd read his thoughts—in her mother's tongue, Nez Perce. He answered in the same. "He can't have more. Not here. Do you know why?"

She nodded.

Sometime next day he saw the sun a failing silver, veiled in ice. The snow began to rise and slide in ribbons. He tied his hat. He tucked his chin against her, bore along the hissing gusts, ice scouring his cheeks; it stung his eyes like sand and melted into tears. He blinked and wiped them, kept the river on his right. It was better on a day like this to move than to keep still.

He'd had to force her to drink tea that morning. Now, helping her to make her water, he saw her wasted thighs, the skin not honey brown, as it had been, but clay. Her breath was worse. She choked. She bleated, trembling.

"Stay with it," he tried to say. No sound came out. He said, "It's you and me. The two of us."

That night he set a twelve-foot pine alight, and slept in falling sparks, and held her fevering close against him.

———

WITH DAWN CAME ease, then quiet. The snowflakes warmed and fattened, idled down. They could be close but had no way to tell; the sky was blank, the horizon sifted into nothing by the snow.

And he'd thought she might not make it, but it couldn't ease those hours. Kneeling at wet coals. The pine's black skeleton was steaming. Nothing lit. Nothing lit. She wailed. He sat and held her head. He'd have given her his life but only gave the blankets from around his feet when she told him hers were cold.

She said, "I want to stop."

"We'll stop. We'll stop the day."

His feet were bare. The snow had quit. Chickadees were peeping in the boughs.

"Tell me Elisabetta."

Elisabetta, the white bear, had danced like a woman if a fiddler played. She'd smiled and swayed her hips. He swallowed. Like ashes in his throat. All the features of his mind seemed gray and flattened. He couldn't remember what to say.

"A long time ago, when I was young . . ."

"On the stony beaches."

"On the stony beaches of the north," he said, "there lived a beautiful white bear. And her name was Elisabetta."

He tried to tell it, as he had so many times. When her breath went still and the color drained, he put her down and climbed the low rise behind him and started calling out for help. He called and called like a madman, until he was hoarse, until the icy snot ran down his face and all his breath was gone. But of course, no one was in this world to hear him.

CONFINEMENT

LUCY WOKE FROM A DREAM of falling dogwood petals, then saw snow swirling past the window.

When she closed her eyes again, a memory came to her as clear as dreaming: how, beside a dappled pool, she'd stood with Luther in the rain of blossoms. Their white skin glowed in the gold-green light of dogwoods.

He knelt before her. Her hands were in his hair.

He had undressed her there, every stitch. Each thing had come away until this moment, standing awed, seduced by possibilities, by the coolness of the air. She, who'd never been allowed bare feet, whose childhood wrists had never shown.

Gravely, she had done the same to him until they lay, twined on leaves, like Adam and Eve in their green and ticking jungle.

She heard the metal doorknob click. It was the midwife, Old Johanna.

They'd held her down against the pillows, Johanna and her strong daughter Anne. They'd folded a square of flannel and pressed it to her mouth that morning, to muffle her cries. Now the baby, squashed and appallingly small, cleaned and neatly swaddled, slept.

"What did you give to make me dream so? I hardly know where I am." Her tongue was very strange. It made her smile.

"Safe in your bed is where. And a little girl to nurse and keep at home. Of what did you dream?"

"Of my husband."

"So? This is very soon."

They smiled together.

"Shall I call him in?"

"Who?"

"Your husband."

"If he pleases."

———

"IS SHE ABIGAIL?" her husband leaned and asked. How dispassionate he always seemed, how fixed. Fixed: the hard high ridge of his nose, the hollows of his eyes. The beard in careful angles, as though he could not help but survey and order the features of his face, drawing points and boundaries. He paced through counties with his stakes and chains, marking off one neighbor from the next, straight through the curves of slopes, unruly forests, all needing to be claimed.

He was Israel, of course, not Luther. Luther was years gone.

"I keep dreaming," she said. "So many dreams."

It was her fourth lying-in, the second in this tall square house in Iowa, with the crab apple tree outside the upstairs window. It was her third daughter, the first to be born in a waning moon and snow. Israel would go down to their big Bible now and record the necessary fact: January 6, 1847. While Johanna boiled the ruined sheets.

But the name. Surely not his mother's. Not Abigail.

What door had opened in her soul?

She heard him ask, "Is Mrs. Mitchell all right?"

The grief seemed almost new. Her tongue was strange. What had they given?

"Ja, very well. I try to make them easy. It's good for both to sleep."

Lucy saw him turn, walk to the mirror. For births, he wore his Sunday suit. He straightened his jacket now. She saw the good shoulders, the silvering curls at his nape. She did know his virtues.

She said, "I was thinking Mary."

What had made her cruel today?

A pie, a pudding, a roast chicken had all arrived. Olive and Samuel had sent five loaves of bread. Anne would come each day of this confinement to feed Daniel and the girls, to see that a mother's work was done.

He said, "I'm visiting the Whitcombs this evening. They mean to go to Oregon this spring."

In her arm, the baby stirred. Mary. It was Luther's mother's name.

"I said the Whitcombs mean to start for Oregon this spring."

"No," she said.

He turned. Her eyes denied him, sought instead the clemency of snow, its gentle ambiguity. It lofted and spun beyond the panes. Here was no straight fall to earth.

A YELLOW LILY

He was warm at last and sliding through long waves of dreams when her voice woke him.

Tota?

His eyes came open, he tried to pull the blankets back. His hands were dressed and bandaged. He'd never meant to sleep.

With one foot on the chill dirt floor, he listened. The ropes of the old cot had sagged so deep, the mattress all but kept him. What he'd heard now seemed more like an echo, a thing said in some other time and gone.

Outside, the black pines roared. Wind moaned across the snow. His hands were aching. His face was stiff with scab. He pulled his foot back in.

The parchment window filled the room with deep gray light. Sacks of meal changed shape in shadowed corners. He saw the kegs and shovels, the leaning hoes. He closed his eyes. Because, of course, he was alone.

Tota?

He surged awake. His belly thrilled and eased. The room full dark. His heart beat through his muffled fingers.

Well, how many nights had he stayed awake? He would not believe in ghosts.

The parchment rattled. His feet were cold.

An arm or leg, removed, he'd heard, could remain so strongly in the mind of one who'd owned it that for years it might go sounding its aches and needs. For years it could exist without existing, not a ghost, but a simple failure of the body's understanding.

That's what it is, he thought. The voice. A shadow of perception, like the light that stands an instant on the eye when a flame has been blown out.

———

HE WAS DREAMING of ice, of men in furs in tiny boats of skin, when he woke again. Light broke in squealing angles through the door. He squinted.

It was the tall one, Mengarini. The one he had seen first.

Sun glared on the snow outside. MacLaren closed his eyes against the light, having seen the tall robed figure, the basin and the cup set steaming on the pine round by the door. The hinges squealed again. The wooden latch fell to.

This hut, he knew, had been the first of all the buildings on the grounds of St. Marie's. It had a hearth as well as the small window.

The man was kneeling now. MacLaren heard wood laid. Ashes stirred. Then something seemed to slip from him, the strangest feeling. In that instant, he not so much recalled his family or the valley he had left, the cabin, barn, the knoll of pines—it was no kind of memory, but a corporeal sensation that a part of himself had just slipped out and been there and come back in the time it took the hair of his neck to stop prickling. He'd felt it go out of his left shoulder.

He'd never considered souls until now, or believed in their material existence.

The Jesuit Mengarini had long fingers and very dirty wrists, as though for years he'd washed his hands and nothing else. He stood over the cot, spoke down in Italian. The sounds bounced out in strings of vowels. He held the tea and offered it.

In French, MacLaren said, "You could put it on the floor."

The Jesuit waited as though expecting some reply. Then spoke in Dutch.

MacLaren would have liked to know where Junie was. Whether the priest Laurent was here. But he wanted more than anything to lie still. He'd never learned a word of Dutch. He said that, and thanked him. He said, "I'll drink it later."

The Jesuit cocked an ear and pursed his lips, a caricature of incomprehension. Then smiled and reached and said, in Salish, the word to sit.

"I don't need help." MacLaren fended him off in Nez Perce. "I don't need help," he said. "I don't need help."

MENGARINI BROUGHT HIM bowls of food. He brought him tea with laudanum. Each time MacLaren woke, his soul, if that was what it was, would slip away and then return. It happened other times as well.

Twice each day he looked up from his cot and saw the Jesuit's dirty robes, the fraying cincture, the yellow teeth. One day the man brought chess pieces and a board to set on a stump between them.

MacLaren sat. He played one game on which he spared no great attention, and was beaten. Mengarini smiled, a kind smile, tried to set up the pieces again. MacLaren only studied the hollowed cheeks, the innocent brown eyes. A solitary man, he thought, with no way to understand the change a family brings.

And perhaps he never had, himself. Only looking back it seemed he'd found, with his wife and children, some fulcrum of the heart he'd never noticed, but it had put a power in his smallest task. So that now the world had lost all base and purpose, or he all use in its relation. So if he moved now, it was habit or pretense, and if he ever laughed again, it would make only a rattling, like shorn metal.

THE WIND TURNED warm one night, and in the morning the priest Laurent was sitting on a round of pine beside the bed.

"*Bonjour.*" His eyes, in the window's light, were very blue. Water ran from the melting eaves. "I've been at the winter camp. You know? The Flathead, they wish we stay with them. Father Point has gone among the Blackfeet. Very brave, you think? But now I hear of you."

A new sound came across the snow, a distant shrill shout. Laughter.

Laurent said, "I have brought some children. To learn with us awhile." Then stood and craned his neck to the parchment square of light as though some joy might be visible through it. So, looking up, MacLaren saw the fleshy throat with its stubble, which he could resent. But when the eyes met his, he looked away.

WHEN HIS HANDS had healed enough, he went out to the woodlot in the mornings to split more pine for their fires, though his blood still raced from the least exertion. The scabs on his back and legs caught in his clothes and wore away and left his skin a spattered pink. His soul, for the most part, stayed.

He took his meals at night with the others in the mission hall, and when he had wiped the table clean, and washed the four tin plates and spoons, and the others had retired to the back room for the night, Laurent would get the chessboard.

"What was the first bed you remember?" The priest asked this while setting out the pieces. When not attending to afflicted souls, or saving them, he collected lives. The chess was a diversion. So Laurent had learned already of MacLaren's childhood home in Scotland, the hills and cattle. How on wet windy nights, the stones that weighed the thatch would stretch their ropes and swing, and clack against the walls.

"It was a boxbed," he answered now. "I shared it with my cousins." They had been gangling boys, all three, overrun with the itch. Giggling in their dark closet, farting, pounding one another's ribs.

"What was your first sin?"

"Not what you are thinking, if you're thinking that."

Consider your evil tendencies, said a book Laurent had left beside his bed, *and how far you have followed them. Consider how every day has added to the number of your sins against God, against yourself, and against your neighbor, by deed, word, thought, and desire.*

He said, "We'd steal the blood from ponies."

They fell silent, considering their moves, the plights of ponies and starving boys.

"What age when you left that place?"

"Fourteen," he said, and there was the rubble and ice of Hudson's Bay, the fort where they had slept and worked and drunk their measure of Sunday rum, and the bear, Elisabetta, who drank it with them and would dance with her long chin across their shoulders, until she was shot one night—he'd never told his girls this ending—for refusing to stir from an Orkneyman's bed, and was eaten for supper the next day.

Tell me Elisabetta.

He said, "It was a miserable country."

So sometimes he would find himself in the very regions he most wished to leave. Even distant memories held surprises. He rubbed his face, and when the pieces were put away, he went back to the hut he slept in. He took the pine round and shouldered with it through the door, and set it in the moon-striped snow, and sat, and lit his pipe.

And marveled, now, at things he'd never noticed: how the trees with their rimed branches looked like the still white pieces of coral an old Kanaka had once given him, which he had liked to study, imagining warm seas and watery forests. So he sat and saw the stars afloat on the surface of the night above him, and felt himself to be as nothing more, perhaps, than a crab on a bright sandy floor.

"The world is too beautiful, eh? Sometimes?"

Laurent had crossed the snow and stood beside him.

"God forgives us what we cannot forgive ourselves," the priest said.

MacLaren rubbed his stiff knuckles. He said, "If there be a God, sir, He is the one to need forgiving."

The priest considered. "And so we must," he said at last. Then said, "The evils of the world all have this source: *tristitia*. Sorrow. It will poison any man who carries it too long. Be careful, my friend."

———

HE HEARD a jingle of harness bells one morning as he paused in his work, and came through the gates to find two dogsleds halted and the dogs now panting and turning in their traces. Four native attendants had helped a heavy man to stand, and now beat the snow from his robes.

Laurent raised his arm, called MacLaren over. He left the sledge of wood he had been pulling.

"Here is the Abbe Franchere, by God's grace. He is touring our new missions. Abbe, Monsieur MacLaren."

The abbe's heavy lips pulled in, dismissive.

Laurent said, "He is a gentleman of Hudson's Bay. Trader. Cartographer. Expert of language."

"Mercenary," the abbe said. Their eyes had locked.

MacLaren answered, "*Oui.*"

THE ABBE had come from France the summer before, to oversee these scattered missions. By ship, around the Horn to Fort Vancouver. By bateaux, up Columbia to Frenchtown. By horse, across the Palouse hills to the northern missions and Coeur d'Alene, where he had passed the winter. A voyageur called Gabriel had brought him here, with three grown boys of the Flathead tribe.

Now, morose and inconvenienced, the abbe shut himself for a week in the back dormitory, writing up his letters. The Flathead boys waited on him. They had given up their names and now went by John, Philemon, Baptiste. Laurent and Mengarini slept on cots in the hall.

Baptiste and Philemon slept on MacLaren's floor. In the evenings they sat looking into the fire, laughing, talking in their own tongue, while MacLaren smoked and read by tallow light the book Laurent had given him: *An Introduction to the Devout Life.*

We must be on our guard not to be deceived in making friendships, it said, *between persons of the opposite sexes. If discretion be lacking, frivolity will creep in, then sensuality, till love becomes carnal. It is sweeter than the taste of ordinary honey; so worldly friendship is profuse in honeyed words, while true friendship speaks a simple honest language.*

"And your wife?" the abbe had asked with greasy lips one night across the supper table. Laurent, sidelong, had watched them both.

Lise. He'd never called her wife, in all the twenty years he'd known her. Although a priest had married them. Lise had borne his children, nursed and raised them. Together they'd cut hay, split wood, plucked geese. They'd made a life together, strong as timbers joined and braced. He'd always thought it was that strong and true.

True friendship is always the same—modest, courteous, and loving—knowing no change save an increasingly pure and perfect union.

"Is she dead also?" the abbe had asked.

And he'd replied, "She was well enough when I saw her last."

AFTER A WEEK, he was still stepping over Indians and the old voyageur had moved into his hut as well. "When are they going?" he asked Laurent.

"Soon. We think by horse to go home by way of the Missouri. To St. Joseph. The abbe and I. Gabriel. The Indians. And you, I hope, also."

"Me?"

"Of course. Ah? You know the way."

THEY BEGAN their journey with the snow still soft by day, anxious to make way as soon as the season would allow. They wrapped the horses' legs in blankets and traveled under moonlight on the crusted ice. At morning's end, old Gabriel would lift the great abbe from his mount, and the Flathead boys would rub his legs and serve him tea. They cooked and ate and went to sleep, the Jesuits in their oilskin tent, the rest pitched under what shelter they might find: a ledge, a bush, a leaning tree.

WHEN THEY CAME, in a week, to the high round valley that had been his home, MacLaren left the others encamped and rode to it alone.

He'd neared it when a drift of smoke surprised him, hazing up against the morning's blue, from beyond the copse where his cabin would be standing.

"Lise!"

The name leaped out, though it wouldn't have been her. But he dug at the ribs of the lazy mare he rode, lashed her with his reins. He arrived, of course, to find no one at all. It was only the steaming thatch.

Crows flew up from bones around the door. The elk he'd hung had rotted and come down.

The pegs had swollen with the damp. The door gave way to gloom. He waited in the jamb, watching the ugly mare scrape her bit along the rail outside. She pawed the wet snow and swung, fretting to get back.

He took a breath and went in to the smell of cold smoke, the dank of abandoned places. The robes were roiled, his things so disarrayed that at first the place seemed ransacked, but it was only as he'd left it. Two half-burned timbers lay along the floor.

He had come with things in mind to do. But when he saw the chair he'd made, he sat in it.

His daughters' dresses lay rumpled in the corners. If he looked, he knew he'd find their dolls and treasures hidden there, and was afraid to. He saw the table with bowls still on it. They'd grown up always eating on the ground, and here he'd made a table, but was always coming in to find June kneeling on the bench, Elizabeth astride it, Alexander in the dirt beneath, Lise on her shins by the fire.

"Sit right when you eat, you three. Or you'll have coals for Christmas."

He'd put spoons in their greasy hands, sat them decently while June asked him, "What will St. Nicholas bring? Is he really magic?"

"As magic as the snow outside," he'd told her. "As magic as your mother."

"She isn't magic."

"Well, she is. She is."

He thumbed the smooth arms of his chair.

His printed books stood on the single shelf he'd made, his row of ledgers beside them. There were twenty, one for every year he'd served or worked, though some were lost. All filled with cramped notations: dates, supplies, routes long forgotten. In winter, he'd let the girls turn through and look for treasure: some array of mushrooms he had rendered, a bird, a snake, a butterfly, a painted flower. They'd found his awkward portraits of chiefs, sketches on the construction of canoes, the styled moccasins of different tribes. Outlines of the forts. Junie liked the flowers. They had known by heart the pages he had written on, when each was born.

The day was passing. He'd come with things to do.

He went outside. The place seemed different in the thaw. He stood above the graves, in patchy snow. Now he didn't like the place he'd chosen, or how the earth had thawed and slurried into them. A winding of print cotton lay exposed. He'd bought it at Fort Hall. He'd been keeping it a secret, red and green for Christmas.

And then he had to go and rest his head against the rail of the fence.

When he could, he found his shovel and dug up sod and laid it on.

He was back in the barn, looking in the dirt for footprints, when Laurent came through and stood against the light.

He looked up. He said, "Someone took my saddle."

"What else?"

"What was on it. Some maps I'd made. My sextant. Telescope."

"And from the house?"

He shook his head.

"There is death, you know. In all the vapors."

"I know it."

He trusted only boiling. He chose the things that would survive it: knives and awls, smaller tools, his traps. Molds and presses, spoons and other plunder. He built a fire under a pot outside, broke down icicles as big as his arms from the north-side eaves and melted them, while Laurent stood over the graves and read.

At midday he got the balky mare and began to haul brush from the river. He dragged whole pines from the copse and piled them on the cabin's warm south wall. Inside, he raked the rushes high, dusted on black powder. He laid on the blankets and the dresses. The bench and chair. He put his ledgers on top, and kindled the base, and lit it.

THEY TRAVELED through the early spring, east on the emigrant road. The abbe complained like a woman. Gabriel sang and swore. MacLaren rode with Laurent beside him on fine days. The priest was full of words: he told the lives of saints, brought up questions of theology, paid out self-deprecating tales of scholarship and ease. MacLaren, hearing, felt all his motive gone, all curiosity. The heart damped out completely.

They broke their journey for a day in a village of the Ogallala, the whole tribe gathering to see the great unrolling of the Heavenly Ladder. He had seen it many times: the old canvas hanging from its rood, soft from use. Stained by instructional fingers. There were Adam and Eve, painted dark-skinned innocents in their conifer Eden; the Angels of virtues and of Temptations, the Protestants with their devilish consorts, crude Sinners tumbling into brimstone, the saved ascending in gold-leaf light. The people watched. They put their hands across their mouths to show their wonder.

And the babies screamed at pale-eyed men but were baptized all the same. MacLaren, from a distance, heard the howling. There was smoke and water. Laurent and the abbe strode fearless through them, trinkets jingling in their cassocks. From one pocket they pulled strings of beads, steel awls, flints and strikers. From the other, small iron crosses on their thongs. And that was how old men and warriors were won. Then came speeches back and forth, in which unlikely promises were made.

The next morning they rode on.

"It is a great undertaking," MacLaren heard the abbe say, "to bring such people to God." The Ogallala, grateful, had praised the abbe for the power this god might give them against their enemy the Crow. They'd gladly hoped to wipe their own soiled backsides on the scalps of those who were less than human, to roast their enemies' live bodies over coals, to slaughter their children, to make their daughters captive.

The abbe, yet new to this country, was most put out.

"Cruelty is a virtue here," Laurent explained. "They win their honor with theft and murder. I have had to put away my lessons on the crucifixion. Always they want to know how it is done."

"They must be improved," the abbe said. "They must be taught some Christian mildness."

IT WAS just April when they stopped among the Pawnee. This time MacLaren said, "I'm no interpreter."

"By gesture, no? To make them understand."

"Ask Gabriel."

He left them to it. Walked instead across the ragged snow. Black meltwater leaked under crusts of ice, the sky was cold white. All winter the world came in only these two colors—of snow and cloud and ice, of dark trees, shadows, crows.

Then, kneeling beside the creek, a star of yellow surprised him. It was a lily, blooming in a sunny crease of granite.

Before they'd married, he'd sent a letter down to Lise. He'd pressed a lily of this kind and enclosed it, playing on her name that way. It was all the courtship he had ever needed. She'd made him the coat he'd married her in, the one he wore today, the yellow all but faded from the quills: her lilies in return.

He packed a pipe and smoked it, looking west across the world.

If sorrow was an evil, he didn't know what evil that would be.

He thought about Laurent, his endless stories. As though he feared the emptiness they rode through. Land and time. For his own part, he had no need to fill it. There seemed more truth, these days, in silence.

A TRUE WIFE

LUCY HAD BEEN CONFUSED at first, opening this letter onto her lap, to find nothing but pleasantries, some note on a mutual acquaintance. She sat alone this April morning on the edge of the bed with the emptied drawer beside her. She'd just packed Israel's socks and linens. Then, tipping the drawer to clean it, she'd discovered this letter folded under the paper lining. It was from Pennsylvania, addressed in her own hand. She had never seen it, never imagined the words of hers that Luther must have left, undiscovered all these years, now under Israel's socks and linens.

She read until she found the reason for its safekeeping:

> And now to a subject which lieth close to both our hearts . . . my thoughts on the matter are the same as when you left two weeks ago, without it is that I think of you different and *love you more.*

She saw her father's garden, then, complete in memory. She remembered writing under the elms. Three weeks before, in that same garden, Luther Ross had sat and watched her from the depths of a willow-work chair as, daringly, she'd perched on the table and read her notes aloud, of a trip to New York City. She had been nineteen.

> You must choose but one who will be a true wife and mother—and if at any time you find I am inadequate to that position do not hesitate one moment to inform me, for a little sorrow now would be

better than a lifetime of misery, for misery it would be, if you have one thought or wish that I cannot fulfill.

Well. What a thing to find, she thought. She folded away that uncompromised and daring girl, and put her in a pocket.

———

THE NEXT HOUR was all apology. The Van Luvens had arrived. Through the window, she'd seen the husband lift his little wife from the buggy and set her on the puncheon walk. "I'm sorry for the disorder," Lucy said now. "You can see there's all the packing."

Mary was awake. Lucy, cradling her, stood behind their visitors, looking through the doorway at the parlor. Daniel had been playing among the trunks and crates, and now began to hammer something.

"Daniel," she said. "Come out."

He peeped, then dodged away, her small fair-haired boy.

"I'll show you the improvements," Israel said.

He'll talk about the wainscoting, Lucy thought, and led Mrs. Van Luven into the dining room. The Van Luvens dealt in furnishings and were looking for a well-made house.

"The dining set looks almost new," Mrs. Van Luven said.

"Yes. The Carrs are taking it on Monday."

Behind them in the hall, Israel was pointing out one thing and another. Only four years before, he'd filled the house with carpenters. As his new wife, she'd watched him stalk, the male imperial, instructing the men in this or that, fingering new joins, fussing behind them with her good broom and dustpan.

Now she heard the back door slam. Caroline and Sarah ran down the hall and bolted up the stairs. Israel called after them. She heard a distant bawl of cattle.

Her body swayed to soothe the baby. In these early months, it did so of its own accord. Reason had no part in the collusion; she swooped and swayed unrestrained while her thoughts clashed in the door frame. Mrs. Van Luven surveyed the brambly window.

Lucy, I'd not like you to break the trust between us.

That's what Israel had finally said when all her winter's reasons were exhausted. When he had denied that hers *were* reasons. On matters of pure inclination, he felt entitled to preside.

"One could easily get more light in here," Mrs. Van Luven told the brambles.

Lucy said, "They're yellow roses." Upstairs a fight was breaking out, the girls in fierce accusation and defense. "They'll bloom in May."

"How lovely. Only the rest of the time, one must suffer them."

The cattle sounded very close. Then Sarah was in the doorway with a pair of pantalettes dangling from an upraised hand.

"Sarah!"

"Mama look! What Emma did!"

"Sarah, please!" But she did see the ragged hems.

Then suddenly the flanks of cattle were passing only feet from the window. More were coming through the fence—she heard the sound of breaking boards. Her visitor cried out. Lucy glimpsed a passing wagon on the road, the canvas lettered with its place of origin. She turned and strode into the hallway.

Israel was on the stairs, still talking.

"Benton County's in my daffodils," she announced as Emma Ruth scowled past.

———

She could have put down the baby and taken up a broom against the cattle. Or stayed and praised the merits of her home. Instead she found her cloak and bonnet, and followed her daughter into the rain.

The cattle had nearly finished passing; it was a small group. She saw the wagons, their sides all hung with chairs and tools and swinging pails. Their own new wagons stood silent in the yard as she passed, and the tent, still smelling of new wax. She'd watched through the kitchen window only yesterday as Israel and the girls had tried it out. They'd bobbed and pounded, tripped on strings, stood up poles that fell again.

Through the barn's dim doorway she saw Emma standing cross-armed by a stall post. Israel's new mare had her ears back and was glaring.

"You're missing old Bob," Lucy guessed.

Emma answered, "Horses don't miss people."

"Well, you watch out for this one."

Israel had ridden in from town a week ago on this tall Thoroughbred, the same cherrywood hue as the dining set he'd bought last year, and now sold at half its value.

"I'll buy you one," he'd called. The mare had quartered and flashed her shoes, flung her head for rein. White foam flew. He'd said, "We can ride together." As though, with five children, she might be at liberty to do so. She'd said as much, and then he'd named her.

Don't break the trust between us.

He was the true grandnephew of Daniel Boone, which he mentioned on all appropriate occasions. His parents had toiled, he'd always told the girls, to give him every opportunity at schooling, so as not to pass along the hardships of a farming life: they'd roughed it on the frontier and come out the better side. So when windows needed washing, Emma Ruth and Sarah and above all his own Caroline must appreciate that there *were* such windows to be washed, not mere flaps of oilcloth; when it was time to walk the road to Mrs. Baker's house, they must appreciate that there *was* a piano, and money for the lessons, and that they were saved—unlike his mother—from tending pigs and corn. And now they must appreciate this most of all: the chance to go to Oregon, and suffer for themselves those hardships that had made his parents such outstanding characters. The irony seemed to escape him.

Don't break the trust, he'd said. But who was she? When her dooryard bloomed in roses every spring? And what was a house worth? Or any place, and all its people, if you could leave it just like that? On a whim, it seemed.

Thousands have gone already, he'd argued. *There is no danger.*

So she had wondered: Did men's imaginations fail? Or were women's too acute? It was just that she knew caution. It was out there like a boundary fence, scarcely noticed until he'd make her cross it. Scribing, steadying, keeping them safe. Predicting grave consequences for trespass.

"Other people go," said Emma now.

Her thoughts were so evident, Lucy saw, a child of ten could read them.

"I know." She looked up. Dark trusses glowed with pigeon dung. The rain came down. The baby stirred against her.

Other people went. But still, beyond all daylight reasons, all petty arguments, was some dark thing she dreamed or knew. It came to her at night: a vision of vacant miles, bright sun, endless grass, sand, circling birds. She saw a grave. With certainty past reason, she knew that one of them would die, and be left out there alone.

"If I lost one of you . . ." she said. But the truest words always swelled and caught before she could deliver them. So no one knew.

She dried her cheeks on Mary's blanket. Then said, "Don't speak of this."

She looked at Emma Ruth: her brown-haired girl of slivers and scabs. Who sharpened found knives on stones, filled pockets with sucked cherry pits, who could not do a tub of dishes without studying the ways of water. Emma Ruth said nothing.

Lucy said, "You cut the frills off your new pantalettes."

Luther would have loved her.

For misery it would be, if you have one wish or thought that I cannot fulfill.

How young we all begin, it seemed. How brave and full of certainty. How terrible it would be to know: not only what we must become, but who we really are.

"Well, hem them up," she said. "Don't leave them ragged."

MEMORY AND FLIGHT

*I*T WAS POURING APRIL RAIN when MacLaren saw the tiny window lights at last, shining like a beacon from the ferryman's house at the edge of the Missouri.

They descended the road in sheets of water to the landing on the river's edge. MacLaren rang the bell, but no one was there, and no ferry either, so they sheltered under the streaming eaves. They leaned against the wall and passed the time in the bitter smell of budding leaves, and at last the keelboat with its white-topped wagons loomed out of the sweeping rain.

The tide of oxen made the shore, lunged up through luminous foam and muck. The horses went wild with fright to see such creatures streaming out of the dark, and ripped free to bolt off westward with trail ropes skipping through their legs. It was half an hour before they could be rounded back and their packs put straight, and more time yet before they could be persuaded onto the ferry's slick deck, where they stood with flattened ears while the river seethed with rain.

They made the eastern shore. All up the road into St. Joseph, the wagons stood blocked and set, with families encamped in the mud and waiting.

So he delivered Father Laurent and the Abbe Franchere to the door of the Peerless Hotel. From the shelter of the porch, they could smell the steaming baths, hear the clink and clatter of bottles and china plates.

"Sleep dry," MacLaren said. He relied on irony and haste, in parting.

But Laurent took his hand and then gripped him by the elbow. "Come, my friend," he said. "Come with us abroad. You would be my guest. There is so much to see. So much you could do."

People moved behind bright panes of glass. In his enormous cloak, the silent abbe watched them.

"You see? I cry," Laurent said. "So easily. Tell me what you will do."

MacLaren shook his head, with John and Baptiste and Philemon all waiting in the rain, not knowing where they were.

He squeezed Laurent's arm, its genuine flesh.

THEY FOUND the trading house beside the river, left the Flatheads on the porch among the others of their kind, the half-breeds and Negroes. In the stink and roar inside, he and Gabriel turned in what they could for credit and got drunk. The close warmth was good after all that cold; it was good to be among these men, their steaming vices—knocking chairs, sloshing cups, shouting, swearing, throwing knives, embracing, seeing who could lie the loudest; good to forget what else he'd learned was possible.

He had been staring into the glass above the fireplace for some time before he realized his own face in it.

HE WOKE on a slope of dank shadow. Stubs and glass. Rotten sacking. One eye was musted in dirt. He lay looking up, and the planks and joists of the trade-post floor made a low ceiling above him.

Two dogs nosed through the refuse. MacLaren sat, dry-mouthed, and wiped his eye. Bloody dirt came out of it. A few other men lay sprawled. Cheap clay pipes glowed like mushrooms in the midden. One lay near his hand, and he picked it up, then found another, until he had half a dozen. He knocked them clean. His girls would bring home ones like these from behind the walls at Fort Hall. They'd file away the stems and stop the holes with sap. They'd paint stars and flowers and use them for play teacups.

He put them in his pocket and stooped out into a thick river mist to find their horses were all gone.

Wagons clogged the place. He thought it was midmorning. He washed his face in a trough and looked around. Orange lights of cook fires glowed along the street into the mist like channel markers. Tents stood pitched at the road edge here, among wagons backed up for the ferry. Men sat in chairs in the mud watching other people pass. Some read books or leaned over skillets or held steaming mugs of coffee.

He began to walk. The buildings were brick, and pillars stood along the street edge, with balconies above. Women had strung their laundry underneath, so that, going along, he was obliged to duck the arms of shirts, the wet wool toes of stockings.

"Renounce your sin," a woman's voice called after him. Bold letters on the canvas of her wagon read: BENTON COUNTY. She said, "Renounce your degradation."

He skirted pigs and men with barrows, children tugging at the ears of sacks. Oxen stood in muddy feeds of hay. He crossed a street where a fiddler played, turned to see a telescope in a pharmacist's window displayed among green goggles and tin ear horns, and bottles of Eye Remedy stacked in a clever pyramid, and a telescope was a thing he had been missing. So he found himself standing inside on the gritty boards, picking things up, and reading the backs of boxes.

> Be sure that you know the Physician as a man of standing, skill, and reliability. To such a man explain your case freely and without reserve, without false pride, and he will either do for you what medical science can do in such cases or else frankly give you the very best advice.

He came out with a bottle of Dr. McMunn's Elixir and no telescope and walked south out of town.

Around midday, he found the horses with Gabriel and the boys camped down among the willows, cooking a skinned house cat over coals. He sat with them, and they ate and talked. They wanted to ride a steamboat. They'd ride a steamboat home, they said, and laughed, and he laughed, and after a while he emptied the foolish pipe bowls into the fire and broke the seal on the white glass bottle and drank it freely and without false pride.

————————

IN A DREAM that night he woke in his own cabin. It was day, clear and fine, and he opened the door with a strange feeling of lightness, of having been gone a long time. He saw the mountains as he'd known them, the meadow with its creek, the copse of pines. His children stood in bright sunlight beside the barn's log wall, and he thought a year might have passed. Then thought it must be more, two years or three, because the girls were there, but he saw two boys—Alexander and a fairer one who was younger.

Lise was in the meadow, cutting hay. He went and spoke to her. "Have I been gone?" The sky was brilliant blue. "How long was I away?"

"You were never away," she said. "You've been here always."

He felt a tingling fear, knowing how much time had passed, knowing he could never hide his ignorance, never step into his life and find out all those things as should have been familiar.

"No," he tried to tell her. "It was someone else. I've been away."

"No," she said. "You've been here always."

He woke with the sun well up and found the camp empty. This time they'd taken all their things—the Flatheads and Gabriel—but left the horses.

He stayed the day, but they didn't come back. He woke next morning after a night of rain and tied the horses nose to tail. He let the brown mule follow and rode up into town.

The sky had cleared to a hard pale blue, and all the mud was steaming. Vapors drifted down the sides of warming buildings. The puddles blazed like mirrors.

On the far side of town, he found a place where stock was dealt, the pens and barn and office. It was early. He tied the horses to the rails and climbed the steps, squinting down across the pens and races. A man's voice carried from inside, and a woman's, the rattle of a stove lid. A yellow dog lay in a corner of sunlight, legs splayed, flews hanging in a scalloped grin. MacLaren stood beside the open door and knocked and called but had no answer.

He stood and studied the riding stock: a light-boned mare, a long-backed sorrel with a bitten hip. A hard-used dun in the far corner caught his eye, its tail chewed down to a stubbled whip of bone.

Then the liveryman banged out, and there was business to discuss. They went down the steps together. MacLaren looked on while the man ran his hands down the legs of each animal and pulled its ears, talking all the while about the mules coming in from Santa Fe. There had been something favorable in the old dun horse, and MacLaren looked again, sure it would fall short. But its frame was not the type you found much on this side of the divide. He studied it.

And then a pale light squeezed behind his eyes, to see the old saddle scar below those withers. The gelding turned its head. The liveryman had asked him something, but the pores of his scalp were tingling.

Thunder sounded, the faintest sigh, from clouds gathering up across the river.

"That dun horse," MacLaren said. "Who brought him in?"

"Depends on why you're asking."

"He ran out of my place this winter. Six others with him."

"And what place would that be?"

"North of Fort Hall."

"Arkansas?"

"Oregon. Who brought him in?"

"Don't think I'll give that animal to you. Fellow gets in a dozen a week with every kind of shift and tale. I'd go broke," he said, "if I listened."

"Who brought him in?"

The liveryman described, at last, a pale-haired man of slight build, with silver conchos down his chevaliers.

It was Beal Beck, as clear as life. The strut and swagger. The winning smile.

"What happened to the others?"

"Sold."

"So what's he riding?"

"Officer's private horse, I sold him. Spanish bay."

The old horse shook its mane, turned, and moved through the mire to water. Now they could see the old Company brand in smudged white hairs on the shoulder.

He said, "Was there a woman with him?"

"Why?" said the liveryman. "Do women run out of your place as well?"

When their business was done, MacLaren skirted the pens alone. From beyond the rails, the horse stood unmoving in the mire. He was nothing but slopes and angles now. Hips so gaunt the hair stood off them.

"Hey."

He watched the matted ears turn to him. In his years of work, he'd judged more horses than men—bought and sold them, burdened and freed them, slaughtered them for meat. By order of the Board of Governors of Hudson's Bay, no man could keep a mount. They were used in common, assigned and disposed of, as was each man, no accommodating personal desire. And he'd been all for the rules, except for this one horse, that he'd claimed and kept these many years.

He turned away, thinking of the pool where he'd led this horse as a round-backed colt. Remembering the wary springing stride, the silver sheen on muscled brown; this horse the very colors of water over sand. He'd stood him in that river, belly-deep, while Lise scratched pictures in damp silt.

The horse has two great gifts: memory and flight.

He'd coaxed the colt in deeper, until they were both swimming. Slipped astride, and leaned, and put a noose around his nose. And stuck, when the horse found footing, when he launched and landed, plunged again; stuck when he had vaulted up the bank, hit the plain, headed toward the grassy hills. He'd run, and run, and run.

What's his name? she'd asked that evening.

You name him.

Drums Roll Over the Hill, she'd said.

Now he waited, courting that great warmth of breath, more tender and more wary than any human greeting. He heard slow steps, the sucking mud. Then felt it, warm, moist, hay-smelling. He turned, the fence between them. The horse pulled back. They had both changed.

The breath again, the prickle of whiskers in his palm.

How many thousand miles had they shared, fifteen years in his keeping? How many journeys? This horse's memory held them all—the mineral scents of plants and water, the cast of light and land, the pull of the earth's pole. This horse was a great geographer, with a recollection for country far surpassing his own.

He slipped through the rails as some end of loneliness overcame him, and then his hands were on the warm dry hide, to stroke, to feel, to free the matted hair, to smooth the soft hollows above the eyes. With the mane in his fist, to slap the neck in broken greeting, to hold him.

From that hour, nothing could go fast enough. No deliberation, no care for anything but this: to find the man so knotted into his winter's loss that the name alone was enough to stop all useful thought.

In clatty boots, he went through likely buildings; shouldered up and down the streets through crowds, fixing on the faces of pale-haired men and men who rode bay horses. He'd gone into one of the larger mercantiles when, through the legs of people waiting, he saw his Dollard sextant in the counter's case. Then saw his flintlock pistol, its butt now wrapped in leather.

He waited, shifting. A man and his son were placing a large order. He knew the workings of that pistol in and out, knew the sextant's every mark.

He stepped up in his turn. "Did you get a telescope from this same man?" he asked, and rapped the defending glass.

"Telescopes are over there," said the clerk across his notepad.

He went and came back, and when he could get to the counter again, he asked for things from the shelves behind: a shirt, drawers and sundries. With those things neatly on their paper, he said, "I have owned that sextant twenty years. It has my name on it."

He stood and waited, then, for the proprietor to be brought out.

At the counter's quiet end, he saw a man in a tall silk hat standing beside an open box. The man had some bright thing in his hand and was turning a clock key. He glanced at MacLaren as he did so, then set the thing to run, and MacLaren saw it was a pair of black tin horses pulling a red carriage. It angled off and nearly fell, and MacLaren caught it, the key sedately turning. He restored it to the counter, and the tiny gride and grind of clockwork carried it heedless back.

"Ever seen aught like it?"

MacLaren looked at him.

"Must have had a case," the man said. "Sextant as nice as that."

He affirmed it, looking away.

"How'd it end up here?"

MacLaren said, "I had to leave my place. I got back, and my outfit was gone. This morning I found my horse at the livery across town. A friend of mine had sold him."

"Well, I guess that's one kind of friend."

"I just want to find him."

"What's he look like?"

"Yellow-haired man about thirty years old. Riding a Spanish bay."

The toy man nodded but was already eyeing the room for other custom. MacLaren said, "My wife left me for him."

The man regarded him. Then said, "It's Bonnie here that does most of the buying. I'll put a word in for you."

HE GOT SOME other things he needed and was out at the ferry by evening, crossing with two families from Illinois. They milled and lugged. The men were awkward and sincere and talked too much. The wives in shawls and bonnets hovered, wincing, fearing for their furniture. One woman had produced a pocket stove as they were waiting, and boiled up coffee, and when they'd run the livestock into the current and set out at last, the families stood and drank from steaming cups and declared the woman a great marvel. MacLaren knelt among his panniers, taking out the things he'd bought and packed in haste: lead and powder, bricks of tea, biscuit, sugar, rice, tobacco enough and for currency. He unwrapped brass wire, needles, a roll of ribbon from greased paper, and stowed them in a pouch he kept. Four bottles of McMunn's Elixir. A sallow daughter chewed and eyed him coldly. From the pocket of his coat he took the clockwork carriage in its printed box and stowed it in his can of flour. When the panniers weighed even, he stood and watched the moving horns of the oxen as they swam.

So Beal Beck was driving for a family. This much he'd learned, and little more. He looked around again at the women in their dresses, the ambitious men now laughing with their buttered bread and jam.

And then turned back and watched the raised head of his old horse, who was treading through the deeps behind: lip raised to show long yellow teeth, nostrils curled, wide eyes solemn and alarmed.

A RENDERING OF FAVORS

BESIDE A TRICKLE OF WATER, Lucy Mitchell stopped to pick a handful of mint and held it to her nose for comfort.

She walked with Mary on her hip, Daniel by the hand. Clump to clump, they picked their way along the margin of what had become not a road at all but a daunting swath of clay a quarter mile wide, churned across these rolling uplands. Their boots slipped sometimes into pocked holes made by cattle, and the standing water gouted up in little geysers. Their legs were soaked from this.

"Is he, Mama?" Sarah frowned back from under coppery tendrils. The leaden light had made her graceful.

"Is who what?" Lucy had been trailing her three girls all morning, not attending to their arguments.

"Is Mr. Beck a squaw man?"

"I don't know."

With Mr. Beck's help, they had crossed the wagons by ferry in the dark of morning, committed them to their runnings again, chained the oxen, and gone forward in turn, along the wooded bottom and slowly up the bluffs as the rain began to fall, as their skirts and hair went limp, as clots and spatters fell from turning spokes. The cattle and goats and sheep had all resigned themselves to progress, and then the last view of the Missouri had glimmered through the leafing trees and gone. The Missouri had gone.

The rain had stopped an hour ago, the air was moist and grassy, black-powder clouds massed and shifted overhead; but it discouraged her, the sight of this vast mucky artery through the green.

"I want to go in the *wagon*," Daniel said again.

"No. You're muddy."

It discouraged her. Because their fate was fixed, and Mr. Beck was now their driver. He rode glinting ahead of them. His high-tailed horse gaped and mouthed its silver bit. Mr. Beck wore a pirate's blue kerchief and leather pantaloons seamed down the sides with Mexican buttons; he wore a new shirt, bright red and stiff with sizing. At noon they had eaten cheese and biscuits while he'd talked in crumbling mouthfuls about wild Indians, dog-towns, rock spires, wonders beyond imagining.

"He is," said Caroline. "A squaw man."

Sarah said, "He can't be. He's from Pennsylvania."

"Well, they are all *originally* from somewhere."

Lucy sighed. Just two days ago, the Gibbses had quit, giving her a fleeting hope that Israel might reconsider; that despite all plans and promises, possessions gone, he might (having now brought them to the country's very edge) finally see and *understand* that for two thousand miles, they would find no house, no store, no fixed light of any kind, but only ugly barren places, the haunts of savages, and at the end of it some mud-spattered town wholly separate from the civil world, ungoverned, unconnected. She'd felt the tiniest hope that Israel, like their driver, Mr. Gibbs, would come to his senses, and not ask them all to forge onward. Over their boot tops in mud.

But Israel would never change his mind. The sight of this vast road convinced her. This was no personal delusion. All the little tracks and trails, the private notions of direction, had joined here suddenly into a highway of such span, a shared fever dream of such proportion, that there could be no resisting.

Sarah and Caroline still argued. Sarah, her oldest, was fair-skinned, golden, blessed with beauty. Caroline was spinster-colored—sallow and brown—with arms and legs like spindles. No clever combinations of apparel hid this. She strode ahead, always leaning into life, pulling like a nervous horse. She was Israel's.

Caroline said, "They're too lazy to work, so they live with Indians. They eat raw meat and get vermin and forget about God, and after a while it makes them crazy until they start to hate their own true kind."

That was Alice speaking, Lucy thought. Caroline's dead mother.

"Living with Indians would not make you crazy," Sarah said.

"Who's Wathindian?" Daniel asked.

"Missionaries live with Indians," Sarah said. "All the time."

"They don't cross-breed," said Caroline, with too knowing a look.

"Caroline," warned Lucy.

"Who's *Wathindian?*"

"*With Indians.*" Caroline turned and flashed. "And it's none of your concern."

Lucy squeezed her boy's small hand. They separated into silence, with no sound but bells and chain and the tread of animals and wagons moving.

At last they met a wooded creek where she thought they must encamp, but found no sign of those ahead. The sun had fallen below the covering of clouds to blaze a large and liquid yellow, so bright that Lucy stopped and turned east again, and saw the new grass flare a breathless green. The plain was empty in that direction, but for a distant wagon and some sheep that shone unnaturally white. The clouds had turned a deeper blue.

Well, look at the light, she thought. But it was a fleeting forgiveness.

THEY FOUND their camp at last, a soggy flat of haphazard wagons lately allied, of grazing livestock, hung laundry. Her hands still smelled of mint.

"Put the trunk down here, if you can," Lucy said. Mr. Littlejohn was an oxlike man with a mat of reddish hair. She watched his twine suspenders spring and ease. Belly hairs curled through his moth-holed woolens. His mouth hung open most of the time, and he wheezed a little when he breathed. But he'd done this thing easily, which Mr. Gibbs had not tried once without assistance. The oxen, freed already, grazed content. And was Mr. Beck obtaining wood? She saw his bright red shirt—he was riding toward a clump of box and alder. So this was something.

WITH TWO WAGONS, with a family of such size and composition, Lucy had insisted on two drivers. Israel had agreed. Abel and Elton Gibbs had come three hours late on starting day, and could not conceal for more than half an hour the fact that they had seldom driven oxen or wagons of such weight. Elton Gibbs, the father, complained of stiffness. Abel nursed his coffee, savored bones, did things one-handed that required two. Then spring turned back, and after the Des Moines, it had all been rain, the roads hub-deep in mud. If this was a taste of what would come, Elton said, he'd tasted plenty. Lucy had sat out in an evening drizzle baking biscuits under an um-brella to appease them. She'd fed them her good pickles. Then they'd rolled the green wagon in the Nodaway with all three girls aboard. From shore, she'd seen the wagon skate and turn, heard her daughters' cries. Abel had jumped to swim it, but none of the girls knew how. They'd clung like cats. Only the dear oxen had saved them.

The morning after that, she'd been carrying the pail down through the mist for water and had seen the old man and his son with their mule already packed. Alarmed, she'd called their names and seen Elton raise his hand. It was his only gesture, after all her work to please them, of farewell.

It put her in a fury. "You knew they meant to leave," she'd said to Israel. "You wanted them gone."

"They wanted themselves gone. We found we were in agreement."

She said, "You promised."

With the help of their neighbors, they'd gone on and camped in a muddy field for the night, a few miles from St. Joe. Her own hopes of warm supper and dry bed were thwarted—they would not take a hotel room, said Israel. Not with the cost of livery and lodgings, when they had all they needed with them. It was nothing less than robbery, staying in that town. So they ate their supper in the wagon, crammed together knees and elbows around the narrow plank that served them all as a table. When that was the last town they might ever see. She'd fed them biscuit and wet cheese, watched Israel empty the crumbs from his plate into his hand and eat them with the familiar tilt that so annoyed her.

"I'll go in with John Kingery for what we need," he'd said. "I'll get you a pocket stove. We'll have tea even if it's raining."

"We need more than just a pocket stove," she'd said. "Our own drivers. That is what you promised."

"Yes," was his reply. But the rising inflection admitted new reserve.

Well, they could not rely on the kindness of neighbors. Not for two thousand miles. When he was gone, she'd taken out her writing box, found pencil and a slip of paper.

Mr. Mitchell, you would know each offense but that restraint forbids
it. If God wills we go through, I will remember, and hold you to a
rendering of favors to our account, until the years have settled it.

She read it over. It was bitter, and it satisfied. She folded it into her Coleridge, where he would never find it.

He came back empty-handed. The VanAllmans helped them drive on
to the crossing and into line. They inched forward all one day, while only
thirty wagons crossed. Then Israel found Tom Littlejohn splitting oak behind the Peerless.

Her first impression of the man had been a smile of individual teeth,
varied shapes and absences. The hand, when she'd put hers out to meet it,
had been large and blunt and hesitant. Then he'd disappeared on some errand. Later, as she was changing Mary, she'd heard a snort and a catching
sound and looked around to find his head inside her wagon.

"You reckon it's a half an hour, lady?"

"A half hour from what?" she'd said, appalled.

"Say five or ten ago."

"Minutes?" And then she'd understood the mournful, dented features.
"Heah."

"Well, then," she'd said more gently. "It would not be half an hour. Half
an hour is thirty minutes."

"I see," he'd said, and looked away. "I never studied clocks at all. Man say
I'ma go on down a half-hour count how many and tell him."

He was offended when she offered to go and help him count, leaving her
to wonder how they'd get along. But today he'd driven beautifully, and was
strong and obedient, so that she could see herself with other women, defending her good fortune.

Now Mr. Littlejohn took each object carefully and set it down, and set
the dog down also. Peg shook herself and sneezed, inflamed with damp, and
sat to scratch her ears while Lucy gouged a fire pit with her heel and called
to Israel for the shovel.

"Why dorn't you like that *other* place?" Daniel followed and demanded.

She looked down at his face. His blue eyes at times seemed very alien.
"Do you mean the town? St. Joseph? Well, that was not our town," she
said. "Not yet. Now get the shovel from your father so we can make the fire."

The light was going. She'd be cooking in the dark if they did not all keep quick.

Her baby cried. Israel brought the shovel. He always smiled before he told her what to do.

"You should have a shawl," he said. His gray beard on this journey had lost none of its precision. He had already gone through camp to see which families had arrived and which had not, had surveyed for water and for wood, had determined—as though it mattered—the prevailing wind. If she paused, he would be full of news.

"I should have dry shoes and stockings," she said. "And time to change into them." She took the baby from Caroline and jogged her. "Shall we raise the tent tonight? The girls were hoping."

"Whitcomb's barometer is falling. I want them in the wagon," he said.

"The wagon stinks," said Caroline.

"You'll have smoke blowing over your kitchen if you put the boxes on that side."

Lucy said, "Israel, there is no wind tonight."

But he squinted at the sky and said, "There will be in an hour."

IF THE SMOKE did not rise straight, it was because it eddied toward her, wherever she went.

"Here come your goats," Beal Beck said as she was cooking.

Drawn up from the willows by the smells of biscuit and salt pork, the goats surveyed the camp. The rits of their nostrils snuffed and flared; long ears stood sideways at attention. Their golden eyes demanded.

Tom Littlejohn said, "Old devil's in a goat, heah."

She took up a pot of scraps and went to them. They had not owned goats before this journey, but she'd discovered an affection for them in these last two weeks. They were sociable, willful, more presumptuous than dogs or children. They plucked rinds from her fingers with a delicate air of entitlement.

"There's a reason we keep them tied," Israel said from behind his paper, but she ignored him. Then the treats were gone.

She shooed them off, but they followed anyway, until a stub of firewood spun through the air and hit Desdemona squarely on the hip. The big doe wheeled, indignant, and the others twitched their hips and strolled, as casual as brigands. They showed the fleshy undersides of tails, the tidy holes. Black pebbles spattered on the grass. Mr. Beck had thrown the stick. He laughed.

By some ingenuity, Israel had produced this man as well, only hours before they were to cross the river. Beal Beck had come along the walk to meet them, with his belted knives and pistol, his fair hair bound by a blue kerchief. A vain man, she judged, with a rough formless face. A dandy. His fine bay horse, he'd said, was bought on money from the fur trade, though scarcely anyone could go it anymore. With prices as they were. A fellow had to be that good, he'd told her. A fellow had to know what he was doing. He'd stood too close, with a young man's need to prove. She had felt herself a woman, in his assessing gaze, and had not liked it.

And now he was talking again (he had driven trotting races in Vermont) while she dished the supper; talking (he had shot a bear in the Uintas) while they waited to say grace; talking (he had known an old Apache) while they watched him set the steaming plate atop his knees and open the edges of a rag he'd brought from somewhere. He took a dirty handful of wild leaves and scattered them across his supper—beans, bacon, honey biscuit, and all.

Emma Ruth said, "PleaseLord we thank you for the food here set before us and ask for youtoguideussafe inJesusnameamen."

They ate.

Lucy watched her girls. Emma Ruth had already broadened her affinity for animals to admit Tom Littlejohn as a friend, but seemed indifferent to Mr. Beck. Caroline, affecting too early some idea of maturity, had taken on a dismal cast that would save her, certainly (if sickliness did not), from the attentions of any man. But Sarah smiled. Sarah stood and poured them coffee. Sarah had grown more helpful by the hour.

Lucy saw afresh through this man's eyes the tall body of her girl, now grown impossibly inviting. At fourteen, it was a woman's body. It swayed and tilted, offered and withheld, mocking, it seemed, a childhood that had scarcely ended.

"I was right about the wind," said Israel.

Lucy warmed her hands around her cup. Beck's two horses and his mule were still tied to their green wagon. So was Israel's mare. They looked at her, ears pricked and hopeful. "I'm sure those horses hope you'll let them off to graze," she said.

But Mr. Beck had been to Santa Fe. He had run a payroll for the mines. He pointed out his crooked nose, which he had broken in a dance hall fight.

"It's the hair they fall for. Don't matter if they're married, what their brothers think, Mexican girls all want to dance with yellow hairs. Dance you so hard, you sweat right through your boot soles. Make little muddy footprints on them floors. You ever drank agave? They got these *cascarones*, little hollow eggs. Things get real hot at the end of the night, them señoritas come around and break one on your head and choose you. Know what's inside those eggs?"

The girls stared blankly.

"Choose you for what?" asked Emma Ruth.

Lucy stood.

"Fine gold dust. And when you wake up in the morning, you got that fine gold dust all over—"

"Dishes, girls," Lucy said. "Before the wind comes any harder."

They protested. She swept them into motion while Beck stayed in their good pine chair with his heels set out before him. The yellow beard he scratched was too thin, she saw, to hide the old craters of childhood pox.

Tom Littlejohn said, "You want, I put they horses out."

"Rain," Caroline announced. The hair whipped back from her face in brown strands. She had her father's thin neck, his round hooded eyes.

Beck said, "Hell, no. This weather, I leave 'em tied. It's a long walk back to the Missouri."

Sarah said, "We have a hair book. If we all go in the wagon, we can show you."

Lucy said, "I think that Mr. Beck might like some time all to himself."

But Mr. Beck said he'd spent plenty of time alone.

IT WAS a relief, an hour later, to leave the reek of lantern oil, the jostle and noise of cards and conversation. In the quiet of the small green wagon, Lucy could still hear them faintly in the large one. But could hear also, now, the low tunes of wind running through the spokes, the luff and snap of canvas. The wagon seemed a living thing, breathing in the gusts.

Lucy settled as the baby chugged against her clothes. One-handed, she worked to free her stays, then rucked her damp chemise. The baby latched and settled.

Lucy, with one hand free, cast among damp bedclothes, tidying things away. Sarah always left a mess, rushing from one thing to the next. Then a corner of old linen caught her eye. She pulled it out and smoothed it.

It was her sampler, the first she'd ever mastered, with its careful letters, its numbers in all styles. She'd brought it, giving up the frame, knowing, even as she did, it was a silly thing to keep.

She was ten when she had made it. She smoothed the satin bricks, the faded red of her childhood house. The elms outside had feather chains of woolen leaves. She'd stitched green grass, that drawn-in day of winter, with the sound of ice on window glass.

She is my delight, she'd heard her mother say that day. In the hall, the boards had creaked. The Christian Relief met at their table every Wednesday, with the sound of scraping chairs, the familiar swing of dresses, the little huffs of women. In the double Windsor chair across the room, she'd bent and looped the careful roses. Blushing from her mother's words, all her instinct was for stillness, so that such rare praise might light as soft as a moth and stay. Only her needle moved.

A woman must cultivate the practical arts, and lend to them that satisfaction of beauty, that the soul might flourish, and the hands be remembered past death.

She had already learned that line by heart.

I could not wish for a cleverer girl, her mother had announced to those four women.

She'll be so useful, won't she? This had been plump Mrs. Holland, whose boys broke the branches off Lucy's father's elms, rattled pickets when they passed. *You'll be useful someday, won't you, dear?*

So the rare dignity her mother had conferred was reduced, by those wobbling ringlets, to a childish thing. And that was how she'd known to adore her mother's stately reserve. Her perfect undemeaning gentility.

And what would you think now? she wondered, imagining her mother's visit, and how she would remove her gloves by the tips to draw and fold the fine skin of them. Mother, in her correct and ulterior civility. She would not know where to sit.

You were right, Lucy thought. *You were always right.*

She remembered going home alone once, after their elopement, to her mother's parlor table with tea put out for two. Just the two of them. She pictured now the window lace, heard the ticking of the Edgemere Queen.

It isn't that far, she'd said, and put her hands across the table to take her mother's. Because Luther had appeared and had been everything she'd never known. Fearless and joyful and wild.

But her mother, snatching, had said, *Don't.*

Because Luther Ross was a carpenter, while she was the minister's daughter, bred down from judges, patriots, governors, generals.

Lucy stroked the old sampler. Twenty-five years had passed since she'd learned that first sacrament of stitching. Her faith in feather chains had long eroded. So now what would she do, if she could do it? When life for so long had been given over to those things her mother had avoided: to making bread and boiling water, to washboards, churns, and irons, with nothing of her own that kept beyond the daily keeping? *And the hands be remembered past death.* So sometimes she had the sense that she was waiting, without remembering any longer what she waited for.

A horse neighed just outside. Mary, sleeping, startled and quieted again. The horse was one of Beck's, still tied in the lee of the wagon.

Lucy heard the moaning wind, scraps of laughter. Distant bells of cattle.

She wrapped the baby, tucked her in a cove of blankets, and left her sleeping.

No Safe Convention

Dark clouds ranked in the west, and a wind rose, so when he rode into another camp near dark, it was with his hat between his teeth, squinting against the spitting rain. Cattle bunched like wedges, heads down, tails to the coming storm. He rode past a line of wagons with canvas clattering like unfilled sails. A pair of pigs lay under one and jumped up as he passed, and Drum shied so he all but came unseated.

Tin plates rolled. A tall white-footed mare stood tied in the lee of one wagon, and then he saw Beck's painted mule beside it, and Junie's roan mare, Sally, and a dark Spanish bay with no white markings.

MacLaren reined in, stepped down. No idea what he'd ask, what recompense he wanted. The thought of questions made him clumsy. Numb-fingered, he worked at hitches and bucklings, swept packs and saddles onto the grass. He hobbled the mule and horse and set them loose to graze.

It was quiet in the green wagon where Beck's horse stood tied, but from the next he heard a familiar laugh, and listened, making out no words, but sounds of talk and gaiety inside: a family, snug against the storm. He pounded the boards, and called.

They all went still. A big man peered out.

"I'm looking for Beck." He pulled his arms around himself, he was that cold.

The man blinked. Child-eyed and a foolish grin.

The hail eased for a moment. The sky lit, thunder boomed again. MacLaren waited, then went to the front and found Beck had come down and was grinning, his hand held up against the weather. "By holy God, sir." Beck squinted. "Look at you."

MacLaren stood. The words piled up behind his breath. Then another blast of lightning flared, and ice roared down from the whole dark reach of heaven, bouncing in white spray across the green.

Beck ducked into his collar. "Come get up out of this damn thing!"

But he could only stand, ungoverned. His throat shut tight to see the man. At last he said, "Where's Lise?"

And though nothing could stand in such a wind, those two words stood, demanding answer. A pink trickle was running down Beck's wet fore-head where a hailstone had cut him, and now the man was coming forward with one arm raised in a broad welcome. And before MacLaren knew it, all the hate he had forsworn was gathered, the dry powder of his rage, it sparked and went. Lightning hit again. He stepped forward in the blast and felt the blow he had delivered and was surprised. Beck reeled back, then steadied and shook his head. He touched his nose and cursed.

MacLaren watched. Clarified by hate. The ice could sail right through.

And then he was on the man again, fist full of crimson shirt and the smell of cotton sizing, of shaving scent, blood from Beal Beck's nose. He bulled forward, Beck fell away, their cheeks pressed together in the pelting ice. Along the wagon, the horses shied and sidled as they drove between them. Beck's skull struck the boards with a dull crack. The Spanish horse swung on its rope and set, and the painted mule sat hard, and MacLaren drove blows, the two of them now deep among those bunched and straining bodies. Against the thunder of the driven canvas, he saw Beck's silent roar and heard his own consume it, unformed, unreconciled; saw the blood-slick nose, pink teeth, the head that rocked against the wagon boards. The horses' forelegs punched the mud like pistons; then, with a rending shriek, the canvas pulled free and was snapping aloft like a great white wing, a sail col-lapsing wetly over while they beat and flailed, and against this glory and release—bare-toothed ice and knuckle, bone and blood—was a dim un-godly shift of goods, of falling glass unmoored boxes breaking staves, like a reef-holed ship capsizing, which he mistook for the sound of his own grati-fication but saw the wall of boards unbalanced now and heeling toward him. Saw the wagon falling.

Out free on the grass, MacLaren backed and stumbled. Through the mist of ice, he saw the flogging canvas, the fallen horses, the wagon on its side, the ribs now bare.

And then he had his knife, was on his knees beside the wreck. The snapping canvas sprayed off hail. He got down in the mud and worked underneath it, blind in the snort and sweat and cut of hooves. He found the first rope and sawed until it parted. The freed horse scrambled up. He did the same again, again, each animal rising to lunge away. He piled the canvas back between the naked bows, in the pelting sleet, piled it back until he found the bloodied head, the dull red shirt, saw the man facedown, unmoving. And it was when he turned the slippery face out of the mud—it was when he felt the give of skull beneath his thumb and was on his feet and shouting for help—that he heard an infant screaming.

———

SHE HEARD IT. Even as the girls shrilled beside her over their game of cards, above the drum of hail, she heard the crash. The call. Her baby shrieking.

They ran uncloaked into the hail to find a man who held her child half wrapped in a pale coverlet soaking and spattered with blood, a white nightdress bright with blood. She took her baby in, she held her—never seen such power of blood, and through it she could see two swimming teeth, the dark oyster of muscle beneath the tongue that filled and disappeared in blood. She turned her over to let it well free, and saw the tiny pearl buttons, the sodden ruff of lace.

Other women had come, and men with lanterns, calling.

Mary seized, her breath stopped dreadful between each cry.

"Come, quick," the women said. "Bring her up inside."

They said, "You three girls come stay with us."

———

OH, LORD, *let her abide with me. Let her abide.*

Under swinging lamps, she sat and pressed her baby to her shoulder. Her own mouth was so dry. Her breath came in ungainly gasps.

"Why Mary's crying?" Daniel watched, his little slate across his knees. Sarah's keepsake book lay open on the bed.

Women pressed against one another, panting, brushing water from their skirts. They had followed her in. She rocked the baby, awkward, finely trembling.

"Look how she wiggles," someone said. "She'll be all right."

"Does anyone know the man who was killed?"

A blanket fell around her shoulders. Lucy pulled it close. Concealed, she worked through her damp clothes one-handed, to offer comfort, to take the bleeding mouth against her breast.

"Was he not your driver?"

"What dor I make now, Mama?"

Mary, Mary, Mary. She thought the name, a prayer, one word, to keep her. The baby jerked and fretted.

"What dor I *make*?"

"Big N," she said, but everything seemed washed in white.

"Show me."

"Well, she cannot show you," said Mrs. Richardson, whose bonnet starch had melted. Now the brim was drooping. Lucy looked away, alarmed that at a time like this, she had noticed such a thing.

Someone said, "N like the gate. Go up, down, up." Then another woman pulled the baby free.

"Mrs. Raimie's taking her to Mr. Whitcomb. So you can rest."

She watched her child carried off and thought: this is how it is. Luther had died the same, with no warning whatsoever.

Poor Mr. Beck, she thought. But no sorrow relieved her.

"We should have something for her nerves. Where is it dear, what do you keep?"

She shook her head.

"Well," said Mrs. Richardson, "I'm sure you should take something."

So she relented. Then sat quietly with the taste of laudanum, following the sensation as it slid through throat and belly and nether parts, limbs and toes and fingers. Slowly, she did ease, while everyone retold it—shouts they'd heard, the horses, the wagon on its side. She remembered having seen a man with matted hair, slung pouches. His belted coat was quilled and fringed.

Women went. Others arrived. In a rustling of dresses, her baby came at last, wrapped in fresh blue flannel.

"Sound as a dollar," Mrs. Raimie smiled; her chin backed into the folds of her neck. "She cut her lip, but he thinks her head is fine. A pretty little scar is all she'll have."

THE WOMEN LEFT, the girls were offered other beds. Alone, Lucy cleaned the lamps, aware of every shape and sound, of Daniel's petulant wriggling, the smells of oil and mildewed bedding. Mary stirred and fretted. A piece of chain clattered in the wind outside, it rose and fell against the wagon boards. Again and again, she saw that moment of disaster, her daughter tumbling, falling through lamps and trunks, bureau and mirror, and was so possessed by this near death that she could see the muddy grave, the lock of hair, the years to come, erasing all her memories but sorrow.

She found a sheet and pinned it, as a curtain, across Daniel's bed.

"Why dorn't Mary has to sleep?"

"I want to watch her. She might be hurt inside."

She moved the planks, rolled down the mattress, made the bed. Each time she turned, she saw the bloody spatters on the shoulder of her dress, and she was not superstitious but it seemed unlucky to put on something fresh so soon. She knew no safe conventions for easing such a worry.

Then all she wanted was to hold her baby and lie down, but Israel's voice was coming. She heard him climb the wagon. Then he and Tom Littlejohn crouched in and hung their dripping coats on hooks.

"Is she all right?" Israel asked. He took up the bloodied blanket, wiped his hands on it, sat beside her, breathing. He leaned and peered. He smelled of mud and lightning. "Whitcomb said she had a bump."

"I don't know. I'm sitting watch."

"Thank him in the morning. You will, won't you? Lucy?"

So she was obliged to respond. "Yes."

"Don't leave her alone again."

She felt Mary's soft hiccuping sighs. Tom Littlejohn claimed the tall-backed chair. Stooped in beside him, the third man seemed a most unwilling visitor. He was the man from the rain, she saw. Who had found her baby.

Israel said, "I think it's time for a brandy."

She'd stowed it under the bed. But he insisted, so they undid all her tidying, got out cups and brandy and sugared cherries. Daniel whined that he was hungry. They put things back and took their seats again.

"Sit down, sit down." Israel poured a drink and passed it. The man reached, then sat on the low bacon box.

Israel asked, "Will you drink, Tom?"

"You gi'n it out sir, yassir, I'd tuck it." He pulled one arm into his sleeve, squeezed filthy water from the cuff.

Israel said, "Mr. MacLaren was Mr. Beck's partner until lately." Then raised his cup. "To your timely assistance, sir."

She remembered the storm, the quillworked sleeve. Now she saw his dirty knuckles oozing blood.

They'd need an early breakfast, Israel said. The green wagon was a shambles, the mare was gone, they'd have to find her. He turned brisk like this, in an excitement, expanding to fill the space around him, moving, directing, preempting all their thoughts, when what mattered was that he had taken up the bloody blanket and wiped his hands on it, and then accused her.

It was you, she thought. Not me. I knew that this would happen.

The anger had stirred inside her while he'd bumped and fussed with boxes; now it roiled. It ached behind her eyes, the back of her nose stung with it, but her place was full of visitors. She eased her neck. Her hand was cold against it.

Israel said, "Are you all right?"

"I am fine," she said, but her voice was quavering.

"Put the baby down," he told her. "Have a brandy."

She bent aside discreetly, wiped her nose against her shawl. Saw Tom Littlejohn pinch his eyebrows up in sympathy.

The lantern swung in gusts. Israel began to fill the silence. She stroked her baby's curls, pulled her shawl to block the light. And found herself watching the man across from her, whose head was tilted back, eyes closed. Whose legs angled off as though his feet yearned toward the exit.

Pity or fear the simple native, but these men had chosen degradation. So she, like Caroline, had been taught to mistrust any Christian who had shunned the fruits of worthy industry, foregone the rules of right relation, slipped over to the darker side, to wantonness, depravity. No, she thought, Mr. Beck had not been a squaw man. Not when set against this one. She saw nothing familiar, in clothes or hands or manner.

She studied the face in its repose. It seemed not so much old, as of an ancient cast, sprung from some antique island of steep-boned men. The beard, a little mixed with gray, looked as though it came and went. Fine unbarbered hair was plaited and forgotten. He was very lean, his whole frame the expression of fatigue, but was strung and ready nonetheless. When Tom wondered aloud whether Beal Beck had any folks, this man stirred without a pause and said, "There's a brother in St. Louis. I'll see his things get sent."

Her brandy was untouched. She found it, and sipped. Then said, "You're wet and cold, the two of you. I'll find you blankets."

––––––––––

HE HAD BEEN a trader with Hudson's Bay, he said, when they were settled again and Israel asked his business. Clerk, he said, cartographer and trader. Draped in a coverlet, his feet pulled in, he leaned above his cup, and she watched his eyes flick under the brows as he answered Israel's questions. He never looked at her. It was a conversation between men, and she should have excused herself but could not.

He had led brigades through the mountains, men who did the work of trapping in the West. Scores of men, he said, but women and children might put the number to a hundred.

"Women and children?" It was a measure of the brandy she had drunk, besides the laudanum. She was never one to ask, if quiet observation might discover.

Now she suffered the briefest glance. Women did more work than men, he said, and did it better: carried burdens, put up camp, found food, cooked, took care of hides, trapped hares and martens, netted snowshoes, minded horses, fixed canoes. She saw then that he was speaking of squaws, not women as she'd conceived them.

"While the men all smoke their pipes," she said. "It's the same with us."

But she'd used the wrong tone if she meant to jest, and was not rewarded, when on any street she would have shunned him. She would not have admitted him across her Iowa threshold, would have burned the blanket she had loaned.

So why did she blush and smell her baby's hair? What put him so suddenly above the man now dead, but that he seemed all economy, restraint, a living education in necessity? Each phrase he spoke impressed her more with its simplicity, its authority, so that she became aware of all their efforts at trimmings and civility—lamp, coverlets, beds arranged just so—even these rude efforts must have struck him as ridiculous, as though they had no sense of the essential; as though, like children, they were unable to cut through it all and choose.

Israel asked, and this man answered, and she saw the Polar Sea. She saw canoes and dogsleds, great wooden forts, the industry of men. She saw beads and scraps of fur, a pouch with a bone button. The Babine, he said. Vancouver. Mary's sink. Sacramento. She saw his teeth, his eyes, and listened until the facts of her own life seemed not facts at all but petty doctrines and conventions. Such simple gravity as this man had was gained only by long and difficult conversance with the world.

He is fearless, she thought.

An exalted sanity overcame her. He was speaking or not speaking, and she heard it; she glowed, she breathed, afraid this sense would leave her. All past failures were inconsequent. Nothing that had once obliged her seemed in any way important. Some other path had opened now; she felt a strength, an awe, to see in this man's face a life of such great scope and deprivation.

And then he rose and handed Israel his empty cup.

"Thanks for this," he said.

She said, "Stay with us while it's raining. I'm sorry about Mr. Beck."

"It was my doing. I'm sorry for the child." Then, in their following silence, said, "I startled the horses."

So she looked at Israel and said, "Then I suppose we're all to blame."

THEY TURNED IN soon after that, let Tom Littlejohn sleep propped in the small foot space where the baby generally lay.

Lucy, in the narrow bed, stroked Mary's hair. The storm was easing. She heard Tom Littlejohn's slow breathing, thought of her own safe harbor, warm at least, sheltered but for steady drips, only somewhat damp. While that man had never lived but in the dark and rain.

He burned in her imagination.

She'd had too much to drink, of course. There had been an hour during which she'd come unmoored, but already it seemed distant, foolish, after the rituals of bed. She had washed her feet and hands. Israel had helped her with the corset.

It was only that she'd never seen, in any man, a state of such transparency. It was beyond bombast or humility, vanity or irony or any trick of character in the men she knew, who feared. Who lacked the true resources.

When one's particulars become at last too cumbersome and are shed, there is only this, she thought: awareness and a ready frame.

The baby stirred. Israel said, "Are you going to sleep with her all night?"

"No," she said, and was herself again. "I think she's better now."

THAT GREAT STILLNESS

❧〰❧

THE STORM BROKE into ragged clouds. The moon sailed in slow passage. The frogs began.

His blankets were wet, and his clothes were wet. His freezing feet had slowly chilled his blood as the night's events swarmed through him. He kept seeing Beck's smile, the arm held out in that affront of generosity. With a smirk, stepping clear around the question. *Where's Lise?* Somehow calling down that mad black rage. He hadn't known it was inside him. How much he'd hoped for her.

Long waves of cold quaked through. He pulled the blanket, remembering the child he'd held inside his coat, how in the storm he'd felt the downy hair and known the small smooth curve of skull against his palm, the surprising weight, the perfect fit as proof that one was made for the other. In the wagon, he had watched the woman cradle that same small head, her fingers spread; had seen those gentle flutes of bones. He'd all but forgotten the grace a woman's hands assumed in taking up a child.

By some strange fate, he'd earned the favor of these people.

He'd sat in the smell of salt pork, lanterns swinging; closed his eyes, more spent than he had ever felt, while all sense of what had happened began to pull apart like clouds, the unaltered stars shone through. But he had jarred something from its rightful place, sent it skidding across the firmament. A man. A friend. He'd answered the questions he was asked, put sensible words together while rain drew soot from the canvas ceiling to drip on them like watered ink.

How many *would* declare themselves? he'd wondered. It seemed that not a soul had seen them.

I should go, I should go, he thought now. But had no idea where.

Lise was dead, or she'd have been here.

IN THE FIRST gray light, he went through Beck's possessions, familiar with the mind that had arranged them. He knew the tidy bundles in their oilskins. Fresh shirts. The shaving kit with lilac scent, the cards, the elk-bone dice.

His hands were stiff, clothes heavy from the rain.

He found traps and chain. The tools were greased and wrapped. New rope lay coiled and tied, half braided. In the tea can he found *reales* and U.S. dollars, some beaver tokens, all knotted in a cloth. He counted what his missing horses had been worth, but there was too little, and in the end, he kept nothing but tea and sugar and other things that would spoil or were not worth sending. He bundled and noted the rest to see it carried east.

A trumpet sounded. Mules brayed in answer.

He found the body where it lay on a high trestle of chairs and planks beside the righted wagon. It was a shape under oilcloth, nothing more, dew silvering the folds. He thought he should take off his hat or pray, but morning had leached all feeling, it seemed, or left none true enough to guide him.

Camp was stirring by the time he found his horse and mule. He saw Sally grazing in the mist, and caught her up as well. The Spanish bay was gone. Piece of flash, he thought. Good riddance.

The saddle from his barn lay in a puddle, his parfleche soaked with rain, only rags and rinds inside it, Beck's old gloves, wet biscuit. Then under all, he found his own small writing box with pen and ink, his ledger in waxed linen, tied with string.

He heard the voices of the family waking, heard the woman murmur. He remembered earnest eyes, fair hair, a small pale face, its pensive peaks. She'd thanked him for his help. She'd told him it was providence.

And then he was packed and riding west into his shadow, the morning grass weighed flat with rain, the nodding horse's dark-tipped ears before him.

ALL MORNING he rode beside the traveled way. The horses splashed through sheeted water. The road was fouled by muddy mats of willow thrown down for the churning wagons. He kept to the sides of hills. On a bend beside a stream, he crossed a camp, deserted now, littered and scored by ashy pits like mortar holes. Black mounds of excrement lay with newsprint wipings.

Soon he came on creeping oxen, scowling farmers plodding through the muck. He passed them wide, but they called out to him, "Hail there, where you from? You know the Oregon? What's it like?" He saw the fine shudder of the canvas. Saw the children peeking out.

HE LEFT the road, followed old elk trails, but his thoughts kept sliding back to lightning, that feel of giving bone. Righting the wagon, they'd pried Beck's body out of the clay, turned him over; the farmers in their oilskins looking down, their backs all turned like cattle to the sleet.

Now old bracken in the hollows wet him to the waist. He judged the light, watched for holes, studied gatherings of crows where they hopped on melting carcasses. The mule would graze and trot, graze and trot. He knew where she was by the sound of her packs, distant or near, the muffled clank of traps and kettles.

HE CROSSED Wolf River the next day and left Beck's panniers at the Agency, noted for St. Louis.

Clouds built up again that evening. Soon the rain lashed down. He dropped for shelter into a gully, sat his horse under dripping oaks among the mossy racks of antlers where centuries of elk had yarded in through winter storms. Now this land was overrun, the tribes all pushed together across the Missouri border. Now those big herds were gone.

That night he lit a fire in a grove above a creek. He held his hands to warm against the flames and drank McMunn's Elixir. After a while, he found the ledger and unwrapped it.

The silence spilled through him, it rose and fell like breathing.

He thumbed the pages. He saw the rendered section of a range. A note scored latitude and longitude, an arrow marked a notch he'd crossed while trapping. Then a paragraph:

> The Elk will flee if his heart be missed by inches, though fleeing only quickens death. He'll race for miles, bleed his strength away, not harbor it as the Bison in some effort to live. Tracked to the finish, if yet alive, he lies in the grass, & the eyes are dark again and unafraid. Some change has come on being more than mere exhaustion. He is overtaken by that great Stillness which precedes the passing of an intelligent Soul.

He threw branches onto the fire with no memory of such an elk. Then turned the pages, looking for what he'd loved: some mention of his wife, his girls or Alexander, Beck or Baikie, Moise Kochem, Mary Tadzahot, old Noonday, the place they used to live. Looking for some clue as to what he should have seen but hadn't. But it was all like this: maps and marks and a few vain lines in imitation of more learned men.

He drank again and lay back. The only thing the pages showed was who he must have been: his busy pride, his self-concern. A man who had not owned his life enough to wonder what he cared for.

So he drank again, felt the silt of opium sift over jagged secrets until the robes began to seem as warm and soft as cattail down.

Next morning he rose and packed again, urged to some part of the world still empty enough to hold him.

———

HE LIT no fires. Eating came to seem ingenuine.

He sat on his heels beside a puddle, the sun a certain gold, seeing how the light struck through and lay the shadows of small springing leaves exactly on the silty floor. And in that beauty, it seemed for a moment possible that whatever force of nature could coax up leaves from nothing might do the same in him. But the following days brought nothing. He was amazed how little breath he needed.

In white light one afternoon he saw the sky begin to seethe and swarm, saw trembling drifts, it seemed, of small floating jellyfish. They fell like snow, and his eyes fell with them, and they jumped and fell again until the trees came over.

And he rode again the next day, but soon an instinct for stillness absorbed him until he found himself in drowsy grass, jacket pulled over his head against the flies. Warm, purified by light, he fell into a dark so fixed he couldn't wake, though Alexander played beside him. He heard the winding of the clockwork toy, opened his eyes and had glimpses, but his lids would fall again. The deadweight of his limbs refused to stir.

He heard the mule snort, high and nasal, giving him her warning. Then voices broke through.

The air roared softly. Light drew him up like liquid. He saw the relic of a mitered hat, a face striped bright vermilion, a necklace made of spoons and Venice ruby. A brass-tacked carbine, cradled.

So he stood in all this thick and pulsing air, lifted his hat to set on his head, but when his hand arrived, there was no hat in it, and he gazed until he understood that it had fallen at his feet.

And when he saw it there, he fell out laughing, sure that nothing so comical had occurred in all his life, the hat on the ground and his hand to his head—he was bent-kneed laughing, hands hanging helpless and all his breath gone from laughing; tears formed, and he gasped and pulled for air, and soon his legs gave out. He knelt, forgetting why they'd come. He stretched his jaw and sucked the empty sky, not knowing what to do, there was so little air. Maybe he'd forgotten how to breathe. Maybe the air was all consumed by laughter.

Courage Once

⌒⌒⌒⌒

O<small>N SUNDAY THEY GATHERED</small> under a hazy sun and sat on chairs and trunks with the smell of bacon lingering: boys with cowlicks slicked, boots cleaned for this one hour; men at rough attention.

"*He* works through our faculties."

The Bible, standing open in Mr. Olmstead's hands, was a source of inspiration, Lucy presumed, as he took not much from the literal text. But he gazed out over them with great authority. His voice was strong and resonant.

"*By* His grace we carry the harvest, to which each farmer has given his toil."

A sudden wind stirred through them, tilting hats, lifting bonnet strings. It would be a drying day. Thrown together now, all shades of faith, and with the need of a quick passage, Lucy hoped there might go among them the kind of tacit indulgence that would permit such work on the Sabbath. Though she'd never be the first to dare it.

"*Within* us He has planted mental faculties, to be developed through application."

She closed her eyes and pictured again the Hudson's Bay man. She had tried, these past days, to keep him near in memory: that remarkable person who, for one night, had shown her what it was to be fearless.

Daniel swung his feet. Israel stilled them.

"*Around* us He has lavished for our gain a country rich in resources, these natural gifts and forces to be controlled for man's own ends."

Was it faith she lacked? Certainly she had less confidence than Mr.

Olmstead in the world's docility. Her first thought that morning had been her lack of china for serving Sunday tea. The forces of nature had certainly seen to that.

She had cried, the morning after the storm, to find the box overturned, her cups and saucers all to smash. She'd pulled out shards still wrapped in paper, jagged angles of azure, hand-painted wheat, gold filigree. Behind each, some friend's memory or fond event.

Israel had tried to sell the set for boots, of course, before they'd even started. "They're cups and saucers," he'd kept saying. "They're nothing you can't spare." He'd never understood that bond, that slight womanly indulgence: to sit on a Sunday with some dear acquaintance, or alone in blessed peace, with steaming tea in china. How she'd always loved the bone-glass clink and rattle, so different from the workday thump of common ware. It was as though the very brittle delicacy put up, in that hour, a shield around her, made her somehow similar, to be treated gently and with hushed regard. Her children had not disturbed her lightly when she sat like that, with tea in a china cup. And men might think that china was only proof of money. But women whose memories were still sharp from harder times all knew that china was most truly about rest, about snug homes with corner nooks, a table where one might sit at ease. She had generally had this, and her mother had looked down upon those others not because of poverty as such, but because they'd lacked the leisure to make use of such fine things as these—the bone-white sugar bowl, the creamer clamshell-pink—that made more fortunate women civilized, and of like mind.

"*All this*, His endless bounty, shall be now to our profit. These stones, these trees, this fertile earth, the timber He has granted, have waited out the ages for our coming. So we must employ our earthly powers for the good, and work in concert as the very hand of God, to put this desolation to right use."

She sighed, reminded of the work ahead. Swept hard along in righteous enterprise, she had no way to convey to Israel the scope of this small loss: in shards of blue, broken birds, a future with no boundary between herself and the rounds of work the days presented. Tin would never do, there was no civility in tin, it could not soothe. No, the china was lost to her, and to her girls who'd stood to gain it. There would be no pretense now of gentility on that far shore.

Mr. Olmstead's head was bowed. She lowered hers, obedient, and with Israel's steady draw and sigh beside her, tried to remember James MacLaren's face as he had leaned at rest. What she'd felt exactly on that night was lost. Now she could only shape him to her own ideal. She preferred him as a father, tall and gentle-voiced. She tried him in good clothes. She sat him gravely in a parlor, amid the rustle of silk dresses. She heard the clink of silver on a china rim.

THEY HAD FORMED into a solid party, it seemed, of some forty wagons. The men elected Mr. White as captain. Israel was one. They crossed a river in more rain, then had a drying day, the evening cold and still. Frost lay sharp next morning. She walked. She cooked barefoot while clots of mud fell off the wagon, and the girls with knives cut chunks of the day's mud from all their shoes and scrubbed them. She went to bed, fell into dreams at once, with no idea where she was. All her nights this journey seemed filled with exhausting, rolling dreams in which she saw and desired and feared things in places she'd never been to, with people she had never known.

In the dark she turned, and when she slept again, she was carrying packages along a river landing. Mary was in one arm, wearing a yellow dress. She set all on the planking, the baby among the packages. She turned to see the river, wide and dull. Then saw her baby fall. She saw her sinking.

She leaped in after. The water was clear, not murky green at all, but a beautiful turkish blue. Sunlight struck on white sand far below. And through the shafts of light, she saw her baby sinking down past columned pilings. Her own skirts seemed to hold the air, to buoy her, and her girl was falling as swift as stone, the little face turned up, pale hair waving. Billowing down and down, the yellow dress now smaller, smaller, pulled forever into darkness.

She woke. Mute. Motionless with grief. The dream ran itself again, stubborn and fixed as any real event, admitting no revision. Again and again Mary fell in billowing yellow, with waving haloed hair.

This child was too great a gift, and would be taken.

The hanging wick threw a faint still light. Lucy crept to her knees, leaned over the cradle, and listened while Israel slept on, undisturbed.

It's just like you not to wake, she thought. She could see the contours of his face.

She wished for someone's comfort. If she woke him, though, and asked, it would render the giving worthless. So she didn't, but lay beside him, thinking about sorrow and all the real grief mothers had endured through time, and could never wake from.

How impossible was consolation, and how necessary.

She thought about the years to come, and whether she could ever bear to lose a child, why mothers were fated to dream this way. Until it seemed such dreams must play a part in hardening off the tender heart, like those chills that toughened seedlings on spring nights, by God's design: in the safety of our sleep, exposing us to the icy blasts of possibility—the unspeakable future, the unquiet past. To make us stronger in the daylight world.

She wondered whether Luther would have wakened.

LUTHER ROSS HAD left the world the day he'd stepped back off the walk at Simpson's mill and fallen. Emma Ruth was five then. Sarah had been eight. He'd died an hour later with sawdust in his hair and men shoveling the bloody sawdust away from where he'd lain. She never dreamed about that death, exactly. But he did come back sometimes, so she lost him freshly when she woke. Or he died in other ways.

They'd been in Ohio then. It was a poor house they'd shared, but more than she could keep. And because she knew she could never take her daughters home to Pennsylvania, she'd decided on the only other course of action. At last she'd crated their belongings, boarded and traveled for a week of trains and inns and slow connections, to arrive in the state of Iowa at the end of a treeless lane she'd never seen before.

She remembered how they'd set their small bags on the verge beside the muddy road, in the jingle of harness bells receding. Then stood, the three of them, their small gloved hands in hers. They'd seen the house across the greening fields, and behind it, the tall gray barn.

She'd known her husband's family only by brief letters. Looking out train windows at strange passing country, she'd wondered on those days of travel what parts of Luther she might find among his brothers. What kind of mother might have raised him.

They'd tied the dog to the pile of baggage. She'd firmed her daughter's hands in hers and set away, with Peg's howls quavering behind them. Chill wind blew their skirts against their legs.

And for all her doubts and hesitation, they were received and warmed, fed, consoled. Five grown brothers took her hands and cried. Such grief, in its frank expression, had alarmed the girls.

She'd moved into the downstairs room and taken on old Mary's care. Washed dishes, milked cows. The corn grew, and she and the girls went sinking down the rows, step by step through steamy mud, through whispering leaves, yanking pigweed, picking earworms. Emma Ruth would laugh, flashing through the stalks, tight with Samuel's girls. Sarah hung silent by Lucy's skirts all day. A girl that tall, they said, should work her own row.

To her daughters, she'd said: *Don't say ain't* (delivering corrections behind closed doors, murmuring in a kitchen corner). *Don't say ruint. Say ruined.* She'd been too proud, too awkward. At sea in another woman's house, having run one of her own. Samuel's regard brought down Olive's silence. The run of middle brothers—William, Mahlon, Cyrus, Darius—still lived in hope of marriage. Old Mary kept reminding her.

"Well, I could never choose," Lucy had replied. She'd kept to widow's black, stayed home from picnics, walks, grange socials.

Still, awkwardness arose. She'd had to pause one night alone, on finding Mahlon propped and waiting in the barn's open doorway.

"I mean to buy that sow off Bill Brewer next week." He'd said this to her flatly, in flat evening light with swallows darting and diving, appearing and disappearing in the tall door frame. Her hands had throbbed with tiny cuts from picking corn all day.

He'd followed her into the cooling room, its trickling sound of water, the bitter damp of lime and pale stone glowing in the dusk. The sound of his clearing throat behind her had raised the hair on her neck. She'd put fresh muslin in the strainer, poured the milk. He'd said, "I know I can't be Luther."

The pail was empty. Bringing it down, she'd knocked the rim against the counter's slate, and the sudden hollow blow had stopped her heart. Like a door's slam in a gust. Like the impact of a falling body.

"No," she'd said. "You'll never be."

Israel came calling not long after that. Lucy had seen him a few times before: a good-appearing man, much older than she was. Then he'd left his

card and invitation, and she had dressed next Sunday and allowed herself to
be driven off for the good noon hours. They'd sat in his boardinghouse parlor, she nearly mute with unease, imagining her daughters there at home.
Where any Ross, old Mary would be saying, was good as Israel Mitchell.
Lucy had been half appalled herself.

She vowed not to be hasty. He visited again not once but twice. Before
two weeks were out, she had a set of books from him: some histories and the
novels of Scott, in ignorance of her tastes. She admired the excellent binding. Riding back by buggy light—the widow with the widower—she'd
judged him kind and dignified, well furnished with ideas. Though they
lacked a common bond of melancholy, it seemed. He was much too pleased.

The next Sunday he had driven her to a house he knew, forlorn and
given up for debt. It was modest, not old, a neat square, double-pitched with
a chimney through the middle. Behind him, she had waded through the circling roar of insects, weeds rustling chest-high to seed. Not many consider
the value of a built house, he had told her. The whole country covered in
cribs and hovels by men thinking to save by their own labor, and it costs
them more than they imagine, and their labor besides . . . The key had
turned, the front latch worked with a clean click. The frame was true. The
door, he showed by silent exaggeration, swung easily.

Inside, it was dim. The weeds, so high against the windows, threw an
underwater light. In the kitchen, a broken pane had let the weather through.
Frail grass grew between stained boards. She had followed, room to room,
he musing aloud how nature abhorred a vacuum, how litter and weeds soon
filled what had not been filled with the better efforts of man. It was a lesson,
perhaps, he'd said. A metaphor one might take to be instructive in the relations between men and women. The vicinage of the heart not meant for long
to remain unoccupied.

"Vicinage" had been the winning word. It had intrigued her, confirmed
her appraisal of his intellect, stirred the prospect of certain unforeseen abili-
ties. What else would he be capable of saying, a man who could use the word
"vicinage" with such assurance?

In the upstairs room they had found a dead meadowlark on the floor:
shriveled eye and yellow throat, the beak sharp, dry, dusty. Lucy had raised it
by its wiry feet, left maggots in a damp patch where it lay. Carried it to the

window, which he'd opened silently. It had fallen through the leaves of a crab apple tree and disappeared.

I've had one chance for love, she'd thought that day. I likely won't have two.

———

SHE WOKE to a morning with all signs deemed right for shearing. They quit travel early, made camp on sloping lawn above a branch of the Nemaha River. It was warm at last, with a drying breeze, and it was not unpleasant to be cooking beans while dogs dashed barking, men whistled, sheep bunched into makeshift pens.

After supper they had brandy with the Whitcombs, and Israel stayed. Lucy brought the children home to bed and was reading when he came out of the dark.

"Come walk with me," he said. "It's a pretty night."

She had just been turning in.

But he persisted, and had flowers. He showed them to her by the lantern's light. "You never walk with me," he said. "It's the finest night we've had."

Together, they ducked the arms of drying shirts. Distant petticoats stirred on their pins. Clots of wool still roamed and glowed along the grass. It was not so bad, she decided, to be out.

They walked over a low rise, and then another, and soon the camp was gone and they stood on a dark swell of grass. She looked up, realizing she'd not seen a sky like this, never imagined the true reach of stars: they filled the whole black span of night like icy sparks spun crowding out, a frozen moment of some great celestial detonation, confused and alien in their arrangement. They chilled her.

"Ah," he said. "What do you notice?"

She breathed and would rather not have answered.

"Well?"

"The emptiness. Our smallness."

"No, I mean the clarity, look. There's no effect of winking."

So she was corrected.

He faced away west and said, "I wish you'd trust, Lucy. That home lies that way. That we can keep you safe."

She said nothing.

"There's a good company of people here. You know them. We're all of us fine. Look, I'll show you how to find your way if you're ever lost." He came to take her by the elbow and turned her. "See Orion," he said. "The upper star of his belt rises due east and sets due west. You know Polaris, of course."

"Of course."

"If you have a watch but no compass, here is what you do."

"Israel, I have no watch. Or compass."

But his watch was out already, held level between two fingers. He squinted at the face. "Come here by me," he said.

She protested.

"Put your eye down here and sight."

"Let's wait," she said. "We'll bring the girls tomorrow. You can show us all."

At last he relented, and they moved on together. Curlews rose piping from the grass, wheeled in pale arrows through the dark.

"We're disturbing their nests," she said.

They paused together, turned back into the breeze. She began, with a step, the way they had come, but he stayed, his fingers locked in hers.

"Lucy."

The gallery of stars stood crowded and did not wink. He put a hand around her waist.

"No." She moved off, by instinct. "Not in the air."

"Did you never? When you were young and lively?"

"No," she said, and took his eyes, her own level and true. "Never."

He said, "A kiss, then."

She stepped and met his lips.

In the tent, she obliged him, thinking of the stars and his hand around her waist. Outside she heard a horse's neigh, the steady barking of a dog. He breathed and moved above her.

Did you never?

But Luther Ross, beside a dappled pool, had once undressed her, every stitch, and his hands had wrung down each side of her neat ribs until he had found flesh, and sunk his fingers, and pulled her to him.

Now the night lamp swayed obscenely, wobbled on its string. She and Luther had climbed Grouse Hill, howled like wolves at the setting sun.

Walked home in the dusk. He'd carried her on his back across the little stream. With her hands across his eyes, he'd jumped and spun until they both fell laughing. In a moonlit pasture, they had skimmed dry cowpats at each other, she in a thin blue dress and racked with laughter. Going home, he'd walked the fence above her, easy as a cat.

Come up with me, he'd said. *Come up.*

She had at last, her arms stretched out and back, and he'd walked behind and held her fingers, lending her his balance. He'd had that balance, enough for both of them. That was the irony.

Now Israel, who meant to please, would not quit until she'd convinced him. So her happy sighs were counterfeit, to gain some peace.

He was heavy, then, and very soon asleep.

Did you never?

And then it struck her that Israel had had a youth as well. Of course. Like hers. Before hardening into this particular form—this stranger pressed against her. He must have danced and dallied, done foolish things, loved a woman in the open air.

Who had that been?

She curled her arm around his resting head. She touched his hair and saw it now: all that time he'd told her Oregon would offer better land, a chance to advance, more opportunity, and she was unconvinced. And she'd never told him what she feared, but he'd never told her this: that what he wished to throw away of hers—house and furniture, town and friends— were his confinements. They were only obligations, when what he wanted in his heart was that flashing mare, and a crowded sky, and what he'd asked tonight. A chance to find lost youth, that simpler joy. He'd come to her with flowers, in hope of something.

She had hardened very much, herself. Her own cares had cramped her into this unyielding shape, this grotesque of her young self. She stroked his hair, wondering what was wrong with her, that she had failed to love again. And wondered what had given her that courage once.

Stolen Horses

THEY WERE TRAVELING WEST, these Ioway, to meet the Platte herds that would fatten in the coming moon.

The outriders who'd found him had stayed by, watching while he'd knelt and wept, laughing like a lunatic. They might have robbed him. They should have left—who knew what he was seized with? But one had knelt beside him, offering water. They'd cracked pumpkin seeds between their teeth, filled his palm with slender nut-green hearts so beautiful he could eat them only one by one. Their heads were haloed in the sun.

He rode with them out of the hills and crested a rise and saw the families in a wide procession. The men beside him whooped and were answered by a great mingling of hoots and howls, trills, turkey calls, raised rifles, whirling blankets, these people having kept through life the sensibilities of children.

In the evening they made halt, and he sat to watch the lodges go up while the oldest crones came near. They squatted, bead-eyed, and touched his hair. The skin rode in folds above their elbows. They pressed the patterns of his coat, pinched him by the arm, and whined their tales. A girl the age of Junie came with a mirror and a bowl of paint. Another brought tea seasoned with sugar and red pepper, and they ran away, but he knew they were watching while he drank and shaved, while he dipped a finger in the paint and stroked his forehead and the length of his nose, and while he marked his cheekbones.

These Ioway had come out from the Methodist agency and some knew English. After the sun had set, they brought him into the smell of smoke and sweat and sour grease, where he sat among the wives and relatives and ate pumpkin boiled with last year's meat. The men talked and laughed. To question was impertinent. No one asked who he was or where he meant to go. A woman, serving, crouched in her calico dress. She slid her canny eyes to watch him. Empty as he was, he feared he would be sick. But refusing food was worse. So he raised his bowl again as the children climbed across his legs. He ate while the camp dogs paced outside and shoved their noses under gaps in the old skirt.

A FINE VIBRATION woke him in the dark of morning. The ground was trembling. And then the dogs began to bark.

A dozen others slept or were just waking. A child lay nestled close against him. Gently, he eased free and ducked out into the morning.

It was horses running up the valley, two dozen or more. Through gray light, he watched the long approach, until he could see their forelocks standing, the flashing metal of their shoes, the red flare of nostrils. A few were ridden, and their riders were young and lithe, and one rode a white-foot mare MacLaren knew he'd seen before.

He watched. The horses slowed as they came near, tails flagging in alarm; they swung their wary heads from side to side. Bracing forehooves cut the grass. But the riders raised a stirring yodel and the whole herd wheeled like flocking birds, flashed past the gaps between the lodges. Girls ran out and answered back, shrill and laughing. The horses swept around again, then slowed and milled, and the girls ran forward to herd them through an opening in the willows and down to water.

THE WHITE-FOOT MARE was one he'd freed from Mitchell's wagon in the hailstorm.

MacLaren sat in rising sun, breakfasting on pumpkin in cold grease while the women walked out among the stolen horses. They spread blankets and sat straight-backed as dolls with legs outstretched, mothers, grandmothers, girls, pointing and chattering, keen-voiced, as the horses, on their slender legs, stepped and grazed around them.

"You'll have the bluecoats down," he said an hour later at their council. "They'll take your boys or they'll take you. When I came through the Pawnee agency, there were five men pilloried there for taking cattle." His hands moved as he spoke. Five. Men. Cattle. The talk passed on. He waited, sleepy in the drone of flies. Outside on blankets, the women clapped and sang.

The talk went on, most in Ioway, and he didn't understand it. At last they rose and bent through the lodge door and into a dazzling midday. Their buffalo chief came out and paused beside him. He was an old man, not above five feet, slack chest draped in beads and claws, sinewy arms in gleaming brass. They called him Closed Mouth, but he'd called himself Walter.

The two of them stood side by side, watching small boys throw sticks at the tin toy carriage MacLaren had given them the night before.

Walter said, "All the peoples say yes. So might be they think we don't need them horse. Might be you take them back that road."

MacLaren shook his head. One of the smaller children broke away to squat. They watched a blue-eyed dog, all ribs and snaking spine, slink in to eat the mess. The boy fell over, squalling. Someone threw a stone.

The old man tilted his chin. "Them Sac make two bits. Might be good rifle, to get from all them horse."

The carriage, flung, rose high and fell, battered with thrown sticks.

"Might be you get a more good thing for us. Might be you talk good for us. You are a smart man, redcoat man."

MacLaren considered this, having found himself once more among shit-eating dogs, naked babies, stolen horses. Among people who, with all the food this country might provide, ate rotten meat and pumpkins. Who had not, in all their history, found use for a wheel or a book.

"A smart man," he said, "would not ride out with stolen horses."

So Walter, cunning, said, "Then might be only you are good."

IN THE END, he took some boys. He packed his own horses and set out in late midday with the white-foot mare on a rope by his side, all of them tagged at first by a small army of children and dogs.

The herd closed up at last and followed south and east across the grassland. They kept a steady jog, and for a long time, there was only grass and sky and the muffled thud of hooves.

Toward evening they settled in a swale to rest. He stood Walter's boy as sentry, and the others stretched out on the naked grass like dogs and slept. He was bending to light his pipe when he saw a stout gray lift its head and turn both ears toward the setting sun.

Walter's boy gave a low whistle. MacLaren stood. Against the glare, he saw in wavering silhouette two sets of long ears striking up, dark daisy petals. Their heads were up, rumps down, in the low Mexican gait of cart mules. They wheeled at a distance and halted.

Walter's boy strode down the slope. The other three, already awake, sat on their heels and murmured. MacLaren found his telescope and aimed it.

They were farm boys—armed but awkward. He saw an old long musket, a light narrow-bore rifle. The mules gaped and shifted and snapped their skinny tails.

They stood off, all silent. The Ioway waited on their haunches, gun butts in the grass beside their feet, barrels resting back against their shoulders. They cracked pumpkin seeds and spit the husks. MacLaren put away his telescope, thumbed out his pipe, and stowed it. He motioned the Ioway to stay, and mounted, and rode out.

The farmers watched him come. Their mules were tired, fretting, dark with sweat. They fired rhythmic snorts like bellows. At twenty yards, the musket rose. MacLaren halted in its sights.

"You stand there. Leave the rifle lie." It was a long-faced fellow. His neck was corded, flushed with strain. The mules stamped and turned, and the rifle swung in a long arc, then returned unsteadily to aim. He said, "We mean to have those animals back."

———

HE WAS ten minutes on the rise, talking them down. Their people were camped waiting at Big Nemaha. They'd ridden the day, spent all their food and water, come more miles than was wise, they must have known, for two farmers out alone on wild-eyed mules.

In the end, they followed him peacefully down the slope. The quiet one remembered him from that night of the gale, and now the other asked half-boldly what he was doing out with Indians, stealing horses.

They drank the water from his gourd. From a woven mat of dried pumpkin, he unrolled the black carcass of a grouse—shook burned quills from his fingers, stripped meat from the bones, and shared it. The men eyed and sniffed. He went and came back with biscuit and pumpkin seed and found the bones were polished. He delicately raised the subject of Walter Closed Mouth's speech.

They hackled. The long-faced one said, "Hell no, we ain't giving them our guns."

He left and readied his packs while they conferred.

When he came back, the same one said, "Give your word they'll ride off and go."

"They'll go."

"It's getting back we're worried of," the thin one said. "All them others quit us."

"Herd on back with us," the other said, "and don't try nothing."

"Make him swear," the thin one said, and the other said, "You take them dirty thieves our guns, and swear."

———

THEY RODE EAST with the herd spread out. Flecks of cloud glared orange behind them. A low sun fired the grass and lit the hair along the animals' dark bellies and shone along their whiskers like gold wire. No one spoke.

They came to the first branch at moonrise. The water ran high, and the horses pushed through the tall grass, sat on their hocks and danced with cautious forelegs, and stretched their necks to smell it. MacLaren whistled and swung the tail of his rope, drove them swimming through. Then took down saddle and packs and sent his horses after.

Under an elm, he found three limbs and dragged them out, tied a loose bull frame and put it afloat. It took three swims to move his outfit, while the farmers watched from the other bank, pouring water from their boots.

He took dry clothes from the final load and dressed while the horses grazed. Then found a cottonwood and settled in rustlings of old leaves. The two men followed like wet hounds. The evening was cool.

"You aim to camp?"

"I aim to smoke."

"I got Van Dusers. We could get us up a fire. Dry out awhile."

He said, "I don't know your names."

"Rufous Leabo." The quiet one stepped and stretched out his hand.

"Vine," said the thin brother, who was sitting. "Vining."

"Vining Leabo?" he said. "And Rufous Leabo?" He pictured climbing leaves. Red-coated weasels or pecking birds. They stared at him, unaware, it seemed, of this embarrassment.

Rufous Leabo took a can from the buttoned pocket of his shirt and set it out. MacLaren heard the matches rattle and found them dry inside.

"Will you smoke?" he asked them.

"Our wives don't hold with it."

"Ah. They'll find you here."

Rufous gave a sideways grin. Vining hunched. His teeth were clattering.

Rufous said, "You been out to Oregon?"

MacLaren nodded.

"Climate pretty good?"

"If rain is what you like."

"Long as they's free of fever. We heard they's free in Iowa, but it found us there. She and I mean to find us someplace clean of that." Rufous Leabo hugged himself with chill. "We had three babies, and they all got took. I told May I'd find us someplace that don't happen."

———

THEY FOUND Big Nemaha by starlight, then crossed and turned along the banks. Under the falling moon, they passed a grove of cottonwoods, some black and broken-crowned, some relics now bleached silver. They passed abandoned gardens, hummocked and tangled with old weeds, and rode at last along an avenue between the empty lodges, low domes crumbling now to show their willow frames. The horses shouldered close, and reared their chins above the backs of those ahead, and rolled their eyes at the dark doorways. MacLaren slowed and reined to the rear, cut out the mule and Sally. The rest went on without him.

Beyond All Bounds

THE GRASS WAS WET with morning dew, and Lucy bore through it steadily. In steely light, she followed the trampled swath the horses had made coming back in the night. It was a game, that was all. She had no other aim. She would follow where the trail led. As a question she might answer, step by step.

Probably he was gone by now.

Over breakfast, she had learned of the horses' return. Israel had spoken to the Leabos. And the men, it seemed, would be engaged all morning. The rain had swelled the river. They were making floats, rigging ferries. No one knew how best to cross it.

And her work was done, so she thought she might go walking and see where her feet took her. There was no indecency in walking. Other women walked. She had left the ugly brogans, though, and worn her dark prunella gaiters with the patent heels and tips.

How far would it be? she wondered. How far was she willing to go? Even her old dog Peg had lost interest and turned back.

A sparrow burst up from the grass. She stopped, breathing a little at the effort of brisk travel. Warm and wet and itching in her dress, she faced eastward to that bright margin of the world—so alone in all this grass, with nothing before or behind but grass, no sound but the rustle of grass, no smell but the sweat of herself and grass. Nestled down beside her boot, a cup of thatch held three speckled eggs, each tinier than a fingernail.

She stood, aware of the tingling in her hands, her feet. As a child, she had felt the same when drawn into some great compelling mischief: breathless and tiny, her heart drumming bright as a bird's.

If she did see him, she'd go directly back and have Israel ride out.

She pulled up her skirts and went on.

HE SAT in gloom, watched the smoke roil through the shafting light and was reduced to this. This dirt. This fire. This spent morning.

His throat could scarcely close for aching. Even the teapot made him sad.

And here it was seeming that no comfort would ever be enough. No solitude. No strength.

He closed his eyes, falling forward in dry fear, falling into all the empty days to come. Into nights awake. Slow stars ticking past the watchface hole in this old lodge of people dead or gone away. He'd lain awake last night with only his mistakes for company. Seeing Lise, sitting on her shins in firelight.

Shall I go? she'd asked. *Do you want me to go?*

By holy God, do you think I do? He'd made her cry. He always made her cry. Then counted on the saving ironies of morning.

But there were none now, and there would never be. There were none.

WHEN LUCY looked up next, she could see the river's bordering trees, old broken cottonwoods and willow. Gray morning had turned a delicate powder blue. She walked on toward what she thought were humps of shrubbery, but saw them soon resolve into a gathering of wattled huts, primitive, domed, clustered like hives. It was a kind of village, deserted in the weeds. A horse grazed, tethered among these huts in a circuit of trampled grass. It raised its head at her approach. She stood in her damp skirts. The morning pulsed and steamed.

SO, HE HAD done it quick, no second thought. Poured the bottle empty into the nog he used for tea. Drained it in two swallows. McMunn's was nothing but draught opium, and more than enough, he knew. And so he was done that easily. And so he was done.

He saw the shadows on the walls.

He went outside and stood. He breathed, in the surpassing light; heard life go in and out. That forgotten miracle. The sky more precious than he'd thought.

He walked out across the grass, and cut his horse free. Then saw a woman standing, distant, in the grass.

SHE WOULD GO back, of course. She should go back. Should certainly go back.

In the hum of flies, she crossed the trampled grass. The horses had returned to grazing.

The doorway was a low dark passage. No sound came from inside. She turned away, began walking among the ruins, this sad small city of some vanished people, almost wishing she had found the place deserted so that she could peer at ease and wander, stand in shadows, ponder the littered dirt. She circled back and stood again outside the doorway.

"Whose village is this?" she called, perhaps to avoid some more deliberate beginning.

"Pawnee," she heard him say after the briefest pause.

She bent to look inside; saw gloom and dust, and the man himself sitting in a shaft of light. His eyes were closed. A pint kettle tilted on the flames of a small fire.

She straightened again, considering the morning, ready with some excuse. None seemed in order. She stepped through the short entrance passage, stood beside the inner jamb. The dust beside the fire was printed with his boots and, in the dimmer reaches, with the wiry track of birds, small pockings where they'd scratched and preened. A stickled fleece and dirty blanket made a bed behind him. Saddles and bags lay strewn. Here was a private disorder on which she had intruded.

The place was very silent. She could hear his breathing.

He did seem changed.

"Mr. MacLaren?"

He wore the coat she'd seen, a greasy oxblood, quilled with faded flowers.

"Mr. MacLaren."

Those eyes turned right on her. The skin across his cheeks was scarred and buckled.

Well, Mr. Kingery had been suspicious on that night after the storm. White Indians like that would steal your horses, sell them back across the river. Agents of the Crown spied out along the roads, allying with the natives, making trouble, keeping good Americans out of Oregon. She had dismissed all this. Such dangers were contrived, she knew, by suspicious men who failed to understand the truer ones of chance and distance, human frailty. In this man, James MacLaren, she had trusted her instincts absolutely.

But now, in his strange gaze, she felt a rising panic at how much time had slipped, with herself unknown and miles away, beyond all bounds. All standards of propriety.

He said something in almost a foreign tongue: did something go.

"I beg your pardon?"

"Your china," he said slowly. "Did it go?"

"Oh, almost all." The question took her entirely aback. She stood in the stillness, aware of everything at once: the beat of her blood, the musty earth, the fall of light through the gap in the old daubing. Outside, the curlew's piercing note.

I've had no choice, was what she'd thought. The speech she'd made as she was walking. *I would not have come, but Israel never hears me, he won't believe, and I can't bear to lose a child out here and he is so certain he is always right when you see he isn't.*

He was saying, "That's flour you pack your dishes in. Put them in your bin."

But then I saw that night. I saw that you would understand. Would know how not to let that happen.

"Your girl's all right?"

In your bin. Now he was pouring tea into a wooden bowl.

"Yes. Should I pack her in my bin as well?"

Because it was a wavering drunkard's hand. He did smile, gravely, as the spout spilled and missed.

Then the tea steamed, and seemed to be for her. The dirty vessel was too large to be a cup yet wasn't quite a bowl. Carved of some smooth burl, its handle was fashioned as a clever caricature of a beaver, teeth sunk in the rim, flat tail curved to meet the base. A tiny eye was set, of glinting back.

But now his head was in his hands.

She was a fool.

"Oh, Jesus," he said, with a helpless humor. "I am done." She watched his head tilt back. "I am going. I am done." And then she saw him cry.

———

HE CLOSED his eyes and opened them in the underwater pulse of blood. Slow dark wing-beats.

He retched, then lay at some point wondering how he might have lived, how different he would be if he had ever learned to welcome any death. At any time.

He tried. In the dust, he saw her boot prints, the place where her skirt had swept.

Then shifting dirt gave way to dreams, such patterns, come and gone before he knew the words. Colors without names. He kept trying to say them and come back.

At some point he was thirsty. He crawled to drink but the air was tangling into golden webs, like sunlight weaving on the bottom of a pool, a delicate liquid gleam. He lay and watched until at last, with great tenderness and awe, he knew it was his soul.

———

LUCY CAME AWAY with spring grass whipping past her boots. A morning wind had risen. She bent into it, skirt and petticoats pulling through her legs in haste to wag in a foolish wake behind her, and arrived after an hour's walk to no disaster but a righteous threesome of girls and her baby on a blanket. Mrs. Richardson called to her, but it was nothing. The wagons were still crossing. So she could forget she'd ever ventured.

The ladies' ferry (she found when she went down to it) was nothing but a wagon box taken from its running and lashed to a pair of logs. Mr. Warren steadied it against the bank. He was standing past his knees in water. His hands were bright with chill.

"Is this the best you've contrived? For women?" She saw Mrs. Whitcomb frown.

The bows of the wagon stood bare. In the bottom of the narrow box, a line of washtubs had been set with small planks across each one, as seats.

Mr. Warren said, "It's safe enough. There's a dozen crossed already."

They raised their skirts and stepped. The washtubs dented with little pops and rumbles. The baby jogged on her shoulder. Lucy pressed the little head against her in its linen bonnet, and followed Jeannie Knighton with Lenore. She sat. Liberty Tuttle, in a dress of wide pink stripes, sat next with open arms, calling Daniel to her lap. Her terrier came at a scrambling leap and raced across their gathered skirts. The dog and Daniel squirmed together, jubilant, in the woman's lap. She leaned to look at Mary's head. She said, "She looks much better, don't you think? She looks all right."

But they were deep, the box so narrow and scarcely caulked that water had begun to rise beneath their weight and well up through the floor. Only the washtubs kept them dry. Lucy stood, alarmed. Her dream, forgotten until now, seemed suddenly an omen. Libby Tuttle said, "Are you all right?" But with a creak and lurch, they were afloat.

Within minutes the river was piling against them, forcing icy water through the boards; it heaved the box half over. Lucy's hand flew up, and she heard the rap of wedding rings on tin. Jeannie Knighton cried out, a shrill little scream, and Lucy could hear other voices but her eyes were full of her own daughter, soft and solemn in her bobbling white bonnet. Such innocence only begged disaster. With soaking hems, Lucy gripped her child, seeing now that she would not be buoyed, only drawn down. She would never keep her children above the pull of water.

"It's really tippy!"

"Daniel, *sit!*" He was not the least bit fearful. The terrier scrabbled and panted.

Made to cross at risk of our lives a very high river.

She'd note it down, hold Israel to account. But the indulgence she allowed herself didn't serve this time; its petulance was in no proportion to this true terror. Head bowed, she waited in the coffin-dark, the rope's steady tug, the rush and suck of water.

And then they had arrived. The men called, the current eased and swung. She pressed her eyes against her baby's dress, furtive and ashamed, and stood. Frank Tuttle reached for her hand, but she declined, not liking him to feel her tremble. She smiled and held Mary out instead.

———

THAT NIGHT, she lay with Israel's arm across her. She never said where she had gone. Those hours would be sealed away.

But she lay and listened to the glassy singing of a thousand frogs, the sighs and whispers of the night. The quiet clank of ox bells. Far off in the air, she heard faint mingled calls, as though a whole strange tribe of people had lost themselves and were clamoring for anyone who might save them. She listened as the sound came nearer, and passed above, and disappeared.

———

IT WAS a gradual finish. An exquisite easing. Slowly, he passed into shadow. Dead-limbed, moon sealed, snoring.

A Pitiable Hunger

⌒⌒⌒

*L*UCY WAS BENDING TO DIP her pail in water when a skunk's sharp face peered out from the muddy edge of the thicket beside her.

Well, you have an easy living here, she thought. With bones and ham rinds and children's dropped biscuits. They had come some miles since morning, and it seemed this river often served a party's noon.

They looked at each other. She saw its black bead eyes.

She set away up the bank, and to her surprise, the skunk came after, loping over the grass, its motion strange and fluid. It was stalking her. It stopped when she stopped.

She hissed. It raised on its forelegs and balanced, tiny fingers spread like stars, tail hoisted and curled in threat, a sinister question mark. She hurried on. In camp, she said, "I have never been chased by a skunk before." But Israel was reading a pamphlet out loud. Somebody of Illinois had employed successfully a method of making butter . . . something standing for twelve hours . . . heated until blisters appear. He broke off.

"Dairying in the West," he told her. He showed her the pamphlet's cover. A grazing cow was pictured in black ink. "Elder Patton had it. By 'West' they mean Illinois."

She saw his satisfaction: her husband, who had made such fools of others by crossing latitudes (as though movement west were in itself a virtue!); whose great-mindedness had already put a pamphlet out of date. Did he wish credit for having left the world behind? She said, "There's a skunk just there," and was glad to see the beans had not burned.

He said, "This man Hale used grade Jerseys."

She picked up Mary and smelled her. Israel resumed his reading.

She climbed into the wagon, lay the baby on the bed, got out a clean frock and linens. "I saw a skunk," Lucy told her. "It was chasing me. It had little hands like stars." It was silly, of course. It was nothing. She hated the way so many women made events of the smallest things and went around exclaiming.

Mary reached wet fingers up and touched her cheek.

Lucy smiled. She oiled the fine pink bottom, pinched the little shoes. And what was all the conviction about goats before they'd left? The choice was clearly goats, Israel had argued, for superior thrift and hardiness. There had been pamphlets on that, too.

But who'd care, truly, if it was goats or cattle, or what she thought about it?

Such a pitiable hunger we all have, simply to be known.

She tied on the napkin.

"All right," she called. "Israel?" She didn't like climbing down so far with a baby in her arms. But Mr. Littlejohn called back, "He left."

"Will you take her, then?"

He stood below and reached and took her baby, little limbs spread clean as a white Christmas star, and it was then that she saw her husband across the grass, smiling, pamphlet still in hand. He was talking to James MacLaren.

SHE WAS the same as he had seen her, he thought, but with the bonnet gone. A turtle-shell comb stuck out of her hair.

They gave him a plate of pale side meat in grease, and cut potato. Two tall girls swept their skirts and sat on a pine box, a third on an upturned crate. They gave him a chair, and he sat with his plate, its terrible meat, and she came by in a sweep of brown and starched linen. She was above; she clatted the spoon and left a pile of glistening beans.

He saw the other families around the camp, their tilting furniture, smoke streaming from their fires, wet clothes sagging on the lines.

A daughter spoke the grace, which he'd forgotten.

Mitchell said the names of the girls, and a few other things, and then got to talking about horses and his purebred mare, the best Kentucky stock. She'd beat anything in a race, he said, and go all day. He called for coffee. The oldest daughter rose. She served her father, served the dull greasy man, Tom Littlejohn. MacLaren held out his cup. She poured, dismissing him with clear green eyes, and he saw she was gracefully built, and blooming under freckled skin. He looked away and saw her mother's eye on him. He put his knife against the pale hard meat and cut.

Coming here across the grounds, he'd passed a man in a rocking chair reading a book while a girl of maybe eight fried up a smart skillet of bacon. She was very brisk to be so young, but when he'd paused to see her, she'd scowled up and said, "Clear off, you dirty beggar."

"Where's the bread?" Mitchell asked.

She said, "I never baked this morning. Daniel, wait."

I have made a mistake, he thought. His eye fell on the younger girl. She smiled. Sturdy, straight, and square, sufficient as a gatepost, brown plaits pinned up. The white of her scalp was gleaming.

He stabbed the gristle and pooling fat, and the world was narrowed down to that, and manageable.

When they had eaten, they put their plates on the grass for the dog to clean, and he and Littlejohn went out to bring the oxen.

"Did that Beck say anything about a woman?" MacLaren asked.

"Ah," Littlejohn said, "he talk all day, hey, e'rathing he say be women. They breast, they dance, put they lip, put they head—"

In the middle of his death, he'd heard a voice say, *Open. Open.* Nothing else was real—no wavering light but the sun striking through the water pail to gleam on the roof above. No soul but what a draught of opium would give. That much should have taken him straight out, he didn't know why it had not. At one point, he'd felt certain that Lise was in this world, because he couldn't find her in the other. It was the one mystery he'd keep.

"No," he said. "Her name was Lise."

"Whey she?" A wipe of the nose against the sleeve. The hand a brutish mitt, a paw. Nothing he had dreamed was real, but he did see now the shine on this man's face, the pores and whiskers, the way he watched for clues. Like a man come into a play without a script.

Open was the word. So he asked, "Did he say, was she with him? In the winter?"

"Naw. Watch out, them pigs come up behime when you sleep. I had my ear bit."

He nodded.

"Get they two." The man gestured at a pair of oxen, a gold one, and one white with black flecks. "They yourn."

THE HUDSON'S BAY man had come, and then nothing was where she seemed to have put it. Plates kept tilting. Spoons fell onto the grass.

She'd heard him say perhaps four words. Then Israel had left them in the sounds of stubbing forks and tin, and because she'd thought of him and kept thinking of him, because she had hoped what she should not have hoped, he was here to shame her.

MACLAREN DROVE not four miles that afternoon before they stopped to fill a washed-out crossing. He found his ax and did his part, soon lost himself waist-deep in leafing brush with only blade and sap, the din of flying wood, filled with simple work in a way he had not been since winter, until the crown of a big elm sailed past the sun and he stepped back.

That evening he ate cold beans and pone with Littlejohn. Watched the ladies in their bonnets, walking back and forth. They waved their hands. They called things to each other. Their waists were very small.

He put his bed down for the night. Broke the seal of a new bottle. They'd made camp in a meadow beside a shallow pond, and he walked out to sit beside it.

The quiet water shone. He sat with his back against the broken limb of an old willow, shut his eyes, felt the ease breathe through him.

A big turtle lay in the long shadows of clumped reeds. Birds dipped overhead. A forgotten piece of cord hung from a limb beside him. He pulled it free, his fingers now alive and curious. Open, he thought, and wondered at the effect of such a word. If something new would fill him.

But nothing happened.

What must she have thought, this woman, who had walked out across the grass to find him? What had she said? He only remembered laughing. And she would never guess how he had grown up hating drunks. All those wet nights, how the rotten thatch would leak. Their bellies ached with hunger. The men were all the same: his uncles and their neighbors, always drinking, always fighting. He and his cousins would wait for a low tide, then scrabble through the rocks, turn over stones and pinch up tiny scuttling crabs. They'd stand in the greasy mud and eat them, no better than a gull or crow. Sleep in the fear their fathers gave them, of the English riding down, firing the thatch, turning them out into the ditches. In truth, the men just killed themselves in boats, and the ones not drowned would drink, they'd drink and sing and then start smashing each other's heads against stone walls while the women looked on, arms crossed. They'd fight with knives and benches, raging through the byres. Hold each other's heads in puddles. Then stagger off together on some dark raid, all differences forgotten, calling out the names of battles cherished for four hundred years, as though they'd bloodied themselves and won or lost each one in person.

You'll go to school, his mother told him. *Go away. You must.*

She had been fair, sharp-featured, but more than that, he'd lost. How young she must have been.

———

"How far does he mean to come?" Lucy asked. The sun was nearly gone. She'd put the little ones to rest. Peg had licked the kettles and come to sit beside her. She smoothed the dog's close brindled fur.

Israel didn't know.

She'd watched a tree come down and nearly kill the man before the second meal. He'd been with half a dozen others, in the brush cutting logs to corduroy. She'd heard the call go up, seen the others move clear and begin to shout. Still the ax swung and still he hadn't moved until a graceful turn and stride, with the rolling green breath of leaves coming past him, limber twigs just brushing his heels. She didn't know what to think.

"Did he ask a fee?" She took the old dog's head between her hands, pulled the silky ears. She had spent all silent afternoon in some attempt to frame excuses she could use, to explain what she had done.

"I told him forty dollars."

"I didn't think him suitable," she murmured.

"What?"

"I said I hadn't thought him suitable. After all."

"All what?"

"Did he not say we spoke?"

"No."

"Well, never mind," she said, and stood to get the kettle. "I wish you wouldn't scold the girls like that. With everyone in earshot."

He asked, "When did you?"

THE TURTLE VANISHED. Copper bells came down like birdsong. Then goats were trotting past, silly udders flopping between their hocks, kids capering after, and he saw the girl among them, Emma Ruth.

He watched. She followed them to the water's edge and stood in a pale blue dress. She wiped her eyes on one sleeve.

After a while she turned and wandered toward him, filling her arms with sticks. The goats came back to her like children; ran their sides against her skirts, snuffed and plucked dry leaves from the bundle she was gathering. She scratched their heads and murmured. When they moved away again, she looked up and saw him, and her face was pink from crying.

There was nothing to say, though now they were not three strides apart. The water shone and lit her edges.

She said, "He's not even our real father."

He nodded, much lighter now than he had been.

She said, "Why did you cut your horses' tails?"

"I didn't."

She waited.

He breathed about it, thinking. "How old are you?" he asked.

"Eleven."

He said, "Someone penned them up this winter without good feed. Starving creatures eat all kinds of things. They'll fill their bellies on each other's hair."

"Who penned them up?"

"That man you had. Beck."

"Were they his?"

"Mine. He stole them."

But her eyes, looking into his, were too honest a blue.

He looked away. He said, "I think they ran down to an old place where I'd lived. Where he was still living. They took themselves home."

"So he never really stole them."

"He was wrong to keep them. He knew I was in trouble, or I'd have come."

"What trouble?"

"I had a girl sick."

He'd thought he could say more, but his throat had fisted shut. He looked off into the light. He heard the goats, their mingled bells.

She ran stray hair behind one ear.

He saw the string wound through his fist. He said, "Did you ever learn a bowline knot?"

He showed her twice, each step, his fingers dark against her naked wrist. He saw the hidden rivers of her veins. There was a nice silence between them.

At last he said, "That was wrong, what I told you then. You shouldn't hear it."

"It's all right."

"She'd have died anyway."

She took the string to try it.

He said, "A girl here called me filthy beggar."

They grinned at this. She worked at the string in silence. "What was her name?" she asked.

"I don't know."

"I mean your girl."

"June. Junie."

She glanced up and down again. "No," he said. "Come up around." Her forehead puckered. She followed his fingers with hers.

When she mastered it, she smiled. And something made him hold his hand up, palm to hers, an invitation, and she pressed her smaller one against it. His own, for a moment, folded over, his joints against her fingertips. And then she turned and went.

———

HE FOLLOWED not long after. The goats lay tethered, chewing their cud. The girl stood by the fire with her mother. She said, "You never teach us anymore."

He passed the low pine box beside the fire. A book lay on it, small and square with banded leather. He picked it up.

Her mother said, "I don't because it's time for bed. I have more work. Now go."

He turned away, his breath grown very slow and dreamlike. The book was open to its marbled lining, and he thought how Lise had always loved a marbled lining, how she'd stare and finger at those swirls and blends of color as though they said more to her than all the printed words they bound.

The woman said, "I saw that tree come down. It nearly hit you."

Something melted when he moved his head, and he waited until the edges of things stilled. He looked at her. The girl had gone.

She said, "People would start wondering about us. If you were killed."

He had to smile.

"You are giving lessons, I hear, in knot-tying."

Well, he had been. He let the pages open. The tiny words came clear.

> The ice was here, the ice was there,
> The ice was all around:
> It cracked and growled and roared and howled
> Like noises in a swound!

He leafed. There were lines all through with exclamations.

"Why did you come?" she asked.

He looked at her. He saw she'd set some shoes beside the fire, all in pairs, arranged by size. "Why did you?" he asked.

She said, "I'm not accustomed to surprises."

"Well," he said, "it is a sudden country." He tossed the book. It landed with a slap, then tumbled. She bent to it. His throat creaked when he swallowed. He walked into the dark.

———

HE LAY after that, alone, pouring back and forth across the night. He tried to close his eyes, to stop. But it seemed like all his days had come alive at once, and he lay weighted, wallowing in all directions, seething with lit moments falling trees old dreams horses good rifles opinions bloody battles children loves a million animals, and the only cure he could think of was to light the tin lamp, pry open ink, and mix it.

The ice was here, the ice was there.
I have seen a Lake, he wrote,

as wide and flat as five days march could cross when it were frozen, a glaring sky and Ice blowing as fine as dust, no Trail or Village in a thousand miles. We marched with our eyes blindered up as Esquimeaux in leather leaving but slits to see & stopt each hour to drink it was that cold. And on one Occasion of such halt the wind quit & sky cleared off to a high bright white & someone said, Look there. Across the Lake we saw an army plain as ourselves, even to buckles flashing. The two Companies were fighting then.

We resolved to battle & die, the Enemy being clearly twice our number & lit each other's pipes knowing that our Bones would sink when the lake unlocked and no one would know where we had gone. Lay upon our arms at ready to do what Damage we could but they showed no sign of coming and after a time Mr. Fidler and Mr. Burland beginning to speculate upon the nature of the light called out finally, One of you fellows go out and test it. John Hall & I walked out from the rest & threw our hats into the air & across the ice four figures did the same, it was only ice, had made a strange Mirror in the air to frighten us with pictures of ourselves.

He paused, then wrote again.

Haloes, or mock suns betoken storms. The heel of his hand was rough and barbed; it scratched along the page as his nib scratched barbed black words. He was peaceful and allowed no exclamations.

. . . all courtship done in Secret. But on those gravelly shores of Hudson's Bay you would see the great white Bears come to laze in the sun one time of year whole Tribes with noses touching & all you could see was the Radius of black-soled feet they would snuff & sleep like that for hours. Otherwise not convening. We could not discern why they would seek each other then, that one time of Summer.

The Book of Wealth

⁓⌒∧⌒⁓

 ℳornings started in a rush and tumble. They always did, this journey. Because they'd agreed on some order, she must be ready, they all must be, or inconvenience the rest. She sat, damp and drowsy, in deep gray light. The baby was still sleeping.

He's out there, she thought. *He.*

She shook the notion free, pulled her fingers through her hair. Outside, Israel called, rousing the girls, his voice martial and inspiring in a way that served only to dispirit Lucy as she struggled with her corset-laces, the self-lacing corset with the little pulleys he had favored, that now were stiff, the stays all stained in lines of rust. Simple bone and lawn would do, but he would insist upon the new thing and order three.

He. His presence had lodged like the smell of smoke in clothing she must keep wearing until she found a way to launder it. What had she been thinking? To summon such a thing?

She fumbled, impatient with her dress, the bodice with the hooks and eyes. Her face felt strange and old this morning. She fingered her imperfections.

"*Mama?*"

Already they were calling. She stooped out, still arranging, tying her damp apron on. The girls were nowhere to be seen. Still in the wagon.

"You need to be up," she called. "You need to be dressed."

"We *can't!*" Sarah cried. "Our *shoes* are gone!"

"I put them by the fire last night. To dry."

And someone this morning had already lit the fire, she saw it flickering.

She stowed her nightdress, closed the trunk, and by the time she arrived beside it, the girls were all hunched barefoot, half unfastened, hands out to the flames.

"Come, come," she said. They lined up to help one another. She buttoned Emma Ruth's blue dress, seeing coals an hour old, and his kettle, and the box on which he'd tossed her book last night. She smoothed Emma's shoulders, thought of her in his company alone. Questions formed, but Israel was coming. The watch glinted in his palm.

"I want you girls out of those chairs and the chairs in the wagon!"

She said, "They're putting on their shoes."

"They should have been on fifteen minutes ago. I found this already." He handed her a fork from somewhere. "Walk all over here, make sure there's nothing in the grass."

She put cold corn bread into bowls, sent Emma Ruth to milk. Put water on to heat. Stowed the kitchen while Israel rolled the beds, while he whisked their tent with his inevitable broom. Brushing her hair, she watched the men bring in the oxen.

"Help me here." Israel always said this.

She turned. "I am brushing my hair." It was one thing she must insist on—to brush and arrange her hair each morning. To wash her feet each night. These small things, she needed.

"Leave your hair," he said, "and help me."

She marked him, with a sudden creeping chill along her shoulders. She put the brush down. Silently helped him fold and load the tent, then went back for Mary, who still slept in her cradle on the open grass. They did this every morning. But not with such unease between them.

She said, "I'm sorry, Israel. She woke me twice last night," and looked up as James MacLaren glanced silently past and was gone.

"He's been a help already," Israel said.

She folded her arms, looked away from his forgiveness. She said, "He drinks."

———

THE HIDE TRAPSACK was already gone almost to mush, from storms and careless crossings. Now the pack mule had buckled her knees in the Blue River and rolled before MacLaren could unload her. He emptied the sack in evening light, poured out a slurry of brown water.

"That mule'm tuck'n got you things wet."

He turned and saw Littlejohn standing with a plate in each hand. MacLaren said, "She does my washing."

The man smiled and frowned. MacLaren took the offered plate. Sweated cheese and pickle, burnt-crust bread, cold beans and pone. Littlejohn said, "You enna cotch ye fish?" Then nodded at the river where it slid over round green cobbles. "They catfish hey, I seem'm."

MacLaren put down the plate and bent to his pile of traps. The steel had grown a soft orange rust. He wiped the first one dry, squeezed, and felt the bow of iron of springs. His fingers, on impulse, tightened. He turned away, hands closing, steel rings sliding slowly, slowly down the bars. Once he'd been able to set these traps bare-handed. Now the bows trembled, nowhere near the bottom.

He let them spring back, felt the ching and snap of steel. Through a slurry of beans, Tom Littlejohn said, "I see?"

He gave it over.

"They big." Littlejohn squeezed and rattled, tipped the pan. The chain swung against the holed belly of his woolens. "You'm like that place? Where we's gone to?"

MacLaren said, "It's always raining."

The man had found his grip, his hands were closing. Brow furrowed. Temples popping with vein.

"Watch out," MacLaren said, and showed the fingers he'd caught once. But the metal jaws fell wide and held. Littlejohn grinned. MacLaren dogged and caught it, set it gently on the grass. They stared down at it.

Littlejohn asked, "They fish out whey we going?"

"All kinds."

"Let's go then."

MacLaren toed the trap until it sprang and landed with a clatter, and picked it up. "It's a long way," he said.

———

THEY CUT POLES after that, and Littlejohn got out hooks and line, and soon they were fishing downriver in a bend of shadow. Littlejohn told about a friend of his called Joe, and MacLaren found himself telling in turn about

Joe Tenney, how they'd netted grouse together as young men up on Hudson's Bay. Tenney was half-breed Salteaux, and had shown MacLaren how to rig long nets and bait them with gravel and willow until fifty birds or so could be run in at one time. The first time they did that, he'd seen Joe Tenney dive in like a wolf and snatch the birds up quick to bite their necks and break them. No blood could spill on the nets, or the foxes would chew those places away.

MacLaren fell silent. The fish lay in fat shadows. On the far bank, he could hear a turkey call. "They're not biting," he said.

"They bite. You wait."

He waited. Littlejohn asked what else he'd done with Joe. So MacLaren told how they'd been on Ogden's brigade together and crossed the desert six days and nights. And though MacLaren and Joe had met when they were twenty, Joe Tenney seemed a man already, generous and thoughtful, with a wry wit and a fondness for wrestling, a native understanding of the country. And after that Joe Tenney quit and went to live among the Nez Perce, and MacLaren visited him once in time to see the man's first child born. She'd been small enough to fit inside a coat sleeve, and Joe had called her after a flower he liked, the first in spring. He'd named her Lise.

The turkeys called again, one to the other. MacLaren stood and handed Littlejohn his pole. He said, "We'll see who fetches supper."

―――――――

MR. LITTLEJOHN CAME grinning into Lucy's camp just as the rice had steamed. Soon she was frying fat catfish in lard. They ate in the roar of frogs and falling light.

"How was it that you came by Beck?" James MacLaren asked from the chair beside her as Israel scolded the girls. They would not eat the skin.

"I don't know," she said. "Israel found him."

They sat side by side in the pine chairs, but he'd not looked at her, nor she at him.

"Did he ever say to you anything about a woman called Lise?"

"No," she said, and looked at him, but he said nothing more. "No." And that was all. She took up the dishes after that. Washing, she saw Israel sit beside him and unclasp the silver box to offer a cigar. James MacLaren leaned

and stared at them. Then, with a few words, he smiled and chose one. Three
more spilled out on the grass. So that she felt, despite her doubts, a flash of
tenderness.

"What did he say?" she asked her husband in bed that night. "About the
cigars?"

"The cigars?"

"He smiled at something."

But Israel didn't remember.

THE ROAD from Westport met theirs that day, angling north and west. Soon
it was a thoroughfare they rolled along, green blooming country crossed
with little streams so she could scarcely see what all the fuss was about, or
how Oregon could be better.

Walking with Hannah Willis, Lucy said, "My roses will be coming into
bloom."

Stands of trees grew by the creeks. Many of their trunks were skinned,
names carved on them, and counties of origin. Shadowy crossings glowed
and fluttered with pieces of fading paper, posted cloth, even folded letters
tacked up in hope of someone going east. The girls stopped once and added
their own names, then Lucy's and Israel's and the little ones. Then Peg and
all the oxen: Pudding and Dollar, Dade, Dan, Bishop, John. Lucy said, "You
should name our drivers, too."

MACLAREN, LOOKING OUT across the evening water of a creek called
Sandy, ate potatoes while Mitchell recited the lineage of his white-foot mare
clear back to the great Snap. Or so he'd been persuaded.

Snap for speed, MacLaren thought. His mother would say that, sending
him on errands. *Snap for speed.* To which the reply was: *Matchem for truth and
daylight.* The one horse had been famed for quickness, the other for honesty
and endurance. Bettors would search the lines of each spring's new colts in
hope that the full virtues of both Thoroughbreds might someday be perfectly combined. And he'd never point out the faults of a horse a man had
bought and was praising, but he ate and thought that if potatoes had a lin-

eage, he'd have listened with more attention: these were finer and sweeter than he'd ever had.

"What are these?" He held up his fork in a seeming pause.

"Carribees," the woman said. "They're from the South. I think Carolina."

"For the rum trade," Mitchell said. "Bred to travel. I ordered seed stock from the Patent Office."

"You grew them?" he asked the wife.

"Israel did. Last summer."

He saw the woman's eyes go to her husband's. Something passed. A hint of accusation. MacLaren said, "The ones we have, I don't know what they're bred for. They're like eating old toes."

"Where do you grow them?" she asked.

"Around the forts."

"Then they'll thrive where others can't, I suppose."

The girls had finished and begun to chatter.

"Why did you choose it?" she asked. "That life, I mean. Living in forts."

"It was a chance to leave."

"You never thought of going back."

He said, "I saw men living to be made gentlemen in that trade, with no more advantage than I had."

"Gentlemen?"

"Of the Company. A trader. A factor." She'd stood. He held his plate for her.

"And that was your ambition?"

"It was no easy thing."

"I see."

But she was right. She couldn't know if she had never seen.

To be a gentleman of the Company: at season's end, to paddle down the river's curve, shaved clean, boots shined, to the blare of bagpipes welcoming you in. Having waited for that day after running men a year or two or three in every kind of country. And then to step out of that bateaux and stride square-shouldered up to the great fort, its palisade and tended gardens, to stride up freely to the smells of supper roasting, private quarters waiting, while all the clerks and laborers spent the evening storing bales, while they fed on shanks and common oats (as he had always done), threw down to sleep on rope cots in the hall.

To dress. To meet, all gentlemen, at McLoughlin's private table, its silver and cut crystal, great platters of duck, lamb, tripe laid out on queensware: China peaks in clouds, clean plates for every course.

None of his family had ever sat to such a table. No cleverness, no luck could win such preference, such food, could ever win new boots or velvet, not where he came from. But he had left that country, and so had others— McLeods and Rosses, McKinleys and Grants—thin boys like him shipped away, in thin coats, and had made good. As gentlemen, they toasted with the best Madeira, roared as loud as any. They cleaved coconuts from the Sandwich Isles with cutlasses after supper. In Christmas boots, they danced along the tables.

She took his plate. "And did you become one?"

He said, "I did."

IN 1832 HE'D gone up to Kamiah to visit Joe Tenney, with a band of Company horses and an outfit. He and Calloway and Gill. They'd arrived to shouts of welcome, a thumping embrace. The girl he'd seen born had grown as tall as his waist. She had a baby brother and she liked the trinkets he had brought. Joe's wife, Mary, served them fish and a paste made out of roots, her flat face shining. Gaps between her teeth.

"I don't know. I got a family now," Joe Tenney told him. "Got a good place here, eh?"

"Come on," he'd asked again. "It's my brigade this time. Come with me."

Two weeks before, MacLaren had stood in John McLoughlin's office, getting that appointment. He'd arrived spot on the hour—mantel clock chiming with a ring like falling coins. He'd stood and studied the carved panels of the factor's desk, the figured blossoms on the Peking rug, his own boots shining in long window light while McLoughlin leaned and read the script of his proposal. The timbers so fresh that the whole place dripped and smelled of sap. Vancouver, the great fort, then greater than any, and McLoughlin was the sole director of all the Columbia District, as far as the Polar Sea. He ruled from his desk with the power of God. No man they'd ever seen had more appeared to fit the part.

When McLoughlin looked up, MacLaren explained, "It's a region we marched through without stopping. Under Ross, two years ago. I'd thought it promising."

"Mr. Ogden does not like that place." The factor's eyes were very blue, his fingernails white and smooth as shells. Come to high office through the luck of breeding; come up through schooling and connections, not through effort in the field.

But Mr. Ogden had never visited this region he proposed. Mr. Kittson had advised against it—Kittson, like McLoughlin, knowing little of the country. With all necessary diffidence, MacLaren had explained these things, standing on blue carpet with his face shaved smooth that morning. "There is a fit interior," he'd said, "behind that range. I believe it."

McLoughlin had thrust his lower lip, protesting.

MacLaren had leaned in turn. He'd reached across the desk for quill and inkwell, sketched a map to prove it. "Outfit me and we'll trap it. There's no risk in this. I give my word. I give my word."

"In this country," McLoughlin said, "there is always risk."

But he was sitting in Joe Tenney's lodge a fortnight later. "Come," he said. "I'll get you anything you want. I'm made gentleman now. I'm a trader."

But Joe Tenney smiled and said, "My brother, I got what I want."

———

THE WEATHER WARMED so suddenly that Lucy's Monday washtub, filled with muddy woolens, seemed improbable. Mr. Luelling's wooden machine counted miles at the steady turn of a wheel—they guessed 180 since St. Joe. Captain Whitcomb and Captain White relied always on stained guidebooks.

Their own Captain White was genial, rail-straight. He rode at the head of their column each day, dense beard quivering westward—more mascot, she had come to think, than leader. A civilized man, rough-garbed for the journey, topped with a poet's low-crowned hat. He looked like Emerson. She'd admired this at first, believing in the outward fantasy: that he was a scholar, farmer, diplomat, soldier, dreaming them all westward, smiling, optimistic. Now she did her washing with the other women, in snatches as they could at noon, and saw how he let slip the practical details and stood with folded arms while the men convened over dinner plates and flailed, high-tempered, arguing about everything: how far to go before they nooned, how late to drive before they camped. How to circle, when to wake. Which dogs should stay tied up. They'd sit an hour arguing that progress was too slow.

James MacLaren, returning her plate at noon, said, "God knows how you came to win a war, you people. I don't know how you thrive as a nation."

They went on. A hundred and ninety miles, two hundred. They crossed a wide Indian path, and some said they were now in enemy country, that the Pawnee were known for their hardness and demands. They ran stock, she heard. Demanded tributes, were cunning beggars and thieves. Late Thursday evening, with Mr. MacLaren yet silent on the matter, she stopped him to ask outright: "Are they dangerous?"

"Are you?" he said, after a peculiar pause that she regretted. He showed more teeth when he'd been drinking.

She said, "What do you mean?"

"What do you think I mean?" he said.

Beside her in bed, Israel said that night that what she knew was all left over from other times and places. "Examine the truth," he said. "In all these years since Fremont, all these people crossing, no white man has ever been grievously harmed by any Indian."

"You think none of them are dangerous."

"Not if treated with respect."

"How can you say that?" she asked. After all, he should know as well as any. He'd been a captain in Black Hawk's war, long before they married. As a child, she'd read accounts of the invasion, those terrible depredations. Who could forget such lurid engravings? Settlers buried to the neck, heads set alight, eyes rolling in agony. As girls, they'd heard and passed down tales of bloody lace, hatchets, looming trees where women were found hung by their ankles and quartered. Scalped babies left screaming under beds. These were Indians, and this was what they did. Who truly could deny it?

"Well, what did MacLaren say?" Israel asked. "Did you ask him?"

On Friday, bright and hazy, they left the valley of the Little Blue at last, and climbed dry shelving hills. Lucy walked, and the wagons rolled, and dust spilled away from the wheels. Israel rode ahead, as always, with the captain and two dozen others calling themselves the Guard.

They passed a grave. The bones of a buffalo. A bleached umbrella tilted in a bush. Josephine Watts, ahead with her three brothers, picked it up, and saw the ribs were broken. She threw it down.

"She's so common," Sarah said, and Lucy shushed her.

They rested in bright sun at what seemed the top of the divide, and had no water, and went on, winding down through dry sand hummocks, sloping clay quite destitute of vegetation. The sun stood high, and the warm air rose and wavered and made the wagons ahead seem tall as buildings. Distant shadows leaped and floated. Hannah Willis walked with Emma Ruth and named the shapes of clouds. James MacLaren stopped once to see they were all right. When they went on, Sarah said, "He had a daughter who was six, but she died."

"How do you know?"

"He told Emma."

They walked on, silent. The sun descended. Still they saw no river. They kept thinking it was just beyond the rise, but then there came another, and then at last the sun was setting and there it was, the Platte.

It stretched away across a wide flat vastness, an inland sea, bright as sheet ember with the sun along it. Hannah Willis came up and stopped beside her as geese began to rise.

They stood and watched this rising, rising from the surface of the water; it was as though they'd come upon the fountain, the primal nation, the origin of geese, the burnished sky alive and netted with shifting skeins. They cried in darkening thousands. The first flew over. Then more, and more, a strange sighing of wind and voices, saying *kala kala kala*. Some passed so low that, looking up, they could see the neat white bands beneath their throats and see their black beaks open and shut, and the living eyes that watched them. Their wings pulled at the air.

"Oh," Hannah said, "they sound so sad. They're crying."

Daniel, gaping at the sky, asked, "Why they're crying?"

Lucy watched them fly. This wonder she had never seen. So wide the shining river. So vast the life: a million wings, a nation interrupted, of hollow bones and feathers.

She looked ahead to James MacLaren on his horse beside the oxen. He was looking up.

She said, "They're not crying. It's just the sound geese make."

Then came the boom and shotgun echo as men began to bring them down.

———

THEY CAMPED at nightfall beside the water, and all she saw next day was sky and grass and sand, and the river rolling right along the ground, with no timber, no bank at all, the water not so much a river as a moving tide of sand. In a certain light, it caught the sun, glittering. It rolled in waves of floating gold.

She and Mrs. Olmstead stood beside it with their pails at noon and agreed that the land was dreary and the water was disgusting.

James MacLaren brought in birds before, but now he brought an antelope, and then another. His passion for hunting was such that she had seen him stand in the middle of supper and leave his plate, having noted some motion in the grass of a far hill. She and Israel would exchange the kind of glance they used when watching Daniel absorbed in some necessary and foolish enterprise. They had plenty of meat already.

"He can't help it," Israel said. They spoke as though the man was no more complicated than a dog—mysterious, in some ways admirable—whose fidelity was thoroughly suspect.

"No," she said. "I see he can't."

———

SUNDAY MORNING she woke to find the dawn a dusky pink. Took up her pails. The camp was made in a grassy hollow, and they had to walk uphill for water, so contrary was the country. The river had put down layers here through time. She angled along, broached the bank. Then saw him, half unclothed and bathing.

His back was to her. Even from that distance, she could see the muscle and the hidden bone, the shadowy run of ribs. He bowed and straightened, pouring water. She watched his back, paired trunks of muscle, the shadowed channel of his spine resolving in the waist's neat curve. The grace of his shoulders, their working depth and breadth sheeted so by water and light that she imagined wings might sprout there. She turned and strode away, her pails still empty.

MacLaren left the camp at rest that afternoon and rode out alone to where the peace of the country drew him, pooled in the hills, dark creases like standing water, this region of the world, to his mind, suffering altogether too much sun. He rode through low bluestem, grama, switchgrass, brome, Adam's needle on the drier ground, and prickly pear, and blooming compass. Great shoulder blades tilted through the dirt like grave marks—buffalo bones more common here than rock. There were hulls of ribs, chalky femurs, porous with time. Rain lilies bloomed in sand.

He cut the fresh tracks of two young bulls in a sandy wash and followed them, and in three hours, he found them grazing in a swale a few miles from the river. He set up on the rise and dropped the first from about two hundred yards. Then dropped the second and spent the next hour gathering fuel enough to keep away the wolves. He'd brought along what he needed.

He stripped the hide of one to rest on. Dined on warm liver. When the fire was going, he took out a volume that Mitchell had lent him, a slim tract entitled *The Book of Wealth: In which it is Proved from the Bible that it is the Duty of Every Man to Become Rich*. But his hands were dark and sticky with blood. He had very little water.

The hills sighed warmth into the valley. He lay with the book on his chest, now thinking that he'd always lived his life in hope of gain. When Joe Tenney, a better man, had lived in hope of gifts and giving.

Joe had joined his brigade at last, through no desire but generosity. They'd set away a few days later, he and Gill and Calloway and Joe and six others from the village.

But for all his own ambition, MacLaren found the region of no consequence. There was no fur, there were no great valleys hidden in that range; it stood a solid mass for eight thousand leagues, defying every precedent of geography. They pressed deeper and deeper but found only small lakes and stony ones, lines of naked peaks as long and toothed as saw blades, dense fir and pines and denser undergrowth. And no fur to speak of, no people of any kind, but on coming out at last, they did surprise some women digging with baskets who ran moaning along the river's bank. It was for this lone forsaken tribe that he'd packed his bales of good Brazil twist, striped blankets, vermilion, awls, kettles, spoon lockets, earbobs, fathoms of beads, fusils, long rifles, lead, and powder. And they were indolent and fearful, lived on roots and small game, had no interest in trapping.

By then his men had developed a great anxiety to be home. So they made north again, dropping down through lowland timber, through tallgrass valleys, into warmer country, on the river of the Snakes. There, one night, he'd stretched himself out and read from his volume of *The Comedies of Shakespeare*. There were only stars, no moon that night, and for hours through the dark, he must have slept with the toppled book rising and falling on his breath, but woke when a spear ran through it and stopped against his breastbone.

In a rush of breath, he'd vaulted into flight. Barefoot, he had dodged, a shadow target on the frosted grass, the drum of hooves behind him, the cries of men. He'd run and hoped to gain the river, each stride another moment he might live. They'd borne down and he had run, head low, arms driving, he had run and run, past all ability to breathe, until his lungs and legs were fire, until he trailed a burning tail like a comet in the night. Arrows speared the grass. A shaft struck through his side. He rolled down the banks, hid in freezing water, in mud and rushes, broke the haft and pushed it through, while his pursuers prowled and were at last drawn off by sounds coming from his camp. The commencement of more leisurely amusement. All night he lay in mud and heard the godless cries and echoes of men not dying.

Past daybreak, the hopping crows had steeled his nerve. They lifted as he neared the camp, circled over on a wash of wings, came down to strut and wait. The men were scattered all about. He had seen Gill's body. Wotolen's boy was in an eddy with an arrow through his neck. The others lay scalped, diminished, like hares shaken and left by heedless dogs. Calloway, stripped and slashed, was dead, and Joe Tenney was dead beside him.

Wet and racked with cold, MacLaren had knelt.

Sinew and stakes had held them. Their hands were black and curled, eye sockets pooled with blood. Tongues and noses cut away. He saw the arc Joe Tenney's head had dug in the dirt beneath him; saw the naked skull, its drying bone, bloody twists of hair and grass and dirt. He touched the cheek.

It smiled.

He'd lurched away, heart jolting. He'd gone to sit against a tree, hearing something very much like laughter.

When he could do it, he'd gone back and talked and stayed beside Joe Tenney. Then killed him with a stone.

––––––

THE DUTY of Every Man, MacLaren thought, and put the book aside. He pulled the bloody hide around himself, and slept.

Blue Beads

"Come," she said. "Feel its hair." She walked, with Daniel, like a visitor in a strange museum. They had never seen a bison, alive or dead. Now here were two, one already skinned, but the hide on this other was as real as life, its foreparts matted with wool, flanks sleek and glossy. Each head alone, she guessed, might be the weight of a man. A dead wolf lay nearby.

Flies hopped and stuttered in pooling blood. She smelled her fingers: musk, the scent of grass and dust. She stroked the great black horns. Fine silty cracks ran from the tips. On the ridge a silent audience of wolves sat waiting.

They had been feeding while the carcasses were unattended, while James MacLaren had ridden in that morning and shown the way out again. As she'd walked beside the little wagon, she'd seen him fire and recharge the rifle as he rode, that poetry of practice. In the space of two breaths, the dance was done, the rifle at his shoulder again. The wolves had sped across the shallow swale, seemed to float, ascending. They'd wheeled along the ridge, hopping, heads down, to eye them. But he had not fired again.

Now she got a blanket from the wagon and came back. Fat intestines spilled. The lungs were drawn, kidneys large as roasting pans. Mr. Koonse held up an injured heart while the old dog watched with civilized attention. James MacLaren used a jointed foreleg as a mallet, shearing through the tall ribs with his little ax in spattering blows; he was silent, intimate, all attention. Each motion came precisely on the next. She remembered Luther with his cabinets, how he'd lean and work, forgetting her, forgetting everything except his hands, his tools, his pure intention. She saw it now, again.

They had come out through the grass alone, with only the small green wagon. Caroline and Sarah had kept with Mr. Littlejohn and the big wagon in the column. But Mr. Koonse and his oldest boy, Alonzo, were here on horseback to assist. The Koonses had raised pigs back in Linn County.

Soon Lucy was in the wagon, piling joints and pieces on a sheet laid in the foot space; Israel raised them to her. The morning warmed. Nicholas Koonse laughed and talked, and James MacLaren smiled back. She envied the ease between them. Mr. Koonse was a pleasure, a favorite with women, a tall gentle man with a small neat head, who smiled no matter what.

She arranged her meat by layers, covering each with cloth. Then heard the men tell Daniel to get in the wagon, tell Emma Ruth to take the baby.

"What?" She leaned out. "What is it?"

Israel nodded along the ridge. She saw nothing but the slope of grass; heard nothing but the children's voices. Then she understood the wolves were gone.

The swale was silent. The horses grazed, unwary.

Then two heads topped the rise: two men, moving strangely afoot, hesitant or lame, who were not Indians. Bare shoulders followed. The bold V of ruddy necks stood startling against the paleness of other skin. The horses pricked their ears, intent as she, and watched the nether parts appear.

Daniel said, "Why dorn't those mans have any no clothes on?"

"The Indians took them," Emma Ruth said simply, and he was satisfied.

———

LUCY KEPT INSIDE with Emma while they dressed. "*Ja, ja,*" the strangers said, and "*Danke, danke schön,*" like caricatures of Dutchmen. Mr. Koonse, as it happened, could speak with them. She found bread, and silty water from the barrel, and a sewing needle. In borrowed clothes, they washed their feet and picked out thorns. They were brothers, Gutteschmidt, one fair, one dark. They'd strayed too far while hunting the day before, been relieved of what they owned by Pawnee, mocked and set afoot to find their way. Mr. Koonse relayed this. Israel called for brandy. *Danke,* they said. *Nein, ja, danke,* laughing with relief.

But there was work yet to do. Soon she had used up all her cloth and sacking. They put the joints and cuts of the second bull atop the first, with no protection from the flies. She had stacked the meat as high as her knees, with her skirt tied in a knot before they could declare it done, and go.

At noon they stopped at a small gravelly creek, lit a fire, and fried fat pieces of meat. Mr. MacLaren had set straight east on horseback, with one Gutteschmidt apiece on his mare and mule, so that he might be back before dark.

"There was a princess, in Bavaria," Mr. Koonse told Emma Ruth and Alonzo while they pulled hot bits from the skillet. "This was last year in the papers. She was sitting in a tall window, winding up a music box, and she fell out. And a cobbler's son was passing underneath, and he caught her. So the king showered the family with every kind of gift. And now they have two hundred acres in Pennsylvania and are living a life of ease."

"That's not real," Emma Ruth said.

"No one would put that in the paper if it wasn't," said Mr. Koonse. "They'd think up something far more likely."

So Lucy was not at all worried, going down to wash. But, on coming back, she saw a distant movement, then saw that it was riders, on horses of every color.

Mr. Koonse and Israel stood to look.

Then she was snatching up the empty washtub, piling dirty plates, gathering forks and knives. The dog looked up from where she lay.

"Come, come." Lucy rushed the children, who were wiping their fingers, unaware. She swept up the baby, got Daniel by the hand. "Up now. Into the wagon!"

She heard Israel call Alonzo to bring the oxen.

She drove Emma ahead of her into the wagon, its slippery sea of meat. Bent and breathy, she shoved boxes, yanked down the mattress.

"Make yourselves safe. If there's shooting, get down and hide." She pulled back the boards, wrenched clothing chests aside. Her strength seemed suddenly vast. "Daniel, there." She pushed him toward the hole she'd made among the boxes, warm meat and swarming flies, dirt, cornmeal grit, clots of moldy things, old onion skins. She saw a sock of Israel's they'd been missing.

Emma Ruth said, "What about you?"

"You hold on to Mary. You keep her quiet." Her words came out like hammer blows.

"What about *you?*"

She piled up things to hide them, standing on the irrelevant meat, thinking of James MacLaren, who should have warned of this. Who should have known to stay.

Outside with Israel she pushed the oxen into place, heaving them on slow cloven feet; they stepped and tangled in the chain, swung their heads with great sweeps of brass-balled horns. Mr. Koonse, on his knees, tried to charge his rifle, but Lucy saw his hands shake so that more powder fell outside the barrel than down it. She went to help. He smiled, a little grimace.

"I'm so glad you're with us," she said, knowing he must regret it. She saw Israel lurch astride his mare, saw him lash her into a surly canter.

Mr. Koonse stood and brushed his hands. They heard the distant keening chorus, saw weapons fluttering with feathers. The fried meat lay leaden in her stomach. The dog stared off dimly, growling. The oxen waited.

She shook her skirts at them. "Get up," she said, not believing they'd obey her. She waved her arms, clapped her hands. "*Get up!*"

They swung their heads, eased into motion, while Mr. Koonse mounted his stocky bay and rode out to join her husband.

IN FACT, they were not murdered or abused in any way, but with no explanation, she soon found herself among an Indian band—the wind coming sideways, all the riders advancing in gauzy silhouette against the dust, squaws and scrawny offspring perched high on laden horses, on great skin-made sacks, on bundles of blankets and robes or straddling the extra width of poles, the combined resonance of dragged timbers sending up a deep choral hum. Old crones rode low sleepy ponies and the young rode behind or on the ponies' necks or on palanquins slung from dragging poles, the littlest in their filthy skins with puppies cradled like dolls. There were multitudes of dogs of all descriptions.

She saw the head of a papoose, round and dark-eyed, its cradleboard slung from bundled poles as carelessly as a canteen of water. She saw young males not much older than her Daniel riding half-grown colts with only strings to guide them. A painted buck rode past her very near, and from her vantage in the wagon, she saw with a shock that he was naked but for a cord around his waist and some strings of blue beads. She stared, taking in the taut uncovered plane of skin, that scarcity of hair; she blushed at what lay open to her view, cradled in the natural state against that horse's sweaty withers; she looked away and back again. His muscled leg hung smooth as a woman's, the foot quite dainty in its beaded moccasin. White plates of bone hung from his ears, and his head was shaved but for a kind of coxcomb into which some feathers had been tied. They fluttered as he turned his gaze to her with a stare more direct and impertinent than any she had suffered in her life.

And why not be confused? If not by lurid engravings, by her mother's cautions of lesser tribes: Negroes, Jews, the Irish harboring strange conta-gions. Of all, the Indian was furthest from God's pattern, closest to the devil. But nothing had prepared her for this richness, for their skin and muscles, for such colors, such reckless adornment; she had not fortified herself for this assault of blue and red and yellow beading, of shell, of glinting brass, the gaiety of bells and calico more gaudy than she'd ever dare. A heat had risen in her.

"Mama! Why you're just not talking to me?"

"*What*, Daniel?"

"Where are those man's *clothes*? I said."

"I don't know." She watched the rider moving off, the neat cleft buttocks traveling in perfect union with the horse's springing back. She had to look away.

"Did the Indians taked their clothes, too?"

Emma Ruth said, "Those *are* the Indians, Daniel."

"The *other* Indians."

"No."

"Will they taked *our* clothes?"

"No," Lucy snapped, ashamed that desire could be so cheaply provoked. But her boy frowned sweetly in concern; she saw how closely he watched for her answer. "No," she said, "but don't you let them near, or touch anything of theirs."

It was her mother's voice exactly.

THEY APPROACHED the camp with much riding back and forth, of delegations forestalling trouble. The Pawnee set up not a quarter mile away. Israel gave meat to all the neighbors and sent more to pacify the natives, so the air soon smelled of roasting; but for supper she served cold beans and bread, not liking to show her kitchen, careful of anything that might prove a temptation.

Her husband, now heroic, roamed like a Chautauqua lecturer. His success that afternoon had swelled him to a kind of thespian largeness. Now he answered questions, gave advice, counseled the wary, while Pawnee prowled in their shameless paint, looking into wagons, touching with impunity. Some, pretending beggary, bobbed and whined in disgusting blankets kept especially, she suspected, for the purpose. Some had dressed themselves in clothing gleaned at other times from whites, the articles unmatched and ghoulish.

Across the compound, Mrs. Olmstead pinned a blanket tight across the openings of her canvas, the whole wagon tilt shut close and safe. It seemed a good idea.

Daniel was gone, Lucy noticed. She found him on the other side of the wagon, feeding crusts to the Watts' barred hens. The hens stilled and squatted in the swoop of her shadow and thrust out their necks in alarm, and she took Daniel's plate and led him. He balked, wailing. Twisted his hand in hers.

"We'll read stories."

She scrubbed his face beside the barrel, pushed free the tide lines of sticky filth, and never saw their approach but smelled them, heard the jingling of bells, her husband's solemn greeting. And would have hid, but Mary was out on the blanket.

"Go up," she told Daniel. "Find your book."

And there they stood, in her own camp, in a careful lunacy of dress and paint: one with vermilion lips and eyelids only; one with painted ears and cheeks who wore, for clothing, a damask dressing gown. Another wore a turbaned headdress and leggings so adorned with tiny bells that the smallest movement produced a shimmering of sound.

She had told the girls to ask their friends if they might share beds that night, as their little green wagon was still fouled from meat. They were away on that errand. She took Mary from the blanket. The big wagon was stifling and maddened tonight with flies. But she would find no ease outside, under the circumstances.

They read poems from *The Children's Companion*. She got out a *Godey's* she had saved, and they looked at fashion plates. She read the captions aloud:

Figure 4.—Dress of rich white silk, the second skirt open at the right, and fastened by a graceful festoon of crimson velvet leaves and Roman pearls. The hair is in Grecian braids, the wreath is of crimson velvet leaves, with festoons of Roman pearls to match the skirt. This is a novel and pleasing style.

Mary beat the bed with spoons, pulled ribbons, shook button strings. Israel stayed near for a time, and then she didn't hear him. Daniel whined and fretted, hid under the covers while flies lit on their faces, all of it so tormenting that at last she brought out the sweet plum wine she'd saved for Independence Day and uncorked it, and all three shared it from the baby's silver cup, and the children fell asleep soon after.

Freed for her own needs at last, she crouched low, quiet as she could above the nightpot. Then poured another cup of wine and drank it, idle and drowsy in the falling light. She read from Wordsworth, chasing flies across the pages. Her eyes walked down the accustomed lines, but the rhymes tonight seemed suspect, set against that leering unclothed memory, his bald existence. A man. In all particulars, identical to those of her acquaintance, but possessed of a freedom so long forsworn among the civilized races that until this noon's awakening, she had never imagined its absence. She had not conceived of any man who could ride proudly naked but for a string of beads.

From the Indian camp she heard raised voices, fierce warbling calls, gunfire. A pocket sewed into the wagon tilt held her bedside reading; she slipped the volume away. Then heard another voice.

She peeked. Mr. MacLaren had returned and was speaking to another Pawnee.

He might have been an Indian. She watched, struck by some fundamental change she could not at first understand: in bearing, voice. The angle of his head, the cast of his eye all belonged to someone else absolutely as if he had changed souls. The quick pleasure she'd felt at his voice darkened to see him speaking by these nimble gestures, quiet words. She had not imagined anyone capable of so thorough a betrayal.

She hid again. Twined up her hair and pinned it.

Flies lit and settled on the bows. The talk ended; soon she understood he was alone. She heard the dipper ring against the metal pail. She waited, thirsty from the wine, amazed by how his smallest sounds could charge her senses. She had meant to go out when the children were quiet. But now, ashamed, she would not.

"Are you going to hide all night?" His voice was low and clear, outside.

She said, "I have been putting the little ones down."

"Your girls are cutting up out here."

Her hands felt warm and damp against her cheeks. She rose, hitched her skirts, put her head out into the buttery light.

"They're all right," he said. "They're at VanAllmans'."

So she descended, walked to the pail and dipped some water. Then stood looking out from inside this fortress of their wagons. His saddle hung on a pole beside her; the wet fleece reeked.

She glanced across her shoulder. He was on his heels, rousing the fire with little curls of grass. A square-cut bottle stood beside his boot. Which explained, of course, the breach of privacy. To call on her like that.

She turned away. In evening light, she studied the Pawnee camp, its sooty tents. Some, low and round and bladder-like, had no doors but were open as sheep shelters. Others were tidy cones daubed with childish figures.

"Must they paint everything?" she asked, and was angry. The wine had made her reckless. She meant, Why did you leave us?

"It all means something. For power. Or remembering. Those lodges," he said, "are all set out like stars."

"Excuse me?"

"In patterns. Constellations."

She frowned up, trying to imagine the point of this: a dozen huts put down in the shape of Orion or the Dipper. Though of course they would have different names. They would see different stars.

"Did it frighten you today?" He shielded the flame and spoke to it.

"Of course." And now he'd cut right to it. Sipping wine, plodding through her poems, she had simply been dismissing memories: Israel out in the dust among them, the voices behind her, their terrible cries. In two words, it welled: Of course. She hadn't cried or known that she would have to.

He looked up and she had to turn away.

He said, "You hide, you women. You're all afraid of seeing."

She scrubbed a sleeve across her cheek, inflamed.

"What will you see?" he said. "Something disagreeable? What are you afraid of?"

She turned and saw him. Her notion of his intimacy with these people had been vague and theoretical. But in tonight's cruel smile she knew the truth: that all this time she had been no more than a hopeful traveler, who, thinking she had only a low rise before her, had topped it to discover more ranges beyond than she could hope to cross. No little conversation could begin to make way into the strange regions he inhabited.

And what was she afraid of? She thought of the leering rider in blue beads.

"With what *morality* do they temper their desires, Mr. MacLaren?"

She had been, to him, the palest shadow. A novelty in a bonnet.

"They are shameless," she said. "Unbridled. They do what they please."

He said, "And why don't you?"

———

HE POURED another inch when she was gone, and drank it off to the bells of livestock coming in to pen.

It was the Dutchmen's rum. He'd meant at least to share it out with Littlejohn. But Tom was at the driver's fire, playing spoons with White's nigger, going clackety-clack. And it had been too long a day of blood and sun and travel.

Old Drum grazed nearby, still wet from the long ride. MacLaren walked out and caught him, labored onto the bare back to reel and right himself.

"You going over?" Vine Leabo called, riding in on his solid gray.

"Just down to the river."

He rode slowly under sky the deep silver before dark. The color of nothing. The river gleamed softly, grass dark along its banks.

He found a dry sandbar and got off. Drum Hill pawed and snuffed, then buckled with an eloquent groan and rolled. MacLaren watched fondly. The horse cast back and forth, squirming on one side and the other, then came up on his belly and sighed.

Across the flat, the Pawnee were drumming, but the breeze had spilled it into insubstantial sound, the line of it was lost.

For his own part, he was growing free and hazy.

The horse stayed there, his legs folded under. His old lips hung down. MacLaren went and sat in the sand beside him and pulled dirty leaves from his mane, pale dry twigs as fine as bird bones.

With what morality?

It was true: by fifteen years of age, he'd learned what some of this world's people could delight in.

He'd seen a Naskapi pull off a captive's thumbs on long tendons, to string through his own ears for bobs. Seen a line of fires built inside a hall, gone in with the people who sat on benches as though waiting at a theater. Seen captives then brought in to run through flames, to have their toes cleaved off with hatchets and be made to run again, splints driven through their eardrums, tongues cut out. Hot brands, clubs, knives, fire, water—he'd seen one night of torture so long and so inspired, so hateless and considerate in its artistry, as had left him sure the minds of such people would forever lie beyond the reach of men like him, who did at least ponder now and then the reasons for things.

That was when he was twenty. And he'd known since then all kinds of tribes, their wildness and wantonness and vanities, seen surpassing cruelty and cunning but also great courage and generosity. And had learned, to his surprise, that few of them would trust the heart of any man like him, who'd left his home and people and enslaved himself to ghosts forever in search of gain, to roam without reason, claiming things that could not be owned.

Kiye' yiktipec, his first wife had called him: Who Wanders. It was not a compliment, though white men, in their ignorance, called these people nomads.

Between such opposites, it was hard to see a hope for understanding.

The gelding sighed and launched up to shake away the dust. Then walked away.

He lay. The evening darkened. He watched bats feed, tilting, wheeling up like leaves in a draft, and he tilted with them and was nearly gone when a whoop and shotgun's blast made his muscles spring. But nothing followed.

He rose at last and steadied. In a dry cutbank, he cached the pistol he carried, horn and shotbag, hatchet—things he judged more likely to be stolen that night than used where he was going. By the forelock, he led the horse and slipped him into the pen made tight by circled wagons. Then went to visit the Pawnee.

———

Two hours among them and he was lost, all players in some grand carousal engendered by kegged Ohio whiskey, brought over from the whites in trade for horses. In three hours he was roaring with the rest; they sang and boasted and gambled. And he was still there when brawls broke out on shouts of insult. Children and dogs long gone to ground. And he was still there when they mounted backward and rode lurching mares through their own camp, dragged ropes, fired fusils, tipped lodges, clubbed their women down with rifle butts, fell over, lapped from the open kegs like dogs, or lay under the stopcock while it ran down their chins.

By midnight only the stout or temperate were moving: some Wolves-in-the-Water still drummed beside a glowing pit of weeds and dung; the ones not able to sit any longer toppled back to lie thumping lazily upon their chests in faltering song while the rest bobbed, howling. MacLaren howled with them until he was spent again at last. Then lay back drifting, warm and self-abandoned, watching flames. The voice on his breath seemed separate, and he listened to it rise and fall.

At some point a woman came and pulled him up by the hand to sit. She gave him her cup. She touched his legs. She put turkey feathers in his hair, ducked free of strings of beads to swing and let them fall across his shoulders. He heard someone laughing. She stood and leaned, saying *"Lau, lau,"* pulling his wrist until he rose, he and she across the tilting ground. He stooped behind her through a doorway, stumbled, and they pitched together in her strange laughter, his lips grazing the numb salt of her shoulder. Goose down sifted over them from a bag blown open by their falling weight.

Against his tongue, he felt her teeth worn short from flattening quills—she was older than he'd guessed. She bit him, laughing, for his exclamation, and then parted before him shameless and clamant in light carried through the walls from the fire, where the rest drummed on without them and swayed in clattering adornments.

In Cupped Hands

⁓⟨⟩⁓

THE MORNING AIR GATHERED and moved into a long breeze. She faced it, squinting across the river's wide glare, its humped greenery, to the hazy rim of that north shore. The sand where she stood was scribed by dragging poles, the deep pockmarks of hooves. A flock of crows had come to stalk the empty Pawnee camp. They quarreled and hopped into ungainly flight, skimmed the ground to light again.

There'd been no sign of him.

She filled her pails. But when she got them back to camp, he was there beside their fire, in strings of foreign beads.

They'd held their camp for two hours that morning, watching as the Pawnee departed. The captains had resolved to lay over, although it wasn't Sunday. Now everything was quiet, and all she wanted was to lie in some re-membered shade, but the other women had taken laundry down to wash. So she went as well, her daughters with vague grievances in tow. Sarah drooped along, pails hanging from each hand as though their use had no relation to her. Emma, stoic, followed with the linens. Caroline's mood was more weighty than the kettle she was dragging. *Oh, you've raised such delightful girls,* the VanAllmans had said that morning. *So polite. So helpful.*

"You sure have a swad of laundry!" called Libby Tuttle, who had only a small basket for herself and Frank.

Lucy forced a smile, hardly better than her daughters. It was the wine last night, or the constant glare. Her head was thick as a pumpkin in the heat. Now it would be soap and lye and the slosh of all these women rounded to their boards. The dirt must be wrenched out.

"She just thinks she's upper ten, you know, and so does he," she heard Mrs. Raimie say, and Mrs. Watts, seeing her, said, "Good morning, Mrs. Mitchell."

She said, "Sarah, light our fire."

"Emma has to get the *bois de vache*." Caroline laboriously insisted on this foreign term for dung.

"I got it at breakfast," Emma said.

"I don't care who gets it. Good morning, Mrs. Watts. Mrs. Raimie."

"I got it twice before that."

"No."

"Yes I did."

"You did not. That was Tom!"

"Mama!"

She turned. All three scowled redly at her, in their pettiness, their un-concern, relying always on her civility. So how did the dress snatch up in her hand? How did it fly into Sarah's face? And the tub of laundry clatter and spill out across their feet?

She walked away. She left it sprawling in the dust.

———————

WELL, SOMETHING LOST had welled inside her, on her knees in the wagon's waxy heat. The meat was gone, and now the blood-pink soap was swirling. She scrubbed with passionate despair. Something lost had welled, kept welling, until it was a yawning desperation, unreasonable, familiar. She wanted to hide and sleep.

There had been evenings after Luther. Scrubbing floors like this. Before that, terrible days deprived of him, with her daughters playing in the other room, or curled beside her under the covers. Too long bereaved to be re-membered by neighbors with gifts of food, Sarah on a chair had cooked them eggs. She remembered Emma beside her bed, saying, *Get up, Mama. Get up.* A pot of peas had lasted them a week. Brushing her daughters' hair might overwhelm her.

How had she picked herself up, decided where to go?

She couldn't remember. Only that she'd done it and put it long behind her. And would again—and would again—but for not knowing what it was this time that felt so much the same.

They would walk away from my grave, these women, she thought. I am nothing. They would not get half a day before I was forgotten.

———————

"WHAT'S WRONG TODAY?" Israel asked her later.

"Nothing," she said. "Maybe too much sun."

Of course she knew exactly what had happened. There was nothing wrong with James MacLaren but that she'd created him, to fill some absence in herself.

———————

HE SLEPT most of the day. Woke in the middle of the night and couldn't sleep again. Vine Leabo was on night guard, so MacLaren went and relieved him. "No sense the two of us sitting up," he said.

———————

HE HAD LEFT his dead men unburied in the valley of the Snakes. Walked six days with nothing but his clothes. Everything else was stolen. Three days from Fort Nez Perce, he'd come across some men of Rad McLeod's brigade, who'd brought him in.

Misfortune being more the rule than the exception in their line, most men insured their families by some exchange of oaths. So he'd sworn the night Lise was born, and thought nothing of it, to take Mary as his wife. He'd sworn to Joe again, before he'd killed him. So he owed the care of that family, and in Vancouver he found he would be taken down to clerk again. He had pledged his pay and all entitlements to meet what debt was personal, and gone up the river to find Mary.

He'd thought she hated him. As soon as he was able, he'd put her into a bateau for Fort Vancouver, with Lise and Joseph, who was only two.

They'd lived in a row hut outside the fort all summer. He hadn't known what to do. Up to then, he'd kept away from the company of native women, as men did who hoped to gain positions, not wishing to be compromised by need. But now those hopes were ended. And he had an obligation.

He brought her things but couldn't touch the children. Her language was more difficult than any he'd tried. One day she started hitting him with a fire-iron, and he threw her out with the supper she was making, and made his own, and fed the children. After that, she lay beside him, and before long they were easy, as married people should be.

She was round and smelled of fish. Her comfort was a revelation.

Then it was August, and John Work's brigade was going down to California.

"I have to go," he told her.

She beat his chest. She called him no-home, ghost. She called him stinking-dog-that-wanders. "Come with me, then," he said. It was a big brigade—eighty men, some with families. They might be gone two years. He said, "The other wives, everyone is coming." But she refused, with words for reasons he couldn't understand. The simplest of his explanations—of debt, of obligation—made no sense to her. Or so she kept pretending.

He had ended it by telling her she'd come.

Traveling south through the mountains of East Oregon, they had gone two days without water. When they found mud at last, they fell and sucked it up in spoonfuls. They'd had to walk when the horses started failing, and Mary's feet were bruised from stones. She wouldn't speak. But her girl drank that water with all frankness and said, in the English words he'd taught her, "Long go, ey?"

That had been a revelation also: the feeling he could have about a child. Already, he'd come to know the tilt of her chin, her thinking frown, the way her fingers darted through her hair to plait it. She never touched him. She kept apart, as girls that age were taught to. Played with the other children, games of sticks and feathers. He never told her what to do or claimed relation. But sometimes she'd come and tell him things, or bring him stones to look at, or clean his boots. If their skin should meet, it was like touching a live deer, or some creature so shy you would remember it.

But for that, it was a dismal tour. The fur was gone from the California mountains—the Russians and Americans had come through first. Fall rains swelled the rivers, kept them idle. They starved one month, had fevers the next. The rogues of all the nations had been gathered under the Irishman Mr. Work, and knifed each other over cuts of meat, shat in camp, beat their wives. They spent down a hundred pounds of shot and powder in six days, laying waste to herds of Tule elk, six hundred animals, for no reason but amusement and to save themselves from carrying so much lead. Then starved in following months for lack of ammunition. Mary fought with Kanota's wife. She cried in bed at night.

But he taught the girl to write the alphabet with coal sticks. Told her stories about caribou and dancing bears. On Christmas night, he told about the baby Jesus, and under the moon, they all climbed a bluff of the Feather River, touched off squibs and hooted, and threw stones into the gorge below.

They had reports from the coast of no beaver, so John Work decided they should go there. For a month, he led them hacking west through forests thicker and more destitute than any they had seen. They made two miles a day and had no fish or meat to speak of. They slid down muddy gorges, wandered lost in fogs. Crossing a river's mouth at last, they saw six horses swept into the sea. And this was part of what they did, part of what he'd always done. But it was more, MacLaren had begun to think, than any child should suffer. He was enraged. He cut down Work, behind his back, as a man who cared for profit more than families.

So they left that useless country, floundered three months more, to come out again into the vicious summer heat of the great middle valley, afoot, half starved, galled by Indians. Such horses as remained were pitiable things not fit for service; nor were many men, most in a similar condition but for Mr. Work, who must have had his secrets. Even Mary had gone gray and thin, drawn into herself, with child. She'd bundle and unbundle their things without a word, do the cooking, lay the beds. One night they were set upon, and all the animals were stolen. The men cut loose and marauded up the valley, set ablaze two villages, used their last lead to slaughter fleeing women and their children.

"Well, how am I to govern the whole damned rabble?" This was Work. The two of them had stood in camp that night, roaring back and forth. "They can go to hell," the Irishman said, "and take every goddamn savage with them." Which the girl, overhearing, had then pondered. Later, from her blanket, she had asked him, very serious: *Who is savage, and who is not?*

The country took its own revenge at last. They rode, one afternoon, through a village of silent bark huts where wolves were at the bodies. Ten, then twenty of them took the fever, with Work despairing to stop, believing they'd die of that contagion. Fits of hot and cold had seized them. Most were too sick by evening to bring in wood or water, could not hunt or strike a fire. Senatoen's boy died, who was only two, then Rondeau's daughter.

Then Mary bore the child in a sheen of fever—a son whose hand closed once around the last joint of his thumb, it was that small. The fingernails as small and neat as fish scales.

He buried them both before two days were out. Gave over doubt and prayed. Spare this one, please. This girl.

She was nine years old and very sick. He rode on with her all that week, her head against his back. The boy Joseph, on the saddlebows, kept asking for his mother.

And then one morning, Lise woke cooler from her blankets, and her eyes were steady. Later that same day, she handed him her plait of hair, which she had cut away—he'd never seen her do it. He took that emblem of her grief, and coiled it into his pocket, and kept it safe for years.

———

MACLAREN WATCHED across the warm dark plains as the world resolved by slow degrees. The oxen woke and grazed. Coyotes slipped back and forth along the river. He saw the early fires lit, the people stirring. They were under way by dawn.

The sun climbed slowly. The air was dry and still along this river. It shimmered at midday. No trees but for the glinting green of saplings waving far ahead, a whole orchard carried in the back of Luelling's wagon. MacLaren drove, eyes closed, head bowed against the dust. And this winter's fever had scarred his lungs and left him with a tolerable cough, but lately it had set in deeper. It ached up from the bottom of his lungs.

The girls walked along, sometimes singing. They climbed in and out of the wagon when he stopped it. Their mother walked. When they camped, she cooked and served, but had nothing to say to him. Between storms of coughing, he ate the supper she had made. He couldn't remember just what had gone between them, and it was nothing to do with that, but since the night with the Pawnee, he felt more alone than ever.

That night he coughed and bent and coughed until his nose bled, and went to sleep on blessed opium, double what he needed.

———

LUCY HAD CAST her vote with all the women: the Platte Valley was hideous country. Destitute of anything agreeable. Their feet were sore. Their faces and hands had burned. From exhausted sleep they'd wake suddenly to a wolf's cry only feet away, it seemed. Then came silence, which was worse. One imagined all kinds of things at night.

At last, on Friday, they came to a wide channel, another river flowing into theirs. They turned along it. This south fork was nothing like the main one; it was narrow and quick, and its banks, after so much treeless country, soon grew deep with sedge and green thickets of cottonwood and willow.

So that was some relief, or should have been.

But something came over her anyway that evening, while she made the bread. Israel had deemed it immediately necessary to change the position of the board rails in the wagon, and wanted her to help. She refused, with enough to do just putting away supper, tending the little ones, baking to-morrow's bread.

"The boards have been in that place since we started, Israel. Can it not wait?"

She saw the poor toolbox, his dusty boots. He would walk all over the beds. He said, "I have my tools out, Lucy, I mean to do it now. I'm tired of them falling down."

"Well, I am busy."

So he continued on his own, though he could have asked either man for help, or even one of the girls. But, stubbornly, he banged and swore, as though the point of the whole exercise was to blame her. To bring her into some compliance.

She washed the little ones. Israel stalked off when he was done, and she went in for fresh clothes and saw the rails were changed by only a few inches, the beds much the same for all that. Luther's hammer, left out, offended her. At last she got the children down to sleep, and went to check her bread, and saw she'd left the rising sponge uncovered.

An oath left her lips, the first in years.

Fat mosquitoes, drawn by the warmth, were wriggling by scores. It looked like sponge for currant scone, with the currants struggling to free themselves. Picking them out, she began to cry. It was ridiculous, of course. It was only bread. But the bugs stuck to her fingers, her fingers stuck to sponge, and soon she couldn't see what she was doing. She lidded the pot with a clang, and left it, and began to walk.

In this heavy heat, the river drew her. Down through the smell of mud and rot. The bank was shallow here. Cottonwoods had sprouted by the thousands through the gravel, but they stood only as tall as grass. Their leaves ticked against her striding boots.

She knelt beside the water. She put her hands into it. This fork was clear, not sandy. She rubbed the sticky flour from her fingers. Cooled her face. Brought one handful up, and another, until she was well. She should be well. The days were mild, travel was good. The danger was only particular.

She stilled, her palms pressed tightly, holding in the water. This clear essence. She watched it seeping out. She brought more up, pressed her fingers tighter, but still the water dripped away, and a third time she tried, with her fingers in a different arrangement, fearing that this might be a true reflection of her trouble: that some essence of herself, no matter how she tried, had been seeping thus away. And if it were lost before she found some place to put it?

It was the toolbox she'd hated. The way Luther's fine and balanced tools were mixed so carelessly with Israel's dull chisel, his rusty nails and auger.

She sat. She wrenched the shoes from her feet, pulled off her dirty stockings, wondering how she ever would forgive it. Not the tools but what they meant. Apron, petticoats. She stood and struggled, she tugged and hissed at her confining dress, remembering those Pawnee women, their unbound breasts beneath their tunics. In a tiny pop of eyelets, she snaked free. Bodice and tight sleeves, this hateful husk. In drawers and corset and chemise, she entered and let herself sink into cool green dark. She had not been drawn yet into water.

She gasped a little at the chill. She stood, the water to her neck, and felt it moving. It was intimate and heavy, gliding past and through, between her body and her clothes. Caressing, cooling secret parts of her. Releasing some deeper grief.

She tipped her head back. The shameful tears were streaming.

Here. I am all of this, she told herself. I am a river. I cannot run dry.

"But you've *been* this way," White said. "So give us your advice."

The guidebooks lay open on the table. They'd called him over for a supper meeting: White and Whitcomb, Mitchell and some others.

MacLaren spoke with them for a time about the route as he knew it.

Then sat while they all talked, while the Negress chopped onion, fried meat. White's wife, it seemed, was above the cooking. Sallow and bruised-looking, she moved like a slow tall bird.

Over smoke and popping grease, the council men talked about Tupper's evil mare. Warren's wife with fever. Tony and Hill were swinging knives again, neither would say why. Sometimes they would pause to ask MacLaren more about the country, and he answered, but his mind was somewhere else, and he fed silent on collops fried in onion gravy and gritty rice while they fell to talk of hats, how Chatfield's father had made a fortune on a new steam press and then lost it in the craze for seacoast silk. They got from that to the Quaker schools and how they might improve things, bending into it as fervent as if there were such a school just down the track from camp.

His plate was empty. I have no idea how to talk like this, he thought. He thanked the women and left.

He got a change of shirt, walked down through bordering willows. The river was steep-banked on this bend, wide and floury green.

You've been this way.

The country was so vast, of course, that one or a hundred or a thousand men could have very little effect. And how, anyway, could one fault a people bringing schools and churches and all the goods of industry? Still, there was always something about newcomers laying claim that made him uneasy, as though he were being robbed some way, or made to give over something he had never thought to value.

As a guide one summer, he had gone with a naturalist, John Burke, botanizing down the ridges of the Bitterroots. Trying the work of Adam. Now he was thinking of that man, with his knapsack and cloth hat, his Harrods best India coat. His passion for describing what was common. Burke found lilies, expanded on the heathers. The mosses had amazed him. He'd unwrap grassy tufts from a collecting paper, fairly trembling. "What is this?" Some hairy piece of green. "Is there a name for this?"

Most plants served no special use to the people and had enjoyed, for all those thousand years, a respectful anonymity. The rest did have all sorts of names, and some MacLaren knew and could pronounce. But they were in the wrong language now, and the wrong form.

"It's a strange urge," he had observed to Burke. "This naming of things."

The ridge they had been walking was too high, of course, for names.

Burke said, "The name is just the beginning."

"The beginning of what? When you've named the last thing? Will the world be yours to command? Will you have Eden again?"

You know the way. He'd only ever done what needed doing. Borne along the current, he'd brought guns and traps and beads and mirrors. Brought men with paper and lenses, men with trinket crosses. Brought Mrs. Warren, down with fever.

Now the river slid through quiet shadows. He looked both ways and shed his clothes. Waded in through fine dark silt, the water warm and greasy. Waist-deep, he scrubbed his hands, his hair, his beard. Then stood dripping, tasting salt and dust, in the sound of evening birds. Three small pink clouds lay reflected on the surface of the water.

You know the way. What could one man affect? Or a hundred or a thousand? If not much, what then excused such plundering and pestilence as had already been their wake? Such disordering of a place so perfect after its own truth, in the name of making some imperfect and impoverished version of another? Did this world so need improving?

He leaned, slid into cool water. Angling upstream against the current, he swam, head down, eyes closed, the world and all its sound reduced to cool green churning. He quit finally, out of breath, to tread midchannel, gliding down again. With the sun behind him, he saw a pale head bobbing at the bottom of the bend. He blinked the water from his lashes.

DRIED AND DRESSED, he walked back through camp. He got his nog and kettle for tea, and the water hadn't boiled before she passed, her hair still wet from bathing. So it had been her.

He said, "Hey."

She turned. He'd heard her argue with her husband. He said, "I don't know what I was saying. That night."

She made no reply, but set up her place on the wagon's rear gate to knead bread.

He got out his pipe and cleaned it. She worked, her back to him. After a while, she said, "None of us seem to, out here."

He watched her leaning on her dough.

"Israel's the only one not tired," she said. "Sometimes I think he'd make the whole world over if God would let him. And start with me." She tucked damp hair with a floury hand. MacLaren thought what a subtle man could read from a woman's bread, if he had seen a few loaves made. This one would rise very high.

She said, "I'm just trying to keep us fed. Clothes clean. Bonnets found. Just hoping not to break too much or lose too much. Just wanting to get through it, and I look around and what's he doing? Like this, tonight. Or he'll have the shovel, trying to get his chair exactly level. You've seen him." She looked at him across her shoulder. Then smiled a small exasperated smile. Waving mosquitoes, she saw the humor of it, and made him smile as well.

He saw that she was pretty.

"Anyway, it must be fine always to do as you please," she said. "No one else to see to."

He took a coal from the fire's edge and cupped it to a bowl to light. Sat and drew the smoke and didn't cough and sighed it out, his hair still wet from the river, feeling again how he'd borne against that current, churning, eyes squeezed shut as though he might swim far enough back through it and be right again, and have what he had known again. A life. A certainty. He said, "Those are good children."

"I know. And I suppose he does have hopes. Israel. He has ideas. He'd be less if he didn't."

"He had an idea to win you."

"Yes, he did." She put the dough into the cast kettle to bake, and brought it to the fire.

"And you agreed."

"Yes."

He waited until she told him: she'd taken the girls to live with their father's family when he died, his mother and his four brothers. Four bachelors on a dairy. All hoping, she smiled. Mitchell had taken her out in a buggy, she said. He'd shown her a house. She trailed away.

"And now you're here," he said.

"Mosquitoes in my dough." She lifted the lid to show him. He stood to look.

"Sustaining," he said.

"What did they want? The men tonight?" She set the lid back carefully.

He said, "I don't know."

She looked at him. He saw her tendrils of damp hair. He looked off, but he had never felt this thing so deep before, this need to speak, to say how far he had been swept from what was good, and the sense seemed doubtful and unmanly.

"Are you all right?" she asked.

Rivers flowed in one direction. Things were the way they were. He pressed his eyes, and leaned his forehead in cupped hands.

Us the Sinners

THEY CROSSED SOUTH PLATTE on Saturday's dawn, and climbed all morning a divide of low dry hills. The runneled soil was almost hard as stone. Lucy stopped with Daniel on a high vantage to rest, and looked back across the watered valleys, the plain stretching east. A white glimmer of wagons showed a party coming on behind them.

"There's the river," she said. "That's where we've been." She saw the bend where they had camped last night, and thought of the great splashing—such a churning, it sounded like someone riding a horse down through the shallows. She'd sunk to hide herself, slipped gliding to the bend to see: a man, swimming hard against the current. He'd stopped and turned and seen her.

"What river?" Daniel asked.

He might have been any man. She might have been any woman. But there they were, together. Neither first knowing it had been the other.

She took Daniel's hand, and they set off again.

They walked all day across the bluffs. In the afternoon they descended with the aid of ropes the face of a steep sandy declivity grown with scrub and gnarled cypress, a terrible dusty job, one wagon at a time. The men enjoyed it. That evening they camped on a grassy bench of cottonwood and ash beside a clear stream. The camp was well used, the grass bitten down, the hills around them bleached and fierce as ever, but the shade was welcome.

———

HAZY BANDS of clouds glowed behind the trees. She heard the clank of buckets, the splashes and squeals of children wading.

"We should all write home!" Mrs. Richardson, their breathless organizer, their town crier, was calling. A trapper's cabin stood abandoned in the trees, filled with notices and letters.

Who would I write to? Lucy wondered. The world they'd left seemed a lifetime away. And there was no accounting for this one now, unless she was dishonest.

The children are strong. The weather is fine. We have come along well so far.

How, truly, could she say why she was happy now?

AT SUPPER she told Israel they were running out of tea, and James MacLaren went off and soon returned with a brass can, three quarters full.

"For us?" she asked.

He affirmed it.

Israel gave Daniel the job of putting it away in the box on the rear of the wagon.

"I'll do it later," she said. "He'll never reach."

But Daniel said he could, so they all watched as he ran to the wagon with it. Watched as he set down the can to fetch a pail, turned the pail over for a wobbling step, and stood up on it, but the can was forgotten. He got down again for the can, all of them calling advice: put it down, use two hands, push it up.

She said, "He can't do it, Israel. The lid's too heavy." Then watched, adoring so much her child's small determined back, the shoulder blades that showed beneath his shirt, his bending knees, his pure triumphant smile as the lid banged shut at last. Israel said, "Well done," so Daniel ran to her in pride and embarrassment, to hold her by the knees. He buried his head in her skirts. And she should have stepped back and made a man of him. But pulled him close against her before she could resist, and said, "I love you *so*," and bent to kiss his dusty hair. Then looked around.

HE DISAPPEARED after that. James MacLaren. As he did most evenings.

Blushing, she'd broken her gaze from his departing back to look up at some ruckus in the trees. The Watts boys had climbed into the cottonwoods and were cracking down old limbs.

Now she stood in her tidy camp. A bonfire blazed out on the grounds, with the sound of tuning fiddles.

"Come on," her husband said. "The girls are there."

She wiped Mary's face while Israel waited, already in clean clothes. Beyond him, Sarah had struck a fetching pose, talking to Vine Leabo, and Lucy gestured to Israel to look. This, she thought, was why so many women allowed their daughters an early marriage. It was so much easier than vigilance.

"Quit fretting," Israel said. "Come dance."

"Are you not worn out?" The baby would loll and fuss in her arms. The same dreary songs would be sung.

He said, "It's Saturday, Lucy. Come dance. You never come."

So she did stand in the sawing of the fiddles, and sighed and sang "One More River to Cross" and "Home Sweet Home," declined a waltz and listened to Nancy Richardson tell about a time in Springfield when she'd lost a gold locket. It seemed so long, Lucy thought, since that April slush when they had all been strangers, when these familiar women had appeared to her not as people but as baffling arrangements of teeth and noses, eyes, of bonnets frilled or shabby, waists thick or neat, dark aprons, fine basques, a brooch, a line of buttons. She'd wondered how she would ever learn them. Now they could talk quite easily, having formed their opinions of one another. Nancy Richardson bent into her tale of the missing locket, and all those suspected of taking it, but then a storm pushed over a big oak in the garden. "It turned out," she said, "it was a *raven* the whole time."

"Well, when I lived in Columbus," Mrs. Olmstead began, and Lucy stood thinking how little point there seemed in any past so far away, and how little point there seemed in talking of the future over which they had not the least control, toiling as they were toward something she could scarcely imagine. So she was gazing, not listening, thinking of that moment when she had run her fingers through Daniel's hair, when she had bent and said *I love you so* and looked up, when James MacLaren's eyes by some rare accident had met hers, when their two souls had locked—she'd felt—like folding fingers, for that instant of relief. Or had they?

And now she saw him again, standing across the lawn among some other drivers. Suddenly, she had drunk a cup of morning light.

She danced with Israel after that. He was a studied dancer, not natural but dignified. She bent to it with him, feeling kind and gay. Now and then she saw James MacLaren. He moved, he talked to people. She and Israel did the same, and when Jim Patton began to fiddle the tune of a call and song she knew from Luther, she looked at Sarah and saw that she remembered also. So they stepped in and began and soon were singing boldly:

Same old man, working at the mill,
Mill turns around of its own free will
One for the hopper and the other for the sack,
Ladies step forward and the men fall back.

They sang five verses, and people clapped and sang, and when it was over, someone shouted out for "Turkey in the Straw."

And then a little while had passed when she could not find him any-where in the crowd, and the inspiration left her, surely as it had come. She put Mary to bed at last and went back for Daniel. They walked together toward the wagon in the dark.

"Did Papa finded our new house yet?"

"No."

She looked again for James MacLaren, though her joy, of course, should not rely on him. But it did.

It did, because she had stood silent in that group of women not—as she had thought—because of anything to do with futures or with pasts. It was because she didn't trust them or herself.

She hadn't been this way when she was younger. Loving Luther, she had never doubted she was worthy of his love in turn. She'd laughed and swirled, danced and teased. But now it seemed she had reached an age when she felt at the mercy of all her stains and imperfections, when she stood and spoke and went away suspecting she'd betrayed herself somehow, afraid her eyes had strayed, that she'd scratched her scalp or made imprudent comments, told stories no one cared to hear. She often had the sense that she had walked away with eyebrows rising in her wake.

Oh, for that youth again. That confidence, when the world's demands were small. And now, if some believed her strange and some believed her silent, if some believed her mean with her affections, it was not because she thought she was better than they were. It was because she did not trust that she was anyone at all.

"Mama?"

And now it had begun to seem that if somehow he could love her, she'd be certain of herself again. She would exist, confirmed, she knew, in those eyes. In James MacLaren's most discriminating eyes.

She pecked at Daniel's laces.

"*Mama?*"

"What, what?"

"I said, *when* will Papa finded our new *house?*"

"Not yet, I told you. It's two months yet."

He looked at her, silent. Time meant nothing, nor distance. "Will the moon be there?" he asked.

"Yes."

"It follows."

"Yes, it follows."

She shucked his clothes, helped pull on his nightshirt. He leaned and wrapped his arms around her. "You're my really best mama." She held him high against her. He said, "Look! I got *so* many *stars* tonight!"

She looked up. The stars that had once crowded her now stood in their silver extravagance. Imagine, she thought, to have such innocence again. To feel entitled, laying claim on the whole universe.

———

MOST NIGHTS, with her children sleeping, it was an effort against nature to stray. But something had untethered her.

She skirted the camp alone, walked through tall sighing trees until they thinned. Across pale ground, dry grass. Small dark cypress grew fragrant and gnarled, each in solitary shadow.

She walked along the water's edge, over broken claypan, the rubble of strange mud concretions. A silent owl swept over, swerved, and tilted up to light on a dark limb.

In the glimmer of night, she took off boots and stockings. The silt was fine and warm, laced with tracks of plover. Gravely, calmly now, she undressed herself, every stitch.

MacLaren, released in his bed, could still hear the last few voices singing.

After supper he'd gone to get that can of tea and seen again how a woman could love her child, and have him hold her by the knees. He'd looked at her, this strange pale woman who would never see June tug at his sleeve or Lispat put her arms around his neck, who would never heft his boy or know the woman he had loved.

No advice would serve. In his camp, he took what medical science offered. Drank and left the bottle in the grass.

And then, in all that crowd of people, he had thought only of her.

Lise. Lise. If you were here. If I were with you, in your eyes. I'd be alive again.

Now, slowly, his life restored itself. His body, until they were in that long-ago dark, he and Lise, between moss and slow turbulent clouds. A thousand miles away beside the lake of the Babine.

They'd left a memory alive that night, he was sure of it. All people did, in places, all the millions who had lived, their flickering revenants here and there: fighting, loving, dying. He wondered how the world would look if he could see them all, the air of every place alive. He'd go and find that lake again, and see his faded ghost, and hers, come out each night in endless repetition of one act.

The clouds, the stars, the lake. She, naked in long moonlight, the rhododendrons' flame cooled into blue, the sound of water lapping. He, kissing her body downward: once, again, again. The hollow of her neck. Between her breasts, that wide defile of tenderest skin. Gentle swale of ribs and belly, navel. The lily parted deep in blossom. Her fingers woven in his hair.

Knowing her then, his wonder, invoked: that even to one so undeserving, the world might offer a rare moment of grace.

He felt them in motion, these ancient lovers. And lay, and listened to the hooting of an owl.

On Sunday morning, from the corner of her eye, Lucy watched him move through camp, in scenes from his own life. He worked, he rested, he spoke to Mr. Littlejohn or Israel, to other men she scarcely knew. She had nothing to say but must know always where he was, and envy every claim.

"I heard you sing," he'd said to her at breakfast.

MacLaren left the camp at rest and found himself midday on a small beach beside the stream. He sat in a boulder's slight shade and, after a while, began to run his fingers through the gravel. Sorting stones the color of coal and bone, ash, clay brick, thinking of the northern beaches where he would sit years ago and do this.

After California, he'd put Joseph with the tribe at Kamiah and Lise in school at Vancouver. He'd been assigned to Finlayson, to push north into the interior, the devil of a country. They'd trade up and down the rivers all summer and fall, then find a cold cove along the coast at season's end. Make a post on the banks to stay six months of winter. That was no place for children.

The ships would come and anchor in the black water of whatever sound they'd built on, and the sailors would row in with packs of beads and blankets; once an artist came ashore and did a sketch of what he called the landscape: the mountains looming up, dark with trees, or bright with naked granite and the water tumbling down. Well, there was a waterfall for every mile, bears as thick as English sheep, but what joy could you get from such a place?

Sometimes he'd get a letter from her. He'd stand with her braid in his coat pocket and look out across the water. He'd find the sun on cold gravel beaches and sit sometimes combing through base greens and browns and grays, looking for the tiniest clear colors of sunrise: honey, claret, ember-orange. He'd made a little bag of them to give her.

They'd sent him down to Langley after that, then made him trader out of Spokane House. He led men into country not dared since Burdoe's brigade was murdered, since MacDonald swore that beaver would be furred in gold before he'd try again among the Blackfeet. By then MacLaren had learned to get through any country. You should see the bloody coast, he'd tell his men, you'd stop complaining. He'd pushed and dealt, spent nights with his interpreters, read Napoleon by firelight, given audience to chiefs, not forgetting himself those years before, standing in McLoughlin's office. The weight of that calamity.

He baled and sent five thousand pelts one season from a place Ross said was too impeded, and was called down to Vancouver at last—having lost all freeness in his limbs, all youth, all ability to smile—to change for work in the Babine.

Coming home to the great fort, they'd stopped and gone ashore in the last mile. Shaved and found fresh clothes. He'd been away four years. Paddled down around the bend and soon heard the bagpipes skirl out across the water to greet him. He left the laborers to their work, went striding up the road alone, across the fields and through the gates and to McLoughlin's hall, walked in while supper was in progress. The table pounded, his presence toasted, they'd pushed back plates and cups and seated him on the factor's right, to a supper of roast goose and apples, blueberry sauce, potatoes, mutton, steaming kale. He'd sat to drink and laughter, the swing of kitchen doors, Queensware platters borne and carried off, news of Ogden in Caledonia and Russians on the coast and a steamship of their own, could you believe, a bloody steamship. A brown girl had leaned past his shoulder with a dish.

"Where's Lise?" he asked. "I should find her after supper."

McLoughlin's knife had surveyed the hall like a compass needle until it found a slender woman who might have walked behind him once or twice already, while he'd fed.

"There." From across the room, she saw them looking.

So in that moment, his ordered world was overthrown. McLoughlin, the old fox, had given him a knowing look.

He'd found Lise in the kitchen when the work was done that night. Sewing buttons on a man's blue coat.

"I'll be factor at Babine," he'd told her, standing beside the racks of pots and pans. Her letters, folded into his bound trip book, had not prepared him. The stones stayed in his pocket. He'd said, "You might as well come with us."

But she'd stared silently at the buttons she was sewing.

She was thirteen, his given daughter.

"No," he'd said. "You're right."

Now he looked at the stones he'd found. None were much good here, but one was smooth and white and shaped as a hummingbird's egg. He put it in his pocket. After a while he stood and went to drink and saw a woman's bare footprints in the silt.

———

LUCY WALKED the next morning, and by afternoon the road became so crossed by buffalo trails that the wagons thumped and banged over lists cut close as if a plow had shared them. No one could ride a wagon, but the girls took to lying on their beds to be thrown up and down for the fits it gave them. This entertainment, once discovered, spread among the girls their age, so their whoops soon sounded against the unsprung jolt and noise of turning tar pails, and brought to Lucy's mind a kind of spreeing not yet imagined by most of the innocents inside.

They camped with the chimney standing distant, a dark hazy spar.

Tuesday dawned brilliant on a gun-blue storm. Silent lightning blinked against it. Thunder flowed softly down the valley and faded in the whine of mosquitoes. Sarah, feverish with contempt for everything, scowled at mothering questions. It was pails and bloody flannels, the same as anywhere, but here was no easy privacy.

Horseflies pursued them south, away from the river, into drylands. Clay formations rose like castles through the rolling dust. Baked gullies fanned from hills. The girls lagged in the heat. Caroline began complaining that there had been worms in the breakfast meat, when of course there had been no such thing. Then started sicking up as if to prove it, while Emma and Sarah and Alice Raimie all stood by.

"There were," Caroline cried. She wiped her face. "I saw them."

"You have to come," Lucy said, watching the green wagon roll ahead. Mary squirmed and fretted on her hip. "I cannot always nurse you. Come and follow."

"No. There *were*," Caroline said. "Stay with us! *Stay!*"

But she had turned away already and was following the wagons toward the deep blue line of clouds approaching.

They ran together at the edge of a ravine as the first drops came popping down like pea gravel on the canvas tops. Rough-locked, the wagons descended the steep incline, ran along the hard clay floor of the wash. Then stopped in turn to water at a crossing where a marquetry letter desk stood forlornly in tall snakeweed.

She left the baby sleeping while the animals drank, and helped Daniel from the wagon.

"I want to go *in*." He drooped against her, flushed and sweaty from napping.

"Don't mind the rain. It cools you." Already the flat planes of stone were darkening like speckled eggs. She saw a walnut bureau standing beside a table on which the finish had gone chalky. He whined again.

"Drink," she said. "Then I'll help you."

James MacLaren had come down from his horse and passed now, stroking the high spine of their gold ox Dollar, and she watched him hold a cleat and swing beneath the wagon with a grace so heedless that she could both love and darkly envy it. On Sunday he had wrapped the reach in green buffalo hide, tacked on with nails, where the grain was giving. The hide, he'd said, would shrink and dry almost as hard as iron.

"Is it good?" she called.

It was.

The Kingerys' wagon, ahead of theirs, made way again along the narrow passage. The rain was coming gently now, after that first gust. It hissed around them. James MacLaren now sat on his heels beside the stream.

"It's beautiful," she said.

He looked at her. Then looked across the stream, the canyon walls. Pale knobs and ridges stood out from the darker clay like the freed bones of giants.

She said, "I grew up in Pennsylvania."

He stood and ran a hand under the horse's sweaty girth to check it.

"I never imagined any place like this."

He mounted.

She watched his face. He took the coiled whip from his saddle and swung it gently. Bishop and Dollar leaned into the yoke. And then she heard a cry and saw that Daniel had been climbing, was halfway up the wagon box and had slipped on wet wood in the oxen's lurch and was dangling.

"*No!*" She ran, dresses cracking in her haste, and came on him as he'd gained a foothold again. She dragged him down. "No!" Without her help. How many times had she said it? How many children had been run under wheels?

"You're a big *bitcher!*" He swung against her, flailed and kicked.

She set him down and struck him hard, then lifted him again, embraced him. The oxen had halted. She looked around at James MacLaren on his horse.

"I didn't see," he said. "I'm sorry."

She felt her child's small bones against her, put her nose into his hair.

———

THEY STOPPED near yellow bluffs. Someone called them Scott's.

It was too hot, this country. He'd spent the whole day killing flies.

He made his camp in the shade of a low bush, sat and watched the oxen rooting dumbly through the wormwood. Tom Littlejohn, ignorant of heat, had beat a picket into the dirt and was throwing horseshoes. Some boys stood squinting, hands balled inside their pockets.

"Have you seen the girls since we were in?"

MacLaren looked around.

Lucy Mitchell stood above him and waved flies. Her boots had cracked along the seams. She said, "I thought they were with the Raimies."

"No."

This day, the heat and work, had left him with nothing at all.

———

SHE WALKED the road east again, her shadow reaching out along the dust, and stopped and listened and heard nothing.

"Sarah Ann!"

She hadn't worried much as camp went up. They were so often separated, traveling as they did with other families. But now everyone was in.

"Emma Ruth, Caroline!"

But no one had seen them, not even as the bacon spattered and the goats stood begging, not even as the beds were shaken, as evening's shadow began to climb the bluffs. She waited, watching.

It was said that darkness fell. But out on these plains, it more appeared to rise up from the ground. Here, among the bluffs, it seemed a rapid tide. If she'd not been so worried, it would have been a grand spectacle: the creeping shadows, the turning of clay from yellow into pink. From pink to dusky ocher. But there was no sign of them.

In camp, Israel was glowering. The sun had turned him pink as well, beyond even the brown they had become. Now the women were convening with questions and opinions. Dear Luelling brushed long floury hands and said maybe they'd fallen asleep and were only behind.

"Ones that age are always taking shortcuts, that's all," said Mrs. Watts. "Get a little grown, they get their own ideas."

Mrs. Wilcox could be relied upon for warmed brandy.

Lucy left a second time, walked out along the road and back again to stand beside the fire. Israel said he couldn't ride the mare, she was played out. Although she believed he was speaking of himself.

"Mr. MacLaren would loan you his, I am sure," she said. But Mr. MacLaren was lying as still as a log in the shadow of a bush, where she had found him earlier. He'd slept through supper.

"MR. MACLAREN."

He opened his eyes. It was dawn or dusk.

"I am sorry," she said, "to wake you."

HE STOOD into his stirrup again and wheeled out with Bob Tupper, Richard Tony, Vine Leabo, and a few others whose hopes or goodwill or good horses inspired them, and at the end of twilight six miles back, they found footprints veering up a gap between the bluffs. It must have seemed a quicker road.

Drum Hill walked softly on the clay and now and then arched his neck to eye a lurking cypress, a shadowy boulder. Dirt cliffs rose around them and narrowed into canyons grown with bayonet and currant. In places, the walls drew closer still, into narrow waists through which they couldn't ride astride but were forced to walk, or kneel on their saddles. Richard Tony took to standing like a circus rider. They scrambled banks, clattered over stones. Bob

Tupper swore and dropped his rifle, and the blast delivered pebbles from the sky.

———————

"GOD BE MERCIFUL to us, the sinners."

Reverend Olmstead had been waiting all this time to intercede in his own way.

"Create in us clean hearts, O God; and renew right spirits within us."

She knelt in late dusk on the glowing earth, allowing these words to be said. As she must. Because she had walked through heat and dust forgetting them, her daughters. Thinking that love lay somewhere else.

"According to the multitude of thy tender mercies, blot out our transgressions . . ."

———————

SHE MILKED the goats at last. She sat in the dust with her head against warm Desdemona's flank, thinking, I did dream this. These rocks, this grass. Before we ever left. I dreamed a grave.

She squeezed the soft teats, and the goat shifted once and put her foot in the pan and overturned it. The milk disappeared into sand.

At the fire she sat with Israel. He'd mounted to go out with the riders, but the young men had told him to stay, and meant it, and he was grateful. Now he fed the flame with twigs and brittle grass, and the flaring light cut lines of shadow in his skin. He did look old tonight. She watched his face and thought how seldom she had done so.

He said, "The oxen's feet are wearing out."

The night was very quiet.

He said, "We need to buy shoes at Laramie. We'll have to shoe them."

She listened for the horses coming.

She said, "I should have kept them with me." Now it seemed so clear: what they had needed was water and shade and rest. They'd been fussing about the water, not drinking, and so the heat had addled them. How could she not have seen that? She said, "I should have stayed with them."

Oh, if she could only sit them by the fire, dab their feet while they ate. Murmur her reprimands.

If I lost you girls, I would lose myself. I could never live if you were taken.

She thought of the graceful bow of James MacLaren's back. Her words in that gentle rain. How he had looked at her.

Israel said, "Come to bed, Lucy. Staying up won't bring them home."

STARS STOOD over the widening canyon. They stopped each quarter hour now, took turns firing pistols. They waited against the jingling of bits, the creaking of leather, silence. Then went on.

The moon began its rise.

The land spread into flatter washes, baked plains of clay. They lost the trail, and no amount of circling could find it. They halted the horses, and he and Vine Leabo and Bob Tupper walked out searching the ground more closely while others held their horses, while they drank from canteens and smoked and talked.

He found no sign, nor did the other two.

They fanned into a line a half mile wide, and took turns calling as the moon advanced above them.

ISRAEL LAY DOWN at last, but Lucy couldn't rest.

The night was bright, at least. She walked south this time, along the little channel of water they had camped beside, and stopped. It was no use.

I will keep thy statutes, O forsake me not utterly.

These words came to her. She was, in the end, her father's child, and raised on sermons. And doubter that she had become, she was a mother also, and therefore superstitious. Where children were collateral, she was convinced of her own sin, and of condign reprisal.

She looked away and pressed her palms together. She closed her eyes and vowed, and she knew this was the price: that they would come, and this would be the price.

There will be no more straying in this place, she promised them. For our own good, we must tread the path together and do right. I will swear it. I do swear it.

THEY FOUND the girls at last, out on the plain, five miles southwest of camp and lying in the dirt. John Tupper's evil mare had balked and flared her nostrils. Then Tupper himself had seen them.

Down the line, they called one another in. MacLaren, arriving, stepped down on aching knees to find they'd risen and were standing in their dusty dresses, fumbling canteens.

The younger men stood by while the girls drank and drank and brushed their tears, while they choked on hard meat and cracker. MacLaren scratched the sand from his hair and walked away.

They put Caroline up with Hiram Hill. Vine Leabo gave a hand to Sarah, who was laughing, giddy. MacLaren put his own hand down to Emma Ruth, who'd followed him, and she rode behind his saddle under the setting crescent of the moon.

He closed his eyes, dead tired now with the girl behind him, thinking of that afternoon, the oxen moving, the boy falling. It seemed like days ago.

And now behind him rode this child who had been a girl, and remained a girl in many ways, but was lengthening into a woman's shape and thinking. It was the tenderest age. He saw how little he had understood it years ago, with Lise as he'd left her in the kitchen, sewing buttons on another man's coat. Thirteen, his given daughter, already taken on a woman's form and mystery.

Even then he'd wanted her. Her skin, her eyes, her solemn beauty. To be with her. To watch her walk. To watch her smile.

I do not like to hear of you being kept at work in the big house so late . . .

He'd gone away north, but the letters he'd sent down had been in a different tone. Though he'd no delicacy to address those things that most concerned him.

There is a good school for girls in Red River, I would send you if you like . . .

And he had not thought before to disallow the company of maidens in his own fort walls, but became an advocate in that year for chastity. Though for months on end, he all but forgot her. A year, two years, given over to his work.

I am coming the month of August, and hope to find you there . . .

Sealed in that final letter, carried by dogsled with the winter's news, was the only true sentiment he had ever dared: a small pressed lily, the first yellow of spring.

Come down on *Nereide*, he'd lain the night at anchor, in a hammock breeding fleas. All next day his business held him. Then, changing in his room for supper, he found the gift she had folded on the bed: a good elk-skin coat, dyed oxblood red and styled on gentleman's blue wool. With fringed epaulets, the pattern of a compass rose, and borders of yellow lilies.

Two weeks later, they were marrying. He in the coat, and she in a dress of her own device, her dark braids shining. Looking up at him with all the faith, all the faith in the world.

She who'd never known a man. He wondering by Christ what he'd done. They'd lain the first night side by side beneath the covers, hand in hand, flat and awkward as if some comic amateur had painted them. Such a charge in the air as any move but their clasping fingers might call down lightning to spear the inches between them. Outside was a half-hearted shivaree, a few of his men sedately banging pots, throwing stones at the roof, a single bawdy song in French. Then quiet. They were left with only the sounds of their own breathing, the small outside noises: an owl, a dog, the rousing geese.

Droll Simon Carr, his clerk, had noted there were fucking laws against it. Then relented, admitting that she was of a decent age and not his true daughter.

Stiff as paint, that night in Vancouver; and so, as they'd shipped north in single berths with men who leered and scratched; and so, on the inland journey; and so, on arrival in his low-ceilinged room, his narrow bed, where she slept with her head on his chest. And so, until at last one dappled night of skin and warm breezes, they had come to it.

What sin could that have been? When love had seemed too small a word for what he'd felt.

THE GIRL behind him stirred and brought him back. The morning was luminous green, the sky red-gold and pink behind the eastern buttress. He saw the wagon's white tilts standing soundly in clear air, fires glowing there like chips of orange glass.

In shafts, the sun rose cold and small under a single pale pink cloud. From all the grasses on the plain, cicadas roared.

Our Time on Earth

⌒◡△◡⌒

They crossed the Laramie, a deep bold stream, green and throwing glints of light.

Water poured against the oxen. MacLaren pulled up his feet in hope of keeping them dry, but the gold ox Dollar veered downstream. Then it was all he could do to get around them while the wagon canted up on hidden rocks and Mitchell sat his mare beneath the cottonwoods and shouted. Blue storm clouds coming on.

So he was wet past the knees before he got them turned and under way, climbing out through deep-cut mud, the spattered dust of the embankment. Mitchell turned and spurred his mare. Across the dry plain, the American fort stood low and white against the lead-blue sky. About a hundred Sioux lodges stood pitched to the south, with dogs and feathered scaffolds. A band of ponies swung their tails and chewed the dusty stubble.

His boots were full of water. Most of the wagons had drawn up outside the gates already, and a great scrambling was in progress: the numb and drowsy had come alive and were fast climbing in and out of wagons, rummaging, arguing, dusting hats, shaking skirts, calling children. And all he wanted was to walk back down to the river's shade and wring his socks and wait, but Tom Littlejohn came hurrying across the grass and said that Mitchell wanted him.

The place was swarming. Fort beggars in their robes plucked at sleeves, beseeching. He saw Tupper and Watts and Wilcox heading up the stairs to private quarters, others already shouting questions from the upper gallery, opening doors as though a month or two of travel had entitled them to any trespass.

He'd have barred the gate, by God, if it were his place.

He turned again to go, but Mitchell saw and called him over loud and urgent, as a man in a fray will do. So he soon found himself on the covered walk outside the trading room in a line with a dozen others, the waters of the Laramie warming in his boots and a clanking sack of ox plates for which he was to settle.

He stood in the doorway. The room was crowded. He closed his eyes, taking in this current of low dark smells: hides and castor, damp clay, timbers. The smell of his life, for as long as he remembered. Here were the same hidden sacks, the beads and blankets, tin cups and bad kegged liquor.

He heard women's voices and looked, and saw them at the counter's end, holding cloth against the light of the small window. Fur robes caught the bands of sun. Lucy Mitchell raised a buckskin jacket, made cheaply for the trade, pulled a sleeve against her arm to measure it. Then said something wry enough to make the others smile.

And then the day darkened, and she looked at him—or beyond him—through the open door. She didn't see him now. Then put down the jacket and called for buttons.

So he heard himself the year before saying, *No, you don't need buttons.*

To his girls: *No,* he'd said. *Go on, you'll lose them.* They'd pulled his fingers, begging, the last time he had taken them to Fort Hall. *Please, please, the silver ones.*

No. When you're older.

He felt the opening abyss.

In the crowd of men, the aching moment, he stood angry for a solid day when some chance thing would not undo him.

He turned, went back through the door, stood on the walk beneath the gallery.

He pressed the water from his eyes while the people walked back and forth across the compound. He breathed the tang of coming rain. Above the gate on the blockhouse wall, he saw that someone had painted the great figure of a red horse, running. He didn't know what it could mean. But stood, taking in the air, the solace of this mystery.

A GIRL of about sixteen came into camp that evening. She was selling moccasins. "She's Kennekoon," MacLaren said to Mitchell. "From the north."

Two men sauntered out of the willows after that, American trappers. Curtis was light-skinned, lank-haired, with gentle, slow-thinking eyes. Willard was some ugly mix of dark-skinned races, missing an eye and teeth, stringy beard going gray. He was a friend of Beck's, and full of news from the Sangre de Cristo and Black mountains. Curtis knew Bill Craig. The girl was Willard's wife. She showed some folded calico she'd bought, and wanted a pattern to cut it to a dress. He took her to Lucy Mitchell.

He'd already done what he could to forget the day, and meant to sleep, but Willard said, "I don't suppose you'd tell me, was you looking for fur, where you'd go. I don't suppose you'd tell me true."

MacLaren said, "There's nothing anywhere worth finding at this year's rates."

"Well, it's all to hell, but I like to do it," Willard said. "I don't care what."

So he went to find his ledger. Lucy Mitchell with her new provisions had been cleaning out the wagon, and Richardson's wife was helping. The rain had gone, the evening bright.

He found the ledger with its maps and brought it back. Curtis, by the fire, said to Mitchell, "There's black coal loose along the ground, a hundred miles just west of here."

MacLaren sat. Willard leaned and breathed across his shoulder.

"Oh," said Richardson's wife, "just look. I never could get anything growing in my dooryard." She was leafing through a *Ladies' Journal*, with a smell of lilac coming off her. So Willard had his one eye on her hems, and the woman turned the pages but was watching Willard's wife, now on her knees with printed cloth. MacLaren looked at Lucy Mitchell, and her gaze shied off. Her husband, by the fire, argued for the great age of the earth. MacLaren went back to his maps. Things swam and settled when he moved his head.

"Where's Beck?" Willard asked. "You two split off?"

"No, I'm trying to be *rid* of those, Daniel."

The boy's hands cradled a sprawl of things, small dusty hands brown but for pale webs of skin between the fingers. Something fell that looked like a butter press.

Mitchell and Curtis argued by the fire. Mitchell said, "No, the question is, what *kind* of God?"

"Gone," MacLaren said.

"I just *want* them."

"Gone? God damn." Willard spat. "Gone under?"

Mitchell said, "The evidence is all around. Why close your eyes? God means for men to understand."

MacLaren stared at the old pages, not able to call up the country. In the swirl of things, it seemed the lines were only lines.

A waft of lilac. "Oh, look what lovely lines that year. In Paris," said Richardson's wife.

"You all right?"

He bowed and nodded, then spat and took his knife to cut the pages free.

"Jesus. No, hell, don't rip nothing out, those won't make sense," said Willard.

Richardson's wife said, "Oh, now, *that's* a good idea for a centerpiece." The Kennekoon, with borrowed scissors, cut and cut, and he'd seen a woman with moccasins just like these, she'd hanged herself in willows.

Where's your mother? he'd asked June. *Where's your mother?*

Willard said, "I can't use these."

"There's no braver endeavor," Mitchell said, "than the pursuit of what is true."

The evening pulsed. A silence fell. In Willard's hand, the pages fluttered.

———

Israel followed her to bed that night, still bright and primed for some contention.

He said, "We'll be into the hills tomorrow. We'll be climbing." She lay, worn out, in the heavy sounds of his undressing, and closed her eyes, the sky still light. The days had grown too long to get through.

"There have been wonders on this journey you'd only know by seeing, Lucy. You must admit it."

Oh, she thought. The fervency of men.

"There isn't so much of life, Lucy, that a man can afford to spend each day in repetition of what he knows."

She sighed and turned. She worried now that Israel would never be content; that perhaps, like so many men they traveled with, he had never been. She'd begun to wonder more and more about the picture he had painted of his former life: a rational and orderly progression, in his telling, punctuated now and then by patriotic impulse. But, removing his narration, his defense, what did he have? Nothing more than a series of wayward halts and lunges, of occupation, of inclination, with this journey the most recent.

So, bravely, clumsily, she said, "I think you would defend any change. No matter how unreasonable."

"Well, that may be," he said. "But when my last days come, I know I'll want to look back and see that I've done a few bold things. Some things I can remember."

She said, "I have no shortage of memories, Israel."

But what she saw in the following silence was a strange clay canyon with rain falling through the light. Orange sky with braids of geese, a Pawnee cavalcade. A man unclothed and bathing.

And surely it was fine for him to speak of being bold. But what good had any boldness done her? With a life resigned again to what was right? To mothering, scrubbing, cooking. To bringing in dry sheaves of laundry and pressing each thing flat again. What was boldness for?

"Lucy, I couldn't let you stop me from spending my own life as I deemed best."

It was a fine sentiment. She lay and combed each word for what she so resisted.

"You mean spending it in the way that you desired," she said at last.

"Yes. I suppose."

"You call it best. When what we had was an opposition of desire."

"Well, why deny everything, for safety? Why is that best?" he said. "Put yourself in that scale, wife. Think: If this is all my time on earth, how shall it be spent?"

So she fell into a black silence, she who had not been entitled to choose which home, which life. Who had gone out by buggy a few times with a man of an age to be her father, dropped a rotting lark from his upstairs window, agreed to marry. Who had accepted, not chosen. Because she was not a man.

Well. Life is not a revel. So her mother said.

"You're dear to me, Lucy, do you know that?"

"Yes," said she who was dear. Not loved. They had always been too reasonable for that.

AT NIGHT SOMETIMES his body would remember how they lay together, he and Lise. Curled like the meats of a nut, his arm around her. Behind her sleeping knees, his own would fit. So he woke in the dark to find his robes piled into the hollow of his belly.

He sat, swilling the bottle in the dark. There was very little left. And when at last he went to make the fire, he saw it was already lit and there were coals, and she was alone beside them.

"What time is it?"

"Early," she said.

His noggin wasn't where he had left it. Without looking, she said, "I think the girls have washed it."

He found it among the drying dishes. Scrubbed raw, bleached with lye. He stood, loose-hinged, while the morning swayed and sighed. And the smell of baking bread had not produced a husband, so he took some water from the pail and drank.

"A dream woke me," she said. "I thought I might as well get started."

She looked up with her curving smile.

He sat and watched her needle flicking in and out. And Lise had been a one for sewing, but the shirt he wore now had come wrapped in paper, pulled down from a shelf. After all these months it seemed that he had not mastered yet this most basic possibility: no one would ever fill her place. And he would ask if this were so, but only he could answer, and the answer was dishonest or he could not go on. He wasn't man enough for consolation.

The needle flicked and flicked.

He said, "What dream?"

She'd been on a beach, she told him, alone with only a trunk of China silks. Wide bolts of cloth, all colors of blue, green, gold, red. She'd made a tent with them, tied other pieces to trees and tall sticks, she didn't know why. She remembered how they'd twined and billowed. It was quiet. "I don't know why I dream so much," she said.

"You saw those colors?"

"Very clearly."

"A pretty dream."

"No."

She said the ocean looked as she'd imagined. White beach, breaking water. "You've seen it truly, haven't you?" she said.

"The sea?"

"Yes."

He nodded.

"But I was so lonesome." She looked away. "I was so *alone*, it was terrible, I'm still—you know how a dream can seem so *real*?" She looked away. "And then a *bridge* appeared, a rope bridge with wooden slats, going up from the beach, it went way up above the surface of the ocean, out of sight. So I climbed, I began to cross it, but it kept stretching higher, and it was so frail, and I could see the little flecks of waves on the ocean, and I went until I couldn't see the end in either direction, and each step seemed more terrible."

He looked at her.

"I knew I would fall. I'd be lost in the sea."

He closed his eyes.

"It was just good to wake and be safe."

On the other side of camp, a dog was barking. People had begun to stir, and turn up lamps, and call out to one another. She went back to sewing and he stood, thinking he should find the horses, and she looked up from the buttons and he remembered how she'd raised her chin along the crowded counter and called for them. Then he thought of the red horse he'd seen.

"Did you see that horse?" he asked.

"Which?"

"Above the gate at Laramie."

"Yes," she said. "It was beautiful."

———

THE LAND ROSE into rolling breaks and hills. To the south, dark mountains wavered in her view like glass. They headed toward them through the heat, away from the river again, through poor grass, cactus, artemisia, low forests of cypress strangely dark under such a blank blue sky. They doubled teams on a rocky pass, and she and her three daughters put their shoulders to the wagons, and by such exertions ascended and went on. And whatever wonders Israel thought she should enjoy, she guessed that what she'd likely die with was the clear recall of each box taken down three times a day, roiled through, put back again.

They had dry thunder. Fires flared on ridges and went out in following rain. All night the grass would bend and hiss and, at dawn, fall quiet.

Carrying her pail through bulrushes that Sunday morning, she raised such crowds of insects that there seemed no air to breathe. She ducked and flailed, smeared handfuls from her hair, her forehead already swollen from days and nights before.

At camp, her daughters had to stand in smoke to braid their hair. They stamped and swung like surly colts.

Israel said, "We'll pack a dinner and go up the mountain for the day."

They moaned and crumpled. No more walking, they said.

"We'll ride. Help your mother. Get a dinner packed."

Lucy said, "Israel, no. What horses? What saddles would we use?"

"Go astride. It's the custom of the country."

"Not the little ones—"

"Pack the dinner, I'll take care of it," he said, and there was nothing she could do.

THEY SET OUT an hour later, she on the mare called Sally, along green banks of cottonwoods and elder. Mary rode tied snugly to her back.

Ahead, the horses dropped and clattered through the stream. The older girls rode Rufous Leabo's gentle paint; it stumbled now, and leaped, and the girls laughed shrilly. Lucy worried her own reins in fear. In camp, the girls had been amused by her tangling skirts, by how she'd steeled herself for this adventure. Mr. MacLaren had arranged the stirrups to a suitable length.

"Just let her go, Mama," Emma called, skirts swinging free above the bunched quarters of the tawny black-legged horse, the hooves and sliding stones. She rode behind James MacLaren's saddle.

Lucy eased her hold, heart still fluttering to be so tall, to have that long gray mane before her, the ears so far away. But the mare set down the bank, carried her carefully among the obstructions. When, for all this time, she had refused a mount.

I only remember slapping along, she thought, in those terrible saddles, and feeling always ready to go over the side. But to ride this way, as a man . . .

It was his daughter's horse, Emma Ruth had learned, and told her. He had chosen this horse for a child, and now the child was gone. It seemed a tender thing to see so suddenly. He reined beside her when they were crossed, and said, "All right?"

"Yes. She's lovely." She smiled, for old sorrows, with extra brightness. But already he was looking somewhere else. She leaned to pat the damp blue neck, and this time his eyes met hers, and then with a jolt, both horses leaped and swept around to stand wide-eyed at her old dog, Peg, who had bitten through the rope in camp and was panting up the hill behind them.

"All right?" he asked again.

"Yes," she said, and she was.

———————

ALL MORNING they climbed the hot shoulder of the mountain, through dirt and crackling bushes. From this vantage, the landscape was beautiful, not something merely to be trudged through. Mary cooed and pulled Lucy's bonnet tails, and bobbed and squealed when they trotted, and Lucy felt the same, felt the power the horse was lending her, to flow up a hill so effortlessly, and she in perfect balance. To her daughters, with a sudden bloom of pride, she thought: you will ride this way now, all your life, and I will allow it. We have indeed come onto new ground.

The dog panted and harassed the horses. The girls slid and bickered and changed places. Daniel, astride with Israel, cried that his legs were sore. And when she was almost sure it was too far, they topped a rise and looked down into a great broken canyon filled with pines. At its head, a grassy valley and the glimmer of cool water.

So they descended, she with not more delight had this been Eden itself.

In the shade of an enormous box elder tree, she brought out dinner, served cuts of cold roast buffalo, bread, salt tallow. There were flies but few mosquitoes. The girls took what she handed them and hiked their skirts and ran, took off their shoes and waded out across the cobbles to a wide flat rock that stood midstream. Daniel found a stick that looked like a pistol. Mary crawled and bounced and tugged her buttons.

"I'm losing my milk," Lucy said to Israel. "I think it's the heat."

Mr. MacLaren was walking off on some errand of his own.

"He's taken a liking to you," Israel said.

She tugged Mary's bonnet in alarm. Then smiled at Israel's teasing, and he smiled back.

She put away their picnic. A little breeze sprang up. At last she walked away downstream to a shady tree, and sat, and brought her baby to her, there:

> *In deepest grass, beneath the whispering roof*
> *Of leaves and trembled blossoms, where there ran*
> *A brooklet, scarce espied*
> *'Mid hushed, cool-rooted flowers fragrant-eyed*

She thought of her parlor table striped in window light where she had memorized these verses, transported to such worlds of passion and beauty as could be found, she'd thought, only in the writer's private mind. Never imagining this place, these true banks no poet had ever seen.

She lay back in the grass, the weight of her child against her breast, the small pinching hand. Smoothing the fine curls, she wondered freshly at the gift of motherhood, at the new strength of her body, and let her limbs fall open, lazy, aching from new use.

To ride like a man.

It was caution that gave life compass. But truly, what had she suffered, from leaving all those things that had always kept her safe? Walls and roof and garden? They hadn't starved, there was no need for money. No one had drowned or been killed by Indians, or by thirst. Her lost girls had not been so far away.

And what if they were now come into a different world, where anything might happen, where nothing old held true or was any longer certain? *And whatsoever Adam called every living creature, that was the name thereof.* So she had learned and taken as truth. But now she knew a man who'd seen things Adam never named.

She stretched her legs and lay, looking up at patterned leaves, thinking, This is all our time on earth. And wondered what else should not be denied her.

UNDER THE PICNIC tree again, she rested in the sounds of her girls' voices. Mr. Littlejohn had made them poles for fishing. Daniel stood with his in sunlight, watching patiently. And now the baby slept, and Israel snored open-mouthed among the crumbs, a pamphlet folded on his chest.

"Has anyone yet seen a currant bush?" she asked. They had brought pails.

"Up there," James MacLaren said.

She looked. A wing of the canyon rose out toward the valley, a tall buttress of brush and dirt crowned by pale blocks as square as lapstones. Cedar and pine grew sparsely on the crest, but below them, in the heat of the walls, was a dark line of shrubs.

She found the pail, picked her way across the cobbled bar toward the stream. The girls stood barefoot on the other bank, skirts tied up and pantaloons rolled. Lucy held her bonnet brim against the glare.

"I am going to pick currants!" she called, but they had caught three fish already. When she passed the tree again, Mr. MacLaren said, "I'll come if you like."

———

IN THE HEAT, she chose her course from tree to tree, like a ship to scattered islands, her clothes too heavy, unsuited to the climb. Out of sight of him, she flapped and cooled like a barnyard hen. In exasperation, untied her apron and hung it from a stub. Her stockings were abandoned under the picnic tree.

The sound of rushing water rose from the canyon below, and she waited, breathing from the climb, until she heard the dry cough so particular to him.

She knew the charge in her skin when he paused beside her. He was warm, as she, and breathing.

She was very fit. She saw this as they walked. When he went on, she fell behind, and they ascended in their small and separate shadows. The soil was strange here, remarkably loose: it caved away in places, light as sponge. It struck her that perhaps they were the first people ever to have crossed it.

"Do you think," she asked, "that anyone has ever been here?"

"The world is old," he said.

They came to the steep wall of an outcrop. Rank grass grew, white sage and everlast, and a line of dark green bushes, bright with berries.

They picked in silence, in the calling of jays. The currants dropped like rubies onto the gray floor of her pail. She tried one—it was tart and sweet and seedy—then another, hungry for them. It was so long since they'd had any fruit to speak of. Then she went to picking in earnest. For a time, she watched only her hands, thorough in concentration.

A hawk's trill broke her industry at last. She paused, saw it tilt in spirals on the draft. Then she was watching James MacLaren.

Did I look like that? she wondered. It was intimate, like finding someone asleep: the face stripped of thought or care. The fine brow a little furrowed. He fumbled at this work, and she was glad to see one thing at which he had no native skill. But something stirred in her, to see this echo of the pure child he might have been. So she ached for how far they were fallen from that grace. To be picking berries, not very well. To be sneaking some, tasting their own fingers. How was it that they could not, as children could, appeal to each other for the simple comfort of friendship, but must always guard their eyes? Wary and walled in pretense.

She looked away. "What was your life as a child?" she asked.

He spoke, haltingly at first. She asked more questions, and he answered as they overtook each other by turns, telling of his homeland, his mother and aunt and cousins. How, for pennies a day, they had won kelp, raked it out of the sea, carried it in baskets to rake dry and burn to ash for English glass. They'd rope down cliffs by moonlight, steal the eggs from sleeping gulls.

"And your father?"

"Taxed off to the German wars."

"Did you know him?"

He shook his head without concern and said, "I think these are clean as I want to make them."

They stood like children and compared, and his smile was quick, because her pail was heavier than his. He said, "Woman's fingers."

He followed her back along the low wall, and she turned and climbed higher.

The stone was different here from any she had seen, fine-grained and sparkling, pink and gray and mottled with lichen. It clinked underfoot like china. Limestone, he told her, and then said, "There's your view."

They'd come onto an outcropping of boulders, tall and steep-sided, scored by wind. She set down the pail. She untied her bonnet and took it off.

To the south, the dark peaks rose. Below, to the west, stood the slopes they'd climbed on horseback, and more like them ranged beyond, diving into the plain like great half-buried fingers. She saw the Platte's dark course. The prairie spread so vast and empty that she could scarcely discern, along the curved horizon, the end of earth and beginning of sky. It was more gray and flat, more wide and terrible, than anything she had imagined.

She thought he would say something, that he would point out the geography, name the faint shimmer of mountains. But he said nothing. The breeze tugged her skirts. She breathed the desolation in like air, not knowing what to make of it: to see that this was a fraction of what they'd crossed, and would cross yet.

"Those red bluffs," he said at last, "mark a crossing. A trail goes north. The tribes all use it."

She did see a rusty canyon's wall among the hills in the rising distance. She nodded, thinking again of her ride that day, how easy and swift that travel had been. She'd never understood this as a landscape in which people might travel confidently, easily, as a matter of habit. "Do you think of leaving us?" she asked. Then answered herself, "I suppose you must."

He didn't reply.

They fell silent, with no reason to linger. Having come to this abyss together, to stand side by side with their innocent pails.

She brought her arms against herself, chill despite the warming air, and rubbed her sleeves. It must be now, she thought. This time. My time on earth.

"I am so glad," she said, "to have you with us."

He glanced off, perhaps dismissing her. They gazed in separate directions, over the gray plain. She said, "I forswore to think of you, that day my girls were lost."

"You thought we wouldn't find them."

"It seemed a consequence. Do you believe in that? In consequence for sin?"

But he had moved already; he was taking her pail. The tin collided, the currants rolled from hers to his. "What sin?"

"You being too much in my thoughts."

He stacked them, and took them by the single bail.

She followed across the clinking stones, bonnet still in hand. He let himself down a tall block, more than she could decently step, and she paused on the brink, looking for some easier route, having now embarrassed them. He offered no hand to steady her.

Scrabbling to earth, she blinked and kept on a step, into the shade of a low cedar, fists tight on her skirt in pretense of a final look across the view, the canyons, the tall snag of a pine below. She stood, ablaze, in the jay's harsh call. She had set herself alight as offering, and he would look away as she burned.

And then her feet, her ugly shoes, were taking her, marching down through rattling grass, over stones and giving earth, her shame now scarving out, now reeling away behind her.

Part Two

Here the slightest mistake is big with fate.

—WILLIAM AULD,
Hudson's Bay Company trader

What Cannot Be Seen

⚜

THAT NIGHT HE WATCHED her boil the currants in a bowl with borrowed rum, flour, and dark sugar into a kind of pudding that, on serving, was consumed entirely in the time it had taken him to pick the first handful from which it had been made.

He was on the second watch that night, so he turned in early to hide under robes while mosquitoes whined and crept. The sun would not go down. And looking at the final bottle, he could feel the roar of absence coming like a waterfall ahead, that queasy fear. It was nearly empty. But he could drink this night, and soon felt better, lying with his hands against his own warm skin, lacings eased until the blanketed dark grew thick with steaming breath, and with Lise, who'd been in his thoughts all day.

With her basket, picking currants. On a horse, behind him. Bathing in the river, that warm Sunday long ago when she had come to lie beside him, tracing swirls and sparkles in the stone, when the light had shone over the lovely muscles of her back, which she had given him, and the curves of her legs, which she had given him, and her buttocks, which she had yielded to him; when she had raised and turned to show those breasts, that belly, thighs stippled now from grit, and then told him she was with his child.

The river's shine so bright his own eyes turned to water.

How do you know? How could you know?

Etku psukse. *I feel it.*

Now, in the probing whine of insects, his blind body wished for her.

———

Lighting his lantern by the coals, he saw the bottle's glint where it still tilted by the leg of Mitchell's chair. So he put it under his arm.

He followed the sound of water, stepped through willows, stone to stone, and arrived on the other bank in luminous spires of milkwort. He climbed the hill, flailing the torn stems of blossoms at the insects still following his heat until a great cottonwood shaped itself against the sky.

Under the limbs, he blew the lantern out. Darkness. He heard leaves and water and the grazing herd: mesmeric heat and rising of a hundred rhythms, slow steps, and breath, and tearing grass. Nothing seemed amiss, but on such dark nights, all foreknowledge relied on sensing what could not be seen. The wary snort. The quickening hoof.

He sat against the cottonwood's bark, unstopped the rum in the now familiar hope that his failure to address the world might ease into simple incapacity.

He brooded on the squandering of currants.

Up in the hot bushes, it was Lise he'd wanted, and the girls, and the days they had spent picking. When they were small, she'd let them play, let them sit and eat straight from her basket. When they cried, she stopped to nurse them, crooned some soothing thing; she helped them with stained fingers. He'd tell her not to do it.

Because what would make them strong? Not that. What would teach endurance? What child was ever tempered for this world by love?

He would save the berries, spread on blankets, and put the girls to sit with sticks, to guard them from the birds while drying. They'd have used that pail of currants for a fortnight.

A gust stirred him back through the leaves, a gathering sigh that trailed away with a dry patter of falling seeds—they ticked down on his hat brim, struck the lantern's metal cap with a hard small sound, like teeth. He squinted in the dark and combed the grass with his fingers, but there was nothing.

The rum, though, was very good.

He lay back, his hands one on the other, and felt the very ghosts, her knuckles in his palm, those peaks and passes, how they'd fit to his. As hills to sky.

How could something lost grow larger? It had grown. It ached inside his ribs.

And what would Lucy Mitchell say, stitching, in her tatted collar? So whitely virtuous, waking safely from her dream.

Wake, she said simply.

No.

Because then who would he be?

At which he breathed dark mothy laughter. Bright berries rained together, two pails into one.

He used to say: I never trust a man who will forgive himself. Would you?

WHEN HE SAT sometime later, Beal Beck was beside him, his face as soft and luminous as blossoms. But the brows still had their devilish arch.

They'd lived three years together, he and Beck, sharing meat and fire, the same lodge smoke and voices seeping through their clothes, boots setting the same steps through ice, eyes watering with the same sheer heights and visions. They'd built the smokehouse out of posts and wattled sticks. Blood, the swinging ax. Now the man sat and said nothing, while MacLaren's thoughts vined aloud and dreamlike as bramble over rotten logs that were his life and Lise, Lise, Lise.

He'd have followed her, but plumes of mist had risen from her heels.

He stood looking at her footprints, knowing now he'd never wanted what she'd given to Beal Beck as much as he had wanted what she'd kept from him.

He asked it. *Why?*

But Beck bowed forward, wrist to his lips, the way he did after drinking.

A wind swelled under the moon, stirred in the limbs. MacLaren heard the pattering again, a clink of bottle glass, and would have reached around but found that he was pitching over, slow as goose down, and his ear was to the roaring night. His face in grass, his thoughts in flashes of dream like lightning.

SHE WOKE DISMALLY in a fever of mosquitoes, the morning dark as usual and full of bawling cattle. Then Israel cut his finger, and Mrs. VanAllman came asking for the rum they'd lent.

"Well, I don't know," Lucy said, looking for clean cloth. "I thought it was returned."

"No," said Martha VanAllman, who was tall and thin, given to sharp words and fits of crying. Israel called out again.

"Just wait," Lucy answered. "Don't bleed on anything good."

Israel blamed the knife, of course, for folding back on him. So much did he despise all imperfection that he'd never see it in himself. The fault was in the tool: the knife, the ax, the wife. "I thought Israel brought it back," Lucy said, still turning up the lids of trunks. "He borrowed it. It was his suggestion."

"Well, there is no sign of it."

"Well, I'll ask the girls."

But the neighbors' rum was gone, a shapeless care while she bound Israel's finger, folded blankets, put away stray plates. Then Mr. MacLaren walked in late and set the empty bottle on a chair.

HE RODE half asleep that morning, hat pulled low, face swathed with linen against the dust. Loose cattle spread away in both directions. He'd fed his breakfast to the dog.

And the oxen went along fine without him, so he thought a smoke might help, and rode off to get some air away from the rolling wagons. He sat his horse and pinched out shavings, made his pipe, and lit it with a lens, sensing, in the growing quiet, a denser drone somewhere. A sound he knew, and heard because he knew it. He turned and squinted, saw Tupper on his evil mare. She ducked and snuffed the sand.

THEY GATHERED a small army of men with good mounts. They milled and shouted, finally set away: he and White and Mitchell and two dozen others jouncing with alarming weapons across the scabby upland, through musky wallows churned to talcum. Wool clotted in the stubbled grass. The horses came up short by turns, thrusting their noses down to scent along the dung piles. The men booted them on, cursing such deep animal persistence as was not satisfied by the snuffing of one or ten or thirty, but would, if not moved otherwise, stop and consider each offering on the chance that one might hold some new clarification on the unseen nature of things, some great and final proof of meaning to be divined from the excrement of buffalo.

The valley narrowed. The men conferred, divided, wished one another luck, the pistoleers riding off to intercept the animals when they began to run, the riflemen climbing the rise as the distant weight of sound grew slowly more articulate, the massed drone that was more than flies this time, it was the choral roaring, grunting, bawling, snorting of uncountable and teeming bison.

"God almighty," someone said. "They sound like a million."

They ate from wrapped parcels of corn cakes and rank side meat. They hobbled horses, checked their loads. MacLaren sat in the thin grass, drank some water. Then lay back, to hell with dignity. Richard Tony laughed.

MacLaren shut his eyes.

Waking under the cottonwood that morning, he'd seen rotted blankets trailing through the limbs, lifting in the breeze like hanging moss. No wonder there were ghosts, he'd thought. But would rather have been dreaming.

He lay in the still heat, the sound of horses feeding, until he heard the hunters go. He knew he ought to join them. Behind closed eyes, he saw the hours to come, that herd of twenty thousand half a mile below, innocent while he aimed through wavering air, its millioned flies, choosing from among them. He'd load and fire, load and fire, load and fire, all in a haze of back-blown powder, and below, they'd wheel to snatch themselves, leap forward in surprise, drop where they stood, great heads slapping the earth. He saw the kick and twisting tail, dust from hides billowing up against the light while calves stood dazed and bawling, while the herd slowly sensed something amiss, something unseen being not as it should and started forward finally, puzzled, lumbering at first, then, tails lifting, rising from ungainly flight into the true collective, sublime as flowing water or as birds. He lay, knowing he would go down at last to a field deserted but for the terrible dead, the more terrible dying—dazed and thrashing, bubbling from lungs—these creatures that were now meat and would be dried on racks into fodder enough to keep a company through five hundred miles to come. He lay, knowing that he would draw his knife between the still-damp teats of cows whose calves stood by, hoping to nurse the corpses of their mothers.

And was so close to dreaming that he almost thought he'd done it, but heard the first shots clap out, and rose and breathed, and took his rifle from the grass.

———————

BY NIGHTFALL all around camp, the dogs lay gorged and twitching. Beyond the edge of light, the warm grass sang.

In his last pair of woolen drawers, his blue winter shirt, MacLaren sat and watched the flames, having washed the clothes he'd worn that day and hung them here on stakes to dry. He reeked of meat, for all that he had scrubbed. His ears still rang from shooting.

Inside the tent, the baby woke and cried.

He leaned on steepled hands, pressing images from his eyes of ribs, tongues, entrails. Richard Tony elbow-deep in a cow he'd killed, raising his arms with a bloody whoop. Half the men had caught the cry and gesture, done the same, yodeling like savages, painting their cheeks with blood. They'd had no need to mark themselves. By the end of the day, they were an army painted red.

The kettle was warm. He stood his rifle, poured water down the barrel. Her white dress like a ghost came out of the tent and climbed into the wagon for something. He saw bare feet.

She went into the tent again.

He poured and scrubbed and emptied, poured and emptied, thinking of Lucy Mitchell, the suckling child, the taste of milk, salt skin. He scrubbed the barrel, imagining the spilling hair, the suckled breast. White lace. It brought him into need.

"You're up very late."

He looked up and saw her standing. The baby arched to see him, as though awaiting his answer as well.

He rinsed his sooty hands and dried them. She went away.

The prairie wolves had found the carcasses. Their yips and squabbling carried down the valley. They always sounded like five times their number.

She'd put on a shawl and came and sat with the babe now pulling at the tassels, bobbing up against her. He watched her fill a tiny spoon with laudanum. The baby fussed and pushed at it, then accepted. She put the bottle on the ground beside her.

He said, "Don't leave that out."

She looked at him and he said, "Your boy might find it."

She said, "I trust my boy just fine," and then she'd stood and there was a damp child on his knee.

The baby looked at him.

He hopped his heel, alone with her, seeing the pretty sullen lips, the sticky curls. She'd grown. She gave him a wary look, then scowled, turning for her mother. He tilted her into the crook of his arm and tipped out tobacco from his pouch. He'd found a cowry bead that morning, and now it spilled out with the shavings. He tried to show it, but she turned away. Her face had begun to screw and sour when her mother came and took her.

He still had the shell between his fingers. When the child was content, he offered it across the fire, leaning.

"What is it?"

"They were raining down on me last night." It passed—pale, tarnished, the tiny mouth a dark indented smile—his fingers into hers. "I was under a burial tree."

She said, "A shell?"

She studied it. He looked away in the sound of distant ox bells, the wet squeak of the baby's suckling fingers.

He said, "I'll pay back the rum."

She said, "Is it so improving, to drink that way?"

He found his hat and put it on and saw the shirt was over his arm, though he'd meant to leave it drying. And he was going but stood; he felt he was seeing her for the first time, but time had stretched the sound and left— it seemed—only the echo of something she had said, a ghost of some idea he'd forgotten.

He said, "I'm turning in."

But, bedded in the thick warm air, he lay awake, seeing the fine skin of her ankles. And more, the places unnamed—all thought denied—the curves of calves and muscled shins, the knees, their salty creases, the long thighs' tingling skin, those shameful leading thighs, their gently curved and lurking bones, soft folded flesh between, savored sin and issuance of life, those deep privacies they guarded. All these, that could be named only limbs.

———

MR. LITTLEJOHN HAD somewhere come upon a mouth harp and rode the wagon pole curled round-backed as some buzzing beetle. But Lucy no longer pretended any interest in these impossible hours of daylight.

She walked, with a tiny ocean shell in the pocket of her apron.

That evening she was putting on beans to warm when she saw James MacLaren walk down among the horses. They put their ears back at his approach and moved off, surly and dull with salt and work and dust. He sat on his heels and waited. Soon they'd settled back into grazing, eased around him.

"What do you see?"

She turned, surprised. Israel had come in from somewhere.

"Your mare is very thin," she said. He had all but disappeared among the horses. She turned away to cook again. Israel stayed watching.

"Why aren't the girls helping?" he asked.

"I've called. They're off somewhere."

And then she knew that James MacLaren had straightened into view because her husband said, "Well, find them," and then told her they would never be of use if she didn't get them cooking, that every other family had girls working and she let hers run free. They'd never be independent, he said. Then asked, "Where's the coffee?"

"In the pot."

"The Council meets at eight," he said to his watch. "I'll need supper soon."

He poured a cup and stood with it, and she poured her own and sat in the pine chair looking at him. A handsome man, she saw. Straight-shouldered, a man of intelligence and intention. Whose children were hers. Who gave and expected, whose talents and follies had emerged through the years to surprise her. Who wanted her. Who wished for her affection. So, blowing across the hot rim of her cup, she could convince herself that every fault was hers, for expecting far too much. Was she so impoverished? So ravenous? So angry that she must think that she had come to love the skin, the hairs of the hand, the dry cough of a stranger? What had possessed her, in those brief moments on the mountain, to think this world might accommodate such an impossible lapse of order? That she might love and be loved in turn, and seen?

No, love could not be some great heedless unchanging thing. It was shifting ground, changing balance day to day. A word, a gift, a memory, a failed intention. We are only people being as we are, she thought. Anything else is self-deception.

"The trail breaks up tomorrow through the drylands," Israel said. "I told White I'd spare MacLaren to ride ahead as pilot. Kingery offered Richard Tony for our driver. If that's no inconvenience to you."

"Of course not," she said. "Why would it be?"

MacLaren turned in early, walked down past skimming ravens to the camp he'd made. A thousand people had come through since he'd slept here last, and no small number had looked across the river at the coming hills and decided to lighten their loads. He passed a wrought chandelier, robbed of crystal. Stained tree stumps stood littered in clay shards. Here were caches of flatirons, boots, sprung books. A parasol, a bell, a garden gate, a kettle. Iron stoves. Tomorrow they'd swim the cattle, raft the wagons, pull the long grade. A two-log float stood beached on the far shore. The water between ran dark and deep.

He unrolled his robes and sat.

The last McMunn's was gone. He made a pipe, fired it with a borrowed match, a high whine now coming on, some necessity of blood that made him want to stir around or take up whittling. He looked at his hands while, above in the cottonwoods, the ravens made that noise they did: a knocking in their throats, like nuts falling on tuned wood. There should be a name for that, he thought.

He finished his pipe and tried to sleep, facedown, remembering how she used to lie beside him at the end of some long day, one arm against his side, her fingers cradling between his legs, to hold him softly. Meaning nothing but sweet comfort. Glad to have him there. He did believe she had been glad once.

A thin grief climbed inside his throat. He breathed it down.

And here was Lucy Mitchell, looking off, her knuckles pressed against her lips. Whose body he had now considered, as Beal Beck had considered Lise's.

Well, men consider. But to act? To take as you please? Another man's wife. Another child's mother. How could any be so bold as to weigh that conduct lightly? Lying on the knobs and hollows of his bed, it seemed a fresh insult.

A dog kept barking. He slept at last and woke in a queasy sweat. His nerves like chain running out of a metalled box.

The ground was harder. The sighing grass, the chittering teeth of insects pulsed with the coursing of his blood. The stars were out.

After a while, he stood and found his shirt.

The dog dreamed and twitched beside her empty chair. The coals glowed. He sat on the kitchen box and filled the kettle, held out his hands to warm.

"Are they still meeting?" Lucy Mitchell asked. She'd come out of the dark with nothing in her hands: no bread, no child, no mending.

"They've found a stack of *Punch*. They're laughing at the pictures."

"They wanted our wagons across by four," she said.

He had folded his arms, fists balled to stop the tremors. Now he held them out again.

"It's a warm night," she said.

"A fellow in St. Joe sold me something for sleep," he said. "But I'm out."

She turned without a word and soon was back with laudanum. "If it serves," she said.

He folded it into his hands.

She said, "Don't leave it out."

She sat. His own chair creaked. They watched the kettle warm. She drew a breath and then said nothing.

After a while he heard her say, "I have not had this happen to me before."

He saw that she was crying.

He stared at the kettle where it rattled and steamed, and she stood and walked out of the light.

———

It is, she thought. Love is some great heedless thing.

She had stood from the fire and left him, followed sloping land down toward the river, through grass, through swinging light, had set the lantern on the trunk of a fallen tree. Now moths blazed in from darkness, began to beat and creep against the warming glass. She took off shoes and stockings, walked out through bitten sedge, tough grass. Raised her hems and stepped into the water.

Love is some great heedless thing, she was thinking, when his footsteps sounded cleanly in the grass and stopped.

In cool water past her knees, she turned. He was sitting on his heels, head low, as though studying the bent grass of her passage. The dark current between them showed the wriggling glints of stars.

It is.

She loosed the raised hem of her dress. Let it ride and fill, and pull under.

Her release. And waited, but saw he could not look at her.

At last she walked out of the water past him, wet cloth pulling at her legs. He rose, and said her name, and stopped her.

She stood. Eyes closed. Frozen, simply being there.

Her hands stole out behind, waiting, as though for a child to gain her.

The warmth of his touch was shocking. The tips of their fingers curled, gently locked. She drew him to her like a cloak. But stayed rigid, upright with fear, feeling his breath on her hair. Feeling, in wonder, the weight and warmth of his hands in hers.

What a wonder, too, the shaking that overcame them. The shaking, as though something grew so terribly inside that it could be neither battened nor released without the gravest danger. Neither battened nor released.

Amazed, she thought: He is afraid.

And suddenly, all her need and doubt alchemized in whole to pity, as profound, as fervent as a mother's for her child. That he could be moved by this. By her.

She pressed her back against him, leaned her head into the high crook of his arm, brought his knuckles to her lips and kissed them, pressed them to her cheeks. In this ecstasy of possession.

Sighing trees. The glancing coolness of cloth. The line of buttons down her back, corset, lace, all shut her in. She dared to turn, felt her head pulled tight to the pulse that was theirs, his hand in her hair, and there was nothing she could say, but held very still, wondering what more strength she might have to give him. Praying she might be allowed some strength to give him.

But he only held tight to her, and this was all. Nothing more was possible.

WILD STONE HEART

⁓⌒⌒⁓

SHE SAW A GREAT DEAL of the night, and when she woke in the morning, her first thought was of him.

The bugle had sounded to gray dawn, and her husband beside her. She sat, light and heavy at once. Closing her eyes, she had the sense that the tent was a raft unmoored; at the back of her skull, she felt the leaden tilt of being swept in slow blind spirals.

The dog, who slept each night at the door of their tent, rose and shook herself. Israel leaned for his clothing. She looked, with fresh sympathy, at the bristles of his ears. He said, "I've lost my watch."

"It's not in your waistcoat?" she asked, leaving herself no time to recall the dark or the river or the moment of his touch. Though she was tempted, beneath her eyelids, to dissolve.

"What time is it?" he asked, knowing—he must know—that she had no way to tell.

"Did you have it last night?" she asked. "Is it under the pillow again?"

"Yes. No."

She watched him feel the pockets of his stained coat and trousers, saw the silvering curls at the back of his head, the thin spot where the skin showed through. The grease and dust were worse than ever. My stars, she wondered, how long since I have cut his hair?

"Shake out the tent," she said. "You always find it."

Out of his hearing, out of his sight, she diffused. A sun had risen, an explosion of light, though the morning was still gray. She strode up from the river, her edges soft with some beginning.

"What are you humming?" Emma asked.

"Nothing," she said. "An old song."

AND IT WAS true, they'd been late rising, later still to cross. Watts' wagon ran under on the morning's first trial, overbalanced and tipped and filled and mostly sank, and all three boys went into the water, and Mrs. Watts went in herself, whooping and splashing in her yards of dress, so Lucy almost laughed. But no one was drowned—not even the crated hens that rolled under not once but twice and rode to shore still fixed in their cages. It took an hour to straighten out, the boys all diving for what could still be rescued. But all was otherwise well, and she found herself to be perfectly fearless when their turn came, and smiling.

So they left the Platte at last and climbed the hills, she among the usual army of sheep, goats, dogs, and children; the women around her drifting into accounts of recipes for which none had ingredients any longer, nor would likely in their lives again. Locusts sprang and beat against their dresses. To the south, the startling deep red gorge of rock widened and fell away, and when they were all silent, they could hear, above the muffled wheels, the soft click, click, click of the oxen's wearing joints.

They made dry halt at evening, spread out along the hilly plain. Richard Tony, with his mouth full, said they were being led the wrong direction. If you wanted water, he could find it for you, fast as anyone. She smiled and served, and all her contempt seemed focused on the fullness of his lips, how red they were, poking softly through the bushy beard.

Suppered, they went on. She rode in the creaking wagon and read to the children until they slept. Near midnight, they stopped beside a muddy spring, got out their tents and beds at last while the oxen roamed crackling through tall brush. She lay, hearing outside the spray of sand, smelling hot horses down to roll, and slowly the camp grew quiet, and slowly she released the night, the day, the morning, until she had set the lantern once again on that dead tree, and saw the water with its silver threads of stars, until she passed him, until she felt his hands again, his breath, his arms around her.

A REMARKABLE DOME of rock stopped them in the grass, next day.

They camped. All afternoon, while others climbed and shouted, whistled, fired rifles, chiseled their names, or went up with buckets of soot and grease, she waited. It seemed impossibly long since they had touched.

He stayed with the cattle. Lingered through camp and spoke with men. Avoided her eyes over supper.

The girls made their beds outside on the grass. She went to sit with them, the evening still bright and breezy, the days so very long. They were sweet to her, and laughed. It seemed necessary to be with them, and she thought of no end of questions. They were glad to answer, and gossiped about the other girls they walked with. For all the dwindling down of their lives, their wearing-out shoes, poor dresses, no rooms to live in, and so much left behind, they did seem as happy as ever, sharing songs and stories. Making themselves new out here, and strong, and she thought she loved them even more than she had before they'd left. Though she'd noticed them much less.

"Oh, my gracious," she sighed, and hugged Emma Ruth's head tight on one side, held Caroline by the shoulders on the other. "Will you forgive me? I haven't been the mother I could have been."

"You're the best we could ever have," they said. "You're not like the others."

"How not?"

"You're just not."

"You're quiet."

"No. Mrs. Koonse is quiet," Lucy said. And then, with shameless solicitation, "I'm just sullen and selfish."

"You're not selfish."

"You teach us things."

"And what was the last thing I taught you?" she asked.

No one could remember.

But she could see how much she had kept back. How difficult it had been since Luther, just knowing what must be done each day and doing it. Then Israel had re-formed the world, with all his requirements and demands. Relieved, she had accommodated. But now everything was changed. For so long she'd banged out the chores of her life on that anvil of mornings, noons, nights. But now she could feel the joy, the ring and heft. Knowing she was worthy.

"Tell us a poem tonight, you never say them anymore."

So she lay, and they lay like little ones against her, eyes closed in the golden light, and she recited.

> *I would build that dome in air,*
> *That sunny dome! those caves of ice!*
> *And all who heard should see them there*
> *And all should cry, Beware! Beware!*
> *His flashing eyes! His floating hair!*
> *Weave a circle round him thrice*
> *And close your eyes with holy dread,*
> *For he on honey-dew hath fed*
> *And drunk the milk of Paradise.*

The wind spun sparks across the evening. The captain and John Kingery sat with Israel by their fire, all still reading articles from *Punch* while, beyond the light, dark grasses heaved and reeled. She wiped her hands, work done at last, and walked through it, and began to climb.

The rock was varnished by the wind. Her boots, she found, were worn too slick. So she took them off, climbed on bare toes, fearless on the steep incline. She put her arms out, thinking about Luther, how he'd walked the backs of rafters. The sharp quarter of the moon shone bright enough to cast a shadow.

When she gained the top, the wind met her suddenly, with force almost to topple her. It dragged away her bonnet, sent it flying.

I have found the wild stone heart of the world, she thought, embedded here in grass.

She walked, toes gritting across the high expanse. Paused over painted names, and graven: some joined by crosses, enclosed by hearts. Some floating white with lime.

Of course, she would not see him waiting.

Along the highest crest, she was surprised by boulders. They stood, carved by the wind, in small dished valleys, on ledges, creating halls and cool crevices of stone. One smelled of excrement. In another, she found crusts and rinds of someone's dinner. Another led down to a view of camp. She followed it, sat on sloping rock, its living warmth taken in by day, given back in this cool air. Saw fires on the grass below, the shapes of moving people, pale wagons looped across the darker grass like a necklace of finger-bone beads.

She waited, hidden, and exposed. Before God, the wind, the night.

SHE WENT DOWN to her bed and lay beside her husband.

"Nice walk?" he asked.

"Yes. It was really very bright. You weren't worried?"

"Not at all."

She wondered where Israel's mind went when he was with her. Quietly, beside him, she had turned away for dreaming.

If he had found her in the dark. His hands upon her waist in that hall of stone. Her trembling as she asked for him, for his hands to find their way. The pressure of his touch, the bite of rock beneath her and her skirts riding up, the hiss of breath. Her hair pulling from its coil.

A woman's hair is for her husband, her mother always said.

She heard Israel's slow breathing, the quiet turn of pages. But she was above, on stone. In their passion, joining, the rest of their lives forgotten.

Weave a circle round him thrice . . .

To leave herself, the shell of a wife, to wash the clothes and work the bread, to see her daughters grow, to kiss her baby's curls. To lie with her husband the rest of her nights, content. I will shed her by some magic, I'll leave her here and ride away with you.

For he on honey-dew hath fed . . .

And then, moving before she could think, the press of naked toes on stone, going down, down, down. Safe now, knowing the great distance between the dream and the intention. Between intention and the deed.

IN THE COLD shadows of cliff walls, MacLaren stopped alone the next noon and watched the swallows dart.

The party was laying over for the day. He'd come out with them to picnic at this canyon they called Devil's Gate. He'd sat while children splashed, while fathers helped boys dam up a hole for swimming. After a while, he'd left them eating, come up through the river's shallows, turned west along this bank. Stone cliffs rose two hundred feet out of level plain. The river came straight through them.

The swallows veered and dove with throaty chirps and buzzes. He climbed over boulders, rose gray granite, the cliff's jumbled foot. He'd come this far, grateful for the distance each new mile had put between himself and whatever he had done or meant beside that river. Even in the light of morning, it had seemed regrettable and best forgotten.

He climbed in the sound of rushing water, until he came out of the shadow and found a warm slope of rock at the canyon's head. He sat in the sun, squinting, counting the hours to evening. Then lay back with his shirt for a pillow.

He had turned a beggar. He had always scorned needful men, how they'd sneak and lie, pinch their eyebrows, making soft excuses. Now, by evening, he was visiting the likely camps. Mattie Leabo gave him something. He'd pass Lampheres', the Turkish mat, and think, Not there. Not there. But here was afternoon again, and those apprehensive veins were waking. There was no reasoning with this.

He heard someone wading. He lay and hoped to disappear, but after a time, light footsteps approached on the stone. Through lashes, he saw the shining legs come near. Emma Ruth in chemise and ragged pantaloons.

She sat, not far from his head, and crossed her arms. Pink toenails, clean from wading. He saw her watch the swallows chitter and swoop in the shadows of the walls.

"You're always sleeping," she said. Her pantaloons were hacked at the knee like a pair of boy's short drawers.

"I wasn't sleeping." He sat and squinted at the water.

"You do, though."

"Because I'm old."

"You're not old."

He rubbed his knuckles. At least his hands were steady yet. His chest spattered pink from the smallpox scar. She could see it.

"Mama says its opium."

"And does she know you've cut your pantaloons?" He reached for his shirt, but she'd taken it.

"I don't like frills," she said. And then, "This smells like a badger."

He took his shirt and put it on. "Go now. She wouldn't want you here alone."

"I'm not alone."

"Go."

She looked up at the wide channel of blue sky that ran between the cliffs, the dark trees clinging to the walls. "If I had a horse," she said, "I'd live out here. I'd ride everywhere."

"You'd freeze the first winter."

"I don't care. It's transcendent."

He looked over. "Do you know what that means?"

"Some things just have God in them. Some don't."

"Who says?"

"I do. I can tell. Animals. People. Even things. We have a headboard we brought. My father made it, and there's a bureau that goes with it. Mama said she could leave the bureau but not the headboard. They match, but close your eyes and you can feel. They're different."

"How?"

"There's like a light coming out of that thing. Or place. Or person. Like they're awake. And the rest is sleeping. You know."

He looked at her, and did know. With her nut-brown hair. Her perfect skin. The square innocence of her shoulders. And it wasn't right that she should be there, but it wasn't lust he felt, except in aching for that youth, that pure healing grace. He could have held it to him. He could have taken it close and held it, if it was a thing you were allowed to touch.

But too late, he saw Lamphere's bag-eyed spaniel wetly scrabbling through the boulders, the old sergeant himself following after, and Henry Chatfield, both armed for birding. They paused below, the old squinting fellow with his stained whiskers and meerschaum pipe, checkered waistcoat with strained buttons.

"Hello!"

"Hey."

"Lovely day!" the man announced, blinking up in his fool cap with the pompon on the top, and their words echoed up and down while Emma Ruth in her underthings sat quietly, while Chatfield in striped trousers tilted his hips this way and that, gazing at the swallows. And MacLaren began to say how she'd wandered up here on her own, but the old fellow was already clatting off, half deaf, in hobnailed boots. With devils of his own, and sly pleasantries to cover them.

"Go," he told her.

Nothing in her was not gentle or good, from the immaculate whites of her eyes to the fingers now unlacing from around her drawn knees. She stood.

Then he reached out, although he would have traded what life was left to keep her pure and safe, he reached out, in the moment before he could stop, and brushed the smooth inside of her calf.

NOTHING

⁓⌒⌒⁓

FROM A WRENCHING URGENT SICKNESS, he fell at last into a kind of sleep, drenched and chilled by turns, dreaming of earthquakes, of pale galleons in the clouds and aboard them a giant race of men and dogs who tried to take him on and away to some blue world. The clattering of his own teeth woke him. He felt for the robes, thrown off in the heat, and thought of Emma Ruth. He checked the progress of the stars, holding on to a pure virtue that wasn't even his.

She had gone with only a backward smile. Lamphere had not betrayed them.

Lucy Mitchell, over breakfast, had watched him, knowing. "Lie inside the wagon today," she said. "Would you lie inside the wagon?"

"No." The tea was foul. He drank it down. His ribs were sore from retching.

"Well, I'll get you something for it, anyway."

"No," he said.

All his life, he'd been the first to rise and the last to sleep. Activity was the sole virtue he'd been born with—enough to earn him envy, sometimes even scorn, among men, as women will suffer among their own for beauty. And now a child had asked why he was always sleeping.

"I'll get going," he said. "I'll be all right."

———

THEY WORKED along the narrow river. A low range of solid rock rose up from it. Dwarf pine and cypress gathered in the creases, and spurs of granite ran into the valley. The river coiled around them. Their trail crossed, and crossed again. One track turned into two, sometimes three. He was one of several pilots on vedette to find the best.

They nooned. White goats had watched from ledges as they passed, and now some men took up guns to hunt, but he couldn't go. Lying in the wagon's shade, he felt like a ship in following seas. The ground would not keep still.

They went on again but quit early in a valley of dark green grass, in honor of Independence. He slept, then woke before sundown to racketing gunfire, whoops, the clashing of pots and pans.

Around the fire, Lucy Mitchell was the very wolverine in the jakes. Elbows flying, pot lids thumping, smoke tears smearing on her wrist.

"Better?" she asked.

A chill wind gusted. He nodded, breathed, feeling very lean and light.

When he got back with wood, the two older girls sat huddled, dressed for dancing, with blankets on their shoulders.

"Dancing tonight," Lucy Mitchell said. "You should join."

Narrow blades of orange clouds hung still as islands. Everything seemed most beautiful. She poured him coffee, then brought him whiskey in her husband's deep tin cup.

He found the men gathered listening to VanAllman, on a stage of crates and draperies, reciting Paine's letter by heart. An American flag lopped dankly on a pole beside him. The women set up trestles as MacLaren watched and drank. The whiskey burned along his empty coils like lye. Whitcomb spoke on Bunker Hill. Then they brought out labeled port and Madeira and good French bottles, started calling toasts to Polk and Fremont and the men in Texas, to the great Willamette Valley, freedom wealth and all.

Some boys were making squibs and rockets. Vine Leabo called MacLaren over where he and Hill had a poker game going with old Velasquez on a blanket outside Lamphere's neat camp. The old Mexican pegged that tent each evening, drum-tight and square, the lantern wiped and ready. The Turkish mat peeked out the unlaced door.

They traded jokes as they played, and bid by caliber of rifle ball poured out of their pouches and shared around. Velasquez dealt his leathery cards.

MacLaren put his finger through the eye of Hill's jug and tried it, and they watched.

"Gets you pretty quick, don't it?" Hill grinned. John Kingery's mastiff had dropped to its belly behind them and chewed a bone.

Vine said, "What's an old dog going over a waterfall like?"

"I don't know what," Hill said.

"Like to be drowned."

They all laughed but the Mexican, who passed the jug without drinking and silently raised.

Vine said, "What's the difference between beans and bullshit?"

Hill shook his head. He tilted the jug and passed it. MacLaren drank again.

"Then damned if I eat your cooking. What's bigger than God and you die if you drink it?"

Squibs popped off in a stuttering explosion. A promenade of girls came by, arms linked, striding brassy through the grass. MacLaren's guts squeezed sharp again, as they had through the day. He closed his eyes and waited. The Mexican said something.

"What'd he say?" Hill said.

"I don't know. Maybe he said you're trying to kill us."

MacLaren blinked watering eyes. He gestured for a card.

"Kill us, hell. He want to be the last one standing?" Hill had his cards, was squinting at the white-haired Mexican. "You know what that is? Hey? Last one standing? That's yellow. Goose shit. Coward. Now Vine would tell you this man here"—MacLaren felt the man's fist nudge his shoulder—"he ain't a coward."

"No, he's not," said Vine.

"Go on, you old nigger," Hill said. "Drink some."

MacLaren heard the jug tilt. Opened his eyes to see the balls roll forth like tiny planets, all sizes, to rest among the others. He folded his sweating cards and tossed them. He was burnt kettle inside, soaked now, the liquor floating bitter black all through his veins. He'd gone too far already.

"You know?"

"Know what?"

"What's bigger than God and you die if you drink it?"

"Your goddamn eye pop, is what."

MacLaren saw the evening sky, remembered those pale galleons, the dream giants who'd tried to take him. In the grass behind them, the mastiff worked its bone with a clacking hollow-mouthed persistence. Beck said someone ought to get that dog.

"You want to know or don't you?" Vine asked again.

"No, I don't. Your go."

Beck, no, it was Hill.

"Nothing," said Vine. "That's what."

Someone guffawed.

And there was Chatfield's English gun, propped against the wheel. The man with his pretty bouquets of birds, each noon without fail. Now there was a passion for killing.

He dreamed the chords of a piano striking. The dealt cards skimmed. The dog let out long slobbering sighs, whet its foreteeth, an idiot sound that grated down his spine until he swept up Mitchell's cup, and tilted to his feet, and hurled it spattering into the dust. Cards fluttered down like leaves.

The dog stood and strode a few paces and thumped down to resume its work in the flattened grass, and Chatfield's gun was three strides off, and then he checked the cap and fired it. The dog leaped out of the roaring dust and tumbled, and rose again to howl away in a haze of falling litter.

MacLaren leaned the rifle and walked away as the two men roared with laughter.

———

THERE WAS an actual piano.

He'd drifted on its sound into a crowd of misty women, a trussed and innocent chorus and the captain's wife, draped as Lady Liberty, leaning in her paper crown, the piano unboxed in her high wagon bed.

Loyal sentiment rang down in untuned hammer blows. MacLaren angled away through knots of people on the grass. The bonfire roiled a watery heat and drew him. Scrub pine and bayonet. He found a keg of cherry shrub the drivers had been drinking. Watched Don Polk pick up a chair and throw it on the flames. Red skeletons of limbs exploded. The shrub was very sweet. Chips of ice flew through the air from buckets. Then Emma Ruth, beside his elbow, had something in a bowl.

"I saved you roly-poly." She'd tied ribbons on herself. "I forgot the spoon," she said. "I'll get it."

"No." He could hear fiddles now.

But she had galloped off somewhere. So he proceeded. Past the captain, in silk hat and tails, the better class here in the middle, between the fire and the dance. Olmstead with his empty plate. Mitchell stood by, smiling.

He nodded, carefully, with his pudding.

Near the fiddlers, he saw Lucy Mitchell with the baby on her hip, Nancy Richardson leaning close to speak, both smiling with cups in their free hands, and he was jealous, and the fiddles sawed, and then swirling bonnets and hats consumed her.

She was dancing when he saw her next, the baby's arm held high in hers like a tiny beau, wild sticky curls, both laughing.

Back at the bonfire, he found an empty chair and sat, and Patton was further gone than he, if that was possible, and started talking, but across the ground MacLaren could hear her voice against the fiddles, above the roaring men, she was singing.

Then someone said, "You goddamn son of a bitch," and hit him in the jaw.

He went over with the chair and rose to his knees, reeling. Pudding all over his hand and something shouted about a goddamn dog. It was John Kingery. So he got up to fight, but there were hands all over him. Someone fired a pistol, and he bulled around and saw, sweeping toward him, a stump of silver pine as thick as an ox leg. It burst against his neck, in a shattering of slivers and punky dust; it was Tupper, and Patton hitting Tupper and Kingery down in the general roar. He turned his back, hand up, dismissing them, listing away.

Mitchell's camp was empty. MacLaren poured cold coffee from the wobbling pot, washed his hand in the cup, drank. The bonfire lit even these bushes. He rested his head against the chair's tall back and felt the dark glide through him. Well, it would lay him out in time and he'd be bigger than God and be Nothing.

So he was sitting with his eyes closed when she passed.

She must have been up in the wagon. He knew her even in the dark by these small sounds alone: her stride, her skirt. She passed. He meant to let her go.

She said, "What happened?"

Wood and dust was all down his shirt. He said, "I've found the coffee." He saw the pale suggestion of her face.

She said, "I have been dancing. I wished you'd come."

He breathed out roughly. As though he could. Could take her hand and dance.

But she stood by as though waiting for something better. So he said, "Christ, woman, go look at yourself."

She was away, then, through the grass. And when his hand fell on her arm, she kept going, and changed course, and she followed him. The scrub snared, and the grasses slowed them, and they crashed through willows with rasping clothes, and breath, and teeth.

She was a torment of cloth. His hands fumbled, and hers were on him, lewdly, her greedy breath, she would consume him, there was not enough of him for this.

The willows leered. There was a crackling of rockets.

And then a lead had opened, they had made their way to flesh. He felt the inward pinch of private hair.

Later he remembered only dark, his shaking hands.

———————

SHE WASHED HERSELF, trembling, when he was gone. Beside the cove of willows.

In the tent, she lay awake, listening to her too-quick breath. Curled, eyes closed, against the drained numbness of her legs, her arms.

Any moment, Israel would come and lie beside her and smell the tinny mulch still in her clothes. Tobacco and the musk of him. She had shaken her skirts, picked through her hair for leaves. Washed, washed.

But what to do with this sense of suffocation? Her breath, her blood, all sensation had gathered into some core at her center: it rang, it buzzed with distressing fullness. She gaped, she yawned like a fish thrown on the banks. She was dizzy.

Over and over, she lived the blow of his contempt. The rushing dark, his hand, the whipping limbs, the burst and flutter of wings. Their clothes against each other. She recalled the urgency of confinement. She had never known that clothes were so arousing.

Yes, she had said. Yes.

Now she pressed her ribs. Not able to lie down, she took a blanket and sat out by the ashes of their fire. Music was ending, lamps coming down. But still she heard the rise and fall of conversation, the punctuating laughter.

She bent forward in her chair. Seized as wood, she could not have turned her head to look for him, no muscle of her neck obeyed. He had left while she lay gasping in the leaves. She had heard the crackling, heard him fall and rise, curse and fall. And so were women cruelly used and ruined.

Tremors overtook her. Then she could not bear to sit. She stood and pulled the blanket tight around herself, shutting out raw painful air, all memory, lay on her side where she found herself, rigid, arbitrary on the kitchen box, not caring that her ear was on the raw tin edge, drawn ankles rattling on hard canvas. She lay and shook in fits. She whimpered. Her teeth welded tight against the clatter.

I am falling, she thought. I am falling. I am falling. I am falling. I am falling.

The Moon's House

MacLaren fell asleep in the hour before he meant to leave, so there was nothing he could do when Tony kicked him but rise and go into Mitchell's camp.

He stood beside the man in gray morning wind, drinking weak coffee, their backs to the roiling willows. The lawn was forlorn with toppled chairs. Ash blew from the skeletons of char where the bonfire had been. Ribbons lopped and snagged.

She started crying while she sliced the bread, and went away, and after a while, Mitchell followed her.

They went out across the roaring scope of land, South Pass, a convexity that spanned horizons alive and heaving. A gritty wind had gathered strength as they progressed: lashing wormwood, streaming from the wheels in sandy veils.

MacLaren had offered John Kingery his spare saddle as payment and apology in consequence of the night. It was accepted. The dog was only bloodied. So he rode, glancing up now and then from under his bending hat brim to see the snowy mountains rising dully to the north.

She came out that evening but was quiet and never looked at him, and Mitchell said it was more generally the case than not with women, to suffer some episode of nervous affliction. It was a temporary weakness, a result of having come so far from everything familiar.

MacLaren agreed.

He took Littlejohn away and made another fire, but didn't feel like cooking. He lit his pipe and smoked, and flicked a stone at Littlejohn to make him talk, but it only flattered him into grinning.

They sat with their backs to the freezing wind, and the flames blew low and scarce. He watched the ragged line of peaks fade into dark, and only the shine of summer snow was left, suspended like the frozen wings of birds.

———

THEY NOONED at aspens the next day beside a shallow creek, close under the range. The white trunks called, conjuring them by twos and threes before they'd even eaten. Into green shimmer and sigh, that forgotten world of forest. Boys with knives set their names in bark. In deep thicket MacLaren found an old beaver pool, sign everywhere, but they'd been gone for years. Trapped out. He crossed the gray tangle of that old dam, stood above where the water slowed across green stones.

It was the kind of country he and Beck had trapped in, streams like this. Ponds with chunk ice running past their knees. They'd chafe themselves warm by midday fires, and Beck would talk about the women he'd known: in Philadelphia, Santa Fe, St. Louis, all the pleasures they would offer. Beck would say, *I suppose you've ate of a woman.*

He never answered. Beck would only laugh.

Then he'd learned what other woman Beck had found.

To hell with her, he thought now. To hell with you both.

He found Lucy Mitchell sitting in green shade with her feet in the creek. The boy played with stones beside her. So he went and stood, and put a cloth in the stream, and wiped his face.

She looked away. The boy stared up at him, blue-eyed, suspicious, from his pile of stones.

He said, "I'll go tonight." He'd meant an apology, but her gentleness made him cruel.

He wanted to tell her: love was a cheat. All hopes, all desires were nothing but pitiful inventions born of our own ignorance and sorrow. The things we sought were never there when we arrived, or never stayed. Love was not the last eternal benediction.

She cooled her hands in water and held them to her face.

He offered his cloth. She looked away through glimmering green, slender aspen columns of pure white.

There was the small tick of stones, where the boy was playing.

But looking at her, at the plane of her cheek, the faultless curl of ear, the hair behind it, looking at the smart wry mouth, the eyes—not foolish, he thought, but sad, and accustomed to the world and the deception in it, and the compromise—he could see this now: that she might know what he knew and more.

The water ran by. The boy came to lean against her dress. "I love you, Mama," he said, and pulled at her fingers.

She said, "I love you, either."

It was their ritual, he had heard it.

"I want to go back," said the boy.

"Go, then. You know the path."

"Come with me."

"Go ahead," she said. "I'll follow in a minute."

————————

SHE WALKED BACK to the wagon alone, her shoes in her hand, and sat on the chair to grease them. An hour had gone. Israel and the children had all eaten.

"Hungry yet?" he asked her.

"Yes," she said. "I think so."

"Seems like you're improving."

"Yes," she said. "I don't know what it was."

"I told you what it was." He brought her a plate with cold beans, dry meat.

She said, "I think it was the altitude."

————————

THE LAND CLOSED upward. She walked this sea of chalk-green sage, frail grass, pale mountains beyond. The track as straight as rails, and sagebrush passing under, crackling beneath the wagon tongues. For hours it ran under, and rang and chimed the hanging pails.

She watched him ride behind the steady tread of oxen. His hat, his matted plait, his shoulders hung with straps of horn and pouches, his stained dusty shirt.

Daniel pulled her hand. She'd been singing little wrung-out songs to please him.

"Now sing 'Old Man'!"

"No, Daniel, no. Enough singing. You sing."

But he wavered, still holding her hand, his face turned to the sky. He'd often walk that way—mouth open, looking into the blue. He'd lost his hat two weeks ago, and the tops of his ears were scabby, his hair bleached almost white. Now he said, "What color is the moon's house?"

"Oh," she said. "Silver."

"What color is the *sun's* house?"

"Yellow, I suppose. Golden."

"What color is the *cloud's* house?"

"I don't know. You tell me."

"White. What color is the *bird's* house?"

"Enough," she said. "Enough. I don't know." He walked easily, but the sand seemed deep to her. The backs of her legs were aching. Mary, awake inside the wagon, beat on something. She could hear mischievous laughter.

"What color is *our* house?"

On the bank, that noon. She had seen the fringes of James MacLaren's leggings, the calves burnished smooth, stained with the lacy salt of horses. Already by then she had come to some relief for this ending. That it would end. He would go, and she would forget it had ever happened.

But now what? Now?

The sun beat. She pressed her neck, looking for the ache, Daniel babbling beside her. They'd passed two Hungarians that morning, packing east on poor mules. A grave with a fence around it, of driven planks, and the planks pushed over, and the grave roiled, not by animals. A woman and a daughter.

People had begun to cache things in the evenings, in false graves. Kegs of liquor. Anvils, trunks of small possessions. As though they might come back and find them. As though they couldn't leave them any other way.

"Why?" Daniel asked. Asking. He filled the miles with questions every day. *Why? Why? Why are those bugs jumping? When can we have apples? What is that noise?* Lagging, tugging. But the world was broken into moments. An owl. A lie. A dream. A dome of rock. Now any answer might be new.

"You just don't *talking* to me!" He jerked her fingers.

She stopped, wheeling. Glared. "What?"

"I *said* there just isn't any no *berries* here."

"No."

"Why?"

"There just isn't much of anything out here." But for small clouds scudding like milk froth. The widest sky she had ever seen, the farthest blue.

When she saw Mary had gotten the lid off the flour bin and dusted the whole inside of her wagon white, she cried.

———

HE FOLLOWED the captain that evening through a raking wind that blew so constant here that all the wormwood was dwarfed by it. Dry grass scattered whirling past their boots. All stones swept clean.

White's flogging tent was dim inside and smelled of oil. Their Negress bent at a folding table, fussing at the tiny stove. The tall wife sat stitching roses on a linen hoop.

"I have a new map," White said, smoothing paper on the table.

MacLaren set his biscuit in the margin. The parchment was much weathered at the folds and showed a wandering line crossed by fragments of rivers that appeared from nowhere and disappeared again among printed names from someone's fancy: *Snow Mountains. Bonark Indians. Thousand Fountains. Utarlah.* Ranges lumped like caterpillars, nowhere into nowhere.

"What's this?"

"The cartographer was with Fremont. In '43." White pressed a fold. "The Hungarians we passed this afternoon offered it to me for provision. So I'm just looking at it. But what I want to know"—he raced his finger along a dotted line that faded into nothing, labeled *Cut off to Ft. Hall*—"is whether you've seen this route."

"There is one like it."

"Is it passable for wagons?"

"It's no track. Twice forty miles, dry. There's a river midway, not shown."

"But a shorter route than going by Bridger's Fort?"

"That route follows water. This one, you'll lose stock."

"If we're prepared?"

He didn't know.

"Is it flat?"

"It breaks up. You come off bluffs to Bear River. With wagons, you'd have to find a pass."

They stood, looking at the map.

"It's a good map, though," White said. "Better than we have."

MacLaren said nothing.

"Mr. Luelling and I sat down and calculated back along the way as it was marked, what we can tell. The mileages seem correct."

"Good."

"Well, it's not the whole picture," White said. "I see what you're thinking. Just the established route." He looked up, with his dense beard, his round brown eyes. "But that's all that matters, isn't it? We go along, cross what we come to. The wider world isn't that important. The given route is all we need to know about. Unless we stray off course."

Outside, the wind pushed and eased. The tent poles creaked on their tethers.

White said, "I thank you for settling with John about the dog."

MacLaren said, "I was out of hand. I don't know why."

"Some got pretty far out of hand. I'd like to keep you up ahead, as pilot. Mitchell agrees. He'll do his own driving on this stretch. If you'd lead the cutoff."

"You want to do it?"

"The season's getting late," he said. " I think we ought to push."

MacLaren nodded. The wife was watching him. Bruised eyes and beak nose, solemn as a heron. Who had worn a paper crown and played piano the night of that wild spree. He saw his biscuit and picked it up.

White said, "It's important we all stay on course."

Their eyes met. The woman looked at him across her linen hoop.

White said, "A woman's reputation can be unmade on mere suspicion. Keep an eye to the wider world. If you would."

HE CAME with them to Sandy River that evening, and it was the same dark blue as the sky in this high flat country. A grove of cottonwoods towered on a bench of gold grass. The wind had stopped.

In this high late light, he passed Lucy Mitchell, hanging out her things to dry. Then stopped beyond, fingering the thin lacy cape already hanging damp and shadowless but for his own shadow across it.

"What is this you women wear?"

"What?" she said. "A pelerine?" Then looked up at him with a still, clear look he had not seen before.

No words had shaped it. No moment had announced it. But even features he had never thought were pretty charmed him now. The freckled backs of her hands, the paleness of her lashes. Her chin, her awkward elbows, her smile.

NEXT MORNING he stood at the back of a crowd of men, listening to the service. Marriage was a team and God their driver, Olmstead said, man and woman in yoke together, working patiently in the service of His will. MacLaren listened, eyeing the men beside him, all yearning, like him, toward needed repairs with no intention of giving up the day. The forge already hot.

She sat beside her husband, her back to him. Slim and fair in her starched pelerine.

And what could it serve, he wondered, this desire of two people for each other? He had not sought it nor thought it could come in his life again. What reason? Or was it only a mute and simple force, seizing the unlucky like gravity? To turn them for no reason, like earth and moon in clockwork thrall.

"I DID LOVE him so much," she said, of her husband Luther.

Her talk was low and quiet, it was urgent. The two of them beside the daylight fire: he braiding rope, she sorting beans, bread baking in the coals. Both watching their own hands.

She said, "I always feared for him. He was so graceful. I'd bring him dinner where he was working, and he'd have stacks of boards or shingles on his shoulders and be walking up the backs of rafters. In the middle of winter. Everything slick with ice. He'd be up on some barn frame. It was terrible and wonderful all at once. I never loved him so much as when I'd see him like that, so easy and fearless. But I was so glad when he came down. I was so glad when he went to making cabinets."

But he'd fallen in a mill and died. Someone swung a board, he stepped back. The pit, the iron track. Not so far to fall. She'd come home—the girls in school. MacLaren watched her tell it, wondering at her ease.

"And the house was cold, this terrible wind out, and we had the meanest stove, any wind blew right down the chimney. I was rattling around with the clinkers and blowing to get the flame up under the flue and the smoke rolling back over me so I was streaming tears, you know. So when I finally heard the knock, I suppose I looked like someone had already told me, I came wiping my eyes, and this fellow at the door started saying did I need help, did I have no way to get there? He could put me up on horseback. I didn't know what he was talking about, I thought he wanted to fix my stove. By the time we got it straight and got there, Luther was gone."

He looked at her. She smiled. Stirred her fingers through the beans she'd cleaned, an odd quick gesture. She said, "I could have said goodbye, but for that awful stove."

He nodded.

She said, "I didn't think there was anything funny until now. I never have told it, about the stove. Not since it happened."

"Not to Israel?"

"Not the story. No. Not this."

They were quiet.

"There is a way death has, I found," she said, "of ending some indulgence. That day before, nothing seemed too desperate. But then this happened, and when I got up and looked around again, everything seemed like such a condemnation. I remember walking through the house thinking, This is the most I ever did for him. This is as far. A few lace doilies. Buttons still waiting to be replaced. Where we meant to go, what I might have told him . . . It's just that lazy day-to-day, but when it ends, you take your own measure. This little bit I did in six years. I'm not a brave woman. I saw that then."

He said, "You bore children into the world and hoped to raise them. There's no braver thing than that."

"No," she said. "That's only circumstance. Though I thank God for them."

"Maybe everything is circumstance. Maybe all the difference is in how you face what comes."

"Do you not believe in will?"

She had words. She had words for things he'd grown afraid to think. "Do you?"

"Of course," she said.

HE ROUNDED the cattle with the others, drove them across the ford to graze the other side and sat in the grove of cottonwoods there. The cattle swung their tails, snatched at flies along their shoulders in the hazy dappled dust; they pulled down leaves from trees, wiped their eyes against their knees, rocked down to chew their cud while he watched them, thinking. He got up and walked along the river.

AT SILENT READING with the ladies that afternoon, she looked through the Concordance, for something, Lord, to save her.

Having eyes full of adultery, and that cannot cease from sin; beguiling unstable souls; to whom the mist of darkness is reserved forever . . .

Her hands steepled to her face, she tried to marshal back some sense of who she was. To take counsel, turn from this course. But as measure of her failing, the words seemed no counsel at all. Even her most treasured poetry seemed frivolous when set beside such dark seductive words.

Beguiling unstable souls.

She looked again at the women silently reading, who had set out, each a fortress, to make godly all that God would show them. To shape the wilderness to His ideal. To make the steeples rise and the very stones to sing the praises of their coming.

Perhaps she'd never been strong enough for that.

So now she wondered: Was it her own grave she'd seen, with buzzards circling? God might forgive human impulse, passion's trespass. But to give over shame? To forfeit what was sacred? Virtue, she knew, was nothing without passion. But passion without virtue?

Do you believe in consequence?

She closed her eyes, cast up her question, heard only the wind in the leaves.

HE WATCHED the sun go down, the cattle penned, the children put to bed. Mitchell had a weekly meeting of the officers.

He met her at the ford in darkness. They crossed deep cobbles, walked side by side through tall cottonwoods, silent, not touching.

"Tell me something," she said. She'd picked up a feather and smoothed it.

"What?"

"What you know. Anything. What you've seen."

So he told how Nihiaway boys would win an eagle's quill by burying themselves in the grass of hilltops, a live rabbit tethered on their chests. They'd wait for hours. Days, until the eagle stooped and struck. They had only instants to seize the prize. But if they gained it, they could keep it, and it would serve them always.

"Am I your eagle?" she asked. "Or are you mine?"

"No, none of that," he said.

"This is the instant, though," she said. He felt her hand take his.

He turned. The smell of her hair was good to him.

THEY SAT against a log in starlight. Side by side, their hands together, under the towering trees.

"Here," he said, and she came into the fork of his legs, her back against him. She was small and light compared to Lise. She was bones.

"SHH," SHE TOLD him. "Shh. This is all we have. You know this is all we have."

She turned and held his head and kissed his eyes.

In her arms, he was a child again.

"Shh," she said, and told him about the moon's house.

There had been nothing, in Lise, to touch this.

———

WITH THE SALT of his cheeks, his eyes, his lips still on her lips, she returned with him across the cobbles. They sat to their shoes in the dark gravel of the bank. Then heard dresses moving slowly through the grass above them.

It was Mrs. Olmstead, complaining to Mrs. Whitcomb of her toes.

"Afraid?" he asked when the women had passed.

He was gentle. She had sensed this long ago. His soul was earnest, generous, and brave, and she was lost in her clothes, she had disappeared, although they moved and creaked.

"No," she lied, only hoping he would not find out how little there was left of her to know.

Sound and Light

❧⌢◠⌢☙

WHEN THE ROAD TURNED SOUTH to Bridger, he took them west instead, where the trail on the map had disappeared. He dragged them like a tail of raveled rope behind him: a dozen slow processions that drifted and spread, crushing wormwood, skirting thorns. They would not make camp until they reached next water, but halted every two hours to rest and drink from barrels, then resumed their way toward a distant line of rubble, and this low broken rim rose with exceeding slowness as the sun crossed the sky, and was a line of distant peaks by sundown. Dusk led dark, and stars came out in a rising wind and began to dim, and by two o'clock they were traveling in blinding sand. He kept course by compass and lantern, but could not choose ground, nor be sure they were together, so they put up until dawn and slept.

────────

MITCHELL'S TALL MARE lay stretched on the ground the next morning, her lips drawn back and eyes closed down to slits. They poured water on her teeth and pulled her tail and tried to raise her, but her ribs stood racked and stark, her teats drawn up to nothing. She groaned and puffed the sand, with Mitchell bareheaded in a dusty frock shirt, with checkered trousers tucked into his boots.

They went back to stand beside the wagon. The goats clanked and milled, and MacLaren thought he'd not looked at Israel Mitchell enough. Day on day, they passed and spoke and worked, always looking at something else. So you could forget a man, though he was right next to you. Now their eyes did meet and were still a moment.

"That rifle is charged," MacLaren said.

"I suppose it's mine to do," said Mitchell. Then went with a kind of tragic elegance to the rifle propped against the wheel, and walked off with it across the dirt.

MacLaren waited, then heard the echoing report. Explosive death, the arching voidance. Dry hooves paddling the sand. How many times had it been his to do?

He looked around, saw himself mirrored in that man walking back with his rifle. And suddenly, it seemed possible to him that we might love ourselves the most when we are suffering and seen to suffer. The pursuits of men seemed only the more shocking, if this were true.

If this were true.

He turned away and mounted.

———

THEY CAME to a fork of the Green at midday, running clear between dry slopes, bordered by lush stands of grass. He arrived before the others to thickets alive with birds; rode down the gravel bank as ducks swam out from their nests and rose running with shy quacks in files of silver dabs along the water. They lifted in a thrum of wings. He stood straight down, knee-deep beside his thirsty horse, and drank.

In an hour, the crossing was full of livestock, wagons, women with pails. He walked the high bank alone. Yellow currants grew here, buffalo grass, a bush with small blue flowers frail as tissue, gone to seed on its tallest stems. The tiny spheres crackled and burst at the lightest touch. He slid down the bank and wet his boots again, walking along gold cobbles. White blossoms floated in midstream on delicate strands of green. He took one into his palm and studied it.

She showed him others, later, that he'd never seen before. He shook his head, at a loss for names.

"Do they have no names, or have you not learned them?"

He didn't know.

"This one is so beautiful."

"I know a man in London you could send things to. He'd give them names."

"How would a man in London know what names to choose?"

He agreed.

"Imagine," she said. "A place without names."

She turned and walked away then, and he kept on down the banks. And maybe it was the light or the river that smelled like where they used to live, but he wanted to tell her then about his girls, how he had walked with them. Their moccasins with tiny bells, their dresses fringed in ermine tails. How they had walked and gathered flowers enough to sit, and tried to make an alphabet. He'd known those names.

A: *Apiaciae*, the carrot. Cow's Parsnip, Swamp Button, Golden Alexander.

Lispat with her high straight cheekbones. He marveled at the way it ran through generations: the bridge of her nose, like her mother's, like Joe Tenney's. Though in temperament she was no one's but his own. "Alexander, he's golden."

"So he is."

He had no way now to tell this thing, so that only he could know how he had held the plants for them while they bent and scratched with pens. Junie had his green-eyed frown, his wild fine hair, her mother's gentleness. Skin the color of heart cedar. Skin so beautiful sometimes the world would stop when he looked at it. She made only lines and wiggles.

B: *Brodiaea*, the grass nut.

"You do it, *tota*. It's too hard."

"You try," he said. But always took her hand to render slowly that bract or keeled or clasping leaf. He told them again, their catechism: *To draw is to see. To see is to know. To know is to name. To name, own. To own, find use. To use, affect. And that is the secret of man's power.*

"What about woman's?"

"You'll have to ask your mother about that."

The grin, the swinging plaits. The press of their small bodies against his. He felt, remembered, wished to tell.

IN THE HEAT of afternoon, he slept. And maybe, again, it was the light or the smell of this river, or maybe it was the thought of his girls, or Fort Hall so near, but it seemed to him that he had made a terrible mistake.

He lay and thought of Lucy Mitchell, the dark, the cottonwoods.

Shh, she'd said. *This is all we have.*

In that night, he had believed her touch, her kiss, believed he might forget the things he'd done, the whole unraveling of his life, that he might trust her to take the man she found and make him good.

Now he closed his aching eyes, remembering, and saw how wrong that was.

———

HE WALKED ACROSS the camp until he found old Mattie Leabo.

He'd come to her like this one time before. She knew his errand, and stood when she saw him, and started around the side of Vine's wagon. May looked up from the pot she stirred, and watched him follow.

"Shall I help?" he asked the old woman when she paused.

She shook her head. Hiked her skirts and found her grip and began her spidery climb into the wagon, a tiny old thing in a morning cap. Her dresses all too big.

"I'm sorry," he said. "I wouldn't bother you."

She said, "Don't think I couldn't tell you if you did. Come sit up. We might as well watch the evening."

So then he was on the wagon seat beside her. She looked over at him with her old bead eyes in their double lids: like a crow's, the lowers almost rising to meet the uppers when she blinked. "A pretty night," she said.

It was.

She looked down. "You broke that hand not long ago."

He nodded.

"It pain you much?"

He looked across the hills and saw the evening wind stroke narrow courses down gold slopes of grass, and come on, sighing, to turn the willow leaves in these near thickets. He said, "It let go, you know. I'd come clear through it."

"I wondered." She sniffed. Then said, "I never liked a haughty man."

"Something is wrong in me. In what I am."

"Yes, there is. There's something wrong in all of us. People are like stones. Weak and strong, but none without a fault. Life gets in and cleaves us, every one. Slow like ice. Quick like fire. Have you not heard stone break?"

He had.

She clapped. "Gunshot."

He nodded.

She said, "There's jagged times. Till hurt wears off."

They sat together, watching.

She said, "This is a real pretty place."

After a while, she turned and showed him the clasp of the chain on which the silver cup was carried at her neck. With clumsy hands, he freed it.

"Nothing knits you up," she said. "That is a fact."

She filled the cup for him and let him drink it.

———

HE WENT into Mitchell's camp to find them holding plates of curling fat-fried trout upon their knees and the girls all shaking their fingers like cats. Fins and bones. When Lucy passed in the pale blue dress, he felt a charge go through him.

" 'Lightning,' " Mitchell read aloud, " 'is occasioned by the attraction of particles of aerial matter conducing to electricity.' "

The paleness of her lashes. Her curving smile. He turned away, tried to listen.

" 'This creates a sudden vacuum into which surrounding atoms are then forced by the weight of atmosphere.' Are you listening, girls?"

"Mary's not."

" 'But the elastic and resistant nature of these atoms causes an immediate correction whereby they expand explosively again to their right configurations. This sudden correction creates centrifugal force which emits both sound and light before their propulsive power is diminished, their pressure no longer felt, nor sound created.' "

Lucy Mitchell brought a plate. He took it and looked down at it. He looked up at her.

Like gunshot.

He looked at her.

———

HE WALKED OUT a while, and came back no better, and now they were eating a kind of porridge. Still eating.

He sat, and into the silence, he said, "The valley we lived in looked a good deal like this."

"Where was that?" she asked.

"North of Fort Hall. We were going down last March with bales and saw a wagon just like one of yours coming up the valley. The first time we'd seen any of this."

He'd been thinking of them: Coos, Moise Kochem, Tillekail, young Amadee, and all the others riding south down the narrow brown-grass valley. The beginning of all of what went wrong.

"In March?" Mitchell said. "What was a wagon doing there in March?"

"I heard later they'd fallen out. Wintered over at the fort."

There'd been John Baikie, Weeks, and all their families; Lise smiling, Beck smiling, the herd all packing bales of fur. Children dreaming of sugar, bells, buttons. Along the shady river bends, bare willow standing red against blue drifts of snow.

"We saw this man driving. Talking to himself. Preaching out in the open air as though a whole congregation could hear. A friend and I pulled out. We got near and saw he had a pair of girls sitting on the seat, one on either side of him. Fair-haired girls. Maybe six years old or seven.

"When we stopped, he started telling how God had shown him a vision of that country. The tilt they had was blown to rags, and a woman on the bed, she'd been dead some days, by the look."

He'd raised his own rifle off his saddle bows by then, but felt more apprehension here among them, telling it, than he had felt at the time.

"And he was saying, 'I'll not be turned back from these gates, if that's what you intend.' And then I saw he was wearing only a shirt and weskit on that cold a day. We were all in coats. Whatever she'd had, he likely had it, too. I said he should find himself some other gates. He said he would not, and when he sent his oxen on, I shot the one. The fellow with me shot the other."

"And then?"

He said, "We rode away."

It was quiet after that. He watched the fire until he heard her leave, then went down for more tobacco and came back to find only Daniel, crouched like some wild dirty angel on his haunches, lighting sticks.

MacLaren sat, having failed in his intention. Having veered somehow or

lost the ending of the thing he had resolved to tell. The point of it. He'd had
a reason for beginning, but then none of it made sense.

He sighed. He said, "Give one of those, hey?"

He saw the small frown, the smeary mouth. Hair like spun gold. A glair
of snot ran from one nostril.

"Give me that."

The boy handed the lit stick. The flame dipped and wavered, went out.
MacLaren leaned to light it again, brought it cupped in his hand.

"Why you have that mouse?" the boy asked.

"Weasel," he said. It was the pipe bag, drawn out on its string from
around his neck. Wrinkled legs and eye holes, the furred strip of tail.

"Why you have a weasel?"

He thumbed and drew. "He's a bag now."

"But why's he died?"

"I killed him."

"Why?"

"Come here," he said, bringing out his cloth. He dipped it in cold coffee.

The boy eyed him, wary.

"Come get your face wiped."

"Daniel, yes," she said. She'd come out of the wagon and was watching,
so the boy stepped in, and MacLaren reached to nudge away the dirt. Then
stood and caught him when he backed and dodged, held him one-armed
around the waist, something he might have done in affection with his own,
but this child wrenched.

"Be still. It's you getting your face wiped."

The boy howled. Then started kicking, clawing at his hand, the cloth.

"Be still." He ran up the sleeve and held it, the small hand balled tight
against the heel of his own. He worked the dirty fingers open, scrubbed the
strange flat hands, those foreign hands, the bones too light, the flesh too
thin, the lines all wrong. "Be still." Vicious, he could feel his animal blood,
this fury at something not his own. He turned him by the collar and then hit
him, and she said, "*Stop.*"

The world hung there, in silence.

He turned and went. The ground uneven, the ground sloping. Grass
tangled in his boots.

SHE LAY AWAKE that night and listened to her husband turn his pages, reading.

"You should sleep," he said without looking. "You said you were tired."

She had no answer.

He said, "I'll wake the girls tomorrow. They can warm the coffee and get something out."

"No. That's silly, why?"

He said he didn't think he'd been giving her enough rest. As if she were a horse. As if to claim her by his dispensation. Though by morning again, such possession would surely resume its usual form. He'd be calling her for this or that.

She turned away, the night too full of opposition.

"Shall I read to you?"

"No." She rose and dressed simply. Outside, she set the lantern glowing on one chair, drew another chair beside it, brought out her needle in the sultry night. The hem of her favorite dress had singed while she was cooking in the wind—the nut-brown wool, much faded. Now she tore the thickened edge, the sturdy hem-saver burned black and frayed. She made a soft plain turn and began it, knowing he was out there.

What had he meant tonight? That strange story, the oxen falling. And then Daniel. A blush came through her fingertips, a tiny moistness on her needle, remembering that suddenness of rage (when all of Israel's anger was never more than indignation, petty tyranny, some childish demand to be pleased), this rage, so wholly certain and implacable as to be more like a force of nature, like trees falling, like lightning. With no clear cause or source.

Of course, she'd had a lick of her own to cut Daniel, for all that.

She watched her work, and plied and pulled it, neatly, neatly, neatly.

When the seam was done, she tied it, and was winding back the thread when she heard the clank of a lantern's bail and knew he'd come.

He lit the lantern from the fire, not looking at her. It jounced uneasily as he turned away, the little flame flaring and guttering in its tin. He was finding something by the wagon. He said, "I'm going."

"Stay," she said. "I'll warm the tea."

He came and sat across the fire from her. He rubbed his face, he was tired. But when she looked into his eyes, it was nothing. She was not there. So she saw what he had said.

"What is wrong?" she said. "Tell me what is wrong tonight."

He said, "I mean to go."

WHEN HE HAD left, she fed the last twigs to the fire. She stared into the little flames, and their crackling was like the crackling of some field of sparks around her, like the blue sparks on lightning nights. She thought of that river where the cottonwoods had been, he had sat with her against him in the dark, his arms so tight around her that she had been as a very boulder lodged in roots, and he had said, *What strength you have, Lucy. What a strength you have.* She had not believed him.

She took the lantern. He wasn't in the camp he'd made by the river. But a band of horses grazed near—she heard them rustling in the grass, and crossed toward this sound until she saw the blue discs of their eyes floating at the edge of her light.

He was standing with his hands on the back of his old horse, the horse with its long neck arched and browsing seedheads from tall grass.

They stood in silence. The horse swung its tail and moved off. His hand slid down its rump.

He said, "What will you have, Lucy? Do you not see what this would be for you?"

"Are *you* afraid?"

"You see who I am."

"Yes."

"No, you don't."

"Then tell me. Tell me."

He would not.

She said, "People are always more than you think they are. Than what they've done. They have reasons. They can be better."

"They can be worse. You can wake up one morning and see who they are and be glad to walk away with nothing but the hope to get clean. My wife did."

"No," she said. "No . . ." The grass chirred, and stirred, and the horses moved like slow dark ghosts with their floating eyes. "It's just . . . I think we are all lost," she said. "Each one of us. Until some right relation."

He said, "I'm tired, Lucy."

She turned, and walked, and the lantern swung wild shadows across the grass.

THE HEART SO QUICK

Under the bone and marrow of the moon, he lay, when she had gone, awake.

He'd seen the corded beauty of her neck, the hollows of her throat, her collarbones. Tender roots of blue milk-veins standing visible at the shift's lace edge. Which, when he'd seen them and remembered, had capsized his will.

Then tell me.

Tin lamp lit. The ink pried open and mixed, the marbled ledger with its missing pages and blank ones.

Mrs. Mitchell,

Mattie Leabo has said we are like Stones, we break along our Faults as loud as gunfire. And if knowing mine will cure one of us of such dangerous affections, then I will tell mine plain, as it will serve us both.

I took for wife, nine years ago, a young woman given as a girl into my care & swore I would protect her. In this, you surely will find fault. But we have grown our own customs here, some taken on the ways of Natives. An infant girl is pledged to some man as helps a family to be his Wife in time and these things are not at all uncommon as they are with you. What I mean to say, she was a beauty, strong built, and of the gentlest disposition you could know. I had two girls and a son by her, Elizabeth, June, and Alexander, and at the time of the matter I had told this evening we were living, as I said, in the country north of Hall a desert place, our headquarters or *Quartier* as the French had called it, a village of mixed races. We were French and Orkneymen besides me and every kind of Brule, Bannock, some Rogues and Outcasts and others good upstanding ones, all with Wives and Children.

You should know that the fevers on the Seacoast had affected the Native people very much, & I had seen in twenty years the Destruction of whole Tribes for you know they have but little defense & so above all things I had feared always for the Health of my own family. & when I was promised & then passed over once again for Factor & could not keep my own counsel in the presence of those responsible for another's appointment over me, to whom I felt superior in every Qualification, I was obliged to quit the service of that Company which had been my whole Ambition until that time, & to remove my family to this more congenial climate. There I fell to my trade in a small way: the provision of men for getting fur. I did the work of laborer, clerk, Trader all, & my Wife the work of camp, & the life in all was good enough.

So you see I did not want any part of that Disease. My thought was of our own protection, the People & my Wife and Children.

I told you what I did.

On our pass home again we saw the woman's grave the wagon the swarming oxen in their yoke with no sign of the others but we saw some birds scared up & circling around the rocks above us. So John Baikie climbed that bluff with me & walked across until we came upon the two girls laid out each by each as died of their father's knife & the man himself with his brains cleaned out of the sand.

He wrote across the span of night, and stopped himself at last and went to cool his eyes. And would have slept, but the reeds across the river were still quiet.

He cut a stob of willow, wound it with strips of tallowed linen he kept in a brass can. Struck this torch alight, and set it flaming upright in the river mud, and shed his clothes. Then waded in with it, the current running slow and cold against his legs. The flame lay over as he moved and curled the hairs of his hand, threw a wavering mirror image, paired spirits of orange in dark river and dark sky. He raised his arms in deeper water, slowed as he neared the other shore, gliding quietly as oil, until he came to where the ducks were sleeping.

There. With heads turned under wings, some warming eggs, some with ducklings nestled. Each drake in his own flat of weeds beside his wife, and fair for taking.

And whatever I could tell you whatever innocence a court of law would find, my Wife had been nearby & knew what Passed & would not speak of it nor could I find ease in myself, you know I have not found it yet. I will always see those girls their yellow hair how it had clumped away & caught to flag in bushes how tenderly they held each others hands it was something I have never spoke aloud for all my long acquaintance with Death. And could not again tonight, but for owing you that truth which will, I trust, defeat whatever hopes you may have entertained, & show what any might yet stand to gain from me.

LUCY WOKE and went out of her tent to find two rows of ducks, singed and plucked and spitted over willow coals, the oxen yoked and standing by. And when she tied her apron, there was the small Tennyson she'd left beside the chair, and four soft sheets of parchment folded up inside it, and James MacLaren sitting by the fire.

A WATERLESS TREK, one sun to the next, was a *journada*. So Israel had told her. This day would be their second such.

They passed dead alkali pools, salt flats. The range of hills had grown. Gaps of yards grew into miles between the moving wagons.

In furtive snatches, she walked, reading what he had given her.

A man once told me (but I did not believe it) to be ware, that Sorrow itself was a source of Evil. If that be so, I have only had as deep a well as most from which to Draw, but it did seem that some dark thing took hold after that Event of which I told you, for in six months my wife was gone. Of my children I have no likeness I could show now, not the locks of their hair to recall them by but that is the case with most I know.

She folded the pages a third time as the light was falling. They made halt and ate all silent while the cattle lowed for water.

"You might as well sleep," Israel said. "We'll go on when we've found a pass."

They made beds in the wagon. She dreamed of him, and woke to find they were under way with a low moon swinging wildly across the open bows, so winding had their course become. At a plateau's edge, she and the girls came out into gray morning dust. They descended, leaning back against the ropes with all their might to help stay the weight of the big wagon, wheels rough-locked and her two little ones yet asleep inside. And in this way they achieved the valley floor, safe, and proud of their work.

By midday they had watered and were resting.

"It's measles," Israel said to her. He'd gone out to speak to some men who were passing south while she chopped cold duck into a batter. Jeannie Knighton's two littlest, Early and Hill, had both, it seemed, come down with fevers.

"No," she said. Though it was a virtue, that he could walk out with perfect ease and address himself to strangers, and hold them until he was satisfied. While she had been taught to consider, above all, another's wish for privacy.

"They say it's measles," he said. "Not alkali. You were saying alkali."

"No," she said. "How would there be measles?"

"I want to make a boat," said Daniel.

She put on bones for soup, saying, "Make one."

"I want *you* to make it."

The girls were already down beside the water, turning over stones.

"Is no one tired today?" she asked.

"I'll make a boat with you. If you like."

She looked around. She had not even heard him there, behind her.

MacLaren got out his knife beside the bank, and made a sailing boat with a piece of bark and feather, then made three more with Narce and his brother and the Willis girl all waiting. Then took off his boots and was cooling himself chest-deep in the river when he turned and saw her passing on the bank behind him.

She said, "That's one way to do laundry."

They'd not spoken since the night before this past one. He had stayed and kept his word and found the pass, and told himself that he would leave when they reached this river safely. He had set down some apology, that long night, and given it. But now she'd left her bonnet in the grass, and the neck of her dress was damp. He waded to shore, shirt streaming, legs draining water. He said, "Did I tell you of the old hermit and his dogs?"

"No."

"He called one Soap, and the other one Water. So when any visitor complained of the dishes, he only said, Well, they were as clean as Soap and Water could get them."

It was a tired joke, but she smiled. Up the bank the children squealed and splashed. Nicholas Koonse stood out to his waist in only linens, now calling to his wife at the water's edge. Mrs. Koonse hiked her skirt at last, elbows cocked in mock formality, and set straight in to meet him. Fell back laughing in his arms and splashed him.

"Look at her," Lucy Mitchell said. "She was quiet as a mouse back home. Now look."

He watched their bare-legged children on the bank. They danced, they shoveled up long sprays of pebbles.

She said, "I don't know how I'll go back. To living in a house. That day-to-day."

He looked at her.

"It's just another scale out here. Isn't it? You see your place on earth. Your own inconsequence. But somehow you end up feeling greater than you were. Do you not feel blessed for living so honestly? Out here?"

"Honestly?"

"Without all those false oppressions. Of society."

"Oppression here comes six foot deep."

She looked away. She said, "I see why you love it, that's all. I know. It isn't wrong."

Then he was afraid she would be old someday, and have forgotten him, and all of this. She'd be trivial as a Lady's Book, and safe.

He wanted to say he'd once climbed a pass and gone to sleep under a tall granite mountain, wakened to a clear howling gale so that it seemed, as he sat watching, that the peak above him cleaved the universe, was hurtling through the dark with him riding at its foot, an ant on a plowshare through the stars. The wind of constellations freezing in his teeth. How small he'd been that night, how exalted.

Every time he thought he understood a thing, it changed.

"I want to know the rest," she said. "I want to read it."

Their silence let in other sounds.

———

MacLaren cooked their trout that night the way his wife had done it, wrapping them in neat grass to steam on coals. They sat and ate while the sky ran gold and red, and Mitchell, in a fine humor, decided on a haircut.

MacLaren left them to it. A rotting bluff backed the camp, and soon he was climbing dust and rubble until the brush gave way to steeper rock. He found a high ledge at last, having gained an hour on the night, and looked out across the valley and the wagons, the river and the low dry hills beyond.

It was carried in him: this light, this scent of soil, this color of stone. Scrub pine, juniper. He'd never thought he'd miss it. It was the smell of Quartier.

I will tell about the man you have known, Mr. Beck.

In the Spring of my Son's Birth came a party of American riders to Quartier. I will not forget that I was standing at the door of our Lodge, & watched their Horses come floundering through the warm snow. Their hooves threw up black spatters of earth, & made a wake of filth across our Valley, when even the Elk had sense to wait for dark. I should have known then what manner of Men I would meet.

But there were we, with the wind lifting up the feathers on our lodgepoles, & the smell of cooking meat & the chatter of my Girls, among the Exiles of all the Nations. But for Mountainy French, the Native tongues had served us, & the girls were forgetting their English. So when these Strangers rode in, & threw down their packs among our hackling Dogs, I held out my hand in Welcome. One of them was Mr. Beck.

You likely knew him as an Easy man & had you known him longer you might have seen him singing Songs telling Tales playing Shadows with his fingers. He made himself a favorite with my Girls. He would bring my Wife a tender saddle of an Elk, kerchiefs filled with bog Potatoes. He would find a patch of Green & stand & fill himself & there was never a dish of Spring or Summer but what he would not be eating Leaves atop it. He could set a fair line of Traps with me, when he learned it better, & carried a good Weight.

So now I have put him in the story for you.

I thought I had acted simply that day we left those oxen dead & that fellow thinking better of his Gates but as I said I never could be easy after that.

He looked out now, and the sun was setting yellow in a yellow sky with clouds piled up. A look of rain was in the west. He thought of his girls, Georgie Tadzahot, their games of dice, how he used to tease them: *Get off your shanks, you Indians, there's work to be done.* Or the pups, how they kept them in a basket inside the dark lodge door so he was always stepping on some tail or paw, there was always howling and calamity and him saying, *Will you Indians keep your damned livestock out of my road?* It had been his way to tease them.

But after that thing occurred, he'd seen only the carcass stink and swarming flies, the pestilent heat. He'd had enough living in a camp of bloody Indians. Which he'd said to Lise one morning, not in jest.

Because more & more I thought how easy it would be for such a thing to happen a Second time a Third these Americans were coming (as come you now) by thousands I had learned & no great time would pass before we suffered for it. As I said the Blood of Natives has the least defense of any People & with their style of living & sometimes their quaint Remedy that Fact turns all Diseases deadly.

But he and Beck had found a valley in their travels together, up in the mountains east of Quartier. Riding into it that first time had struck a chord of home in him so strong it seemed his life had owned that destination all along, that it was meant for him though he had never been there, and they'd put up in deep grass beside the stream. That night he'd smiled across the fire at Beck and laughed as he'd not done since before they had left for Hall that spring. A valley—as the child Emma Ruth had put it—transcendent in his mind; it welcomed him. It promised safety. They'd honed their axes the next morning and ridden up the hillsides to cut dry pines and skid them down.

> Already that summer my Wife & I had been less easy with each other. Some Women will keep things to themselves & between us there was more quiet nights than had ever been & I had found more cause to Work but when I told her I had found a better place & we would go to live away from Quartier she did not welcome my Idea.

The sun had gone without his notice.

He came down at last and found Lucy Mitchell shaking the linen from around Mr. Littlejohn's shoulders.

"Are you next?" she called.

Mitchell himself was barbered and clean, and the boy had lost his curls. Now the girls raised their heads from where they sat at draughts and started cheering.

"It's bad as that?"

They clamored all together.

"No," he said. "It'll have to grow out, it'll be in my eyes then."

"So keep it cut." Sarah, sly as a goat, looked over her shoulder at him.

"I'll have no one to do it."

"We'll keep it cut," said bony Caroline.

"Oh, *you* will?"

"Mother would cut it anytime," offered Emma Ruth sincerely.

Sarah slid a wooden game piece. Then looked at him. "Do it," she dared, and bent her will, narrow-eyed.

"All right, then."

SO THE BREEZE was on his neck, sitting watch that night, with the yips of little wolves in the hills, and the laughter of the families spilling out from the camp's glow. Hearing the ghost of a chord from somewhere, a bell or kettle, he thought of the piano boxed inside its wagon, now seeming like a dream. That there should be such an unreasonable and precious thing borne muffled in its crate, over all these miles.

The things we carry with us.

They'd ridden out and back four times that summer, he and Beck. Putting up walls. They'd thatched the roof for want of cedar, built a smokehouse, dug clay. Then Beck fell off the new barn wall and broke some ribs.

They rode home and rested in the first good chill of autumn. Days growing cold. He thought they might trap out the way and back next time, but come the day to leave, Beck said, "You know, I think I'll just stay this once and make a little more use of these fine women."

It was that kind of thing he was always saying.

"Well, spare a bit of mine. I'll be home soon enough."

Alone, he'd put up rafters on the barn, made the cabin's door and furnishings. The larches, hidden all summer in green stands of pine, were flaring into gold. So sometimes a thing surprises you by showing another color, while all else stays the same. Then you see the difference must have been there always.

Coming home, he was setting out a final line on a creek he'd seen. Wading upstream past his knees, a hundredweight of steel and chain and fur all shouldered, he fell into a muck hole past his waist, and in the freezing water he had lost the willow squeeze he used as tongs to bend the trap jaws open. He got up to his next set and found this. Small accidents often lead to larger ones, but in the freezing water he had tried to set the next bare-handed. And never felt the moment when his hand slipped, only the sudden twist and spring of iron. His echoing shout.

He floundered out, chain dragging. Knelt in the spent grass alone, his forehead to the yellow frozen leaves. Under that blind curve of belly, fingers crushed and dripping blood. A roaring in his ears, a weight of iron.

He cut his pack straps free. Tried to kneel on the great springs until the jaws would open, but he kept unbalancing.

He swore. He made try after try, edging in and out of black. He remembered calling. *Lise. Lise.*

After a while, he set his knife against the joints of his own knuckles. Breath hissed through tears, through dripping snot, and he thought of all the scores of men who had lost fingers in this trade. But he couldn't do it.

He took himself to the base of an aspen. Knelt balanced against it and bent the bows enough to free himself; left the empty trap sprung shut at last on the bloody leaves. He tore his shirt for binding, walked down three miles to the meadow where his horses grazed. Hopped and cursed into dry leggings, fumbling all the ties and fastenings. Broke camp an hour later, riding out with his hand held up against his shoulder for the pain.

It was a long way home, and he rode all day thinking only of his hoard of rum, how he'd lie beside the fire, how she'd get out her pouches and set him right. It was all he wanted. Past dark, he put up in a grove of aspens and tried to sleep.

But the night always has a way of making small things large. So that night he'd lain awake thinking of his pointless life: his, John Baikie's, Amadee's, Joe Tenney's, all the men he'd ever known, the Company men cast away like him, thrown out in childhood to this place, and spent their lives forever throwing themselves back at it. All with some abiding sense that they deserved it, so their only honor was this wretchedness, these aching miles of water, greasy logjams, tangles, thickets. The cut of leather trapsacks on their foreheads, the cut of snowshoe bindings on their feet, the iron weight and dealing death to that race of peaceable enterprising intelligent animals they would murder as their right. Loving such a life as offered proof in currency that fortitude, not tenderness, was what made men. Loving such a life so much they could not quit it, and do some more sensible thing.

That night he'd seen how hard and cold that life had made him: a grudging, unyielding man, too much away. He thought of Lise, her welcomes always better than any commonplace of days together. Those nights reunited, he and she, teasing while the breath around them evened, the children stilled and slept. How they rose to take each other: silent, hungry, the sliding robe their only modesty.

He woke resolved to change, rode the last miles at a long trot, and at midday dismounted among his yelping dogs. But the lodge was empty, the fire run down. He could hear Alexander in old Noonday's lodge, and June.

He ducked in to find them playing with Cecile's puppies, the old woman chewing leather.

He was pretty well spent, and the smoky light of that lodge confused him. Junie hopped beside him, asking what he'd brought, Alexander watching, Cecile toddling through the smoke with her arms around the pink belly of a pup almost as big as she. Noonday had pulled a line of rawhide, he remembered, like some great tapeworm from her mouth, to wind onto her frame. Her eyes, all the while, steady on him.

"Where's your mother, Junie? And Lispat?" His voice had come out burred.

"They're playing tea, and they won't let me—"

"Who?"

"Lispat and Joisette. They said I couldn't, and *ne-ica* said I could."

"Noonday, where is Lise?"

The old woman's hard look-away said bad doing.

"Junie, where's your mother?"

She hadn't answered. He'd asked again, but he'd frightened her, holding her shoulder, rattling her. She'd seen the bloody windings on his hand and started crying.

Anyway, he'd known. The heart so quick sometimes, before the mind.

Now he looked around. Bear River, the dark field, the grazing cattle. He could see Lucy Mitchell's shape approach against the paler grass. She'd put on something dark, a kind of cowl or blanket, but he knew her even from that distance. When she came beside him, he saw the baby held against her breast.

———

SHE'D CUT his hair, regretting it even as her scissors worked, though once begun was as good as finished. But he looked awkward, now, and shorn. It made him even more a stranger.

"What is Fort Hall like?" she asked him.

He had borrowed her Tennyson from beside the fire, and returned it. She had read his letter of the night. The weight of memory. Then Mary had wakened crying. So now she was answering, had been answering as she walked, her body with its little milk.

"White," he said. "Mud brick."

"It's British."

He didn't answer. She let herself down to sit, half turned away in the grass. Not too near. Holding her child, that milky breath.

"But we'll be able to resupply?"

Again he didn't answer. In every silence, it seemed possible that they were coming to the end of things.

She'd been so sure one night that knowledge would bring them closer. That only understanding could ever truly comfort, bind, satisfy. But now, to sit beside him, to remember how they'd touched, made that whole idea foolish. That any past of his or hers would ever change the scent of skin, would alter gestures, shape the words they chose. The eye, the brow, the hand she loved, seemed more distant than before. He went away and wrote and wrote, and it was somehow not for her, and now he was exhausted. Diminishing in her sight.

She said, "Don't do all this writing. Not for me."

The grasses sighed.

She said, "I'll give the pages back."

He said, "They're meant for you."

And then he looked at her, and she saw the ear she had touched, the cheek, the neck. And saw the hair, oh, how it was given up for her. How vulnerable he seemed, and she remembered that first night, when he had been afraid. And loved him then with such keen and sudden tenderness, with such aching grief.

———

HE SAW HER shift the child against her, fold the blanket closer, and thought she might go, and didn't want her to.

"I don't know where I was," he said.

"Did your wife betray you? Did Beck?"

He nodded.

He'd left the children in old Noonday's lodge, left the horses for Lise to tend. Walked far up the river to a flat of warm thin sun and put his hand in water. For hours, he'd lain there looking at the crumbling banks, dusty grass and wormwood, the sky with brown birds flitting here and there.

"What did you do?"

"Went off to think. Came back after dark. She was sitting on her shins beside the fire. The girls asleep. I asked where she'd been, she said out getting a deer. So I asked who killed it, and she started crying."

He'd put his robes in the visitors' place, away from her. Behind the fire. They'd lain and listened to each other's breathing. Alexander, rumped up in the blanket swing above, kept peeking at him, so finally he'd called him down to sleep against his chest. He remembered lying with his bandaged hand propped up around that curve of his boy's head, thinking, At least I have you. Blessing that he had his children. That he'd always have them.

He saw Lucy Mitchell, her little girl breathing, sleeping against her now.

"And what did Mr. Beck have to say?"

"Not much." He'd found Beck squatting on his heels next morning, digging his knife into the dirt. Cunning and abashed, like some thieving dog.

Lise's face was puffed from crying. She wouldn't look at him.

All the day before, lying beside the water, he'd kept seeing them in his mind, how they might have looked together. Beck's yellow hair, white legs spraddled on some filthy robe, her brown ones wrapped around him. Their breathing. The sounds she'd make, which had always been for him. He couldn't think around that one idea. It was everywhere. He'd thought all day beside that creek and didn't know anything by the end. What he was to her. Why either of them had ever done the things they'd done. The whole world seemed upside down.

Get out of here, the two of you.

Love had always been too small a word for what he felt. So how could he have said that no part of her had ever seemed imperfect to him? Her small straight walk, her shy smile, the space between her teeth. The high ridge of her nose. Her knees, their rough brown skin. All beautiful, for being part of her. He'd never said it. He couldn't say it.

That morning she'd been jagged as a mountain. All her gentleness was gone.

He said, "She went off and came back that evening to cook. I gave my blessing. If they wanted it."

"What did she do?"

"She asked me if I wanted her to go."

By holy Christ, woman, do you think I do? He'd shouted that, then watched her duck out, in dust and smoke and overturned tea.

"What did you say?"

He shook his head. He said, "I always made her cry."

He looked out across the grass, the dark bluffs cut against stars. After a while, she stood beside him and said good night.

Alone, he touched his shoulder where her hand had lingered.

THE KNOWN WORLD
UPSIDE DOWN

*H*ER HAIR WAS FALLING OUT. Each day it seemed her brush was filled with more. She'd pull it free, watch it float, thinking it could not possibly be growing in as fast as it was coming out. Thinking she was much too young to be abandoned by her hair.

An air of abandonment, though, had fallen on them all. She saw it as she looked around that Sunday meeting. Men and women hatless, collarless, some even shoeless. Women whose factory cotton had worn out, dressed all week in best delaine; men likewise in best wool trousers, chalky, stained, no memory of what a tie was for. They'd patched and hemmed, turned things backside to. Or failed to patch at all. There seemed less need for it, though holes were growing more and larger. The whites were going gray, and yet she was content to rest, or dreamed she was.

She had seen him climbing through the rocks.

HE CLIMBED toward sunrise.

He kicked down a place against a boulder, east facing, sat and breathed the yellow light, and everywhere were birds, the cheer and call of morning birds, their pure desires. He sat and heard all those bold trilling tongues and wished that he could understand each one. Sun soaked his clothes. He faced into it, shut his eyes, let his hands be idle.

Lise had stayed with him in the end.

She'd struck the lodge for him the next morning. He'd meant to winter in the village—the valley was too high and cold—but the need had come to be away. He'd brought in horses, called the dogs. Together they'd packed the pots and pans, books, clothes, provisions, the Christmas things still in their paper from the visit to Fort Hall.

"You'll like that place," he told the girls. "There's a grove of pines near the cabin, you can climb in."

But riding into that fine valley, the yellowing grass and tamaracks standing on the slopes like golden candles, he'd turned to see them and read no special joy. In the cabin's gloom, he'd struck fire and looked around. The wattled hearth, the chair, bench, table, beds. He'd smoked and sat, the goodness gone out of what he'd made. The girls helped Lise. She was silent. She wouldn't look at him.

The nights stretched out, with winter coming. *Good for love*, she used to say. Now they lay awake, not touching. She cried sometimes. He let her. They pulled, in turn, the corners of their robe, which stretched and settled into the trough between them.

In November a pair of women came by his place alone, Gros Ventres, with children and some bundles. They asked if they might camp there, and he spoke with them. They told him earnest lies, said they had bad husbands, but he didn't know what the truth might be.

He'd opened the ledger now in sun. He was writing.

These Women with their Babes moved off & camped about a Mile down from us & we forgot them, I wanting no more to do with members of this Tribe especially. Some know them as Big Bellies as they are famous beggars or the French say Demanduers & if they were too welcome I would soon find myself feeding a whole Village. They will hear & flock like Magpies. But these kept quiet to themselves & one day I saw no smoke from their place & rode down with a ham of Deer to see, & the One who was with child I found her dead by her own hand hung by horsehair rope from a high Limb, & three Children left alone, not all hers. There were Twins about two years yowling like Catamount cubs but the other was quiet and fine, & looked up at me with all the faith in the World.

Had I then put pistol to their heads & done it would have been a greater Mercy & in some former year I might but as I said those two fair girls were hard on my conscience & in this instance I saw some offering perhaps & chance to address that Sorrow & show myself now ready to Live by Trust not strength alone as I thought my Wife despised. But when I brought them home she would have none of it.

Have you no mercy? I asked, & told her, This is how we will make ourselves safe among these People. For they were difficult, warlike, and not many Men would care to live alone in the valley I had chosen, but Disease and the White God had humbled them enough I thought.

But there is great Superstition around twin children & she had not unlearned it. They will die, she said. They will bring ill luck.

I told her, Get soft meal with sugar & we'll watch how well they eat. & they did eat well & quieted. She said, I'll take the babe but you ride the others to the Mission. By the time I had got back from burying the Mother she had the cradleboards down & ready. We strapped one on each side of my saddle & the joggling of the horse soon put them both to sleep.

I rode late into the night & then put up awhile to tend them. But the Moon early coming into full I determined to ride on the night while the babes slept bundled & when dawn came I got them down & felt them to be warm. The spots I guessed were from the closeness of their boards all night. They fretted and wailed—I cursed their Mother for leaving them & wondered again why she would do so but they are a wild inconstant People, in no way hardened by their proximity to Nature, if they are glad they whoop it up, if angered, they avenge, if sorry they will not hold back but mourn & wail & hack their bodies even take their lives, & some will leave their Babes alone in willows. But I was most concerned by that day's noon to see these Infants their distress & see the darkness of their excrement the chill & suffering come on by night.

I put up camp not knowing what to do. The more distant from my family the more concerned was I about them. I did not dare to think of illness then, but saw the wrong I'd done in taking them so far from any kind of safety but Myself. & spent the whole night troubled by that pride, & by the fretting of the children. All the noises of the night seemed as threats—the river's roar & washing of the pines the wolves in their forays, cold air coming from the North—all these things no different from any other Night but kept me sleepless, & in the morning one Child of two was dead.

I waited paced very troubled next day & the second Child had scarcely stopped breathing before I'd lain them one beside the other, piled their Bodies in river stones, then thought better & laid on a bonfire atop that as well & lit it. & turned back rode hard as I could & arrived to find all well. The horse & I both much drawn down.

I thought you would be home tomorrow, said she. She knew how far the mission was but I said I met a man who took them.

The babe's all right? I asked. She said yes, it was sleeping.

It was supper & the rest were eating. I remember my wife looked a stranger in the house that night, sitting in the chair I'd made her. She would always use a floor. I sat my place at the table & she sat also.

There is a big snow coming, said I.

She had fried up bread in groundhog's grease, served broth potato, but he'd had no stomach for it, although he hadn't fed since morning, and scarcely lain the past two nights to sleep. But he'd not wanted her to think this. He'd fussed getting salt, and had a little broth as she was watching.

"I am done in tonight," he'd said, seeing again those two small faces, their blistered bodies. It was all he could do to betray nothing in her presence.

"But the babe's all right?" he asked again. Yes, she said. They called him Tu-ye, a blue grouse. But while she ate, he could think only of the bodies he had left under that pile of stones.

In the fire's heat the wet Stones will split. Riding away I had heard one crack as loud as pistol fire. But she had no questions.

I have told you she was a Beauty & seemed more beautiful that night with her faraway eyes her quiet face. There is nothing dark in her, which you know from your Emma, but only pure still purpose as is its own kind of wisdom, & most can never gain it. It was only then that I thought of my clothes.

I excused myself from her & went out. I fired the great Kettle &

brought up water from the creek. I found a change of clothing & out in Snow & Moon I washed with steaming water & laundered all I had worn, & took my Coat & weighed it in the river while my hair & beard froze up like Lime.

The rest you could guess it was the Variola or you say the Small-pox & I had brought it in. I slept very hard that same night & when I woke midday my Wife had gone. The girls were very quiet & I got down molasses & cooked up a mess of Christmas candy though it was four weeks early & vowed to myself I would be as good a father as I was able & never let my sorrow show or let them think she would not soon be back. But the things she took left me no doubt. I have not seen her since.

When he was done, he looked around. Stretched his legs along the dirt, blinking out across the level day, this high noon light, the small hard shadows hiding from the heat. A place so adamant as to deny the likelihood of any other.

He listened to the birds.

———

"A FAILURE of imagination, is what it comes down to," Israel said that afternoon. The officers had declared a common meal, with everyone so tired of the fare they were living on. Beans and flour and fish. He said, "Or inspiration."

She said, "There's a reason those things fail." He had committed her to making India pilau.

The men got a great fire going. Mr. Kingery killed a sheep, and by four o'clock had spitted it, the flames still high, so the men all stood around the terrible splayed limbs and watched it scorch, watched the smoke-shine blacken on that flesh. She stood and shifted as her own smoke blew, and only her old dog Peg sat by and watched her while she ducked and stirred.

"Did you find Letetia?" Lucy asked. She had quit, to help Caroline find her hairpins. "She was looking for you."

Caroline wiped her nose and nodded.

"Are you all right?"

But her forehead was not hot. "Well, get up," Lucy said. "Move around."

He had put four pages in her hand. At one o'clock, right in her camp, and no one had been looking. They were the last, he said.

Now she stirred and chopped, and talked with Daniel through the alphabet. "Letter G," she said, "what's that for?"

"Grass."

"Grass, very good. And Ground. Goat. Glad. Gay."

She'd read the pages, nursing Mary in the wagon. All he had written and not written. Then read it through again.

"You know grass can *fly?*" Daniel asked.

"Fly? No, tell me how the grass can fly."

"Not grass from the *ground.* Grass a *bird.*"

"A bird?"

"*Grass!* He thowed a rock and got it dead."

"Oh, *grouse!*" She laughed. "The prairie hen."

"He got it with a rock. Up there."

"Yes, he did, he brought it down. So now it's in my pot. What do you think of that?"

"Pretty good."

"Do you like him?" she asked.

He wrinkled his nose.

"Come," she said, "I want to hold you."

He did, and she held and breathed him in, so sad and grateful and ashamed, and when he squirmed away, she had to wipe her eyes.

The pilau, at last, was cooked. She'd carried mint these many months, now poor and dry, of course. She damped and freshened it, arranged its leaves imaginatively. Placed the platter with the other offerings: of fish pies, stews, boiled prairie hens, mince, and yellow currant sauce. The women scudded all which ways, or had pooled into knots of conversation.

"Pilau, what a wonder! And with *mint!*" said Nancy Richardson. "You know, there were always possums in my mint, I never knew how *wild* they were for mint."

"Possums?"

"Well, *yes!* Were you never bothered by them?"

A warm wind was up. They stood silent, 120 or more of them, shoulder to shoulder and ranged around the bounty.

She ate, standing beside Israel, with Phil Apperson, Nicholas Koonse, all waving forks, outlining barns, the pens and races they would build, talking out their plans to the very set and hinge of gateposts. Soon they called for paper, and she brought some. They hovered over it with pencils, counting, measuring, sketching timbers to be squared, what height the walls, what animals housed, what feed stored. They never tired of it.

She walked away. She found James MacLaren speaking with the old Mexican Velasquez. They fell quiet when she neared. All day she had thought of nothing but his story. How little cure there was for tragedy. But she would offer any gift, her whole soul, if it would make him glad again. She wanted to say that.

But how can a soul be given?

Instead, she told him what Daniel had said, and watched him smile. He had tried her cooking, she saw. There was the stewed grouse, and should have been onion, she said, and an egg.

"It's only pilau," she said. "Mace and nutmeg. And cloves. The last of the sultanas."

He nodded.

She never saw the sun go down. They gathered plates and washed, and soon the fire's light was keeping stars at bay, throwing moving shadows like a lantern show against the sagging canvas of the wagon tilts.

G is for Grass and Gay and Glad. She stood beside her husband and looked across the fire, admiring this man she loved. He stood beside Tom Littlejohn. She stood with Nancy Richardson. He listened to Bill Patton. She talked to Tilda Koonse, thinking he seemed as well that night as she'd ever seen him, very straight and handsome in his coat.

G is for Grouse.

And now he laughed so well that she believed she saw some teeth she'd never seen before, and they were good ones. And he held no cup, and was not drinking when Israel took her by the hand and led her off to bed.

MACLAREN STAYED AWAKE too late that night, and rode on in advance next morning beside their Captain White. Some had been complaining these past few days, citing regulations. They'd had disputes about a choice of camp. Some were asking to be rid of others who were not keeping pace.

So he scouted on ahead, up a side branch near the next low summit, and found a good fresh camp at the valley's head, not used. When he got back to the main trail, White was there. They had stopped and were talking together in the road as a faint clangor came out of the north. Soon they saw a wild-looking cart heading toward them down the hill, the driver hallooing against a sound like tin pots ringing. An outrider, on a spotted gray, trotted alongside. So they waited.

The thing on wheels had been a wagon once. Now sawed in half, it reeled and swam behind two short stepping mules, the driver on a chair up in the bed. A pot and ladle hung from the naked bow and swayed, unplayed now, colliding gently as the cart drew up, and an English bird dog came out from under the wheels and put its nose in the air and narrowed its eyes at them.

"Hey, American!" the carter called, and the mules shook their heads and gaped.

They exchanged names. When MacLaren said his, the carter claimed to know it. They had onions and flour, and MacLaren bought a cucumber off them for the price of a U.S. quarter, and got the news from Hall.

"Grant's still there?" he asked.

A confusion of curses affirmed it.

He bit into the cucumber. The end was bitter. He spat and reached it forward on his palm and fed it to his horse. "Anyone down from Quartier this season?"

Well, Quartier was bad, the carter said in Mountainy, it was bad all up those valleys, and shook his head, and White asked if they had sugar.

"Yes, yes, we have."

"Bad, how so?" MacLaren asked.

"*Mauv' malade,*" the rider mumbled sideways, and wiped his nose. Then spat through missing teeth.

The carter had stepped to the rear to flop open a sack. "Smallpox again they got," he called. "Some run away, some stay. How much you like *sook?*"

White said, "Just a little, what will you charge?"

The mules in jangling traces began to move while the carter dug, and MacLaren grabbed the near one by the bit. He called, "Did Beal Beck come in this winter?"

In curses, the carter affirmed it. A wrecker's yard of language.

MacLaren said, "Did a woman Lise come down with him?"

The carter only grinned. To White he said, "Two bits for poun', I give two poun', eh?"

"No, no, that's robbery. That's ridiculous."

"You hunt the bird? I have very good dog for you."

"*Oui,*" the mounted one said.

"You know her? Lise?"

"*Oui, elle la,*" the mounted one said, and spat again. "*Elle a Quartier.*"

MacLaren's hand tightened on the bit. Although the man was ignorant. And the carter was shouting to untie the dog for White to look at. The mule slung its head and lobbed long lines of drool across MacLaren's leg, ran its nose across his pommel, inquiring after salt. The first of the canvas tops hove into sight on the bend behind them.

"He is *loyale, ça va?*" the carter cried, on the ground now, with the dog on its string. "To stay with always! So small price you can pay for that, eh?"

MacLaren waited. He looked down at the dirt. The sun struck his burned neck, and he remembered her hands, the chill of scissors, how he had welcomed that shedding of something, that unburdening.

And now it was back.

COPPER BELLS

ISRAEL WOKE HER. He said, "The oxen are gone."

She heard the muffled voices of others, the clink and slap of saddle rigging. The air still brought the night smell of pines, a tang of damp.

"Who was on watch?" she asked. The stars were still out. The lamps already lit. "Were they stolen? Was it the Frenchman?" A pair of traders had stayed with them that evening, one had played his accordion late into the night.

"No," Israel said, "I'm sure they strayed back to join the others."

They had separated last afternoon, with much argument, and had made two camps: one on the main trail, and one a few miles up this narrow valley. She said, "I'll let the girls sleep, then."

"Make use of the morning. Tom and I are riding down. We broke a slider yesterday. MacLaren says he'll stay and fix it."

SHE CLANGED the oven, made sure the sponge was going. The dawn had turned a flat deep blue when she started up the stream to meet him. There was flour on her hands.

She was too old, of course, to be finding men in bushes. She feared she must be callow or, if not quite that, then embarking on something that would seem pitiful to her someday. But she slipped, anyway, through the springing branches, with Mary on her hip still reeking of the night, and found him standing in a cove of grass.

She neared to an awkward distance, having come this far. The dark little stream slid along, white riffles gleaming in blue light.

He said, "I heard a thing yesterday. So I should tell you."

"What is it?"

"My wife. Those two from Hall have seen her."

Lucy took in a breath, suspended. The baby cooed and plucked her dress.

"I didn't know," he said. "I kept thinking she'd be gone."

"That she'd died of smallpox."

He nodded.

The camp was so quiet. There was only the hush of wide flat water rushing by.

"Where is she?"

"The place we used to live, the Quartier. I don't know. It might be rumor."

She jogged the baby, looking at the hills, in sudden need of holding back.

He looked at her.

She smiled, or tried to, with Mary on her hip. But nothing would come out.

He reached, then, and she went to him. He folded her against him. She breathed him in, knowing this was what she'd wanted, more than anything. This enfolding care. This kindness. She felt his jacket with her cheek. She heard his heart. His breath. But the baby's squeaking thumb was too ridiculous. They pulled away, smiling. She leaned into his open coat and wiped her nose against his shirt.

"Hey," he said. "It's clean on."

She burst out soggily, half laughing.

He let himself down to sit in the grass. She sat beside him. The sky had brightened. Across the stream, a gold light touched the ragged crest of hills.

"If there is an order to things," he said, "I don't know where I am in it."

She sat, and heard the little copper bells of the goats down in their camp. And she wanted to tell him how she had lain awake last night imagining their lives in years to come, creating lives that they might live in confidence, without sacrifice. Perhaps as neighbors, or he'd help them on their place, which would not be in town. It would be a piece of land, timber and farm, and he'd be needed. She had seen it easily, made it good, forgetting just how possible things seem while lying in the dark.

Mary, on sturdy knees, was creeping toward the stream. He rose to get her. Lucy followed.

"Have you seen what she can do?" She put Mary at the water's edge, pressed a pebble in her palm. The stubbing fingers took it up and flung. For a while, they watched the ungoverned arcs, the splash, her daughter's laughter. Then Lucy felt him touch her hair.

From that moment it was a dream of grass and water, hands and breath. Quickly, quickly, she devoured, and was, in kind; no part of them did not crave union; she breathed, struggled toward it, went down blind, only wishing to feel, to feel—on the velvet flicker of closed eyes—that no harm could ever come to them, the world closed down to nothing but the smell of grass, the weight of him, dark motions of their hands and bodies.

Cool air touched the skin above her stockings. He was sinew in his clothes, ribs and belly, and she quickened to this hunger and was pushed, elbows furrowing the grass, arching back, the pale green tips of willows waving in the paler blue, the drone of bees, wild music, bells, spread knees upraised; in this desire so absolute, so far from any former life, that she quickly bloomed, as she had learned, but then was stricken further: in his motion, his knowing push and push, his finding of her center, something deeper had begun to gather terribly, beyond ability to govern. It voiced, despite her, *Oh*, and *Oh*, and now she grew impossible, a surging fish; her body seemed to take on its own life, leaping, running hard against him. Hands gripped and pulled, a terrible demanding, she arched and drove, and drove herself, then seized in one ecstatic conduction, the sound was nothing she had made before. She closed her mouth against it.

Her daughter had crawled nearer, was pulling at green tufts, and Lucy closed her eyes, appeased in warming grass. He moved away.

He stood, and then the distance made them separate and a little sordid, straightening their clothes, so it almost seemed unlikely that so brief a thing had actually occurred, and that was some relief.

She rose and turned, and rubbed her legs with leaves.

———

"WHERE WAS YOU, Mama?" Daniel, sleepy-eyed, stood beside the fire. She set down her pail, filled, as it should be.

"Bathing your sister, little goose," she said. Already she heard the clang of tools.

The goats, dry udders flopping, were marauding for some unguarded delicacy. They'd already found the grease, she saw, her can licked clean, and only one more Sunday's worth of bacon to fill it.

"More wood, Emma," she called, putting the kettle on to heat, working hazily at breakfast while Mary leaned on the pine box and bobbed and crept along it.

A shower of dry willow sticks came soon enough.

"Is Sarah up?" she asked Emma, not looking around.

"I don't know."

"Why are the goats loose?"

"I took them grazing."

"They've eaten all our grease."

The batter cakes she'd poured were smoking on the hot dry skillet. She pried them off, still raw inside, and scraped the iron. The kettle had begun to steam.

"Take that, Emma, and pour a little water on my skillet, just a little," she said, and kept scraping, expecting a dribble, a puff of steam, and when she felt it come scalding across the backs of her hands, heard the hiss and splash, the billowing steam, she could not pull away.

HE RAN, hearing her breathy scream, the voices of her children. He plunged her hands into cooling water.

Then the fluttering women came, and he gave way, shaken, his mind already going far too fast. He took the piece to Cullen that needed fixed. The forge was hot enough. He stood by in the hammer's ring and sparking iron, undoing that moment again and again, when he'd looked up to the sound of bells and seen her daughter Emma Ruth see them.

"Good enough," he said. The iron hit the cooling water with a hiss and billow of steam.

He worked under the wagon after that, furious with himself, dirt falling in his eyes. Dirt falling, the piece not fitting, not fixing what he'd said he'd fix until he was hitting, just swinging hammer blows and striking blind.

MITCHELL CAME IN with the oxen an hour later, was scarcely in earshot before he started shouting to get the oxen chained, get them chained or they'd be held up in dust all day, the others down the road were already under way ahead of them. The girls told what had happened at the fire, Emma Ruth still crying, while MacLaren yoked and pulled the oxen to the poles, while he forgot things, dropped things, thought of what was done and how to do what he should do and undo what he never should have done. Who knew what he'd been thinking. To let that overtake him. To let that overtake them.

But no lightning struck.

"She's sleeping now," said Mitchell. And they set out.

THE TRAIL GOT into his lungs that day. He coughed. His head was aching. He looked in once and saw her drawn and gray in the dust of the wagon, and her bandaged hands glowed white. He'd made her old in just one day.

Another company had stopped on the head of the range, with no level ground for miles to come. Quite a few of them with measles. So their own party halted just below at only four o'clock. Emma Ruth passed and passed again on errands, made much of the goats, much of the dog, and never looked at him.

It was best, he thought, to do it now.

Mitchell being a man of appointments, MacLaren had to walk him down between one camp and another, and stand in his path to say, "There's a matter you should know. You may know it."

"Yes, man. Speak." He was friendly and vague, the white of his beard and hair standing strong against the brown his skin had taken. Well, you are a handsome man, MacLaren thought. For all your pride.

"In confidence."

They walked down through yellow brome, waist high. Dry lightning had started a fire on the western mountains. Now the sky had filled with birds. He watched them fly, and stilled himself. "Do you know?" he asked. They stood in silence and he felt the shift occur, and knew the man had understood, as he had understood that day with Lise. He said, "I don't know what I was thinking."

Mitchell swept the flat of his hand across the tall brome, knocking the seeds free.

"Whatever you hear," MacLaren said, "it was my doing."

"What will I hear?"

There seemed no true and decent words for what they'd done. For what he'd taken. He said, "I mean you to forgive her. I'll go. If you forgive her."

"If I forgive her?"

So he felt a fool for even hoping to undo this thing.

"If I don't?"

They stood with other possibilities between them, while birds swerved through the yellow sky. Mitchell blinked and brushed the seeds from his palms.

"Go," he said. "Go."

———

SHE CAME OUT when they'd made camp, impatient with confinement, and sat with Mary to help Tom Littlejohn clean fish.

It was scarcely evening, she saw, but already the morning seemed like something from a different life. A greasy light roiled over her wrapped hands, strange and visibly moving, and across the west, the sky was orange, the high sun misshapen, pulsing crimson. Time out of joint.

She held a trout, looked at the pure gold button of its eye. Mary, watching, pursed her lips and said, "Uh-oh. Uh-oh, sis."

"Yeah, she talk, lookat that!" Tom Littlejohn beamed and snuffed at this accomplishment, and she loved him for it.

"Uh-oh, fish," she agreed. She'd thought all day of their morning beside the stream. "So now he's supper."

He said, "Pettis County, we use to get us scoze 'um suckers. Haul in be size that yer." He held his hands so wide she had to smile.

They worked quietly, in the tinny smell of scales. When they were done, he stood wiping his hands clean, looking down the valley.

"They'll pen the oxen tonight, I think," she said, following his look, and that was when she saw James MacLaren riding away with his roan mare and mule.

———————

"WHERE'S FATHER?" Sarah asked when they all sat down to supper.

"I don't know." She'd moved through the evening suspended. That she could breathe, even, seemed remarkable.

"I don't want fish," Caroline said, and the old dog chewed her tail, hissing through her wrinkled nose. They both looked, then looked away.

"Don't tell me what you don't want," Lucy said.

Sarah said, "I'll go find him."

"No," she said.

Dusk came, and dark, until the fires on the hills glowed orange. She had found a final letter.

In the green wagon, Sarah and Caroline bickered.

"Will you quit stepping on my bed?"

"I didn't step on your bed. Mama!"

"You did so, you went all over it."

"Mama!"

They'd never even asked why he was going.

She sat combing Mary's curls. Touching the pink puckered skin, that little scar, she remembered the dark and the rain, so long ago.

"Sing, Mama," Daniel said.

"No. Not tonight."

So he began alone, " 'Chickens cluck on Sourwood Mountain, hey ho diddle um day.' "

His little voice was true and sweet, and he jumbled the next words, dogged and sincere. She joined him, knowing then that no matter what might happen in her life to come, she would not forget this night of fire on the hills, her boy's pure voice. How alive and raw she was, how fleeting and deeply fortunate seemed love in any form.

Someone must have seen them. Israel, she guessed, had learned.

She put Mary to bed, set Daniel on the wagon tongue, unlaced his boots. They watched the burning hills.

"Is that fire coming here?" he asked.

She sensed Israel behind her, and turned and saw his shadow against the sky.

"No," she said. "The river will keep us safe. It's all right tonight, I'll watch you."

She put him in his bed, pulled his blankets close. Outside again, the stars were dizzy as she leaned. Israel had gone to bed. On the wind, a smell of rain and ash. By lantern light, she put away the kitchen, wondering. Who, how. What had been said.

Then climbed quickly back into the wagon. Pushed and pulled among her things until she found the sewing box.

"Lie down," she told Daniel. "Go to sleep."

She opened the box but found the letters safe inside.

She sat and breathed relief, wondering, was it the laudanum that day, or was she such a child that all she could feel was sorrow? Not guilt, not shame, the wreckage of a life. How could nothing matter but the two of them, and grief?

I'm not afraid, she'd said. *I'm not afraid*. And she was not.

She put his final letter with the others, and closed the box, and went out.

Inside the tent, she knelt in that mundane world of apron ties, the ungartering of stockings. Obliged, as ever, to ask Israel for help. Buttons, eyelets, everything was worse, her hands in bandages. She heard his breathing, felt his fingers at her back. She thanked him. Then took her place. He had left his watch too near her head. The seconds ticked; she lay and listened.

───────

HE RODE OVER the pass and quit that night on the first waters of the Snake—a bold creek in its brushy bed, walls of knobbled stone. Fire glowed down distant slopes in lines that ebbed and floated in the dark. Orange smoke seethed across the ridges.

He laid out his things, kettle and cup. Brought up wood but had no appetite. His breath seemed half composed of sighs. Fell asleep to flocking dreams that wheeled and scattered into nonsense, and woke not knowing where he was, but heard by the sound of rattling cans and steady thump of hooves that the horses were loose and making free among his packs.

He lay half propped beside the ashes, trying to summon what he needed from those organs as familiar as his lungs or heart: of will, intention, desire.

Nothing. It seemed his very soul was gone.

It's a dream, he thought. I'm dreaming.

But no life or death had ever seemed more real than this despair.

———

A CHIRP and tiny flutter woke her. She'd come into the wagon and fallen asleep, she saw, propped in her blankets, her head on Daniel's bed. A small brown wren had flown in and perched on the long salt box beside her. Charmed, she watched it turn its head, blink the shining bead of its black eye. She saw the pulse that quivered through it, and felt the same in herself, a hum that came of too much feeling, too little rest. His pages were closed in her bandaged hand, hidden under blankets.

I am sorry for all of this, he had scrawled, *you see I should have gone sooner.*

She'd smoothed the pages last night, grateful for this solid thing. This evidence.

> Lucy I have never known you as I would. I told him you were not to blame. My Wife you know was more dear than I have said. I could not tell what I hope to know in finding her, if any thing could resolve what I have done. But if she is gone or is as well without me, then I will look for you again, for sometimes Fate makes possible those things we most would wish, if only we were patient.

She heard, outside, the clank and clatter of pans, the voices of her family.

"Coffee's boiling, Emma. Tell your mother."

The wren took flight through the circle of hazy blue.

To Drink from Empty Cups

By DAWN HE KNEW he had the latest fever from the camps. The horses were on their pickets, but Cut Ear had gotten loose and found the flour.

He brought her up and scraped the gummy dust from her forelip, slapped her on the neck. She swung her head to bite. He gave her back his elbow. She snapped her tail, put down her ears, and so evil was her look and so sorry her honk, he smiled. But had a brutal ache behind his eyes.

By sunrise he was riding past a camp of Bannocks. Dark women mounted and rode trotting after him, holding up outrageous scavengings to sell: parasols, old fusils, foxed books, while dusty dogs wove through their ponies' moving legs. Everything about the world seemed comical. He laughed. Then felt himself close up like a fist.

The plain was deep and sandy, the hills scabbed with juniper. He passed bloated oxen, dead as trestles, and thought of Mitchell's sweeping hand, how the seeds sprang free. But Drum walked gladly now, and MacLaren did feel more like himself. As a sailor on the sea. There was a kind of emptiness that always freed him, and why he'd had that terror in the night, he didn't know.

But no sea had ever felt the morning's heat, the yellow sky, the sand, the wind; he was sweating through his shirt. Past trains of strangers, hard-drawing teams, plodding women, droves of ganted cattle, he swung wide, hands in his pockets, with no need to guide the horse.

By evening the road bent toward Fort Hall. But he reined upriver to the east, away from it, and had to catch the mule and Sally to lead them—they both remembered going to the fort. They balked in the road, stretched their necks and turned, and when a rope ran underneath Drum's tail, it was a sudden circus: snorts and farts, up-flung dirt.

He stepped down at last to get his hat and had to lean against his saddle while the day paled. The fort was only a few miles away, and he couldn't bring himself to go there. All his intentions had seemed real enough—the people he would find, the places he'd go back to—but what could they mean when he'd lost even the little nerve it took to visit a man who used to trade him flour? So it seemed the years to come might be shaped this way, by places he'd slip past, people he'd avoid, than by any decent thing.

He mounted and rode on.

By evening the fever had turned to rattling, the cords of his neck so wrought he couldn't turn his head. Teeth as loose as cribbage pegs. He clamped them tight.

I should eat more liver, he thought. Or be like Beck with his fists of sorrel, always hunting something green. Good for the blood, he'd said. A man intending to grow old.

He squinted. The sky was ashy white.

He swam the river without stopping. Crossed the cinder plain by dusk, while his clothes dried on him in the heat. He could still make out old tracks of journeys baked and glazed by seasons. Mules, horses, travois poles. Some were his. Now and then, he saw the scribed tracks of wheels, that single wagon.

Well, you find yourself some other gates.

The slanting moon.

He coughed by fits. His throat felt like hot stones had been run down it; he was thirsty and afraid to swallow, so he rode, kept riding, until the world reduced to that, a fear of swallowing, and he thought he should make camp, but it was too much trouble in such glare, and no intention held. The horse kept going.

He saw her scalded hands. His fingers on her wrists, the water in its pail. It was the last time he'd touched her.

———

HE FELL FORWARD at a stinking pool, slid down in starlight to drink. He thought he'd dropped his rifle. He undid the girths, hands rattling, tried to take down pack saddle and all, but the hard straight rail of the mule's spine held it. She lashed and bit. Then stalked into the dark. He heard freed cinch rings jingle on the stone.

He lay beside the trickling water, in the tick and pop of cooling rock, while the horses clopped and drank and worried through the bushes. Drum got down to roll. He heard the thud, the pushing sand, the grunty shudder as the old horse stood and shook the leathers of his saddle.

The saltbush moaned. He was cold and wished his horse would come and stand beside him. He wished his horse would take him off to somewhere good. That horse was a great geographer and knew the pull of places, the smell, the cast of light. Of future, he had none. Of present, only senses. But the country of his memory was vast in scope and intricate with feeling.

HE SLEPT at last, and his dreams were all of water. He bent, and streams turned into sand. Cups fell from his hands. He woke to a floating rim of moon and stood. The frozen lake he found was in fact salt clay, and across the dazzling white he saw a greasewood shrub. He walked. He came to it at last and knelt, began to dig beside the roots. Through soda, yellow clay; he lay and scooped out handfuls, brought up more and more until he struck the liquid silt, put his hand into the pit again and felt the shape of something pliant and familiar. A nose. A mouth. A weed of hair.

Lise was looking up at him through muddy water. She blinked and gaped. He broke away with a thready howl.

Then lay, heart pounding, in the sound of someone's breath. A nudging at his leg. He squinted to see morning sky and the pale belly of an antelope, its centerline of nesting flies, saw the small bare teats, twig-slender legs, strung tendons so close each hair had life. She twitched and stamped with a click of cloven feet, head down, licking salt from his leggings. He stirred. Quicker than sight, she wheeled and sprang away in small exploding leaps, sand and brushy cracklings fading like long stitches into silence.

He sat and knew the horses would be gone.

LUCY'S HANDS, overnight, had puffed into angry crimson things.

Mrs. Raimie came to see her when they nooned, shook her head in a good Christian way, brown and wholesome, went off and came back with a tin cup of something white—linseed oil and laudanum, she said, and powdered lime. She tore linen into bandages, not speaking further.

So Lucy slept the day and woke to the familiar noises of camp. Israel had taken on the cooking. She heard his voice, the clatter of pans, her children's conversation. She pretended they were strangers. It was no effort to lie still.

Sarah brought water and a bowl of supper and sat on the edge of the trunk beside her. "My tooth is hurting," she said. "This one right back here." She gaped and pointed.

"Well, wait for morning and show me. It's too dim now."

Her daughter sighed. She said, "It really hurts. My whole throat hurts."

Lucy said, "I'm sorry." There was rice in the bowl, and boiled dry meat.

"I hate this place." Sarah slouched against the wagon's wall. "It's stupid and ugly and there's nothing ever good to eat."

It had been her speech from the beginning, though she'd quit complaining for a while. Lucy said, "I know."

"Oregon, Oregon, Oregon. Why did they keep saying Oregon was pretty? And now we are in Oregon, and it's the ugliest place I ever saw. I wouldn't live here if I was a snake."

"Oregon is big. This part is the desert. We go through it, that's all."

"I think it's a lie."

Lucy picked a little, tried to eat.

In the quiet, Sarah said, "Do I look more like you or Daddy?" She came to this in blue moments. Remembering her daddy. The answer was always the same.

Lucy said, "You're tall like him already. You're strong."

"I'm not strong."

"You're very graceful."

"But everything else. My hair and eyes and the way I am."

"You take more after me."

Sarah crossed her arms and looked away. "I know," she said. "I wish I didn't."

———

ALL NIGHT Lucy slept and woke, her hands on fire; she couldn't keep from whimpering. But by morning she ached from lying down, and rose and dressed with Caroline's help, and came out into the world.

Israel overplayed it, a robust parody of himself. She watched him take up beside the oxen with a kind of extravagant manhood, as though he'd never had help nor need of it. She watched him take a cloth and wipe the oxen, those innocent locutionary racks of bones, their drooling noses; not powdering their sores or checking feet as James MacLaren had, but wiping them down all over as though it were that other presence he meant to wipe away. She wondered if he'd want to do the same to her when he came in need again of her attentions.

Would she apologize? She would not. All she'd done, she'd meant to do.

To give credit, he was not mawkish. There'd been no scenes. He allowed her to despise him, if she did, though she doubted he deserved it.

With the children, too, he seemed to spread himself, to grow larger, as though occupying some vacant claim. When they arrived that afternoon at the Soda Wells, he spent an hour having Daniel count out stones, and made him do sums, as though she'd never done such a thing nor ever would.

"He doesn't know his sums yet," he told her. So she saw her infidelity would color every failure. Probably in his mind, it would account for most of them—his or hers, real or imagined. In the meantime, she was to witness his competence as a father, to understand how little need he had of her. So she saw the horror of appropriation. He tried to joggle Mary on his knee. A week before, she might have laughed or teased him. Now she was repelled.

And of course there was her own new awkwardness with the women. The Soda Wells was a grazed-down place full of bubbling holes, green or slimy orange, or fizzing with airy water. Mires lay hidden under hardpan. They liked the soda water very well, and everyone who still had sugar brought it out, and also citric acid, and walked among the wells and sat laughing in the shade of the peculiar trees, drinking gassy drinks, Hannah and Libby and Dear and Nancy Richardson and the rest, and Lucy did likewise, and imitated their nibbling of biscuits. She said little, smiled much, moving carefully across the thin clay crust of their companionship, not knowing how much ran underground, which next step might take her punching through and into the scalding mud of new contempt.

AFTER THAT, she didn't walk with them, but busied herself at private tasks. By evening she found herself pretending errands, turning to drink from empty cups, so she could avoid their passing eyes. She dreaded laundry.

And through all this, she carried love around, a small smooth comfort like the shell inside her pocket, something all her own, compelling her to reach and touch and touch again. It was not the end, she knew. It was only a matter—as he'd promised—of patience. And if Israel was feigning fatherhood, the same could be said of her own mothering.

"Don't run around the fire, please," she said, but was really looking at the empty chair, Tom Littlejohn sitting in the grass, silent as a dog, as neutral, a great still sack of a man in the whirling center. She was studying the Indians who roamed through camp each night now, and was not afraid of their bright teeth or the dust of their skin, their covert dreaming eyes.

"Do not step on your sister, Daniel." But she still saw the kind creases of James MacLaren's gaze, and saw, from a height, the earth laid out before them. Listening for his distant particular cough.

"Emma Ruth, you never stowed the dishes." The Watts' hens had strayed and were pecking around her fire. Old Peg stood and growled. Emma, passing, struck out with her foot and scattered them all.

By the next day, measles were in force among them: the Willis children had it, and Jeannie Knighton and her girl, and Davis Beagle, and the Whites' driver, Isaac. Some from Madison County had buried a child the day before. They slowed their travel. She kept the girls from visiting.

———

Afoot, MacLaren had tracked his horses in the blaze of day, strayed from some course, and was consigned in warping air. A single insect hissed. He stood absorbed by this and believed the sun to be the cause of it.

These stones had never been disturbed. He turned and tried to think, but desert was no friend to memory.

We are lost, each one of us.

He broke his joints and moved, his throat so inflamed that water would only have been agony.

The day stopped.

He saw eternal wormwood. He was on his back then, aching in its tangled shade, flaking bark. Leaves crackled on his scalp. Sun flashed silver through the dusty twigs, down the furrows of his eyes. Why he'd left the comforting slime, the green dripping lip of rock, he couldn't say, but out of stubborn habit.

This is how men die, he thought. Stubbornly, out of habit.

Chill on burning stones, he apologized. Saw her curling smile, pale lashes, saw those eyes, the ravening soul. Like suited cards, he'd held the mate. He said, "You are too polite." And regretted most not ever having felt the intimacy of her scorn, of which only the most enduring love is part comprised. She raised her chin at him and smiled.

MAN AND WOMAN

⟨⟨⟨⟩⟩⟩

*I*SRAEL PURCHASED A MARE in the middle of the following day.

The road had taken them past a crude settlement of stick wigwams, the usual rabble of children, savage dogs, shrewd-eyed braves. The American animals they offered seemed generally broken down, so Israel chose a native type, but even this was a wormy thing, slab-necked, coarse, scarcely taller than a donkey, and it cost him two shirts and a skirt of Sarah's and a black lace parasol she'd been glad to part with. There had apparently been some suggestion of taking Mary in an even trade, or Israel was joking. They did eye the golden hair, although she'd shortened it. He bought moccasins for Daniel and the girls, and led the horse away without more incident, and after a while, they halted and tried to saddle it privately. She stood and held the creature, not complaining, though it walked in circles and pawed and dragged its muddy nostrils across her dress while he fussed and fussed to get the rigging right.

They reached Fort Hall at the tail of that same day, a small whitewashed affair with a pair of towers at the front, flags flying, lonesome on the scorched-looking plain. All were disappointed. They circled and made camp down the river to the west, where a little grass still grew, and Israel rode up to the gates with a few of the other men, and came back saying all entry was refused until the morning. He said the Madison party had suffered two deaths, and meant to stay put until more were well, and he'd heard from them that the Hudson's Bay factor was a thief and destitute of human feeling, and would not buy an ox for any price and sold no flour, sugar, nor any necessary commodity but kept all stores for private trade and use. Would not shoe a horse, fix a wagon, tolerate the presence of dogs or children, though you could see the walls were swarming with local Indians and their miscellany.

"You'd be bitter, too," she said, "if you'd lost the country. Why should the British welcome us?"

"We'll pitch them on their ears if they don't, that's why. I'll run for office on it."

So there was great stirring and talk and discontent. She washed her feet and soaked the last dry beans for breakfast, with dusty shrivels of meat.

"You know of the Whitmans," he said behind her without preamble.

"Who, the missionaries?" They had come out to serve the Indians. They were Methodist, she thought, or Presbyterian. It was the type of enterprise her mother might have gathered funds for once.

He said, "I've decided to apply there for the winter. I thought I'd offer to teach their school."

A mission. She looked at her scabby hands. "What about Oregon City?"

"We're a month behind where I thought we'd be. The oxen are run down. We can't recruit them. The winter will be on us."

She looked at him, thinking of that man and two girls, the dead wife, the oxen James MacLaren had shot. They had wintered here. Outside these walls.

He said, "We've used too much of everything."

All spring she'd been afraid, and then she had forgotten: how slowly they were traveling, that they might arrive in sleeting winter, spent down in every way, and find no home. Now here was danger, and she was still sailing in some silly dream of love. So it seemed they were reversed, and he could see what he'd denied for all this time, while she'd begun denying what she had always seen.

"All right," she said. "If you think that's best."

He said, "A pack train left this afternoon; they're headed for the Whitmans'. I can ride ahead. Catch them with a letter."

"All right."

"So you'll help Mr. Littlejohn drive tomorrow, until I'm back."

"Yes," she said. "All right."

He wrote his letter without more discussion, and rode away on the surly pony.

So she lay alone that night. It was impossible, of course, not to speculate on a life in which he did not reappear. She'd done this sometimes, as an exercise, wondering how she'd manage. How widowhood might go differently. This time, she resisted, but did get out the letters, to hold the wonder of that careful formal hand. When she closed her eyes, his face seemed very clear. But only five days had passed.

I'll not see you again, she thought. It seemed more widowhood than any.

But she resolved to bear it. For what had he taught her but to let go of all those childish expectations, which, unmet, bred bitterness and despair? What had he shown but that she was strong and able to meet life truly, without wrong compromise? It was something she had seen in him, that sufficiency. That fearlessness, even in the face of tragedy. It was something she could hope for.

She thought of calico, flour, how good it would be to get a few provisions, make some shirts for trading. She'd been wanting to see this fort, to see the faces of the people there and think that they might know him.

———

So in the morning after breakfast, she left the girls in charge and set out walking, with jingling coins and a cowry shell in the pocket of her apron.

A warm wind pushed her along. Fires were still burning in the mountains. The ground had been cleared around the fort, so what she crossed was dirt and dusty stubble. She could see the Indian settlement, the herd of grazing horses. The fort itself stood in smoky light, worn flags flying from its blockhouse.

Walking, she was aware of herself acutely: of the contours of her shadow, her scabby hands, the hardness of her legs, how flat and lean she'd become. All womanly shape had left her. She felt burned away, distilled to essence, unafraid.

And when she did approach the walls, and knocked at a small door beside the gates, it opened. She stated her business to a broad gentleman dressed in serge, the factor of the establishment. And she was not jeered at nor berated, not sent away, but escorted to the trading room, where she spoke to another man who brought out bolts of cloth. She stood quietly under the timbered ceiling in the presence of gunpowder, traps, beads. She chose her goods and paid.

"You want these done up," the clerk said.

She watched the hands as they folded, wrapped, tied her calico with string. The cough she heard outside was half obscured by wrinkling paper.

But it was his.

Then her head was ringing with the sounding anvil, she was rooted. She had the childish urge to slip away or sink behind the door, wanted more than anything to beat her hands against the jamb and call his name.

She took the parcel numbly. When she turned and saw him pass outside in the shadowed gallery, she squeezed it tightly, crackling, and said, "Ahh."

He stopped, turned.

She was so brittle. To move would break her.

But her boots had taken her, and now their voices, knowing what to do, were speaking, back and forth. She said shirting, calico shirting. He said horses. He had lost his horses, and they'd come back here. He'd followed them back.

"But you're off now." He looked at her defending bundle.

"Yes." She'd never blushed so hotly.

He nodded. But her feet were still.

He said, "There's a place to sit. If you wanted."

She followed him, blotting her eyes with a furtive wrist: across the compound, through a door into a hall. In sudden gloom, they lingered among empty tables and their benches. Then, by some consent, passed through another door.

It led into the blockhouse. A ladder stood inside against a square of ceiling light. They climbed into an empty musk, a stink, a swarm of fur room flies. Then passed back through another door and into a gentleman's chamber. A window faced onto the shaded gallery. He crossed the room and shuttered it.

"Is this all right?" she asked. "Is this your room?" Her skin sang in long waves.

"It's Archie's. He's away."

She looked around, saw someone's desk and papers. A crudely fashioned chair. A bed, a box, a bench. Log rafters and cobwebbed shingles with sunlight spangling through. She closed her eyes, scarcely remembering what it was to stand inside a room, to stand in someplace covered from the sun.

"Israel has ridden off for the day." She put her parcel on the bed.

"Your hands," he said.

"Look. They're fine, they're healing."

They stepped together, like uncertain waltzers.

She said, "You're warm." His eyes looked hot and bright. He was older than she remembered.

He touched her hair, the secret pins.

"My poor hair," she said. "I'm sorry."

The bed was wool and fur. She sat on the edge of it, aware of her dust, suddenly afraid. He was pouring water from a pitcher. He brought a tin cup full. She took it, grateful.

"Have you found your wife?" she asked when the cup was empty.

He shook his head.

"Here." She patted her skirts, recalling that night when she had sat against him; and was surprised when he did turn and sit on this plank floor and lean his back against the bed as she had asked, into the cove formed by her dresses. She touched his hair. His neck was burned. She put her cooling knuckles against it.

He was picking at the laces of her awful brogans.

She said. "My stockings are so bad."

But her shoes were coming off, and he was pulling her dusty stockings with their holes, and had gone to get the basin, clean water, a cloth.

"No," she said. "Let me."

He sat. She pulled off his boots. Slowly she undressed him, as she might a child, but she was trembling and the door was bolted. Boots and leggings, sweat and dust. She smiled to see his linens, and didn't touch them, but knelt beside the basin, dipped the cloth, and squeezed it to the wiry hair of legs, knees, so that water ran in channels down the bones and muscles. Muddy puddles formed around his toes. These are his toes, she thought.

He took his shirt off for her.

She stilled, to see him unclothed but for those ragged drawers. It was alarming, this matter of possession, of light, the terrible and proximate truth of this body, in this room. He was foreign bones and skin and sinew. Her throat was tight with it.

He stood. Behind him, she raised the dripping cloth. She washed his neck, his shoulders, the angry constellations of disease, now healed smooth. They did not disturb her.

He said, "I was never good to look at."

She thought he could not have been more beautiful. It was only the coldness of this possibility, of seeing how much he was a stranger. She rinsed the cloth and raised it, attending to known work, the work of washing.

In the center of his chest, she found a small blurred figure: two standing lines, a thumb's width apart, hatched between with short diagonals, like fletching, or the laddered awns of buffalo grass.

"What is this?"

"It wards away death," he said.

She leaned her head against it. He stroked her spine very gently.

And then their hands, together, moved. Her clothing, piece by piece. The hooks, the eyes, the buttons, leaving her exposed, her breasts, her belly. The bones of her hips, he kissed them. Her pantaloons, gray and frayed. The patch of curling hair, he pushed his fingers through it. He felt her, and she pressed against him.

She sat, because she trembled. He washed her feet, her calves, her knees, her thighs, washed the issuance of her, gently, then kissed her there. She drew her legs around him, pressed her fingers through his hair. She felt the bones of his skull, the heat of it.

He kissed her breasts. She raised her neck above him.

A rifle shot—its sharp concussion not far distant—made her flinch. She looked around, awake from dreaming, into light and shame. "What is that?"

He was listening. They heard a second shot, a third.

"Shooting match," he said, but the spell was broken. He stood now, very naked. She had not seen this happen. She looked away, breathing.

"I would help you to get dressed," he said. "If you say it."

To touch is to see. To see is to name. To name is to own. He had shown her this. She stood and raised her lips, and met his frightening teeth.

He lifted her from the floor. In his arms, she felt as airy as a bird. She wrapped her legs and held him.

"Shh," he said. "What are you smiling at?"

The rafters paled. She closed her eyes, she felt, heard, smelled. On the bed, its woven wool against her back, against her thighs, soft fur. On the wind, the ringing anvil, snapping flag. In the air, the rich foul smells, meat, musk, bitter dust. His fingers skimmed her skin.

Smoke and sweat. When at last they joined, she pulled and met him, reduced to senses. With no memory, husband, children, life, aside from this. The coves between his collarbones, the dark totem; the caved and urgent loins that she commanded, the sharp bones of his hips, the wiry armature of desire. In slowness, she observed the speckled skin of his chest, the muscles of his arms, his upstretched neck, the eyes half closed, intent, his hands placed close beside her.

He bowed his breath against her. They moved easily, as if they had always done this. Fervently, as though they had just met. There might be only this one time. And this, their only obligation.

They took to the floor. They shook down dust from the shingles.

SILENT TOGETHER, they lay spent and slippery in the heat.

Above their breathing came footsteps on the gallery walk. They watched the shuttered window, she beside him on the planks, on the rumpled blanket they'd pulled down. Even the shadows seemed thin and bright. But it was quiet. It was quiet.

They heard the steps departing.

She put her palm against his skin. Some sorrow or release had moved him.

"Shhh," she said, and rose to straddle him, to hold his face until he pulled her down against him. She felt the shaking of his chest. His teeth against her hair.

They lay, with no words, no awareness of time. She thought of the yellow slopes outside, dark cypress trees standing in their own pooled shadows, evenly spaced, like gumdrops, like topiary pawns.

AT LAST he said, "I'll take you with me, Lucy. We'll take the girls, he has no claim on them."

She was quiet a long time, imagining such a life for daughters. What life? The little ones, of course, could not be hers; Israel would not allow it. No one could allow it, and she could not be fugitive with children. But could go alone.

The children would grow up, after all. Very soon. And what she did might be done by death at any moment. The world was filled with children who survived without their mothers. They would survive. As she would without this man.

Who needed most?

She lay, spun out lives for herself, one after the other. Each one wrong.

He sat. His back was to her. She lay her cheek against it.

───────

THEY JOINED AGAIN, gently. She memorized his eyes, his chest, the lines of his flanks. She could see the place between them where they met. She had seen it only once before, a long time ago.

And for the first time, she felt that nothing in her life was so likely permanent as this—it was not lust nor even love but the truest act of creation, their bodies by some will of God or nature that day joining. As though they had been meant to make a child. A child, perhaps, a drop in the pond to ripple unnumbered years, a child perhaps whose seed might go a hundred generations, a thousand, unbroken, into a future unimaginable by them. Generations, generations of children, men and women, all sparked from this one act. Her womb, his loins. It was possible.

And for all her fears of what could happen, she had never seen, until that moment, this most obvious and miraculous of things: that she was here. Alive. Existing now because, since first creation, there had been such lines, unbroken. Children all surviving. Men and women.

He put his hands beneath her, brought her higher, found the very center.

She held his arms. She saw their ancestors, his and hers: the cobbled streets, gutters of filth and vermin, stone cottages with candlefish for light. Mercenaries shipped to fight and lie in the rain on battlefields. Mothers fevering in childbed.

Life is not a revel.

But that she had come to join with him, think! How unlikely. What revelation. Against such odds, what gift of hope. That God might take some lives before their time, but granted more unlooked for, so that the story of mankind might weigh in favor not of tragedy but promise.

To ward against death.

She pressed her fingers to that mark, she breathed her love for him.

What they did as Man and Woman, this was the only defense. This life, her life—this act. Not sordid lust nor defiance but sacred union, which in this moment, in their quickness and completion, was spangled with the light of miracle.

This she would keep. A stolen child. It had to be.

He kissed her eyes. He kissed her lips.

She said, "Do you love me?"

He could never say it. She knew, though, that he might.

They lay twined after that. The air was close and hot. Strands of her hair stuck to his shoulder. She closed her eyes and fell away.

———

SHE JERKED AWAKE and stood. The sun had moved.

His eyes were open. She saw them sharpen, saw his body chinked with lines of light that filtered through the roof.

She pulled on her stockings, unsteady.

He dressed, then stood with her. He held her hands. She heard him breathing.

She said, "He means to lay over for the winter, with the Whitmans. At the mission there. He rode ahead today to post a request."

"The Whitmans?"

"Why?" she asked. "Do you know of them?"

The time was beating in her veins.

He unbolted the door at last and looked outside. She stuck the pins into her hair, then remembered the parcel she'd been carrying.

"All right," he said, and let her go. And then the door was shut behind her.

She went down the main steps alone, into the dusty compound. A clay well stood there with a bucket and dipper. She stopped, and cooled her face, and drank.

"Lucy."

She started at the voice so that she dropped the ladle from her lips—it fell and glanced the pail beside her. She turned and looked at him.

Those round eyes, their tidy hooded lids. The angled beard.

"Israel."

When he turned, she followed. She walked away from there, behind him. The grass passed under his shadow. Each step was strange to her, each step a moment in which she might stop and speak, in which she might turn back, each step, each moment delayed until the next, so that she must, to some observer, have appeared to be a woman, walking.

Part Three

Love is hotter than anywhere I have known it. When they love here they love with all their mite & sometimes a little bit harder.

—JOHN LEWIS,
Oregon immigrant

STONES INTO DUST

⚬⌒⌒⚬

"WERE YOU WITH HIM?"

He had stopped, as she followed, and turned. She gave no answer.

He set away again, but the sand had slowed them, like the thickened air in dreams. They walked in silence. She didn't bother to keep up.

Again he stopped and turned to her. She could see his sweat. He waited in the dirt, under that smoldering sky, the wagons not far distant among shimmering cottonwoods.

She arrived and stopped and took his eyes steadily.

He raised an awkward hand, then, as though under some command to strike her, as though the situation required this response, none other. She held his eyes.

How unfairly she despised him.

He stepped and she shied, but not enough.

———

THE SKIN of her cheek still stung as she followed him into camp, as he clapped his offending hands. "Gather up," he shouted. "Gather up, we're going."

Half dreaming, she did her part, wondering what the girls must think, but they'd set to it, and she was dank beneath her drawers, beyond offense. Empty ash pits and flattened grass of vanished tents stood mingled with the ones yet occupied. She noted, for the first time, the dissolution of their company.

She tied on her apron. Her hands had cracked and were seeping. Dirty plates, cold kettles, she jumbled them into the box together. The tent knocked down and folded—she drifted to it, familiar in the motions—he on one end (shaking, sweeping, folding neatly), she on the other. They lifted the hateful weight and stowed it while their neighbors watched across the rims of cups. He went with Littlejohn for oxen. Lucy found a bait of rice and caught the ugly mare, scrubbed off the clotted sweat while she flinched and struck, and adequately saddled her.

ISRAEL CHOSE a solitary place that evening: a brushy draw near sulfur springs. The girls balked at this. They turned, protesting like unpenned sheep, voices high and worried. Here were ridges and sand, jumbled stones the size of houses.

"Look around," he said. "What do you think we have anymore that the Indians would want to steal?"

She cooked and served, moving her daughters by commands of single words. He scowled at the pages of his book, shouted silence to Mr. Littlejohn on his mouth harp. They took their places at the fire.

"I am going to tell you something," he said to her daughters when they had quieted for grace. "I want you to listen."

Side by side on boxes in the orange light, heads bowed to bowls of beans, they looked up and listened. The air was full and ominous.

"When your mother left you this morning, she'd not been planning to return."

Their eyes fixed on her. Her skin burned with the violence of it. She would not bear to see them change.

"Israel, that is a lie."

Daniel frowned up at her, not understanding.

She said, "There's no cause for you to tell them lies. I would never leave you girls, not any of you children. You know that I would *never*."

"Then tell them where I found you."

Silent, she saw wool and fur, the beauty of that shuttered light. Her skin. His release. If they could know those hours. The selfishness and sacrifice. She took a breath to begin. To make them understand.

And then said, "I was talking. I'm sorry you were waiting."

They were looking at the ground, having drawn away, and she from them, a moment before the certain injury of truth.

"Tell them who was with you."

"Israel."

Emma Ruth put her hands against her ears.

"Tell them in whose bed."

She would not have this lie. The bowl overturned.

"*Tell them in whose bed!*" The words followed her into the stones.

AMONG THE ROCKS she found a crevice in which to hide, and loosed herself there, undignified in grief against the sounds from camp, of tinware, the clatter of pots being washed, and then heard Mary crying, her baby crying. She stayed and buried her ears.

She stayed up there. In dark hours, closed her eyes, summoning her children, needing their faces and the strength of their need as she had felt it in her blood and heart that morning, when she'd known she could never leave them. But now they came to her no better than flat shadows, the merest ideas of children, who turned away or slept or quarrelled, and whatever love had stirred her to this end, she could find it nowhere in the darkness, so it seemed that she could leave them as easily as shutting a poor book, with as little recall, and all she saw was his face. And knew that if she woke beside him that next morning, she would have the life she needed.

By midnight she was resolved. No one was awake. She brought the Bannock mare from her picket by the stream, and tied her to the wagon. She found the blanket and the saddle, carried them, laid them gently on. She was only arms and hands and legs, drained of anything but motion.

She tightened the girth. Carefully quieted the jingling bit. But when she raised the bridle, the mare abruptly shied, swung, shoved her against the wagon in a rankness of old sweat, stuttering hooves, and dust. Lucy ducked free somehow, in the thick of it, and stood, unhurt, heart pounding.

"Mama?"

It was Daniel's waking cry.

"Mama? Mama!"

SHE WOKE with her boy still in her arms, and went out to find the bellies of the clouds a flawless pink.

Mr. Littlejohn snored. The girls still slept. Israel was awake and moving in his tent. She freed the goats to graze, got soap and hairbrush from the wagon, took the pail.

The springs of this place trailed off to a shallow creek. She skirted the verge of marsh grass, crossed black water silvered with oil. Climbed a low spur and descended, pushing through the waxy limbs of willow. On her heels beside the bank, she reached past slow manes of algae, drowned leaves, and drank.

She wet her face, wishing the water were cooler. Cupped it to her eyes, remembering this from Luther's death—the poison of grief, its dreamy soporific. Mosquitoes whined around her.

She soaked the brush, let down her hair, and swept it. *My poor hair*, she'd said to him. *My poor hair*, and saw them together in that room.

How many times would she live each moment of those hours?

She pulled until her ears stood bare, braiding, twisting, driving pins with more force than was her practice. Fresh air cooled her neck. For her children, she would be correct. She would make things as they were.

She lingered at the bog edge until Israel set off to find the oxen. Then she strode into camp. Daniel, in boots and nightshirt, stood and said, "Why you came back?"

She lifted him, smoothed his hair. He wrapped his legs around her waist, pressed his hand against her cheek. She saw his eyes: blue irises ringed with deeper blue. So are innocents empowered to divine.

"I'm finished washing. Who is getting wood?"

He said, "Mary's awake. She stinks."

He followed her to the tent and watched while she brought Mary out and stripped her, bundled the reeking clothes, worried how the red skin flaked and cracked with no salve now, no grease, not even milk since the goats had dried up. She popped a clean frock on and buttoned it. Daniel clambered on the bedding.

"No, not in your shoes!" she said. As though it were an ordinary day.

LUCY WAS DESPAIRING over breakfast when Caroline said, "Shit."

She looked up. No child of hers had ever said that word. At least not in her hearing. But Caroline was turning, pulling her skirt to see the back. All but their Sunday dresses were worn to gauze. She had torn this one, it seemed. The petticoat showed through.

Lucy said, "Just wear it back to front. Keep your apron on." Each word felt costly, as though spoken out of illness.

Caroline brushed dust from her sleeves, saying nothing.

Lucy poured dry peas into an empty pot and stirred for stones. They had not much else, and peas would take too long to cook. Mary wobbled against her dress, grabbed the pot rim, reaching. Reaching, reaching. Lucy gave her a spoon.

"Sarah, light the fire."

Silence.

Emma Ruth led in the Bannock mare, who eyed them, low-slung and baleful. Peg growled as a formality. The old dog had become a terrible thing, dull fur and architecture, the back of her tail raw from some disease. It seemed whole lifetimes ago that she and Luther had nuzzled the round pink belly of the pup he'd brought her. Before real babies came.

The backs of her hands were seeping. She said, "Good morning, Emma."

"Morning, Mama."

"Well, one of you will speak a civil word. Sarah Ann?"

Sarah Ann was fooling with her hair. She'd not found the matches.

"Sarah Ann."

The sullen glare. He had written it large, she thought. Israel had written it very large, and this would be her punishment.

"I am still your mother."

"Just leave us alone, Mama."

"When the fire's lit, I shall."

But Sarah was already gliding off through low gray sage, and Lucy tipped the baby in her haste and strode, stretching across the empty space between them. Her hand ran out and caught her daughter's arm and jerked and turned her, but a woman's face came twisting, arm swinging, and Lucy's swung, too. They batted, close as angry geese, until Sarah backed and ran.

"I hate this place!" She fled into the lumps of stone. "I *hate* this place!"

Mary, in the following quiet, howled. Lucy pressed her palms together and turned to find the matches.

———

HE'D LAIN most of one day out somewhere on the desert floor. Three days ago, or four. Stood in the night and walked again, not half a mile before he found his packs where they'd fallen, and some water in them, and from there had walked a day and spent the following inside a room in bed. Coming out that next morning, his head had still been ringing from the fever, but he'd forgotten it all the moment he'd seen her in the doorway.

Now he crossed the river in morning dark. He rode as breaking dawn slid down the hills, slowly over scrub and stones, brown grass, until a thousand bushes stood all crowned in angled gold and the world was reaching shadows, swaths of light.

He had closed the door behind her. Gone down to supper that night before, only smiling, taking jibes, nodding at puns and clever allusions by men he knew or didn't know, with boils on their necks, fingers missing, canted eyes from too much drink or sun or lonely brawling. He was a man like these, he'd thought, or had been that night, his eyes still burning fever.

He bit the flaking skin, now, from his lips.

And he wished she hadn't gone, but in the light of this dawn, he did feel the kind of peace he'd heard of only in men who claimed they were redeemed. But his hair was shorn and would not hold a feather.

She'd always chosen right, he thought. As true as any compass. He would keep that with him.

———

HE RODE a day and then another, through the gates of narrow canyons and into an earlier life, curing meadow grass, trenched valleys, the river flat and winding. He knew this country well.

It took him over half a day to find the place. The wagon had been robbed and burned, the metal taken. Chunks of cinder marked where it had been. He found the skulls and scattered bones of oxen. The woman's grave was marked by a tilting plank, her name scratched on it. He made a camp, then climbed into the rocks to look for the bones of the mad emigrant and his two daughters.

He cast around where he thought they'd been. Then made wider circles. He found one finger bone. Then more. A leg bone, chewed by rabbits. The father's jaw. Then found a child's skull, clean but for the dried-up lump of brain inside it.

He kept looking until dark, putting bones into a sack he'd brought, until he'd filled it. Then emptied those in a pile on the sand, filled the sack again: ribs, a piece of curving vertebra still stiff with meat, clavicles, long pipe bones of feet, until he couldn't see and stooped at every stone or bleached-out twig that seemed to glow against the ground. When he'd done that much, he carried it all down and made a fire near a tall yellow rock.

He had asked John Grant their names before he left. They were on a paper, but he didn't need it. By lantern's light, with punch and mallet, he drove by memory deep into that soft stone their names to stand until they wore away.

Robeson

John

Alice

Loving

Zeal

1846

He ate a little. Then took the small spade from his pack and started digging. A low wind had begun to moan along the valley, and carried off the soil he moved. Stones rang as he struck them. The dust and sand blew off in ribbons, in pale streamers from the blade. It scoured free and hissed out through the heaving sage.

———

That evening the wind came up. Lucy had followed the wagons into a camp of rack-boned animals, tattered tilts, and argument, and knew they'd found some neighbors.

Water trickled in a rocky ravine. Sheets of fine dust swirled with leaves. She made what she could of supper, fed the children in the wagon. And meant to make her bed in the wagon with her little ones, but Israel had pitched the tent and said her place would be with him.

She obeyed. They lay, listening to the wind, the low roar of sage. The canvas swelled and eased.

Israel's hand moved under the blankets, came to rest on her hip. She lay very still.

She wondered, What does he wish? While she lay wishing for James MacLaren, whose bones and breath she loved. With whom, on a night like this, she might burrow close and feel defended. Wind shrilled strange chords through the tent strings.

He said, "Seems like you're free enough with others."

She said there had been nothing free about it.

The tent flopped and swayed on its pins.

He said, "Well, there's nothing free here, either. So get out."

She lay, unbelieving.

He said, "Go out of my bed."

He made no move to help as she stood and claimed a blanket. The goose down was all one piece, and he was on it. Well, she would find something, and sleep beside her little ones, in this new life. Downy hair and sour-sweet reek would justify enough.

"If I find you with the children, we'll leave you in the dirt," he said.

She went through the doorway on her knees, dragging the lone blanket.

And so are our true natures revealed, she thought.

———

SHE MADE her bed like Mr. Littlejohn, in the poor shelter of the wagon, and listened to the wind hiss through the sage. The air was warm and heavy, it sighed and ceased like some great ghostly breathing. She covered her head, and the world was dark and desolate and filled with dust.

She slept uneasily, and when she woke, the wind was stronger. She heard the clatter of a falling pail, a laundry tub overturning. The goats bleated. The wind came from the west now, low-pitched and scouring, driving little stones like hail. In dust and starlight she sat, and her blanket lifted and tumbled off. She reached but missed, had to jump and catch it, drag it back, battle it down around her like some live thing. She huddled, watching the still form of Mr. Littlejohn, and saw no way to sleep.

She crawled from under the wagon and stood, turning, the blanket wrapping her like a shroud, and walked until she found shelter among some boulders.

Curled there, she worried for the children, and worry bled into dreams of floods and falling timber.

When she woke again, the night was brighter, full of sound. She could see things lift and move. Pails tumbled, porringers rolled, saddle blankets dragged as though pulled invisibly, lopping; a flight of clothing tumbled past. Canvas tilts popped and shuddered on their wagon bows like rattling mill wheels. She heard men's voices, saw them move like ghosts in their gray drawers, heard Israel's voice against the roll of iron wheels, the rattle of chains. Tents were pulling free to flop and flounder like sea things, dragged across the writhing sage.

How strong could wind blow? Yet it strengthened. The bells rang on the oxen. Something rolled over her, hissing like a snake, and she jumped, flinging, snatching the rattle pods where they'd caught in her hair. In fear for her children, she began to walk back, but the sand and stones were too much. She took shelter again, gripping her blanket tight around her. She heard cattle moving.

Please stop, please stop.

She turned again, ankles stung by gravel, and the blanket lifted on dark wings and sailed away.

She found their wagons in a line of half a dozen, chained together. She called for the goats but could see nothing.

Inside the wagon, it was blacker still, but its shelter seemed such a relief, even with the creaking wood, the furious racket of the canvas. Blind and deaf, she ran her hands along the edges and lumps of things, found wood and cloth. No one heard her voice or answered. She sat down in the center well, closed her eyes, and slept while the wagon rocked.

When she woke, the wind still blew, but it was bright, and she set out, not aware that she was dreaming.

She saw a huddle of figures in bright ball gowns, far away, and came on them, and found women who knelt in the wind pounding rocks into meal. She asked for water. They gave her a bowl, and drinking, she saw that it was blood. They said, *Live with us.* Their skin was dark from sun. Some had no teeth.

She forgot her children.

She lived with the women, pounded stones to dust, and this sustained them. When one was thirsty, another cut her hand and filled a bowl for the first. They lived this way, drawing thin and corpselike, and the sun never moved. Their teeth fell out. They kept them, rattling in their pockets like shells. Their hair blew away in clots.

One by one the others disappeared. Their going was a great mystery. At last she found herself alone. She drew her own blood and raised the bowl, weeping, and in the surface saw reflected not the face she knew but the white-toothed grin of a wolf.

HOME

When he woke, the wind had stopped. A comforting weight was at his back, as though someone slept beside him. But when he stood, he found it was only drifted dirt, that he'd been lying half buried beside the grave of bones. When he stood, fine sand poured from his blanket. When he emptied his boots, dust trickled from his coat sleeves. He shook and beat himself, scratched it from his scalp, and while the sand fell free, he thought again of Lucy Mitchell's scissors.

Two days' ride brought him almost to the Quartier, and the first sign he saw was Noonday's lodge, set out alone on a bend in the river. He knew her old construction well: the frame's upper part stood covered in old sheeting. The lower part was cattail mats, held on by a crazywork of leaning sticks, the front walls thrown back to catch the breeze.

He took his horses to the stream, and loosed their girths, and hobbled them. From where he stood, he could see her sitting up there in the shade of her lodge. She'd cropped her white hair. She wore a dirty blanket on her shoulders. He climbed the bank and stood beside the bare poles, but she didn't seem to see him.

"Noonday, do you know me?" He called her this, the name his children used. She had another name, but they'd forgotten.

"E-he," she said. "I know him."

Her face had fallen long ago with wrinkles; they spread out from her eyes, and her nose was soft and withered, almost pendant. But her skin was newly scarred.

He sat on his heels. He'd often seen his children in this lodge. She had held his boy and crooned his name, running her blunt fingers through his hair. *Lek-stam, Alek-stam,* over and over, while the girls sat on blankets and played with her old buckskin dolls, with tiny baskets she had woven as a girl. And he knew the year must have changed him, because something stirred in him at the sight of her; he had the idea to embrace her but knew she wouldn't like it. He might have asked a hundred things, but he'd forgotten what they were.

She had a crusted bowl of flour gruel beside her; the flies were hopping on it. The fire was cold, and there was no wood inside the door. Her pots lay in the dust. He stood, walked out until he found some sticks and twigs, and brought them back and lit them. Then went to get his kettle and tea, and water from the creek, and returned to sit across from her.

She was from Asotin. Her English was about as good as his Nez Perce.

He said, "You had the breaking out."

"I had, *e-he.* He cook up my eyes in that big pot. I saw him. *E-kce-ne.*"

"Who cares for you? Georgie? Or old Gregoire? Does old Gregoire feed you?"

To that, she snapped her gums, and snorted like a sheep, and gave out nothing.

"Have you food enough?" He pushed some stones toward the flames and balanced his kettle to boil.

"How long," she said, "since you go away from here?"

He said, "About a year now."

The fire burned. Finally she said, "Well, them Blackfeet got all them gun."

"Do the Blackfeet come here, Noonday?"

"Long time ago," she said. "Because they got they all them gun. My father, his three brother dying from that thing. So our people know they got to have them gun the same. All the woman cutting off she hairs from that thing. Go to get them buffalo."

"Your uncles were killed getting buffalo. That was long ago."

"So why we want them gun same way. Why all them horse we give to him, he want, them redcoat men. *E-he.* All them beaver. My grandfather had a pretty wife."

In the folded shadows of her eyes, in the boiled-up remnants of her eyes, there was no creek, he knew, no longer any sky or fire, no slanted poles, no horses grazing. She'd been keen-minded when he left. Now the men she talked about were dead for half a century or more. The war with Blackfeet, the first traders with their guns, that was long ago. She sat in silence while he took the kettle off and put tea in to steep.

He said, "Noonday, do you know where is my wife? Is Lise in Quartier?"

"*E-he*. All sick."

He found his cup for her, and poured in tea and sugar in almost equal parts. He sat on his heels beside her, took her hands. His own were clammy. She raised the tea and smelled it.

"Was she sick here?"

"*E-he*. That yellowhair take them came-away horse. Stealing all them horse."

"Noonday, did she die here?"

"All the people is sick this time. All sick, forget it." The tea was still too hot. She dipped her finger and tasted it. "So we are asking him *soyapu* for that cross-stick god. All that good power for them guns. God so big, to go with guns." Her old hands wavered. She brought the bowl to her lips and sipped.

"Did someone go, then? To the mission? Were they going for a Black-robe?"

"*We-tu*. Wrong story. She walk away to find you. Find where is her chil-drens."

Sitting with his steaming nog, he saw the beaver's onyx eye had fallen out. He trailed a finger in the dirt to see if he could find it.

"Mak-calay you got some sugar more?"

He got her some.

"I come this place to die. But you cook now. Feed her good this day."

———

THE NEXT DAY he gathered her few things, wrapped the robes and some mats, and put it atop the load his mule was carrying. He set her up on Junie's roan. They left the lodge poles standing bare on the creek's bend, and he led her on that horse into the village of Quartier.

It was more desolate than he remembered. He saw the pounded dirt, the malingering dogs and dozing ponies, the detritus of bones and dragged-off blankets, ruined buckets, hides stretched up to dry. The seams of Weeks' lodge were falling into rot. Noonday's daughter Georgie was dead. Georgie's husband, old Gregoire, was out somewhere. Moise Kochem was gone, and Coos, who used to trap with them. He found Marie, Moise Kochem's wife, but she'd grown dark and hard, like something left buried in hot sand; he scarcely knew her. Some of her teeth were gone. He didn't want to ask about the children, though she was holding one who had been born the spring before.

He said, "Noonday wants me to take her home."

Marie looked away and said she'd tell Gregoire.

After that, he found John Baikie the Orkneyman rubbing down a piece of bull hide. Old Baikie with his face like dried cod, his wild gray hair—he never stopped working but talked through his pipe now. Lost his second wife that winter, he said. Lost his boy Tom. MacLaren had trapped with Tom the winter before last, the first the boy was old enough. He'd been a good tall boy.

He stood and listened to this hard news, the two of them on that glaring clay, strewn dung, offscourings of the dead. Both knowing the horror of that disease.

"Did Lise come through all right?" MacLaren asked at last.

Because of him, she'd brought the sickness down to them, and now everything was changed.

Baikie said, "If living's all right."

They had been friends, he and John. They'd argued a hundred nights by firelight over the heights of ranges, over Shakespeare's plays, the qualities of dogs. He said, "I mean to find her."

"Well, be away then."

THEY RODE until the valley closed into mountains. He'd taken an old saddle from the village and laced the stirrups short. Noonday rode it, a bobbing white-haired gnome.

It rained one day, and he could feel summer ending. They climbed through forest, dense, damp, the horses' hooves punching through red needles to the winter black. A dead underworld lit by fungus, bright boletes and coral, sulfur-colored slime. Silent but for the chitter of squirrels, the clack of hooves against half-buried rock. He rode, head down, one hand held out to break the way through brittle underlimbs, the bitter dust of old fir bark. Noonday put her head to Sally's mane and kept it there. Halfway up the final pass, night overtook them, and he halted on steep ground beside a spring, made a fire and some food, and the sweating horses staled and cooled and stood around them, chewing dry needles until their mouths foamed brown.

The next day they climbed to the forest edge and then, as though passing through a curtain, came out into the light, a wide valley surrounded by taller peaks. He drew his old horse up and looked across it. This place, his place, to which his soul had kept returning.

He crossed thin mossy ground along the meadow's edge, then rode into the sun. Rich grass swept his stirrups, and the hungry horses nodded, nipping seedheads as they walked. A breeze ran through the knoll of pines. He reined in under their shade and halted, looking up through the limbs, recalling how he'd promised his children this place, with trees to climb, a place to make play lodges.

A jay swooped over, and the old woman raised her head to listen.

Lis-pat, Noonday had called his girl. T'soonie, Lispat, Alekstam. In Quartier, she had set tasks for them. Made them bathe in the cold creek each morning, made them run up the dirt hill without stopping, to get strong. Made them go at night to find their animal helpers. Things Lise had never learned, or had forgotten, or was ashamed of.

"All right," he said to her. "We're home."

The old woman sniffed the air.

They came out of the trees, and a band of deer started and wheeled from the place where the cabin had stood. They splashed down through the creek and started up the far bank again, and when they paused among the aspens, he fired on a yearling doe and saw her fall.

He made camp on the grassy level near the mound of clay and sticks that had been his chimney. He took down Noonday and his packs, set the horses grazing. Bled the doe and brought her back. Cut the hams away to hang, and carried them to the smokehouse.

He pushed the door open into gloom, saw the dusty floor, a pale fringe of grass. Wasps droned in the rafters. He went out to the old woodpile and gathered a mess of chips and grass and brought it back and made a smoky fire to drive them out, and it was not until he'd stood from that, and closed the squealing door, that the sense of where he was at last came to him.

"How long Mak-calay you stay this place," the old woman barked out.

The smoke was seeping from under the door to curl around his feet.

"I don't know."

He walked through the grass for stray chunks of wood and carried them back. He got out his ax and built the supper fire.

While he worked, she started telling him in her own tongue that it was bad, a bad home, this place. There was something wrong with him to want a place like this. Something wrong with all *suyapo*, wandering like ghosts, everywhere and nowhere. She rocked in the grass.

He was stringing the tender backstrap onto long pine splints. As she spoke, he looked across the green valley with its aspen and stream, its bands of elk, a sky like heaven's belly, mountains all around. Someplace clean was all he'd ever wanted. He said, "I have two children buried over there."

"*E-he*, I know them."

She was leaving her daughter's bones in Quartier, but that was different. Georgie had been grown.

He watched the flames creep and the smoke roil up. The sun stood just above the slopes, and he was hungry, so he stood the splints across the flames, not waiting for embers. Her voice spilled out and crackled like fat on the fire. A home was not something a person chose, she said. It was given. Born to you like eyes, like feet. It cannot be changed. A person cannot take the eyes of some animal he liked or the feet of some animal he liked and make them his. This is a no place, she said. It belongs to itself. It has no stories. For home, each part is like a body, each bend and crossing and hill is a place on the body, with heart, with legs, each place has a name and a story, each place has a name for something that happened in old time, and in that name and story is the people's greatness and proof of their favor in creation.

A home has people, she said. How can you know what is the best path alone? Without the words of old people, without the words of friends who knew the first name you were called, know the things you have done; how can you understand the right way? To marry? To fight? To mourn? How can one person sing or dance or fight? If your heart is bad, how can it be fixed, how can you ask for punishment, if no one knows your story? If no one saw the bad things you have done? If you go always among strangers, how can you be good? Without bones, without songs, without strength, you are a shadow who wanders, dangerous to others, not long in the world.

He was watching the warming meat, how the smoke and heat bleached it gray.

Beside him, she let out a shrill call, a long turkey cry. It raised his flesh. He said, "What was that for?" Although he was used to these people, or had been. How bent they were, how unpredictable.

She wouldn't answer.

But what if a home was taken, he wondered. All the better places claimed by those with power? What if your own people had hoped you would avoid the misfortune of living there, then what? What had he been born to? Cold crofts, pinched stony fields for which more rent was due than could be raised. Rain, rot, drink, salt gales. The English riding down. It was nothing to him, where he was born.

Here, he'd had a house and barn and copse of pines. Horses and dogs and a family. He said, "A family is people enough for anyone. You can go see people anytime you want, and not have to live on top of them."

The meat was a murky brown on one side now, half raw on the other. Out in the field, Sally turned, untangling her line.

Noonday held out her hand at him, and he thought she was asking for meat, but she said to him in English, "What is this?"

"What is what?"

"I have hold."

"Nothing." He looked at her old hand, cupped and dark as a beaver's paw.

"I tell you some thing in that hand, you say no."

"No, there's nothing in it."

"Why you think is this a home. Same thing. I say no."

He ate, then was restless and walked around the place.

He found the graves under tall grass—the sod he'd lain had taken root. Alexander, Elizabeth. All spring, all summer, in the earth alone under roots of grass, the hooves of browsing deer. He thought he ought to make his bed beside them, although his children were nothing, he knew, but black meat and bones, like any dead thing. They were gone. But he went anyway, and dragged his bed, and lay as awkward as a suitor, in the grass.

Even there he couldn't sleep, but lay for hours. He saw himself building the burned cabin new. Fencing graves, bringing Junie so they could all lie here together.

He had believed that force of will could make this place a home. Now he thought of Lise's empty face when she had seen it. His children here, abandoned. How he'd lain on the floor of a room last week with Lucy Mitchell in his arms, light blazing through the shingles. Believing in that hour that love was all it took to anchor you in the world.

Every time he thought he understood a thing, it changed.

How We Learn to Leave

*I*SRAEL CALLED HALT ONE MIDDAY as they traveled alone. A broad stream cut deeply through the plain; the water roared over rubble and boulders. There seemed no way to cross directly.

She found dinner. Israel, without a word, had walked up the trail that turned along the banks. His plate was ready, she had nothing to cook: cold pease, dried buffalo, hard crackers. She beat the pail and called, beat and called, but he never came, and when she'd eaten her own few bites, she walked out looking.

She found him up the river, standing beside what looked to be a frail corral in miniature. Gnarled staves tilted crazily in a circle. Low brown figures moved inside it. The air brought a smell of carrion. She went to stand beside him.

The staves enclosed the unearthed body of a man, his cropped white hair embedded with dust, and the motion she had seen was that of half a dozen feeding vultures. They flopped across the corpse, ducked to probe it, pushed red naked heads far into the rents they'd pecked in the baked and dusty skin. One pair hopped and tussled in a gruesome dance among the strewn entrails.

It was the driver Velasquez.

She stared. Israel took his plate from her and turned away.

———

THEY RAN UP the stream all afternoon and made a rocky crossing. Starting down the other bank, they sprang a wheel rim on the big wagon and ran badly for a time, until the Whites came on them. They had a bar, and helped to pry it on, and wound rope around so it would stay. Tom Willis and his wife caught up as they were getting under way again. They all walked together, and no one spoke to her but Mary, in her arms, who was learning to say Cow. Hat. Sun. Shoes.

The camp they made was no different from any ground they'd seen that day—sage and tufting grass, the creek rushing in its deep ravine. Mr. Littlejohn made their fire against a low outcrop of rock, and Lucy set the girls to supper. They'd heard some news from up the line: Hill had killed Velasquez in some altercation, perhaps at cards; that he had taken Richard Tony's horse and made off bareback, and not been seen since.

But Lucy had no time to think of this, with the baby crying. She had only a cold spoonful of pease on hand to soothe her, but Mary pushed it away. Lucy left her in Sarah's care, helped Israel and Mr. Littlejohn to get the big wagon blocked and the wheel off. All evening she went from fire to children to Israel's demands for help—to hold or lift or pull or hand him something. Together, they rolled the great wheel down the cobbled bank, to soak and swell in the stream. But when she thought he was done at last, he started on the other side, the wagon balanced up on planks and borrowed jacks, the daylight nearly gone, his supper on a plate in the dirt beside him. The little ones were tired, and she not able to put them in their beds, and now he'd tallowed the axles with her last candles, for want of other grease. When he asked again for help, she refused. "No," she said, "I'm done."

He turned and looked at her and said, "By God, woman."

She turned away with Mary fussing in her arms.

He said, "If not for me, these wagons would be in pieces."

The words sank slowly down. *If not for me.* She was a woman covered in dirt and grease and rust. Her feet were wet. She closed her eyes and turned and said, "Do you want my *gratitude?*"

"Yes!"

"For what? For forcing us to leave our home?"

"God *damn* your home! I could leave you in this camp tomorrow morning, Lucy, do you know that? No one passing for a month would take you in. Knowing what you've done. They know, and if they don't, they'll hear it soon enough."

He glared across this space, and she glared back. She hated his eyes, his beard, the neat chain that kept his watch, felt the hate she'd always been too reasonable to feel, and now she did not fear. "Who knows?" she said. "What do they know?"

The girls had learned to disappear.

She said, "Do they know what I know? That all this journey you did nothing but trot ahead on a pretty mare all day, enjoying the scenery? That all you ever did at night was go from one camp to another, sit around smoking cigars and talking, lest anyone forget how much you know? Sit reading found magazines while a better man did that work you're claiming, and never asked for help?"

Her hate made it true, and she knew with fresh pain, remembered: *he* had kept these wagons good. James MacLaren had watched and known and taken care of all of them. It was true. It was true.

Israel wheeled away.

She walked back to the fire. The goats had blown out of camp that night of the wind, disappeared as completely as if they'd walked into her strange dream. Everyone had searched to no avail. Now, instead of their friendly begging, a flock of crows had come to light. Perched on the outcrop above the fire, they stepped and hunched their shoulders, assessing her poor remains of peas and rice and sour meal. Waiting.

She plopped Mary in the dirt, took up the skillet, and lunged at them, sweeping two-handed, as though it were a broadsword. The crows lit and stroked away, jeered beyond her reach. Mary bawled. Across the camp, Mrs. White shouted, "Insolent Nigra bitch. Liar. Keep out of my kitchen. Keep out."

All the things that had been weak were breaking.

Lucy made the children's beds outside, washed their feet and faces, tucked them in to sleep. Then put her irons on to heat, with the clothes from last night's wash still damp and wrinkled in their tub, and built her little press: a plank across two chair backs.

At last she set to the comforting work. The chairs swayed gently. The damp cloth steamed.

Israel came into the fire's light. Stood near her, watching. Rocking and pressing, she never looked up; the chairs swayed and creaked. She waited, sensing they were at some junction, that they had fractured and could breathe. That if they spoke, they might patch something into working order.

She said nothing. She said nothing.

He kicked the chairs, viciously, and they went over, the shirts and clean linens, press and all. She stepped back, the hot iron in her hand. She looked at him. He stood a moment, then leaned and righted the nearest chair. She righted the other and set the board on top. She shook the dust from the shirts and folded them.

SHE STAYED UP while Israel went to bed, then made her own bed out with the children. She woke slowly, much later, to Mary's wailing.

The child was blazing. She twisted in Lucy's arms, reached, pinching. Half addled from sleep, Lucy feared that she might have failed all day to give her water. Then remembered the cooling creek and bath, tin cups held to lips. She had done all right, as well as any other day.

An owl cried somewhere. The little breath was quick and rasping. Lucy thought of those mining vultures, red naked heads designed by God for worming into bodies.

She remembered poor Velasquez.

Israel, the toppling chairs.

And then Mary seized, right in her arms—her limbs went rigid, curling. Her head rolled back, dead-eyed, a nightmare child. She'd never had a child this hot.

"Israel!" she cried. "*Israel!*"

She watched, helpless, this thing she held that had been her daughter and now was something else, not even human.

"*Israel!*"

Then something was restored. Mary blinked and softened, let out a dry sad wail.

Dusty linen lay tangled at Lucy's feet. She dragged it over to the fire. With Mary in one arm, she stirred the coals, felt in the dark for twigs.

I should have wakened sooner, she thought. I should have known she was so sick. It was only luck they were together; she would never have discovered it most nights.

The kettle was empty, the pails were empty. She found water in the dishpan with a rag, and began to cool her child, who cried and squirmed, tried to push the cloth away, turned to her empty breast for comfort.

"Israel!" She wiped her own eyes. "Israel!" The prairie wolves were howling in the distance. It seemed a long time before he came out in shirt and drawers.

She explained. He rubbed his face. He took the pail and set off toward the water.

She sat waiting, listening to all the sounds of night. Her eyes fell shut. She had a guilty wish to sleep.

He set down the pail when he came back, and handed her a dripping cup.

"She's dry," she said. "She never wet tonight. I did give her water."

They watched her twist away, push the cup, the water spilling. "Her hands are just fire." She stroked the cloth across her little girl's neck, reached under the nightdress to smooth her thin back. It was terrible, to hear that wail.

"It's probably measles," Israel said. "Keep her cool."

"Are you going back to bed?"

"Were you?"

"No, of course not."

"Then I've done what I can do. I'm tired. Wake me if there's something more."

"Israel."

"It's measles, Lucy. There's nothing I can do."

———

SHE DOZED and woke all night, and rode the next day, sitting watch on Mary.

In the heat, she took off her own blouse and pantalettes, as some had begun doing in the privacy of wagons, and sat bare-armed in only skirt, chemise, a dusty corset, looking back at passing scenery. They ran along the rim of a deep gorge, black crumbling basalt, the river running dark and glassy three hundred feet below. Too far down to drink. They saw no sign of game. Israel refused to hunt. Lying on the bed inside the wagon, Lucy found all her wishes bent not toward her daughter's health nor her own restoration nor on some love that only days before she'd imagined was eternal. No. Her dreams were fixed visions of velvet rolls and jam. Cake with butter icing. She'd break a watermelon if she had it, gobble it quick as a duck and polish it to white rind. She was amazed to find that she could run her arm inside her corset, laced as small as it would go; she slid her fingers up the sweaty cave between her ribs, and would have wept for a peach, but she was too dry for weeping.

———

THEY CAME ON a larger part of the main crowd that night: the Appersons, the Olmsteads, Mr. Koonse and his family, and Beagle, all camped along the vast ledge that bordered the Snake River. The girls went glumly somewhere. Israel called Daniel, and they disappeared and came back as she was putting the last cornmeal to boil. She heard Daniel calling, "Mama, I got a fish! I got a fish!"

She stood. He was running ahead of Israel and the girls, or trying to run, with the largest fish she had ever seen. His arms were wrapped around it, its tail flopped between his knees, and he stumbled on the grass.

"I can't do it!" he shouted. "Come get it!" And then dropped it in the dirt.

She walked to meet him, where he hopped and bobbed, his fists balled up, saying, "Come, Mama, come, come, come, I want you to. The *Indians* are *fishing!*" She sat on her heels to admire the dusty slab of its side—he must have dropped it several times already—the tail as large as her hand, the dull eye the size of a penny. Great hooked jaws, cruel barbs of teeth. She could almost cry for delight. Then Israel and the girls had arrived, he with two enormous silvery fish slung behind his shoulders. So she thought she would say no, but Daniel danced and tugged.

"All right, quickly. If Papa keeps the fire. And we'll come back to cook."

A stripe of orange cloud hung in the west. The air was clear as bottle glass.

"Anyone else?" she asked.

Her daughters confirmed her exile. So she set away with her boy, his dirty hand in hers.

She crossed the flat, listening to his chatter, and found some reserve of cheer with which to answer. At the breaks, the walls crumbled into thorny cobbles. He let go of her hand and trotted downward, quick as a goat, and she descended after, warning him of snakes, wishing her girls had come. That she could have a chance to mend things.

She had been foolish. She had been. But no matter what she'd done, there would be something. There would always be a point at which they felt betrayed.

All week she'd thought of what she might say if she were brave enough. If they would listen and possibly understand. Which they could not.

It's the disillusionment of youth, she would say. We all suffer it. Realizing our parents make mistakes. They can sin, they can be every bit as imperfect as a child. And when you see those failings, the love that made you feel so worthy grows tarnished, suspect. And that is when you start to find what strength and goodness is your own, and what is not, and what are your beliefs. And through all, we're still the same, the mother and the child, the same people. It's only part of how we learn to leave each other.

They reached the valley floor, its softer slope of sand. Brush huts stood, and skin huts, and racks of drying fish. Here the river fell through a narrow channel in the bleached basalt. In the dusk, it churned and glowed, and the mist rose from it. Daniel pointed and she saw them, the Indians fishing on the rocks. She slowed, surprised by so many. She'd come only to see. She said, "It's close enough." But Daniel pulled her on.

Soon they were near the spray and the roaring, the smooth white-stained basalt populated with dark children of all ages, dogs, round women. Naked men stepped out with perfect agility, to sweep the leaping salmon from their arcs, and the salmon struck, flipped and bounded on the rocks. Tall children pounced with clubs and knives. Mr. Littlejohn, among them with his crazy laugh, took up a fish by its gills, slapped the round silver back. He admired it from every angle while the littlest children darted back and forth, fingers outstretched in a game of touching him, and wheeled off screaming.

Mr. VanAllman, loaded with fish, nodded curtly to her in passing. Daniel had run right up to a squaw, who stood to touch his golden hair.

"Daniel!"

The woman reached for the smallest in a pile of fish and gave it to him.

"Oh, no," Lucy said. There was nothing she could give, she had no money. She waved her hands, declining.

Daniel raised the fish to show her.

Silent, Lucy untied her apron and came forward to offer it. The woman talked at her approach. Her teeth were very white. Lucy smiled back, thinking of James MacLaren's wife, of Lise, and for the first time she felt nothing strange at all between herself and this small woman (who was not beautiful, whose hair was thick and matted, whose hands and dress were bloody with gutted fish), nothing at all but a kind of gratitude and kinship. The woman admired Daniel's hair, called out, and soon a naked girl of his same age came forth splay-footed, leaning back beneath the weight of a chubby infant. Lucy reached and took the baby up, admiring his fat feet and fingers, when her own child was so frail. She tried to say so, how fine that baby was, how healthy, jogging him on her hip. And sociable, too. He didn't cry when she held him, but looked with perfect composure.

In the failing light, they climbed back out of the canyon with Mr. Little-john, carrying more fish. Fires glowed in all the camps, and theirs glowed brightest. She came and sat. And then she saw the carved pieces of her furniture in flames, and the others he had split and piled, her precious dog-wood. The girls were very quiet.

"We have too much weight," he said. But his voice was thick.

Then she looked at him and saw that he had loved her.

She turned. Some part of her had cleaved away. She covered it with her hands.

She went into the wagon for a while. When she was ready, she came down again; what she brought was also heavy, and it was his. So they stayed up, silent, with Mary flushed and effortful in her cradle, while Lucy cooked the extra fish until it crumbled, tried the oil into bottles, pressed the meat into a sack; while Israel leafed the pages of his books and, one by one, set them gently on the flames.

———

MARY'S EYELIDS had become shiny, thin and membranous like the pale puffed throats of frogs; too still, now, to be dreaming.

On this fourth morning of her illness, Lucy walked and carried her baby across a buckled landscape. She'd fashioned a canteen of string and an old bottle, but by midday it clapped empty at her back. She was so hot she could think of nothing but the relief of shade. The bleached sky stood soiled above their progress like stained linen. They were spread for miles.

Sweat coursed down her unstockinged legs. Sand crept in and slipped out again through broken soles, and walking, looking at her child's pale face, she recalled her grandmother's dread of porcelain-head dolls, and for the first time knew why. It was this waxy pallor, these pegs of peeking teeth.

A panic overtook her. She stretched her strides in the soft sand, faster, with the wagon so far ahead, until the sinews of her legs were burning, until she was close enough to hail. Mr. Littlejohn failed to hear the first time, and the second, until she was beside him, one hand banging on the water barrel's hot staves, its scorching hoops, saying, "Tom, Tom, we must have some water, Mary must have some water this moment, will you halt them, please."

The water, of course, woke Mary. But it seemed that she was failing.

THEY CAMPED at nine o'clock beside a churned-up trickle—the first water they'd seen all day. An ox had died downstream; the air stank and seethed with flies.

Mary was slack. Her head lolled back. A tiny breath whistled in her throat, and Lucy checked her eyes again and worried that her limbs seemed cool.

To Sarah, she said, "You watch her while I work. You sit here, that's your job, do you understand?" And thought she could carry on despite it, but her hands were shaking as she got out the kettle. She could not think about a grave out here.

She thought of James MacLaren, who had lost three children, and when she begged, it was not to God but to this man who might have shown her. *Please, save her. Please, please, give me strength.*

She would have put her face against his shoulder.

It seemed lately she was always crying.

She'd wiped her nose and was warming a slurry of watered fish when she heard Sarah say, "Mama," and such was the tone that Lucy's breath went tight and she fell still as stone, the flies upon her, and then came Israel on some gust of petty tyranny to tell the girls their wagon was a disgrace, that he was going to a great deal of trouble to haul such possessions as they had, and if they could not respect this fact, they'd carry their blankets and walk and sleep outside all night.

ISRAEL TOOK HER to lie inside the tent after that. Ashamed, she was ashamed, she'd broken the handle off the skillet, swept it up in a fit of anguish and brought it down against the kettle, the clanging had set free some cry of whatever had built inside, she'd cried out and there must have been fish spattering down, but she'd heard only the ringing of the iron, she tolled it like a bell, flaming sticks and embers flying from the force, and she cried out and cried, and there had been dusty shoes around her.

And now a dark bed. She had never learned what Sarah meant to say.

———

"MAMA?"

She woke much later in the dark.

"Mama?"

She saw the lone shadow in the doorway of the tent.

Her breath, her hands, conveyed her grief—they must have—but Emma Ruth said, "No, Mary's sleeping, it isn't that. Father has her."

Lucy opened her arm then, as she would those years ago, when her girls came creeping. She'd had to teach them out of it, with Israel.

"Are you sick now?"

"No," Emma said. She was crying. Her girl who seldom cried.

"What's wrong?"

Emma said, "You know when something's on you in a dream and you can't get out and you can't yell."

"All right," she said, "stay with me," though something in her resisted. This child was too big, she had babies enough, there could be no return to snuffling and creeping. She heard her mother say it: *I need strength from you, daughter. I need strength.* But to have this one back in her embrace. How could she not welcome it on any terms? Lucy held her, stroked her hair. Smoothed the tears away.

Emma said, "I wish we never came here."

"You've been happier than any of us."

"Everything I liked is gone."

Lucy held her, silent, in wandering memories of goats and men.

"Mama, am I good?" she heard at last.

"Shh," she said. And then, "Yes, of course. Of course you're good."

Outside, they could hear the Whites' bird dog, its idiot baying.

"He left because I saw. I burned your hands. I didn't mean it."

"You what?"

"That morning the oxen ran off."

A flood of light threw her back to morning, grass, the cove of willows. A sound she'd never made before.

They lay together stiffly, in the bark, bark, barking of the dog.

Lucy said at last, "That isn't why."

"Somebody can do wrong," Emma said, "and still be good."

"Yes."

"I'm afraid for Mary to go."

Lucy nodded.

"Mama?"

"What?"

"I don't want to marry. Or have babies."

"I know," Lucy said. "I expect you'll do it anyway."

AND MARY WAS no worse next morning, but their big ox John wouldn't rise.

The girls ran out with water and a pan of musty peas. When Lucy went to see at last, Emma Ruth was kneeling beside the huge dusty head.

They waited. The girls encouraged him, stroked his flanks. At last he took heart. They watched his cloven hooves gnaw sand, and Israel gathered everyone to crouch and push against the spine until John righted and could rise. They offered peas again and were refused. At last they coaxed him toward the camp, and he followed a step and then folded his knees and sank.

The children cried. There were impassioned pleas. She left them, and by the time the wagons were stowed, the ox had revived enough to yoke, and went slowly all day without failing. But anyone could see his time had come. Things would have to change.

SHE NURSED MARY with sips of molasses water, and that evening they arrived at a crossing of the Snake some hundred rods in width. Thick willow crowded long sandbars in the channel. And she did not begin by making camp, but lay Mary in the shade and called the girls, and together they knocked out the pins, let down the wagon's gate, and began.

They rolled open the Brussels carpet, gathering tobacco leaves as they went. They took out boxes, trunks, bed planks, chairs.

What they chose to leave that evening might never be replaced: Mary Ross's rolling pin, her molds for candles. Spools and chain, shears, the pickling barrel. Without the washboard, their clothes would not come clean. Without irons, they'd be slow to dry, unfit to wear. They were nothing without their pleats and sizing.

Then Israel appeared to oversee it. The scythe, the saw, the ax and maul, the gate latch, the dear crystal candelabra. The Bible, she said, could not be left. There was the wooden sewing box her mother had given her, with painted roses, clever compartments. She took it aside, went through it, discarding scraps and wads of wool the girls had saved, then came to the old sampler folded in the bottom. She smoothed it on her skirt, to say farewell. *Lucy Arnold Sampler.* She was not a child any longer. Of course she was not.

From the button drawer she took James MacLaren's pages, and rolled and hid them neatly in her stockings, the last good silk ones with their pink embroidered blossoms. She had married in those, twice. She kept her scissors and three spools of thread, some needles, a few buttons rolled into the calico she'd carried from Fort Hall, and left the box, the beautiful box, among the other furnishings.

They dined on their good dun ox who'd looked so fine in April, the largest and gentlest of all, who'd let the children ride him around their yard at home when an ox was still a novelty. Now they shared his meat among the families. They'd consumed half a dozen animals already in this way, in portions given out by others.

Mr. Koonse came to thank them for the meat. Caroline and Sarah, on some private whim, had arranged upon the carpet all the articles that Israel intended to abandon, in such a way as to resemble a well-appointed parlor with no walls. Mr. Koonse was amused by this. His wife had been delivered of their latest child sometime the week before, and he held the infant bundled in one arm. Lucy watched this, envying his wife. No man she'd known had ever cared to hold a baby. He dragged a chair to the fire and sat talking to Israel about the crossing. There were deeps between the islands, he said.

The laden wagons might capsize. He thought they ought to put a ferry on the narrows above. Something safe, he said, for the wives and children.

Lucy sat, spooning Mary a little marrow tea, and listened, watching while he held the child, while he smiled gently, while he nodded his neat square head as though no hardship were in any of it. He shrugged at this worry and that. But even the Koonses had grown wary of her. She'd become some other kind of creature, dangerous, and allied with something else. Of all her dreams, that one, at least, had truth.

It seemed the unaccustomed meal had poisoned her; she shut her eyes and ached.

"Where dorse my bed be now?" Daniel whispered up from beside her elbow.

"Beside your papa in the tent," she murmured. "It's all made there."

"Why orn't *you're* sleeping in the tent?"

"I don't want you catching measles," she said. "I don't think I can manage it."

"I want to sleep with you."

While she bedded Daniel down, the men rolled their empty wagon out of camp, piled it with cut sagebrush, set it alight. She stepped out to see the smoke and flames roil up. It drew people, the young still awake, drivers, and others. They gathered like moths as flames licked high and peeled away and sparks flew into the wind. No one thought of singing.

———

Mary breathed another night beside her, but in the morning Israel came into camp with wet clothes clinging, his hair plastered to his skull. He sat and said that Nicholas Koonse had gone under his horse while swimming a line out for the ferry and was lost.

"What do you mean, lost?"

"We're looking for a body."

The morning seemed airless with the news. In silence, she and the girls loaded their chosen goods into the small green wagon. To the sand they left the Brussels carpet, the table and chairs with books and boxes, and the good side table. It scarcely seemed to matter. Worn dresses and shoes lay in heaps. "Leave all of that," Israel said. "Just leave it." They wore their Sunday clothes with moccasins.

"All right," she told the girls when they were done. "Find one last token." She watched them among the dear and unnecessary articles—they picked things up and put them down—feeling more mortal than she ever had, with Nicholas Koonse's death a clear visit from each private future, which must, in this moment, be divined, each fate secured by the proper choice of articles.

Sarah kept the hair book, Caroline the treasured Coleridge. Emma Ruth put the sampler in her pocket.

Lucy folded old Mary Ross's blue dress, their grandmother's, to give to Mary. For Daniel, she had kept the *Children's Companion*.

She sent them to the ferry after that. But stayed behind, knowing which final weight she must relinquish. Understanding, on this voyage of sand, how sailors became so superstitious.

———

SHE FOUND ISRAEL after that, alone among the ashes of their wagon.

He was reclaiming nuts and bolts, the pins and rings and clevises. He had a sack already perhaps twenty pounds in weight, and was not half finished. His trousers were still damp from swimming, clumped with dust and ash, and he stood and bent, stood and bent, dragging his lunatic trove. She watched.

"No," she said at last. "Israel. We shouldn't."

His hands fell still.

She watched his back. She'd never seen him break like this.

He upturned the filthy flour sack. Gray iron rained into the ashes. A curved piece caught her eye—the hook she'd fixed inside the front bow at the outset of their journey. Staring at it, she saw the windy night so long ago, when a man she'd never seen before had stepped into her wagon and hung his coat upon it.

She stayed until Israel turned. She picked it up and smoothed it clean, seeing a house with a door and this hook fixed beside it. How she might take it from one place to the next, with always the hanging ghost of James MacLaren's coat.

She smiled at this thought. She carried it into camp, the iron warming in her hand. Then set it on a chair they'd left, and walked away.

THEY CROSSED with no other misfortune, camped on the north bank, and unloaded all their goods again to dry. She boiled tough ox meat, though the stink from the kettle made her wretched.

Mary sat, much cooler. Lucy gave her tiny spoonfuls of boiled flour, thinking of the morning, how she had pulled the letters from the stockings she had kept, and sat beside the fire, burning page by page the lines of ink his hands had set down for her, their blots and smudges, their smell of him. Though she would keep the story always.

We are alive, she thought, after all. We are the spared. So the world seemed precious in all its demands, in its threat and beauty. Its sweat and filth and glare. She could love the very snakes coiled in the bushes: it was so much better than not being here at all. Lucy fed and fed her child, and it was nonsense, she knew, but she liked the dark symmetry of the possibility: that Nicholas Koonse had paid for this child. That she had paid for another.

THAT EVENING Rufous Leabo found the body some two miles down the river, farther than anyone thought possible. She was still sitting up when Israel came back. The saw and hammer were quiet.

She looked at him.

At last he said, "What have I not given you, Lucy? What would I not give you that I had?"

She sat for a while, looking at the moon above the western ridge as soft and yellow as the yolk of an egg. "A choice," she said finally.

He said, "I don't see what difference that would make."

She nodded.

He rose and left. She went down to the river's edge, walked through the little garden of wavering candle flames and lanterns, and stood beside the coffin.

THE GRAVE WAS made in the still of morning. They rose and dressed and left the youngest children sleeping. In procession on the talcum road, they followed the coffin, their smooth soles patting the way like arrows. Rabbitbrush glowed in long dry shadows. They stood to the service on a rise above the river, and their mingled heat drew blackflies in increasing numbers, and the drone and stutter and tickle of those insect feet was so distempering that none could help but jerk and fan and flail their hats beyond the psalm and through *he that believeth* and *the promises of God are yea and amen* and *in the shadow of Thy wings do we rejoice.*

Within the hour, they were teamed. When they came to the grave in the road, the first oxen moved roll-eyed to skirt it, and had to be led across by force. The rest followed, each less reluctant, each wagon canting less. By the time the loose cattle had followed, Lucy knew there would be no trace. This land being so complete in its intolerance that even graves must go unmarked.

FAITH

MacLaren walked up and down the river. He climbed the small streams feeding into his valley, until at last he found a stone about two hundredweight that had split clean along a seam into roughly even halves, and knew it was the one. He went back for the mule, and led her scrambling up beside the water, and tied her to a sapling pine in steep yellow bracken. He rolled the stones to where she stood.

What he'd found was dark gray and flecked with mica, tapered on one end and round at the other, like a drop of hanging water. He lifted the first and fit it in a pannier while the mule protested, then hung the second, and when he went to lead her, she refused. So he left her to think, and crossed over to the falling water. He sat and filled his pipe and lit it.

Summer was going. In the creek's tender green, yellow monkeyflower had begun to fade. A woodpecker swooped and lit on a dead pine, lightning-striped and laughing. He saw the red crest, the neat diamond of its back. It cocked its head to listen. Then cast off and fell winging through green shadows.

He went to the mule and led her skidding downward.

Even a good split post of fir or tamarack would rot below ground in two years or three if set in a forest, four years or five on open ground. He pondered this in the chisel's ring, chasing slowly the curved script of his daughter's name: *Elizabeth Anne MacLaren.* He'd begun with too much ambition in this, he thought. As in most things.

And old Noonday had quit eating, wouldn't take even the salted broth he boiled for her. Now, blowing the spall from the letters he cut, he could hear her in the sun and quiet grass, humming some sad old chant. Her voice rose and fell, and sometimes the lowest notes were only whispers. In Scotland as a boy, he'd heard women sing old laments very much like these. So perhaps there was some commonality of music, as ancient as life and death.

THEY RODE OUT as a wind came up, the first leaves blowing from the aspens. The shadows seemed paler already, though he didn't think that August could have ended. But he knew the sweet smell of seasoned grass, the calls of geese.

He'd built around the graves with stone, a wall, not certain when he'd be back.

They crossed the low northern pass, descended to the river valley: it was the same trail he'd ridden with the infant twins, the same he'd walked on snowshoes in December, carrying June. Now the deer were fat and offered themselves, and Noonday ate again but had a cough. While he cooked by evening, she would sit and tell him things from long ago, the same stories circling on themselves, crossing back and over, like string wound onto a ball. One night she sat on her shins for an hour, talking, and when he helped her up to bed at last, he was surprised by the heat in her hands.

Next midmorning, he passed the hill he'd made of burning stones. He didn't look for it but knew the place.

A home has stories, the old woman had said. *Each hill, each river's bend, takes its name from something long ago.*

Well. His home would span a continent, by that measure. But someone had to care. Someone had to know it. It took someone else to name your life and keep it. Stories that your children told their children after.

THEY CAME to the mission three days later, at evening.

The buildings stood forlornly in a stump field. No lodges were near, no horses grazed in the shadows of the pines. He saw the low shed where he'd stayed. The tiny graveyard with its crosses, more of them now. The palisade gate stood open. No children chased balls. He heard only the thunk of split-ting pine, ax and block, the solitary sound.

"Hey?" he called. "Hello?"

Behind him, the old woman talked nonsense while Sally grazed. His own horse snatched for rein. He got down, and tied the mare to the garden fence, and saw a tall fleshy man in robes approaching, ax in hand. His face was pink and moist from work.

MacLaren called out, "There was an Italian here, Mengarini."

"He's away now."

"And who would you be?"

"Carnahan. What's your business?"

He said nothing. The Irishman leaned and pulled the air into his sweaty robes, worked his collar like a bellows, and the dust rose off as it did from the backs of cattle. A fervent man.

MacLaren said, "Who cares for the graves now?"

"I would. If time allowed."

"Where is everyone?"

"How do I know, the bleething savages. Some on the hunt, eh? Some moved off," he said. "They're closing this place down."

"I'm MacLaren."

"Ah, now," said Carnahan, and showed his musty teeth. "I've heard of you."

THEY PUT NOONDAY in the hall on some blankets near the hearth. MacLaren brought his robes and covered her. It was dim, with a low fire burning, and Carnahan had lit the tapers in their spikes, filled a pot with something. MacLaren put on water of his own for washing and went to tend his animals.

When he came back, the pink Irishman had set a supper on the planks. On two plates were boiled peas enough for a child, a few small potatoes, what might have been an onion. MacLaren looked at the steaming fare. Two spoons. He said, "Well, I've got a ham of deer out in my packs. I should have said."

He made tea as the coals burned down, tried to get old Noonday to drink. He cradled her head, felt the soft lobe of her ear, in fingers he'd thought had lost their feeling. He looked up at Carnahan and asked if there was any news of Lise, but the man had never heard of her.

The tea spilled down the old woman's chin.

He asked of Baptiste and Philemon and the rest, but none had returned from that journey, and Mengarini was gone as well. The man went on to tell of other news in other missions. DeSmet was near Spokane. Blanchet near Walla Walla.

MacLaren asked, "Have you heard of the Whitmans?"

"Oh, sure, they're in a mess now. The bishop means to buy them out, I think."

"What kind of mess?"

"A Presbyterian one."

"You have a deal of news for a man so far removed."

"I pass the time. I pass the time, and people come and bring the world to me."

MacLaren put the meat straight in the coals and buried it. They watched it cook while the Irishman ran on about his garden, how the natives took from it, how he'd come to his appointment. His voice was gentle and fluty. Then he asked MacLaren about his time since winter.

He said he'd helped a family out to Oregon.

"A useful thing, very useful. And they're safe?"

"I left them at Fort Hall."

"A disagreement?" He was sharp with interest, and read the reply, but then MacLaren said, "No."

"But something?"

MacLaren nodded.

The Irishman sighed.

They sat awhile in silence. As the meat began to flavor the air, the Irishman told about the flesh he'd lost since coming, and stood and measured his own middle with the piece of hemp that served as cincture and showed where he used to tie it, and where he tied it now. Then got from there to the Blackfeet, the trouble they'd caused all summer, and the mission up at St. Ignatius. MacLaren smoked. They both drank tea. Then the man started back on the earlier subject, and implored MacLaren to feel the uppers of his arms and would have had him feel his thighs as well, and that was when MacLaren stood and got the shovel, pulled the ham from coals to hearth, and whacked it with a sound like pistol fire.

The black ball of meat bounced off the stones and onto the swept clay floor. MacLaren picked it up and did the same a few more times until the ash and char were gone and the meat inside was tender. He knelt beside the stones and sliced, with juices running pink and fragrant. He put the pieces on a trencher, stood while the Irishman blessed them.

"I find, in my own experience," Carnahan said, "that when I believe I've run out of sustenance in the daily effort of living, what I've truly run out of is faith."

They ate in silence. The potatoes had gone cold but they were sweet, and MacLaren thought of Lucy Mitchell. He said, "A woman I knew once told me that ironing was an act of faith."

"Clever woman," the Irishman said.

By MORNING Noonday was too sick to move.

MacLaren walked the grounds, waiting while she died.

Past the garden sprawled with mottling leaves, tilting stakes, rife weeds. Through a gate hinge he had forged himself that winter out of hoop steel. He saw the wooden crosses in the graveyard and could not go in yet.

He passed into the log church. It seemed a folly, silent with its lime-washed walls, littered in forgotten garlands. By whose hand? For what occasion? He skirted slowly the plank benches, paused at queer pictorials dabbed out brightly in a wild childish hand. Here were canvases of fire, saints and angels in blazing visits through the trees. Horses and men looking up in awe. He had seen the Frenchman, Point, who made them. Who spoke to his heathens in figures and hues, his own eyes so emblazed a blue they'd seemed to light the coves they were set in. Yellow, blood vermilion, violet. The true gold of wings and halos here did seem enough to persuade the darkest savage. MacLaren stood envying the pure crude madness of the work.

Genius was this, he decided: not refinement of what others had begun, not improvement on a thing done well, but this flawed and connate impulse leaping out beyond all margins of convention. It was as though, through scope and faith and fearlessness, some people found in themselves new forms of human ore, and mined them, held them out for lesser men to marvel at or scorn.

And standing before these pictures in this crude and foolish chapel, some idea formed and began to rise, so that he sensed the church to be a vessel, and this vessel had rafted them all across the sea: not only Jesuits and Presbyterians, but all the white-skinned race. He'd been blind, he thought, not to see it. It was the church: the genius of this faith had joined and held them in a league across the seas and centuries, made them different from those here, who would not willingly leave their homes. If his were a wandering people, a conquering people, at the heart of it lay this: not ships, not greed, not mere discovery. These things are a part of it, but it is the faith, he thought. The borrowed genius of these stories is what binds us.

These stories. No matter if he knew them anymore, believed or cared. They were in his mind as clear as his own life: Adam and Eve, Noah and his Flood, the angels above Bethlehem, Judas in the garden, the Crucifixion. Not tied to any place, the words of God in all their forms were in the minds of his whole people: they drew down faith like lightning, lent courage like strong drink. And so we take them anywhere, he thought, and think that we belong, since we are all His children.

His mother's gift had been a Bible, with her last and holy kiss, when he'd heard the call from the quay at last, to come away. He had come with all the rest, and everything they'd needed to know was in that Book, and faith would fire blood if they could only feel it. And the men who knew the word of God, and what must be done in birth and union, war and death, had come as well. And such was the power of the Book, and such was the power of the great white tribe who owned it, that all the lesser tribes had soon wanted to find out for themselves what words were in it.

Who was right and who was wrong, and who destroyed and who made greater? He didn't know.

He went in later, to where Noonday lay in the light of the parchment window, and found Carnahan praying over her.

"Don't do that," he said. "She had none of your beliefs."

The man quit, simply. Indifferent or knowing. Together, they looked over the woman, so small and flat a bundle that, but for the ropy arms at her sides, one might take her for a child.

"What relation is she, exactly?" asked Carnahan.

"A friend of my wife's," MacLaren said. And then, "A friend of mine."

THAT NIGHT, in moonlight, he walked around the palisade wall and came to rest in a place where he'd sat so many months before, listening to Mengarini's tales of oranges and bright sun, of dolphins and blue water. They had sat together here, and barefoot boys had shot their arrows up at wooden discs, but he had shut his eyes. At times since then, he'd thought he'd found new strength. Now he wondered if he'd returned at last with little more to show. Of Lucy Mitchell, his clearest memories were shame. Alone, he knew he would forget what he had loved in her. What had been so wondrous in the moment seemed elusive here tonight, except that he was easier in himself. Except that knowing her had somehow made him better.

But even that idea seemed suspect. If he was stronger, he had no proof: he'd come to feel too much for an old woman who wanted anyway to die; he had promised to see her home and failed; there was no one here to welcome her, or to know what next life she might hope for, or how to get there.

He leaned in the shadow of tall pickets and watched the Irishman come out and walk in the moonlight like some lumpen benign giant.

"Hey," he said.

The priest found him. He circled in the weedy dirt as a dog might and lowered himself, sighing. He'd brewed a barley beer, black and sweetened with molasses, and drank it from church pewter. He passed it over.

MacLaren sipped. Dark as tar, it matched his mood. He thought of Protestants and Catholics. The shriveled garden, the empty church, the old woman dying of disease.

Carnahan belched and said, "Thank you, Jesus."

"What for?" MacLaren asked.

"Ah, for the moonlight. For taking all my sins."

"I don't know how you do that."

"What?"

"Give away your sins."

"Well, what else are we to do with them?"

He didn't know. They drank and listened to the night. After a time, MacLaren said, "Tell me, why did you come here?"

"I was sent," the Irishman said.

MacLaren held the bitter beer between his teeth and passed the cup again, thinking of old Noonday and her stories of how days had changed. Of his people in their ships, their old corruptions, intrigue and greed, blind charity, inquiry, disease, all offered in the name of just improvement.

"So was I," he said at last.

IN THE MORNING the old woman lay stiff in her blankets.

MacLaren walked to the river. Sat on his heels looking down through wavering light. A pair of trout glided, hovering above their rippled shadows.

On his belly, he leaned in, hands set, felt the cold shrink of skin to skull, pushed deeper. He had a moment's impulse to breathe in, to slide forward into that mottled world, to become as the sturgeon in the dark and weightless depths, to be carried.

What was it, to be so simple?

He raised and blew and rubbed his teeth. He wiped his eyes and stood and walked back across the grass.

HE DUG Noonday's grave all day, beside Junie's, facing east to the rising sun. That evening he washed and dressed her, pushed her knees back to her chest, as he'd seen these people do. Folded her arms and bound them, cut the tendons of her heels so the feet would lie against the shins. He wound her own blanket around her and stitched it tight. She was light as a child. He lined the grave with old mats, worn robes his own children had once played on, tussling with puppies or hearing her tales. He gently lowered her to sit, and put her bowl and spoon beside her, and the knotted hanks of string on which she kept her memory, her shells and pins and knives, the bag of all her hair she'd saved, the clippings of her nails, her birth cord in its beaded pouch. But this seemed insufficient, and he cast for something else to give, some late blooms perhaps, but found not much. He came back with a few balsamroot, their yellow petals dropping. Set beside her, they seemed worse than nothing. But he let them do, for sentiment. And knew no prayer to help her pass into the next world as she would hope, but asked her to look after June.

It was indulgent, this father's hope. That the dead required company. He stood beside their graves and cried.

———————

A BAND of Sarsi rode down the next afternoon, saddles filled with meat.

They set up lodges with the sound of life again, children, horses, barking dogs. MacLaren shook the Irishman's hand, and wished him luck, and rode away.

He found the old trail west into the mountains, *Inola-a*, climbing through dry pines and aspen. All day he rode until the trees were stunted and bear grass grew in shining tussocks, blooms as white and tall as tapers. He crossed low crests, through grassy valleys, climbed again. Small trees gave way to steep meadows. On all sides the jagged walls of mountains rose and changed their colors with the day, through hues of rose and gray and white. A country driven clean by wind and light.

In a high bog, he followed tracks of moose like postholes, brimming oily water. Scrambling up a hill of rocks, he found a good camp ringed by boulders. Tamarack and hemlock had carpeted the ground with needles.

He built no fire, and at twilight raised his rifle as a big cat slunk along the rocky slope across the stream. He watched and watched, and at last he fired.

In near dark, he brought it back across his shoulders. The tail swung below his knee. He hung the carcass, skinned the pelt to sleep on. The fur had grown in thick already. Winter coming. All evening he had thought of Lucy Mitchell.

It was so quiet.

He split a haunch, roasted it by dark, and ate it, imagining her there with him. A waltz had come into his mind and stayed. He closed his eyes and let himself believe he could have led her, dancing.

———————

NEXT MORNING he climbed again, into a country of pure light and color. Low twisted hemlock. Frost had burned the tender leaves of bilberry. Broad falls and carpets of red and gold flowed down against white granite. The horses trotted soundless on the springy heath, across crests where stones broke through like tilted teeth, old grave marks guarding doorsteps of pushed gravel, marmot burrows. The blue so near to heaven he could almost see the stars by day.

At the top of the final rise, he drew rein; saw the world spread out below him. He whistled for the mule and waited. Ridges and valleys fell in shades of blue as far as he could see.

Then something in the light surprised him, or in the world as it lay spread.

Behold, he thought. Though no such word had ever stirred in him before.

But he saw the splendor he had known, the stones and sky, the animals and plants. He, alone, its witness.

Behold: that the world could assert itself in perfect form, despite his imperfection.

In this moment he was light with some unlooked-for grace.

And he'd always felt he stood in shadow, looking out onto the light; his whole life, spent always on the margins of a great Creation that could only suffer him.

Suddenly it seemed possible that man, no matter what his kind, was only man. That for all his cruelty and his blind destruction, he might be no more failed or fallen than a beaver with its dams. Than a cougar with its prey.

Behold.

Could a man still carry all the weight of what had gone before, of what had been and what would be, and yet step forward, innocent?

He had never given over any of his sins. But what if he could own them for a moment, the same as every other part: his hands or eyes or dreams, his hunger or his love, knowing only their necessity?

It seemed a wondrous thought. It filled his lungs.

He gave a cry as wild and without origin as all his savage brothers: it was turkey, eagle, horse, it was elk and wolf in one. Drum Hill bunched and turned. MacLaren slapped the sweating neck. Smiled down across the valleys thick with trees, the imbricated slopes.

Then, with the changing light, the sense was gone. Cut Ear was coming up the crest, her packs askew. But the moment had been gift enough, and proof of some divinity.

A Supplicant Hand

⊙◠◠◠◠⊙

LUCY WOKE ONE NIGHT not in her bed but sprawled in the wagon where she'd sat to rest while getting Daniel down to sleep. In this dry desert night, she heard small rustlings, thumps like someone looking through their things, sat blinking in the dark, until she saw the glowing teeth and white blazed face of the Bannock mare, neck stretched and face tipped sideways, foraging with her lips across their blankets.

They had left the river bend where Mr. Koonse lay buried, and cut north by west across another endless plain of sage. Nothing for food but dry biscuit and a little rotting fish. When they could find water, it was pooled among green stinking stones in some dry channel, and that was what they drank.

Next morning Mrs. Koonse's infant died. They'd buried it by noon and made away.

She walked and carried Mary.

She passed a lone wagon overturned on level ground with all its furnishings. She passed springs boiling over rocks that dripped with red and brilliant yellow. She passed Mr. Kingery beside a fallen ewe, and bent to help, amazed how close the bones seemed underneath the wool. The animal had no strength at all, rocked limp, dust sticking to its staring eye. John Kingery, on his heels, took off his glasses.

"I'm sorry," she said. She set her fingers in the tines of her own ribs. The sagging corset was abandoned.

What a strength you have, he'd said. But she was failing to endure, as her mother had failed. She would grow old and bitter as dead cottonwood, she would grow unlovable, wrenched beyond her confidence in life, doomed to reliance. She would dry into something brittle, thorned, wounding.

Was it two weeks? Three? It seemed so long ago.

By evening, a cooling wind augured storms. Shorter days were coming.

Now, every night by starlight, the horses and mules prowled, if they could, through untended kitchens. They pawed latched boxes, flung out flour sacks, fed stealthy on dried peas, cured fish, worried through the dampened holes where dishwater had been pitched. Trampling cutlery, flattening tin cups. Each night it took more care to keep the goods from harm.

AT THE BASE of a long bluff, they found the river Boise. They crossed and ran beside it and had trees again. In a grove of cottonwoods, some Indians came with small salmon strung on willow hoops to trade. The fish were dull and swarmed with flies, but they cost only a ball and measure each. And so were they provided. That night Lucy lay awake in the wonderful sound of leaves—the muggy air here bred of grass and water—in the thick late whine of fat mosquitoes.

The Boise took them to the Snake again. Quite accidentally, they found themselves gathered one evening on the banks of that last crossing with a good number of their original party, some they had not seen since arriving at Fort Hall. The Madison party had crossed the day before. Some of both trains had split earlier for California.

The Leabos were here, the Raimies and Luellings and VanAllmans and others, the Whitcombs and Whites, but she could only fear it. These days most exchanges had the same effect on her of fish; they seemed not to sustain but to run straight through and leave her squatting in the bushes. She felt a necessity for lying still. At rest, while the baby settled, she heard the caustic rattle of their voices:

"I saw she'd be in trouble with it, but what was I to say?"

". . . their extravagance."

"They had some cake or pudding every night that first month. Now they're asking to dip into our stores . . ."

After a while, she rose and took the pail for water.

At the river's edge, she sat on her heels. White flowers grew rooted in the current. Lucy picked one out and set it in her palm, but the wonder she'd once felt was gone. She was dry now, the life pressed from her. Memory was not sustenance enough.

Come back, she thought. Come back to me.

Of course he would not. That morning she'd wakened, knowing the particular spasm of the womb she felt that signified the seating of new life.

She scratched Peg's ears and rose and headed back to camp, but old Mattie had set her chair in the broken shade of a tree to smoke, and called, "How are those hands of yours?"

"My hands?"

"Where you scalded."

Lucy set the pail down and went, giving her hand into the old woman's.

"That looks good. I knew a boy who died of a stove burn size of a ninepence. It went bad clear up his arm. You got by all right."

"Thanks to Mrs. Raimie."

"Good woman. She's here now."

"Yes, I know."

"Dull as cabbage but good."

Lucy smiled.

"Your one's got some vinegar back."

"Mary has. Yes."

Mattie said, "That was a good man that was with you folks. I know a good man."

"Yes," she said, and her eyes filled, and she was ashamed.

"You got to rally up, though. Go scratch and bite like all the others."

Lucy said, "I believe there's enough of that around our fire already."

"Well, nice is nice. But the little whoop-up gets you through. That or salt. Look at any mare. The ones that kick are best for longest."

THEY STAYED the following day to rest. Lucy moved distracted through her work, and after breakfast called the girls. With Mary and laundry and the lone washtub, they trudged behind her. She took them slipping through bushes filled with birds, while they complained of heat and distance. Why could they not wash near the others?

"Come on," she said. "Bear with me this once. We'll find a better place."

And then, coming out on a little trail she'd tried, they found it: a sweeping bend, steep-banked on the far side but bordered here by a wide band of silt. A heron launched and flew croaking down the river. She walked onto a beach alive with bobbing butterflies. Sweat trickled under her corset, stood beaded on her brow.

"These goddamn shoes," Daniel said quite plainly. He'd sat down behind her and was tugging at his laces. So followed a lecture while she knelt and picked the knots.

Sarah had set Mary down and slipped off her own moccasins. When Lucy turned, she was ankle-deep, staring at something under water. Her arms bent strangely up beside her head, as though she were arranging an invisible hat.

"What are you doing?" Lucy called.

Sarah said, "I have green hair."

The other two waded in to see. "Show Mama," Emma Ruth said.

Sarah said, "It's only fooling."

"Let me try," said Caroline.

They laughed, the three conspirators.

"What?" asked Lucy, and Sarah said, "Come on, then," as one might to a bothersome child.

Look, they pointed, when she'd come in beside them. Look there, in the water.

Sarah said, "Let me, I do it best."

Then Lucy saw how their shadows fell across the gravelly bed, and a clump of waving water-grass sat atop the shadow image of her daughter like blowing tresses, and the shadows of her hands combed through them; Sarah swayed like a mermaid as the river grass was swaying.

Lucy said, "Well, look at that." An eerie chill ran through her. Caroline said, "Let Mother try, move, let her try."

So she was ushered to stand with tresses of grass.

Daniel said, "If I catch a little fish, can it live in our bucket?"

Emma said, "Can we try learning how to swim?"

"Yes," she said. "Let's do."

Soon they were all splashing and whooping, dragging one another down. They dunked and twirled in clinging petticoats, then took those off and paddled like spaniels in chemise and pantalettes. They whirled the sheets into luminous balloons to light like bubbles on the water. They bared their chests (not so flat as they had been once) and used one another's ribs for washboards, squealing. They wrung the clothes at last, and marched like half-clad wantons into camp together.

But that night, Lucy couldn't eat her supper. Sun and glare and swimming had built some pressure until it seemed her skull was being forced from the inside.

From White's camp next to theirs came the reeling argument of women, the clash of cookware. The captain begged for order, and Lucy turned to see their Negress, Eva, fling a handful of sand at the captain's wife, who had whipped free of her husband's staying hand to snatch tin cups as fast as she could fling them in return. A dipper spun out with deadly aim. A water pail bucked tumbling along the ground. The Negress took it by the bail and filled it with the tinware she could reach, then wheeled and coursed off like a hare with these possessions so that Mrs. White—charitable supporter of abolition and advocate for the education and advancement of Negro women—took up the camp ax and made a howling chase, skirts wrapping and tangling on her legs.

No wonder her poor baby had cried. So Lucy thought, wakened by her own moaning. Her throat felt scalded. Eyes open to starlight, to voices, the low flames of morning wavered and lit the forms of women cooking, but she could no more rise and take up her work than if she were locked in ice.

They made to cross the deep ford at dawn. The men, in an effort to save time, had chained the wagons together like a train, one to the next. It had sounded reasonable, but now seemed very dangerous. She felt the rising water, the lurch and skate.

"Where's Mary?" she asked, but no one heard. If the chains were set wrong, if the wagons rode too low, it would pull their oxen down and drown them, so now she watched the poor animals struggle, heads upthrown, dark noses turning side to side; she heard the roar of voices, names called out, water welling through the floor. If one link burst, they would be lost.

And then they struck the bed again. She saw the oxen lurch and rise out streaming, their spines and hips and heaving flanks. She heard whoops, wild yodeling, Tom Littlejohn's roar. Saw brown skin, deep eyes, her husband's even teeth.

"That was the last!"

She pulled her blanket, not having seen the depth of his former doubt.

"That was the last big crossing," he said more reasonably.

She smiled, but the wagons were still moving to draw the others through, and he was gone.

———

Dirty mountains rose abruptly to the west.

Mr. Littlejohn sat the wagon's forks, keeping time with his jaw harp's buzz. Lucy, floating above the jolt and sway, believed no music to be more suited to such country—an exiled blur so bleak and dry it could have its origin only in some ancient desert. Her teeth seemed hot as hearth tiles. Flies crowded her damp eyes.

They crossed salt-laced flats. Tracks scribed the fragile crust. She thought snow must have fallen, but as they neared, it became a rotted feather bed. So she saw this still heat verified: only their passage disturbed the airy down, which puffed, lofted, settled in their wake. It was the last thing she remembered.

———

A river one night, dark and whispering leaves, a cool cloth for her face. How long had she been dreaming?

A poultice of onions on the neck, said Mrs. Raimie. Or fly to the moon for a dipper of milk, either was as likely. The thought that she might pass from life before she tasted an onion one more time, or a pear, or a ripe tomato: that was grief.

———

In deep morning, she woke to an alarm, smoke, and flickering light, and slept again, forgetting it was not a dream. Later, Sarah said that Captain White had suffered the grease in his wagon hubs set alight, and had found the skinned pelt of his English dog laid out like a lap rug on the seat.

She slept and woke in the wagon's tattered walls, night brightening as they tracked across the moon where it had fallen in a wide brown valley. The ground glowed white. Loose cattle stood licking at their shadows.

———

AT DAWN they halted in gray thorn, alone.

She could rise, find an apron, and get down, but the bones of her fingers seemed too small. The kettle's clank was lost in vastness.

She sat with her ear against the wheel hub and closed her eyes.

Something bounced against her dress softly, like a pebble. She felt another and opened her eyes to see locusts climbing. She watched their wondering heads, cocked legs with neat chevrons she had never loved before. She studied them as they walked across her, felt the bones of spokes against her back, watched her daughters tend the baby, watched the wind flare through the fire. Her girls moved in a dusty choreography, gusts pulling at their skirts. They rose and sat and rose again, dodging smoke, flicking insects, picking worms from flour. The oxen crackled for browse, hideous in their sunken skins.

"I want milk," her son declared. His eyes were glittering blue.

Sarah, mother now, said, "There is no milk, you know it."

Emma's skirt and moccasins appeared. Lucy squinted up, accepted muddy water in a cup.

"Why's Mary getting milk?" said Daniel.

"She isn't."

Lucy closed her eyes. Sticky combs of locusts' feet wandered in her hair. Sarah brought flour gruel.

"Why's Papa's orn't eating?"

"He rode ahead for water."

The dog had come to beg, having chosen her for weakness. The brown eyes bored into hers. Well, Lucy thought. Now pets and people are so keen they might consume each other.

"Why Dollar's nose bees red?"

Lucy, with no appetite for glue, relented. Peg took the cup by the rim and sank, stretched taut, holding it neatly between forepaws. The spoon rattled.

"Hush, Daniel. Eat."

But, rising from her rest, Lucy looked to see the poor ox standing with his nose slimed crimson. She said nothing, only took off her last good apron and went to wipe the drooling blood.

THE SUN SET, rose, set again. Land moved steadily past. Only Pudding and Bishop had not drunk the desert alkali. Of those that had, only Dan survived but was too weak to pull.

From her bed, she watched brown canyon walls slip back and down, walls gouged and shaped by forces she could not divine. For an hour, she lay watching a fluted outcrop resembling nothing so much as a raised and supplicant hand. It sank and sank until the yellow grass consumed it.

ONE NIGHT she smelled pines, and a man who seemed unlike her husband came in beside her and raised her head to drink. She did seem to remember, from long ago, a talkative, confident man who mastered any space around him. This man now wore a gray cloth tied over the dome of his head. He was quiet, with his ragged white beard, and his gaze seemed very deep. When her throat would not admit salt broth, she closed her eyes, and felt his finger stroke her brow, and was moved by this affection.

Then next evening she was well again, quite suddenly. She came out into mountain air. A good pine fire warmed the dark, threw orange light into limbs so high their battered wagons looked as humble as loaves of bread. Her teeth were tender. But she ate the roasted strings of meat from an ox the Whitcombs shared, and had never been so hungry. Gold needles showered from the larches. She drank clear water from a spring and thought the strange tang in the air would be from that, until Israel said it smelled like snow.

"Snow?" she said. "What month is this?"

THEY LOST their oxen in the forest, spent a day walking after them. She climbed, with her sinewy girls, over logs. They pushed ahead of her through dead growth, snapping limbs free with strong hands. Consulted, squinting, with attention to the light, spread and collected again, searched the needles for cloven tracks. She loved them very much, these women her girls had become, though Tom Littlejohn found the beasts at last in a small paradise, a secret cove of grass and faded flowers.

That night, when she stood from the fire and passed behind her husband, her hand was pleased to linger on his shoulder. In cold sweet-scented sleep at last, they sprawled unguarded, side by side.

FREE AIR

*H*E DESCENDED IN PINE FOREST, the river now west-flowing through steep canyons. Aspen and gold cottonwood glimmered in the valleys. He rode through willow marsh, down beaches, crossed bars of small smooth stones.

Blue thunderheads built one day above the canyon, and the sky blinked white. Thunder rolled out and back in echoes of echoes across this steep theater of stone until the sound seemed to lodge inside his ribs. Spare drops drove down like nails. On the walls above, pines sprang in gusts, hissed and flung their cones while the old horse carried him neatly down the narrow bank, slid splaying into growths of willow, hopped tangled drifts of wood, leaped onto boulders.

The rain came harder, sidelong in gusts. His shirt stuck to him, and rounding the corner, he saw the canyon close completely, saw frothing white narrows too choked and deep to try. The route was lost. He turned, drove the mare and mule scrambling back again under icy veins of lightning. Thunder boomed. He pinched the water from his nose and set the old horse climbing.

This wall was as near to vertical as he had ever tried. They clawed up through shale and brush, raising dust even into falling rain; MacLaren stood against the tangled mane, let the horse lunge upward. Behind, the others blew and steamed. Sally rolled her eyes, trying left and right in hope of easier paths, legs trembling. The mule stopped, staggering on the pitch, and brayed. Her knee dripped blood.

"Hey, come on," he scolded. "Come on."

He climbed until they broke onto a knob, then found a rotten shelf running high above the narrows. Sally crowded, skittering wild-eyed at his leg. He flicked her back with his rein. Drum lilted along the steep ledge with the river boiling sixty feet below, as white as barn lime. Made the corner to find the shelf inclining into a narrow slope of scree between a cliff and a straight drop.

"Whoa."

He studied it. Then eased the reins.

The old horse crouched and stepped along, and the deep flaked stone slid out in dusty runnels gathering, gathering to break over the edge below, soundless in the roar of water.

They reached a broken pine on safer ground and breathed. He reined in, with Sally right behind. No mule in sight.

Then fire spanned, a blinding flash, a hazard of exploding bark, splinters, bunched leaping terror. Wet reins jerked through his hands, the air sucked into a mighty detonation.

Cut Ear came bolting from around the corner. On scree, she hit slick underlay and fell, and then the surface of the whole slope broke loose and was carrying them all down, the mule on her side going down and him shouting deaf as sky while Drum swam up the sliding wall of shale, as the mule, borne down, lay helpless, and he was helpless striving upward in the rolling dust, and watched the cast mule slide down and down and, soundless, ease into free air.

FOOL HENS WATCHED from windy pines on the day he rode off the pass and into a high prairie and a smell of baking camas.

A pack of dogs bounded out in silent menace, roached and stiff, but he feared them less than he feared speaking, he had been in these mountains so long. He would have turned back into the trees, but the women who had stood to see him were already sitting to their work again.

He reined in, uncertain, in this thin clear light of afternoon.

The women sat on modest hips. They dug out corms with sticks, brushed the wiry roots and slipped them into woven bags. He watched a girl with a beautiful neck, heard the tinkling of her beads as she bent and probed the earth and looked up at him again.

HE CAMPED ALONE beside a stream of rusty cobbles, and rose to breakfast on baked camas wrapped in cornflower leaf. He had bought two packages, each the heft of his fist. He ate the dark fragrant mass, thinking of those women digging. Fat babies in the grass beside them, wearing deer-hide bonnets.

He'd seen no one in more days than he could say; had grown content again to be a mystery to himself. He only spooned and ate. Then chewed a pine twig until it frayed, and cleaned his teeth, and packed his camp.

He rode all morning across high benchland, until the forest steepened. Then slithered downward through thin grass, red dust, wildflowers gone to seed. Clouds drove shadows down the canyon walls and across the river below. He honed his hat brim in the gusts, and saw the distant river bend this horse had stood in long ago, that day when Lise had named him. Around that bend was Kamiah, her home.

BY EVENING he was riding down the valley floor, past plots of spent wheat, sprawling vines. He knew the place but for these signs of agriculture; knew, as he passed, the great longhouse with its smoke and the light blazing through its gaps, dense rhythms rising from it like a nailery as women worked at their stone mortars. And he thought Lise would be here, but rode suspended, passing by so quiet that even the escorting dogs were silent. He'd willed himself invisible.

He'd come all this way to find her. But faced with this valley he remembered, these cottonwoods and pine, these old convincing dwellings, grazing horses, drying meat, it seemed a great mistake.

He was different now. If he were to find her, she'd be different also, and whatever went unsaid would belong to other people.

So he rode, sealed in the coat she'd made him, his pocketed hands gone cold with possibility. From the longhouse came a howl, and voices joined in laughter, and he heard the hammering of stones again.

HE MADE CAMP above the river. Sitting in the night, he wondered if his horse remembered it.

On the pass, after Cut Ear fell, he'd spent a long time in only the company of horses. His thoughts, like theirs, becoming few and simple.

He'd lost his packs into the river. Gone back and made a camp, spent a day groping through the roaring water for what he could recover. Fed on mule's meat while the horses rested. He'd slept and smoked, regretting whatever intemperance had been driving him in the days before.

He'd let the days pass, known the hours by the sounds of birds. Felt, for the first time, perhaps content.

Now here he was, a man again, and full of longing.

Two flames hovered on dark water. A canoe was gliding, one torch on its bow, one on its stern. He watched the silent men who paused and listened, and then one lunged to spear and strike a salmon lured upward by the light.

DRUM WAS DRINKING from a creek next morning when a voice called down, "I'm looking for a goddamn file, I don't suppose you have one."

MacLaren looked up. He'd been in thought so deep he hadn't seen the stony track, the low dry shelf where a cabin stood in dappled shade.

"I need a file, goddammit. My damn kids tie them onto goddamn sticks and won't admit it."

MacLaren saw, near the cottonwood's trunk, a man's white beard, the boulder of a belly slung with beads and elk teeth. So he found Bill Craig.

They'd traveled the same parts and knew each other, though MacLaren had never seen this home. The American welcomed him, and he found himself riding up into the shade as half a dozen mallards waddled out from coves among the cottonwood's big roots. He tied the horses to the limbs to rest.

"The girls raised those up," Craig said, nodding at the ducks.

MacLaren could hear children playing up the creek.

They started toward the house. The ducks flapped ahead and ran under a canvas awning where a woman sat. They splashed across her washtub, and she slapped them with a bunch of soaking rushes.

Craig said, "Dog ran down a nest a couple months ago. I was never much a one for poultry." He bent and snatched a passing drake by the neck, and settled it in the crook of his arm and smoothed it. The dark woman said nothing.

Craig said, "I was just having coffee when I spied you."

They stooped together into the gloom. The house could not have been ten feet by twelve, more storeroom than dwelling. Nets and bags loomed like dead things from the rafters. A crock lay overturned in a dark corner, the dirt floor deep in litter. Below the single window, a sprawl of rifle parts lay in the table's light among cold chunks of bread. Bill Craig set the duck on the table and sat, and MacLaren sat, and they watched the treading feet with their silly webs, the small crooked nails. The duck stepped and blinked its round black eyes, picking daintily at the bread, clapping its raised bill to swallow.

"Your wife's with Finlay now, I guess you heard that."

"No," MacLaren said. The suddenness squeezed through him so his eyes felt small, and the meat of his body seemed to shrink around his heart.

The duck shook its tail, snaked its head to frabble in the cooling coffee. MacLaren said, "Which Finlay?"

"Jocko's Nick. Said he'd been under you once."

MacLaren shook his head.

"Well." Craig's eyes took his. MacLaren saw the veiny whites, the greens ringed in suet yellow. An old man's eyes. Craig said, "He's been at Nez Perce, but he quit McBean, or McBean fired him. I guess the Whitmans have him working at their mission."

"You see her, then." It was necessary, as he spoke, to fold his arms.

"Naw," Craig said. "Just heard."

There was nothing he could say next. The chair creaked under him. He looked at the wall, the crude shelf fixed to it. A bottle of matches stood beside a bowl, and between them moved a mouse, its whiskers trembling. On tiny feet, it probed and felt, a soft inquiring shadow.

He said, "You need cats, not ducks."

Craig caught his glance and swore, knocked his chair back, swept the duck from its showplace, the feathery stock of it under his arm like a fusil. The duck quacked and paddled the air. Craig raised the bird and aimed it at the corner of the shelf where the mouse whisked back and forth. The duck snaked its neck in alarm, while Craig swore further and instructed. The mouse dropped to the floor. Craig stamped his heel and missed. Then pitched the duck out in a flurry of wings and slammed the door. They heard the scrabble and growl of the defending dog. By which MacLaren was reminded that in the natural order of the world, peace was nothing but an accidental lapse of conflict.

Craig resumed his seat. He searched his nose and flicked it. Then said, "I had a file, you'd help me put this damn rifle together. She'll give you supper, you want to stay the night."

THEY SPENT all afternoon trying to make one poor rifle out of two that had been fair, while MacLaren's head rang with the thought of Lise with Jocko's Nick Finlay and Lucy Mitchell all living in the same place now, maybe passing one another every day, never knowing their connection, and what wild fate had seen to that. Craig talked on about the Spaldings and the Whitmans and their missions, his opinions simple, virulent, devoutly native.

"One thing I can't stand," Craig said, "it's a goddamn stiff-necked Presbyterian. They first came out, they found Old James, you know what?"

"What?" Isabel was Craig's wife, and Old James was her Nez Perce father.

"Old nickel-eyed bugger and his wife found out James could sing some hymns. He'd learned them at Red River, the school there. So they say, Sing a hymn for us. So he does. You know what they done?"

"What?"

"Give him a biscuit. Like a goddamn trick dog. Then you know what?"

MacLaren had raised the free barrel to the light, and was sighting down the bore. With one end to the midday sun, the ring of shadow could show the barrel to be bent or true. He turned and angled it.

"What."

"Meek got him to go over and sing another and get a biscuit for him too."

"And he did." Joe Meek was Craig's fellow, a wild American trapper.

"By God he did. Shows you what kind they are, though. What the hell they're thinking. You want a man to know God, be there one or whatever. What's a goddamn biscuit got to do with it?"

The Spaldings had made a mission for these Nez Perce on land that

James had given them just down the river, but now all of James's people were regretting it, and wished the Spaldings would be gone.

They took the rifle out to fire it, in the smell of boiling fish.

The sky had clouded over. The children came down from the creek, all sizes, dragging sticks and spears, two girls in sack dresses and the boys with no clothes of any kind. Craig fired and loaded the charges, and MacLaren heard in the intervals the woman's low voice and the children's high ones. And Craig must have seen him listening, because he said, "Stay you here, I'd show you some cousins any man might take a heap of shine to. And they to you, by God."

———

IN THE GROWLING dusk, they ate fish with their hands, and crumbled smoky *op'pah* loaves, he and Craig at the table and the children all sitting on sacks or in the dust. Isabel would not be seen to eat, but served and was silent. MacLaren looked out the window. The cook fire still flickered orange on the canvas lean-to roof. He kept thinking of his wife and Nick Finlay, and did remember some scrawny dark boy from years ago, in the Babine. The first year he and Lise were married. Jocko's Nick.

"What do you know of Joseph now?" he asked. This was Lise's brother, the boy he'd taken to Kamiah when he was only three.

"On the fight," Craig said. Then said he'd gone down with some others to California. Something about Sutter's Fort and stolen horses. Something about a Delaware who'd come through to tell the Nez Perce what had happened to the eastern tribes, making himself a chief by saying all the tribes should join to rise and fight the Americans before it was too late. He'd led Joseph and some young men down there, hoping to gather a rebellion.

"Do you think they'd ever come around to it?" MacLaren asked. "Would these Columbia tribes ally?"

"Not if hell froze," Craig said. "But if they did, I'd fight beside 'em."

MacLaren nodded, and Craig kept talking and the words slid by, a river of words. He tried to listen, and maybe Craig was a tedious man but he was passionate, and MacLaren remembered himself once being the same, how he'd known the news from every quarter. Now he listened more to the murmurs of the woman and her girls. Those true mysteries he'd missed. Or never mastered.

Craig rose at last and, from the back of somewhere, brought a bottle, perhaps of Scotch, on which the dirty label had been hoarded.

They poured. It raked like the devil and stank of molasses. The children came in turn to kiss their father, and he dandled the smallest on his knee, a boy, and asked about the day.

"Eugenia caught flies. We fed them to Pambrun."

That boy was six or seven, MacLaren guessed, cinnamon-haired but otherwise the image of his mother. He got to his knees in Craig's lap, put a hand on his beard to whisper into the hairy ear.

"Three?" the father said, in mock surprise. "You fed three flies?"

The boy nodded, solemn.

"This particular Pambrun," Craig said, "is a trout."

MacLaren nodded, looking out the window. He'd watched his own girls on their knees beside a pool once, gazing down as sunlight flashed and tangled on their skin. He remembered that rapture, the child's affinity for fish. A sigh of thunder broke the thought.

"He'll be fat enough next week," Craig said. "We'll fry him."

"No!" the boys cried. Craig winked at MacLaren. MacLaren, in his cruel chair, smiled.

The children nestled in their beds like kits. In the dark corner beside the table, the dog turned and fanned its toenails in the dust. The door squealed at last and softly clapped, letting Isabel into the night.

"Is she all right?"

"She don't stay for guests. She'll be back when I need her."

They poured and drank, while Craig talked of other men they knew or half remembered. The lantern's shadows made their hands look larger.

Silences grew and lengthened. A small rain scurried over the roof shakes above.

MacLaren thought of Cut Ear, sliding soundless into air, knowing how that fall had felt. He felt it now. A gust spattered drops through the open window. Craig said, "Old winter's on his way."

MacLaren let his head back in the final silence, in the night, the lives here arranged in each comforting particular, the lamp, the rain, the breath of children. He rubbed his face.

Craig tapped the empty tin of his cup. His glance caught the light. He said, "Shit for a life sometimes, ain't it?"

MacLaren breathed agreement.

"You got Hobson's choice. Move the dog or share."

The ugly chairs moved fumbling underneath them. Craig blew out the lamp, and stood, and pulled the door. In the open jamb, he owned the pale rectangle of night like a mountain, and pissed into the rain.

THEIR THOUSAND DREAMS

LUCY WOKE ONE MORNING and found ice in the buckets. They'd crested the Blue Mountains in snow. All yesterday they'd labored at the mercy of stone ledges, declivities, fallen logs, Lucy walking with Mary on her back, as no wagon was safe, and all hands were needed for this work. When they came to stumps or boulders, she'd set her feet and heave with her daughters at ropes tied to the axles, to help the oxen ease the wheels over. Or they hauled on the wagon's side to keep it from overturning.

The seams of her best prunella boots now gaped and grinned. Her feet were in a shocking state. Her washed stockings had been frozen on the line that morning, hard as palings. The children had laughed at them.

"Remember clove oranges?" Emma said. "Remember chocolate?"

There was not much to cook. They built a fire anyway, and drank hot water with the rising sun. Some coats had gone missing. Mislaid, perhaps, in the desert heat, along with all memory of cold. Or left purposely, with other ridiculous things. Frank Tuttle wore a ruffled length of his wife's petticoat as a cravat. Mrs. Watts had scissored slits in long patch coverlets, and now her children all skimmed footless, tied at the waist with linen, roaming through the forest like pied gypsies or colorful nesting dolls, with the first jay's call and the needles tinkling down onto the snow.

AT ABOUT TEN o'clock, Israel's thumb caught in chain, on a downhill slide, and burst open. She heard him shout. They pulled aside while the Tuttles passed and halted, while Lucy bound the bloody purpled skin, but Daniel began catapulting pinecones at Mary from the forked end of a limber twig. Before she knew it, she'd snatched the twig and smacked him over the head, in front of Libby Tuttle, though she scolded her girls for such things. Then went back to tending Israel in the din. The Tuttles' feist trotted in from somewhere, sniffing at the food. Old Peg launched from under the wagon, and then there were snapping teeth and shrieks and flying hair.

Lucy sprang up. She and Frank kicked the dogs apart, dragged them away by the ruffs, and got back to find Daniel snuffling in the crook of his father's arm. She sat again, dizzily, the worst kind of mother. And worried also that the want they suffered would cause her boy some lasting harm, in the way that dogs and horses turned mistrustful if starved while young, and would remain so. Mr. Littlejohn gnawed a biscuit, gazing up at birds.

And what harm would this do, she wondered, to one unborn?

"Ride the mare, and rest your hand," she told Israel. He'd chained and unchained rough locks a dozen times that day, while Tom Littlejohn beat the poor oxen. "Let Tom take your place. I can drive them well enough."

THE RAIMIES KILLED an ox that night and brought them little collops that she could not boil long enough. They had no salt, no bread. They sat and chawed stiff meat until their jaws gave out, then spat them for the dog or swallowed the lumps whole.

Next dawn they climbed the final ridge and dropped all day through thinning pines, down across brown grassy slopes slick and scarred from a thousand wagons. The yoke rode up the oxen's necks, and they ducked their heads and twisted. Their poor haunches sagged. It was the final range, she hoped, skating down the soggy mats of snow. Though more did seem to stand on the horizon.

By evening they had leveled out into a chain of high valleys where pretty streams coursed over pebbles. They climbed and fell again for hours, until the sky was marbled orange, and still went on, into another valley, where surely they would stop.

"She's crying again." Sarah had been waiting with Mary beside the trail. "She's hungry."

"Go ask the Whites if they could spare a biscuit."

"You ask."

They were bickering when they heard gunfire, neighing horses. They listened, soon aware of a slow rolling through the ground. Animals running. Emma stepped onto the moving tongue and balanced.

"Horses," she said. "Horses!" She waved and whooped.

"Where?"

There. Across the grass and blue light of evening, riderless and running down their shadows wild and shining as God had made them. There were flying hundreds, every color, dust and seed thrown up in a gold haze behind them, and the thunder sounded up through Lucy's feet and filled her as they neared, and neared, and swept by in a turbulence of wind and earth, leaving her rapt, amazed that all the joy in life might be summarized so readily by the air beneath those thousand hooves, by streaming manes, the streaks of light across their hides.

Through the settling dust, she could see a rough camp of Indian lodges where the wagons had drawn up. She saw cook fires, barking dogs, men capering on horseback. And could only bless the joy and promise of new food.

ISRAEL BROUGHT OUT his guns that evening. They'd not seen much daylight on the journey; all of them were rusted. Lucy washed their muddy clothes while the girls rubbed and polished the useless weapons, and Israel went one-handed about his stores of lead and powder. By evening's end, they'd traded all of them, feasted till they ached, and were provided with a store of dried salmon, a white speckled mare, a sickle-hocked gelding of nondescript brown, and a basket of small potatoes.

THREE DAYS LATER, they had the letter they'd been waiting for, brought south by men transporting flour. It seemed they would be welcomed at the mission.

At a parting of the trails, they pulled aside to say farewell. Lucy was surprised by Mrs. White's sudden clutching embrace. Liberty Tuttle, now heavy with child, said, "I sure wisht you could have seen this baby come."

"She'll be a beauty," Lucy said, feeling sharply this betrayal, to have contracted privately to leave when they'd been together for so long. Their noble concepts of the common good had come to seem a fallacy drawn up in prior innocence. They were all for themselves now, truly, and for no one else.

THAT NIGHT, alone, their picket lines were cut, their livestock driven off.

It was Kiyouse, of course, and Lucy had never felt such fury, stalking back and forth next morning through the camp, while her husband walked out with Tom Littlejohn, both of them unarmed. Furious because the country was full of them, no telling what danger.

In those past few days, they'd seen many camps of them, small collections of huts with poor plots of garden. Filthy women, wily children, indolent young men with gleaming horses tied or under guard. They'd followed down the road, wheedling for something, or slunk behind like wolves. One, laughing, had surprised Caroline in the bushes.

She thought of Grand Ronde, where they'd been so friendly. Welcoming, trading good food for those useless guns. The dark men had admired Israel's marksmanship (remembering this, she was freshly amazed herself at how he'd shot the nubs of potatoes right off their sticks, with one thumb in a bandage). The Kiyouse had been great fellows then. Joined in songs and dancing.

But in fact, they were not great. They were devilish actors, cold, inhuman. They reveled in dust and blood, in theft and death, and despised all who did not. Despised them even as they smiled and begged. She could read it in their narrowed eyes.

Don't you *know?* she thought now. Can't you see that we cannot go back? That we have *nothing?*

Doves mourned in the limbs above the river. Dry leaves twirled down to lie along the banks, to lift and scratch across smooth cobbles.

She'd liked the white mare very much, had named her Isabel at once without knowing why the name had come to her. Emma had ridden her bareback all yesterday, and now Caroline wanted to, and she was gone.

How could anyone ever choose to live among such people? She wondered this, kneeling beside the water. She thought of James MacLaren, who perhaps had found his wife and would go to live once more among the outcasts of all the races.

She tried to picture him but nothing came, no face, no voice. She struggled, wiping water from her arms, to bring him nearer. To remember his confidences, his eyes, his brow, his broken fingers. His shoulders and his waist. The hair she'd cut. She closed her eyes until his breath was on her neck. Until she had him firmly.

She washed her face and dried it, then walked back into camp.

MR. WILLIS RODE in at midday with the oxen. They'd shown up at the main camp that morning. He brushed off her apologies, and she had scarcely filled his pockets with roasted potatoes when Israel rode in on the Bannock mare he'd ransomed, with Mr. Littlejohn on the stumbling brown. The pretty white mare was gone. By then it was four o'clock. Still, Israel meant to go on.

"There's no point," she argued. "We should stay the night."

But Israel had meant to travel, and so he would, and so they did, and kept going while the sun went down, and the sky turned gray and blue and the stars came out, until the road was just the palest scar floating on the dirt.

There was no water anywhere. The sage grew tall here, flaky and abhorrent; it clawed as she passed. Her heels gave into soft burrows in the sand. They'd lost the road somehow.

At last Israel halted and told them all to quiet, and they heard what he was listening to: the distant cry of geese. By these, at midnight, they found the river.

SHE WOKE on a bed in the open, in the pink of dawn. She took the pail, left Israel sleeping. She wished to see the river, but a narrow slough lay between it and their camp. The slough stretched as far as she could see in both directions, thick with sedge and willow. She found her way down, in hope of a crossing, and walked its muddy border. A flock of small herons roared up from a log as she passed, rose away in a scarf of white. The log all but bridged the black water.

She stepped onto the slick wood, lightly, and balanced along it. When she could cross no farther, she held her skirt and stepped down. She felt a pride in doing this so readily, slogging shin-deep through muck, when back in Iowa, she'd picked her way around the smallest puddles.

Moths in the saw grass clung with dewy wings. She pushed through, climbed the rise. Sand sugared her muddy shoes. She saw the padded prints of wolves, the quiltwork tracks of lizards.

This air seemed filmed with moisture, the distance pale and muted. She had a sense of sea. And breaking over the rim at last, she did behold it, with her pail. The true Columbia. She slid down and down the shady bank to the gray sand of the river's edge. So, she thought. We are here.

The stark vastness of it took her breath. The breadth and depth and strength of water was like nothing she had seen. Brown barren hills rose on the distant shore. Three gulls cradled past her on the breeze. They turned their heads to look, as though surprised. She was so far from any life they had foreseen.

She stepped in to rinse her shoes. Little clam shells lay beneath her soles. Minnows swept by, as fine as grass seed.

She thought of her secret child, and wondered if it moved, and thought of the great distance behind her. How long a journey this had been.

I will hold you to a rendering of favors to my account, she had written once. *Until the years have settled it.* But now she wondered how she had ever believed there could be some accounting. How would she have found a weight for wind, or heat, or love? What equation would make sense, involving water flowers, rotting cattle? Flies and lust? Did it matter, in the end, who came willingly and who was compelled? All were changed alike.

This shore. They'd come by thousands to see it, and now its great indifference confirmed the common madness of their dreams. Nothing welcomed here. Nothing spoke to any aspiration. What strange human urge had brought them?

And then she saw. It was the same thing she had known about herself, dreaming of James MacLaren. As Israel must have known in some way, too, when he dreamed of Oregon: that out of some deficit in themselves, they had invested those things they dreamed of with qualities they could not possibly possess.

She stood, then, and was very small with her pail and dress. Reduced to the essence, the simplest form: awareness and a ready frame.

Once she'd walked across a plain of grass to find a man whose essence had been this. Now here she stood. And understood it. She had endured.

With her feet in the water, she sensed him, very near.

The river was not actually deep. The floor was sandy. Her skirts dragged, clinging to her legs. She walked, bending forward in her concentration. When the water reached her waist, she let the pail go and walked and walked, a long way out, and still it was only to her neck. And when she stopped and turned east to the bright margin of the world, she was so alone in it, there seemed nothing before or behind her but this water, no sound but the sweep of water, no sense but the salt of grief, and water.

SHE MASTERED HERSELF, of course, and was useful again, though the pail was lost. She continued the journey in wet shoes and riddled stockings, wearing the wet dress. The morning dried it.

They found the road at last, and walked all day. Indians followed them, calling out in broken English, saying prayers they knew. They laughed, blasphemed. Emma threw a stone. Lucy apologized to Israel three times about the pail. Her eyes felt swollen.

And then, through the terrible sage, came a glimmer of green fields and small squares of white, like cubes of sugar, and a long rail fence. The whole scene quickened her breath unpleasantly, she didn't know why.

She stopped. Her ribs squeezed in, like fingers locking. She sat in the dust, afraid she'd cry again. Tom Littlejohn, at her arm, said something, and Caroline said, "What, Mother? What?"

It became clear, with Israel's patient questioning, that what she needed was to wash her feet and to find some more appropriate attire, and thereby summon up her courage. So they camped beside the road, though it was three o'clock, and pitched the tent, and she lay down inside it, while the girls got out the trunk of clothes and Israel walked ahead with Littlejohn to announce themselves and to bring water.

She lay. The tent was warm. She was very tired. Half dreaming, she had an idea to sew the wool of her ruined stockings into gloves. This seemed a comforting plan. She drifted off in the sound of breaking sticks, the kettle's clank.

Israel returned. She went out, refreshed a little, and saw the girls had dressed as well as they were able. They'd found a gown for Mary, and Daniel looked as good as a boy his age could look for long. They begged Israel to let them all go in, and Tom said he would take them.

So then they stood together, only Husband and Wife, in the quiet.

She looked at him. She could look at him now, because he was changed, and so was she.

"How is your thumb?" she asked.

"Sore," he said. "But Whitman's a doctor."

"Should I do something now?"

"No," he said. "Thank you."

She nodded. They could see the children walking, the Indians coming to flank them on each side.

"Are they all right?" she asked.

"They're fine."

She watched her girls walk with the Indians beside them. Sarah stopped, hands on her hips, and Lucy heard her distant voice as she scolded, waving them off with fearless authority. They did move off.

Israel said, "I think I'll lie down a minute."

"All right."

She brought out her clothes and draped them on the trunk's lid. The blue and white dress she'd kept clean. She had a grayish petticoat, and the wedding stockings, white silk with blossoms. But they were wrinkled and dusty, so she rinsed and draped them on the wagon's tongue to dry. Then washed her feet, and washed her shoes, and put them in the sun. She pulled the pins from her hair. She gathered the fresh clothes against herself, all but the drying stockings, and crept into the tent and undressed.

"Come here," he said, half sleeping.

She lay down beside him, in the warm crook of his arm. She pulled a corner of blue dress across her unclothed belly. Though her frame, it seemed, still kept its secrets.

"Better now?" he asked, and stroked her temple with his unharmed thumb.

"Yes, I think so." She gave a rueful smile.

"I don't know why you'd balk at meeting Narcissa Whitman. Of all things."

She said, "My mother was a minister's wife."

"Your father was a minister?"

"Yes. Israel. You knew that."

"Did I? Well, I doubt she resembles your mother."

Then they were quiet. His breathing slowed. She thought of the river, of what she had seen and thought that morning. "So, we are here," she murmured to him.

He stirred, almost awake. "What?" he asked.

"I was wondering if it's anything like you imagined. Now that we're here."

But he was sleeping.

SHE WOKE to flies and the tread of moccasins. To a leg, a shadow of movement, drifting white. Of embroidered silk.

She bolted up in a rush of breath, and out, with Israel's call behind her. Scandalous, in nothing but a flopping corset from which the hairpins flew, a charred stick in her hand before she even thought (and the kettle upset behind her), flying bare-legged through dry grass.

The Kiyouse had come to squat around the camp. As she rushed at them, they startled up, dusty as dogs, wide-eyed, some laughing, some gabbling as she ran among them. One grabbed her hair. She screamed and flailed, she beat him while he laughed. He kicked her legs from under her, so that her teeth caught against his reeking skin, his naked chest, and she hit the ground and scrambled up, but they were bounding away and dodging through the sage. She set out in pursuit, but more hands caught at her—fingers fixed around her naked arm—and she heard her husband's voice, felt his grip control her, and she could only turn and strike his chest in gratitude and say, "My stockings, my stockings," while he tried to catch her hands, to hold her safe, in mute apology.

To Go Now and Attend

MacLaren came down off Craig's trail at last and found himself before the sun was even up, amazed and sitting his horse above the Spaldings' mission.

Small eastern trees were planted in nice rows, as tall as a man and leafing. The river gleamed. On this wide bench above it, the Presbyterians had built two halls of logs and boards. Beyond, he saw a mud-brick residence, limewashed, into which a dozen windows had been cased and set, trim painted green. Fruit trees grew behind the pickets of a garden. He sat in wonder, looking around: at shops and sheds, a race and housed wheel for grist. Stubbled fields, bare turned earth. He'd almost forgotten what the industry of man could accomplish.

He was passing a new building's frame and the smell of sawn pine when a voice called, "What's your business, sir?"

He saw a broad neat-featured man, very strong, with dark hair tied back.

"None," he said.

"No business?"

"No."

"Well, I guess that's a sorry state."

He supposed it was.

"You could take the other ends of these timbers with me and do a day's work for the Lord, if that would help."

MacLaren said, "I could put in an hour."

The carpenter's name was Jackson; by noon they had the roof up over the mill, and by midday they'd set to sawing bolts from cedar logs to split for shakes.

———————

SPALDING WOULD PAY him in potatoes, MacLaren learned that evening, the same as natives. He sat with Jackson by the creek, where the man had set out wires to catch eels. They draped the eels on poles above an alder fire, and smoked and ate them.

"They're good people," Jackson said. "You'd not want to see any man or woman work harder than they do, and they won't say it, but these Indians have all but worn them out. Five years ago they had brought all these people to the Lord. Seems like more go bad each day. We have two good cows. They came back crazy last week, someone cut off their ears and tails. I hate to see that kind of cruelty. I don't understand it."

MacLaren watched the dark-eyed man, his strength and pent vigor, thinking these Spaldings were lucky in their carpenter.

"These last two years, they've just gone bad. Tore down fences, filled in ditches, broke out windows."

"Why build more, then," MacLaren asked, "with them telling you to go? Why not find some other place?"

"Well, there's good Christians still. The whole tribe divided. The Christian ones moved down the river about five miles. Timothy sends some horses up on Sundays, and the Spaldings ride down, and Reverend says the sermon."

"And the Whitmans?" he asked, because that mission and this one were a pair, the Whitmans not a hundred miles away, among the Cayuse. "Are they faring better?"

Jackson said, "These Nez Perce are the good ones."

———————

THE NEXT DAY Spalding himself returned from somewhere and came to see the work. A stern-looking man with a tall domed head, he wore a black coat and buckskin leggings, and left again without asking of MacLaren who he was or why he'd come, so that up on the roof again, MacLaren wondered aloud to Jackson whether it was common for men to wander down out of the mountains and look around and fall to working. Jackson said it was.

At midday they went up to the house. A crook-backed domestic brought them dinner in a large unfinished room built onto the main residence. They ate at a table with the sky above, pine planks stacked seasoning along both walls. A boy and girl played behind the pickets of the garden fence.

The next day Eliza Spalding herself came and held out a thin undemanding hand to MacLaren and learned his name. She was a plain-looking woman with fine white skin. She said, "How long is it since you heard your last sermon?"

He looked beyond the potatoes on his plate, remembering Lucy Mitchell's pelerine. He said he supposed it had been two months now.

"May I number you among us, then, on Sunday?"

He didn't even know when Sunday was, but looked at her, thinking of Jackson's stories: how the people here had come insultingly, danced naked in her schoolroom, torn up the pages she had made them. Just that morning he had seen this woman stand and gaze among her spindly apple trees, as though awaiting something distant to appear—her thin shoulders fallen in, arms crossed, hand to her chin—so he'd felt exiled himself in that moment, to see her with her back turned to the light.

He said, "All right."

HE RODE with them two days later. The Spaldings had an infant, and a boy about six years' age, and a daughter about ten. This girl wore a cloak and wool bonnet and stood beside a small bay horse, and MacLaren heard her call very easily in Nez Perce to a man who came to help her mount. During the ride, she told MacLaren that her name was Eliza, like her mother's, and that when she had turned ten, she'd go to the Whitmans, to school.

"When will that be?"

"Three weeks," she said.

"I know a girl your age there," he said. "Her name is Emma Ruth."

They spoke for a good part of the ride, much of it in Nez Perce. Young Eliza told him about Timothy, the chief of this Alpoway village, and when at last they crossed in the canoe together, she waved gaily at the Indians gathered waiting; when they landed, she leaped and ran to be taken high into the embrace of a handsome Nez Perce man. She put her arms around his neck, and hugged him, and called out that he was Timothy.

MacLaren smiled. He saw a log house with turned fields where potatoes must have grown. And Timothy was a man of MacLaren's own age but of such striking natural elegance, such gravity and kindness in deportment, that MacLaren, on taking his hand, could not help but wonder what kind of life or gift had shaped this man, and said, "My heart is glad of this meeting."

When the Spaldings rode home on their borrowed horses that evening, MacLaren stayed, smoked, and ate while Timothy's boys eyed him over their shoulders. And such was the intelligence of this man, and so carefully did he listen, that their conversation soon turned to those intimate matters of which MacLaren rarely spoke or had not at all. Balanced as he was on a troubled edge these days between an old life and some uncertain new one, it seemed that if anyone could understand his heart and help make something clearer, this man could. So he told of his children and Lise, of the Americans and Lucy Mitchell. They spoke of the Presbyterians and their missions. Maybe Craig was right, MacLaren said. The whites did not belong here, the Americans could not belong here.

"Would you keep them out," asked Timothy, "if you had that power?"

"If I could undo their coming," MacLaren said, "I would."

"Why?"

"You know why."

"No."

They spoke in Nez Perce, and when MacLaren had made himself as clear as he was able, Timothy said, "I also have two hearts. But from the time of being a child, I saw those people had good ways. They have power. Our old life was small. I felt very foolish when I saw how much we had not learned how to do, and we were able to do these things and did not. These white people are your people. You should not wish them gone. They bring strong ways. To make food. To heal. To understand God. To write. To know. To remember. I see this always. I think we will be strong by staying with your people. I think those who oppose them will suffer. And what you say may happen, bad things may come. But sorrow and fear make men stand crooked. With trust, I can stand straight."

They sat after that, and the firelight was beautiful on Timothy's oiled skin and on his strong fingers, and his eyes were clear and the power of his vision so uncorrupted that MacLaren felt his own shift strangely. So for those hours, it did seem that the world demanded only patience and trust in the goodness of God and man. And when he woke in the morning, MacLaren remembered the cows with their ears cut off, and the schoolhouse windows broken; but during those hours, he had felt hope.

He walked out into the dawn. In these long dry months of fall, the river had waned to leave wide cobbled beaches. Spiderwebs in dewy silver spanned dry stalks of grass. Geese lived on the islands.

———————

So HE CAME to live in the big lodge at Alpoway, with Timothy's people, in the time of year he thought to be October. He was welcome. There was a winter to pass, and a long spring in which something unforeseen might come about. Until then, he went by morning to the river to bathe, and sat in the sun and smoked with other men, and went with them to geld the past year's colts, and rode into the hills to hunt.

Alone one day, he saw a bench of land where a creek came into the river, and saw it could be a home. He made camp. That evening he stood in spent grass beside his horse, remembering a dark fullness of summer when Lucy Mitchell had come with her lantern to find him. It seemed that something she had said that night had changed him, but he had no memory of what it was, or whether he was still changed because of it. It was an effort, now, to recall any of his remote and various lives.

He thought of the mission to the west, how mysterious and unlikely it was that Lucy Mitchell and Lise had both come to the same place. He considered whether they had bottled him up somehow—impersonal as a rock slide across the river—whether he might have continued to Vancouver if it had not meant passing that mission and these two women. Neither of whom he had kept, it seemed, nor quite released.

But no, he thought. He could go anywhere. He could have gone anywhere else. It only seemed that he, like they, had come finally to some unpredictable rest.

So he killed a deer next dawn and brought it home to people who did want him, and ate with the families in the big winter lodge. He watched the children play on mats. The lodge was well made, perhaps eighty feet in

length, with the fires of each family in a line down the center. A gap along
the ridge let out the smoke, and afternoon light beamed through it and lay
in a long stripe across the floor. They told the time by its travel. In early
morning he lay in the sound of breathing. He watched soot feathers wave in
the rafters, studied hanging sacks of pemmican, the furs and drying moccasins, steel traps and old cradleboards and sheep's-horn bows put up in
gloomy corners. A young white female dog had chosen to sleep at night
curled quietly by his side.

And when he woke with her fur against him and found himself thinking of his girls, and of Alexander, it was not with fresh pain, but more with
a kind of wonder, as he would have felt in running his fingers over a numb
scar formed on a wound he'd thought would never heal. Because they
seemed to have sat down somewhere in very bright sun, his children, cross-
legged, with Elizabeth holding Alexander by the belly, making him keep
still. Junie's hair had pulled from its plaits and blew across her eyes. They
seemed to be somewhere far north by the sea, or on a mountaintop, squinting in some white cold light. Each time he thought of them, they were sitting
like that, in the way of dreams, denying any change or further vision. Watching from their stone pile, they seemed content. Maybe only his shame said
they were, for he was more or less content these days himself.

ONE DAY a man appeared from the west with six horses, all with packs un-
laden. So MacLaren went out to help him cross the river and to hear his
news.

He was Montagnais or French Cree. They unsaddled the horses while
this man said that Whitman needed flour, the place was full of Americans
and they had no food, and Spalding was to send some.

The man said that for his own part he thought it was a waste of time,
the Cayuse were dying of black measles, and they hated the Whitmans and
their Americans and their American God, and they wanted them to go. The
Catholics would buy them out. They'd be gone within a month.

They put the pack saddles in the big canoe to cross them dry. The
horses were to swim it. The man sat on the gunwales and produced a pipe,
and MacLaren said, "Have you news of a woman named Lise? Or a family
named Mitchell?"

"Your wife, Bouchman took her. She live at the fort."

The words confounded him. The man had not even looked around. MacLaren said, "You're Finlay." It did come to him that he'd once had a young man like him flogged for theft.

Finlay grinned around unkindly. "You are like your wife, eh? Too many men. Then you forget."

On the river sand, MacLaren, with the wood-framed saddle in his grasp saw how he could raise and swing it, how the rings of the flying girths would catch the man high and low, too quick to step away, and the hurled weight of the frame might bowl him over, and he'd have a start on some revenge. But Timothy was watching.

"Did she want to go with this Bouchman?" MacLaren asked.

"I don't know what she want, God damn. That why I kick her out."

———

MacLaren walked away and spent a troubled night with the white dog beside him, and next morning he borrowed Timothy's plow and harnesses and set out for the place he'd liked. Timothy said he could cut that earth and have it ready for spring planting. That he could build a house and live his life quietly, as he wished, and they would help each other.

Drum and Sally had never pulled a plow, but the soil was light and rich, and enough rain had fallen that the sod broke easily. The white dog slept in the sun or watched. By the end of four days, the whole field lay in coarse uneven lists that curved with the curving of the bench, and when he climbed the hill on the evening he was done, and looked down, it resembled nothing so much as a striped mussel shell, and should have pleased him.

But nothing else had changed. He was not less easy at the end of his labor than he had been riding out. What had come to be a gentle field was raw and overturned by worries; it was Jocko's Nick Finlay driving a plow around and around inside him, and all day each day, as mute as dirt, he'd followed it, turning up no fruitful words but only the old fixed stones of hurt. His hair was long again and getting in his eyes.

He rode up the river canyon after that, deep into where the pines began, and labored for another week, cutting a raft of logs to season and float down when the water rose in spring.

One night tiny sparks of falling ice swirled down and woke him. He'd been dreaming of Lucy Mitchell. She was old and white, and lived among tall marble halls that he knew was Oregon City. He'd felt a great joy to see her again and a great sorrow that she was old before him, and a wonder at what she'd done. She'd shown him a school she had caused to be built, and a tall library, and there were buildings going up all over, mills and other grand works of man, while all this time he knew he was unchanged and had accomplished nothing.

By morning the sky was thick with snow. He sat and watched the falling flakes melt and disappear into the river.

He packed his horses and arrived at Alpoway that evening, shaking the snow from his clothes and going into the lodge with its steamy smells of wheat and boiling deer meat. There he found Jackson the carpenter.

Eliza had turned ten, and Jackson had gone west with Spalding and Finlay to take her to the Whitmans' school, but now Jackson was back alone, bringing word of trouble. Timothy turned to MacLaren and said, "This man says Marcus Whitman will be killed."

MacLaren sat to listen.

Jackson told him, "Tiloukaikt's young are dying of measles. There's bad talk. He's sending riders up and down the river, to get the other tribes to join. He wants war down to Oregon City. He wants the Americans out."

"You left Eliza at the school there?"

"He'd promised her all this time. Now she won't hear otherwise."

"And what do you think?"

"I think there's trouble coming fast."

"AND WHAT ARE your thoughts on all of this, Mr. MacLaren?" Reverend Spalding's wife, Eliza, asked him the next noon. Because he'd thought fit to canoe the cold Snake with Jackson that morning and offer what assistance he could.

They'd stepped out of the world of thin snow, silver light, into the dim warmth of this front parlor where a green settee was waiting with dread formality to seat them. MacLaren had listened quietly, still smelling of fish smoke and old sweat and snow. The lines of his hands were etched black.

He said, "Craig and Isabel will harbor all of you. It's good ground up there, it's defended on three sides. On any sign of danger, I'd go there."

"You could hardly name a place that I would find less congenial." Her eyes were bright in the window light. Her brow was very lined, although she wasn't old.

"He's spoken words against you, but he'd never see you killed. And you have enough loyal people, but in a war, they could not hold this place. Nor Alpoway."

The maid had come with tea on a tray, and two Japanned cups, as he was speaking. There was a tin bowl of sugar and a silver spoon.

The fire shifted in the grate. She said, "It's the Catholics, you know. They've turned these peoples' minds against us."

MacLaren said, "I am going there straight after this."

He held the tea, not certain what she thought or what he meant to do. A flock of crows had settled in the limbs of a black cottonwood outside the window. He could hear them faintly through the glass. In the west, silver clouds were bringing a new snow. It was coming.

She said, "My husband has stood in our church for twenty minutes with the muzzle of a gun held to his cheek. Did you know that?"

"No."

"I watched it. Those were our people once. And they held him as indifferent as if he were a dog to be shot down."

He nodded.

"Last year five hundred of them stood outside our house with torches. They pulled the doors from the buildings. They smashed things. They stole the eggs from our hens and crushed them. They said they wished to tie and whip me."

He saw her green eyes, the white hand at her throat.

She said, "They were so promising at first. If you had heard them weep. Their souls flocked to Jesus like doves to the window. We showed them how to make all of this. We gave them hope."

He said, "I wonder if you know these people."

"Do I know them?" She took his eyes, and the rooms of the house were quiet. "Have I written hymnals in my own hand in their language? Have I taught them to weave? Spin? Write? Have I held their babies, sat in the dirt to eat of their food?"

Even the crows had lifted away in the somber afternoon.

"Yes," she said. "I know them. I know that above all, they are full of *wind*."

"You should go some other place. I don't know why you think you shouldn't."

"Our Lord feared not, Mr. MacLaren. No good comes from fear. No morality is governed by it. We must live by Him in love, and in the knowledge that our selfish actions oft prove fatal. But love preserves us, here or in the hereafter."

He thought, This country does attract fanatics and torment them.

She said, "We are moved by our responsibility to these people."

So he felt his duty ended. He rose, with his hat by the crown, and settled it. Such loneliness had surged again, in her presence, that he pulled his brim against it. She sat and looked at Jackson, both holding sugared tea.

"Who will attend to them," she said, "if we do not?"

He said, "I'll go there."

He'd put on his coat when she came behind him. He was opening the door.

"But God knows the hearts of little children," she said. "And calls them to His side. In that we may rejoice."

He slipped on the frozen steps, and fell hard on his hip, and swore, and stood and brushed himself.

His horse was tied to the fence in muddy snow. MacLaren freed his reins, rubbed the dried curls of sweat. The strong sweet odor steadied him.

"Wait," she called. "I'll get Mrs. Johnston to bring you food."

But he mounted and heeled away.

HE HAD MEANT to begin the journey west at dawn, but the snow was holding off, and there would be a moon; he doubted he would sleep.

He cleaned his pistol while Drum ate a feed of wheat, and the sun was still up behind the banked gray clouds when he set out.

On a good fit horse, it was three days' ride, 120 miles if he did not lose the way in snow, and they'd been ten miles east and back already. He climbed the first creek in falling light, the snow deep in this canyon. By dark he'd come out on top of the low range, the old horse easy and scarcely blowing. He dismounted anyway, and led him afoot across the barren hills while a full moon rose. His hip was sore, and his elbow, and he remembered falling on the step. He thought of the reverend's wife, and of her girl sharing rooms with Lucy Mitchell's daughters. He thought of how he'd meant to stay at Timothy's, and of this new imperative he felt to go now, and attend. And he wondered what it was that moved a man in ways he least expected, so that he might resolve one day to stay and the next to go; so that he would resist a thing he loved once, or cherish what he had disdained; so that by night he hoped, and mistrusted by day; except there was some mutable notion of necessity.

———————

HE SLEPT COLD and rode the next day under lowering clouds. With hands in his pockets, he played the hidden shapes of things: compass, pipe, a pair of rifle balls, a tin of Jackson's matches. Snow and sky were an equal gray, and his thoughts turned after a while to what he might be doing. There was Lucy Mitchell and her girls, young Eliza, Lise and this man Bouchman, and Timothy, Whitman, and the Spaldings, who'd come to do their good, the Cayuse whose children were dying as his own had died, and the one thing he might surely do for all of them was to go to their chief, Tiloukaikt, and speak in council on this matter of war.

What would he say? For it appeared to him that by some terrible accident, the genius of each race was opposed at its foundation. He believed it was an accident.

We cannot choose, he thought, the people we're born into nor what they teach us. So that opposition exists, and appears to us as evil. It is a part of life, and sorrow is its natural consequence.

He would not count for the Cayuse all the wrongs they'd suffered, or would suffer, from the greed or ignorance or charity of this other race. From accident or fate. They were their own authorities.

So what could he say to stop this war? What counsel against rage and sorrow?

But that he knew the people they opposed and had come to love them also.

Ideas will not save us, he thought. Not right or wrong, not peace or retribution. Our stories are all we have. The only thing that can ever save us is to learn each other's stories. From beginning to end.

Now he understood the priest Laurent, who had collected lives: a man who would find the particulars, if he could, of every man he met, would not hesitate to begin from childhood, wondering how each had lived, slept, and learned, loved and suffered, given, earned. Dreamed. Believed. Noonday's empty hand had turned. She had said it, too.

For every life we know, we are expanded.

There is no forgiveness without stories. There is no dignity. There is no way to speak in other tongues but that.

He was considering this when the sun set gold and gray.

PAST NIGHTFALL he rode to the edge of a Cayuse camp, on the banks of Tosheh Creek. Dogs barked. It was a new camp, hasty, and he heard high voices of alarm. He waited in the dark, still mounted.

"You people," he called in Nez Perce, "I am a King-George-Man."

A small woman met him, almost a child. She was holding an old fusil. From shadows in the lodges, voices, shapes around the fire, he believed they might all be children.

"Why are you here?" he asked. The men, he thought, must be at council.

She answered that some were sick. That many children were sick and dying.

"I'm riding to the mission," he said. "I'm hungry. I saw your fires."

She looked uneasy. Drum Hill shifted, pawed the thin snow for feed.

"Where are the women?" he asked. There should be women, he thought, in a camp of sick children.

"Killing." She looked away. "They are killing the *soyapus*."

He pulled Drum's head up, and when he turned, she raised the fusil and fired.

The ball struck his hip like an ax blow and half unseated him; his hat was off in the jump. He caught it, doubling from the pain, the wind already in his eyes, and felt the old horse lean and stretch, gain speed through the open camp. He could hear his own voice. His head was in the horse's mane, roaring, and the snow reeled under and Drum still lengthened, casting downward through the belt of trees, and they were out again on the open hill and he was cursing.

He cursed. He gripped his hat, pounding downward in the filmy dark.

Each stride was like another blow, and he thought he ought to see about the blood, but his arms had gone as weak as a child's, the reins slipping. He couldn't stop the horse or see enough to tell.

By the time they reached the crossing of the creek, he had begun to float. He reined Drum in and stood him. Steam rolled off the sweating neck. MacLaren breathed, and the old horse trembled, rocking with quick shallow breaths.

The wind had stung his eyes; he wiped them. His hands were shaking. He untied his robe and blanket, untied the slapping saddlebags, and pushed them off, and saw that he had dropped his rifle.

He must have dropped it when his hat had gone. He must have.

Bloody Christ. He drew the cold air hissing through his teeth. Breathing was the devil; for no reason he could see, something stabbed sharp above that bone of his hip with each breath. Blood all down his leg. *They are killing the* soyapus.

Well, the pistol was still with him.

He sent the old horse clattering up the stones, away, cold air grabbing at his throat to think of the kind of slaughter he would find, the cries coming from those grounds. Bloody Christ he thought, but Christ had nothing or maybe everything to do with it. He saw children dead and Lucy—he'd been up the river plowing, of all the senseless things—and Lise—cutting trees when he should have come. Should have come days, weeks, a month before. By God, he was no man.

His teeth were dry. The wind raked down his lungs and choked him. He should have seen the danger.

Now it hurt.

Drum had fallen to a shambling walk, and that was agony, and a gallop had been hell. He closed his eyes and roared it, furious, one great black word, and then another.

Then they were running again.

The low moon glowed muted through the clouds. It lit the rolling snow-fields, threw shadows wild enough in draws that Drum Hill bunched and bounded as a deer, leaping the dark places. It was hard to balance and stay light and keep himself from bracing in fear of pain. It was the fear of pain that made pain greater. He kept one hand on the foaming neck, watched the dark ears, sat as well as he could. They crested a rise, gained speed again downhill, the gait now rolling, imprecise, the horse near bottomed out, but MacLaren did nothing to steady or slow him. Sometimes he glanced and saw that blur of spreading dark. Blood had cooled all down the inside of the leathers. Maybe it had stopped.

His eyes burned. He wanted to sleep. They went on, went on he didn't know how long; he kept closing his eyes, and when the horse hit something, he was suddenly thrown forward.

He caught himself, fell back into the saddle as Drum rose stumbling from his knees and staggered, rhythmic breath convulsing like a bellows, steam and lather.

It was too far, MacLaren thought. They were too late.

A kind of black began to squeeze behind his eyes.

This is not the time, he thought, but he began to float above himself, and the sound of the horse's breathing dimmed and muffled.

He came clear when he hit the ground, but could only lie there. Slack hand, dull idiot lips. He thought, This is not the time.

He saw the reins drag off across the snow, the tail departing.

Whoa, he thought. Whoa.

I should breathe, he thought. He did. He breathed a shallow stabbing breath, breathed another, kept his eyes open and soon was on his knees again, looking at his bloody hands.

He got his hat. He stood. Drum Hill stood out there watching, legs trembling, ears roving back and forth. The taut gut shuddered in and out.

"Whoa."

The horse, alarmed, made wild by this run, stood wary.

So there was no time to rush things.

He took a breath, looked around. They were almost out of the hills. The plain stretched, moonlit, a pretty sight, low bluffs behind it. Darker trees where water wound through streams. They'd come a hundred miles since this time the day before.

The horse stood. Balanced on that thin blade edge. Memory and flight.

MacLaren packed some snow onto his hip. Then ate some.

He started walking toward Drum Hill, and Drum began to walk with one eye cocked. Reins dragging.

He stopped. He said, "Ten miles won't kill you."

The horse inclined his ears, not agreeing.

"Whoa."

He tried and failed three times to walk him down, the horse alarmed at his halting gait, jerking away at the last moment. By necessity or inspiration, he resorted to lying in the snow, eyes closed, until he felt hot breath glide across his palm.

He clambered on at last, glad that no one saw him.

"Go," he said, and got a killing trot, and then a gallop, but by the time they came to the ruts of the road, they were swimming slowly through a dream.

A rail fence began. His eyes stung from the wind. He wiped them and could make out roofs of mission houses, see a glint of fires on the grounds. He let Drum walk, but could hear nothing over the wet firing of the horse's breath, the black gurgle of the millrace in the ditch beside the road.

A bare willow stood on the waste below a hill. He reined away through clashing stalks, halted in behind it. He stepped down. Drum staggered as he did. MacLaren tied him.

"All right," he said. But he had no plan.

It was quiet. He thought he saw small fires burning in the yard, by the sides of buildings. He had no sense of the scope of things or where they stood.

The darkness deepened in a passing cloud.

"All right," he said again, and started walking.

There was a square house. Another, beyond, was tall and narrow, and in that one, the windows flickered. He heard one burst its glass. He made it to the gate and rested. Studying the yard. A cart was overturned. Bare sapling trees lay cut in tangles.

"Finlay!" he called. "Tiloukaikt!"

All authority was feigned. His breath stabbed short. In Nez Perce, he called, "You Cayuse people!" He let the red coat open as he started out again, so they could see the cut of it and know him.

Now came voices. The shadows were not empty. From somewhere in the yard, a man said, "Oh, Jesus, come quickly."

It seemed very far to walk.

Dogs slunk away at his approach. He made out a stain of melted snow, the reek of offal, signs of common butchery. A cow, by the smell, or an ox. The bones and meat were gone.

The voice had come from beyond that. Near the house, he saw the form of some other fallen creature, but it was an overturned settee, with a woman sprawled and frozen, and a man beside her who lived enough to speak, and another who was still.

He dropped beside the man who'd spoken. A bloody hole glittered. Guts trembled out. Shot in the back, MacLaren thought. The hand was cool. The man was breathing but did not seem to see him.

"What's happened here?" he asked softly. "Can you speak?" He felt a powerful desire to lie in the snow beside him.

The dying man said nothing.

I'll get to my feet, MacLaren thought. His hands were in the snow, and he would get to his feet, but he wanted to lie in snow. He would get to his feet on a count of three, and counted to himself, and stood, clumsy. He took out his pistol and checked it. The moonlight brightened, but his hands were cold and fumbling. He closed his eyes. Then gathered himself and called out boldly in English, "You people! I'm an agent of the King! I'll speak with Mr. Spalding or Mr. Whitman. I'll speak to them now!" In Nez Perce, he said the same.

The house startled into argument. He heard voices from the rooms. He stood his ground. Then, from the attic above, he heard a child's voice calling.

He went around below the window, called up, "Who are you?"

It was a young face in the open pane, no child he knew. He heard more children's voices behind her, and cries.

"Are you children up there?" he called. His throat was tight. He craned his neck to see. But the face was gone, and three Cayuse men were coming out the door in front of him.

"Are the Mitchells there?" he called up. "Are they with you?" He'd stepped back with one eye on these men, who had grown to five approaching. He held up his hand to delay them. Having more important interviews at that moment.

An older girl had come, and called down, "The doctor and mother are killed. Mr. Kimball is all bloody." She said, "We don't know what to do."

"Where's Eliza Spalding?"

The dark men were coming on, though, and he tried to circle away beneath the windows, but more had emptied from another door and were coming across the snow. He had the pistol in the one hand, hatchet ready in the other.

"I'll get you down," he told the girl, but had no hope of it. There seemed no one here to help. No army in a thousand miles would stand against these people. He called, "But say again, do you know Daniel Mitchell or Emma Ruth? Do you know a Lucy Mitchell?"

"No," said the girl. "There's no such here."

"Stay back," he said. Because they were all around him. He said, "I don't know what you've done."

They swept into sudden motion, regardless of his aim, and the pistol roared and kicked, and he wheeled, and there was Jocko's Nick coming up with a knife and another Cayuse swinging a shovel with great force before he could turn clear. It caught his ribs above that hip where the ball had struck. He fell to his knees, not even screaming.

Then hands were grappling, and somehow he was up and lurching free and swinging. A stone club came at his head and he dodged it, then failed the second time and met it. A sharp light came with the blow and cracked all the bones of his head.

My eye is knocked out, he thought. He was in the snow. They were pulling his coat, his arms and legs. His body was theirs, it would not obey. He tried to speak.

He opened his eye once and saw the doorjamb as he passed beneath it.

"Is my eye out?" he asked them. On his back, on the floor. They had tied his hands in front of him. He sat in swirling lights, tried to stand, and fell onto cold furniture, retching.

So we'll all die here, he thought.

He woke again, curled on the planks. He tried to feel his eye, but his hands were numb. They were tied. Torches and candles moved in blurs of light. He squinted.

"Tiloukaikt," he said. But there was no answer.

"Who is there?" he tried again. "What are your names?"

But they only banged away like carpenters in the echoing rooms.

He thought of war riding down the valley. Having committed the first unthinkable act, these people had no need to stop, no reason. They were lost and would take as many as they could, in the missions, on the trail, and that would be their victory.

"Come, Lord Jesus, come quickly," said the man in the snow outside.

"Where is Spalding?" MacLaren asked. He was suddenly mad for water.

From his good eye now he could see they'd piled the furniture, knocked the doors from their straps, were breaking up kindling. They would burn this house and all of them inside it.

He heard the children singing softly in the attic.

"You men hear me," he said in Nez Perce. "Hear me."

There was glass all over the floor. He saw one man's gaze shift to him. Saw firelight on skin. An arm in dressed deer hide. Torchlight glinted off the shards of glass like constellations.

"My wife was a woman you know," he said. "Her name was Lise."

Jocko's Nick.

"Her name is Lise."

One man stopped.

He wanted to speak because stories

But the words slipped and laughed, they were gone.

"Her name is Lise."

Another glance exchanged. Jocko's Nick was a son of a bitch they knew that.

His mind cleared then. He said, "One year ago this day she walked away when snow was falling. When our children were all dying."

They were a listening people. They were a listening people and he knew to speak. They had no books no letters but when a man was speaking they would stop they would listen until he had said what he'd begun to say, they would sit and hear him. To do otherwise was not

He had thought it would be easier.

He summoned himself.

"My three children died. Her three children. I had no way to stop it. I carried the last girl in my arms, I walked across the mountains to those Blackrobes but on the way she died.

"Then a wise man told me sorrow is a poison. I did not believe him."

He talked. He said what he could think of, so they would know his life, how he had come in anger among these Americans they opposed, and how a woman and a child were kind to him. How he woke and saw what harm his sorrow had caused. He said he knew these people. Some were made to come. Some could not go back. All feared the Cayuse as the Cayuse feared them. He said, "All people need forgiveness. And if these must die, they must. But those who cannot forgive children will not easily be forgiven."

Still the children sang. He heard their voices through the ceiling.

"Hear them," he said. "They are standing straight, these children. They have no sorrow."

———

AFTER THAT he sat on the cold planks. The wind came through. He'd forgotten himself while he was speaking, but when they moved off to another room he began to shake and it was all the devil, he was racked and nothing he could do. For a while he could hear himself crying and he thought he could hear water.

A clock chimed two. All quiet. He was mad for water.

He lay in swimming shadows, it seemed, awake, awake, but hours must have gone. It was later, and he looked out from above some agony that seemed to be someone else's. Upstairs, the children cried and whispered very loud. He would go out the door for water.

Later, he saw a man in a blanket come down the stairs and pass out of the door. Stooped and carrying a pail.

The clock chimed three.

A cat walked yowling through the rooms.

A place in his mind said he was dying of the cold. The voice insisted. It made him rise. He walked on his knees to a coverlet and pulled it from a corpse. It was frozen in one place, shaped by blood to that dead shoulder. He wrapped himself.

When he fell asleep, he dreamed the sound of gunfire.

———

HE WOKE to a gray room of corpses, wreckage, unhinged doors. Children were coming silent down the stairs, were passing through.

Somehow he had risen.

He followed them to the door. They stepped across a fallen man; he was lying in the dooryard in a stain of blood, MacLaren thought it might be himself. The water pail had spilled and melted the snow. He touched his eye with the backs of his bound hands. It was in its socket. Pink water seeping out.

Of course it wasn't him. He was standing here.

He stood and watched the children following their captors across the grounds to a house. Their mothers called from windows. He watched the faces, but he couldn't see them, he listened to their voices and none was Lucy Mitchell.

He won release then, with a cutting edge of glass. No one stopped him.

AT THE MILLRACE, he fell and put his head into the ditch. He clawed the ice out and drank and drank.

He was much better then. He lay beside the sound of water and saw the bare hills and the birds in the blue sky. He had broken his hand once

The good part of his mind said, You should go. You'd better see what you can do.

Sometime later, the horse was yet alive, tied to the willow tree. He saw the stiff sweat. Deep hollows above the eyes. But the eyes themselves were bright. They had watched him coming. He leaned at last. Put his ear to that broad cheek, held his hands under the flowing breath to warm them.

HE HAD a sense of skimming as he rode away this time, very slowly. Smiled. Gliding above the snow. Beyond the fence, a flock of birds burst from the stubble, wheeled and scattered. But he was spent.

At a fork in the road, he could not remember. The horse had waited. He got on again.

ANOTHER TIME he had fallen in the snow.

By evening he found himself outside the fort at Walla Walla with a handful of cold against his head.

He sat in the factor's office. And spoke. And believed he had said something about settees. For here was another.

"You were there?"

The wall behind him doubled with books. He was certain he had made these shelves himself one summer. A great number of books. The clock on the mantel counted.

"I've sent the Cayuse orders to desist," the factor called McBean was saying.

"How?"

"Mr. Finlay came in at dawn with some alarm. I sent Mr. Bushman. His woman wanted to go as well. I sent them out this morning."

Which shattered what was mending, he could feel. In his head. He'd been startled into laughter or did not remember laughing but heard an echo of it floating on and on.

"I take it you never saw them."

"Mitchell," he said, and stopped. All the words had wheeled and scattered.

There is blood coming out of your ear, McBean said.

They have gone down the trail, he said. The words getting small.

Who?

He'd spoken words last night. To save them. But now he could not.

. . . warn them.

but the words disappeared so fast, he couldn't find what he'd been saying

McBean said, I'm preparing a boat for Vancouver.

I need to go by land, he said.

Sir, McBean said, if the Cayuse are after you, you cannot stay here. I will not be part of this. You'll be straight on the road if I find out, with not so much as a biscuit.

The Americans, someone said. Or it was him.

It's the last of November, sir. They've passed, if they are passing. I'll give you a bed now, but I'm no surgeon, I have no care to be.

MacLaren saw the whiskered sturgeon.

Do you know where? he said with sudden clarity. And then forgot what he had hoped to learn.

HE SAW the bed and stayed in it briefly and it was gray coming in through the window when he rose and put on his coat with all the bones of his face pulsing fire on their seams. His beard was wet from the pillow.

He put on his coat. A knifing of ribs almost stopped him.

His fingertips crackled with dried blood. He brushed it off. He put the hat was gone somewhere he put on his coat and went out to the yard where the horses were saddled and waiting

I'm off, he said. I need a horse.

But it was dark if he had been speaking to someone. He was alone the instant later

A new snow had fallen. His were the only tracks.

He walked out of the gate. Ice-cold sand numbed his face there was snow along the fence rails in the setting moon. He had forgotten that the world could be so beautiful.

His hands were warm at last.

It was good to go afoot, unburdened. Such a lightness had come over him. The white bushes slid past, away, both sides of the soft track. He closed his eye as he went, with no sound of his feet in snow

Oh he would warn anyone he saw. His tongue moved inside his mouth, practicing. Up rising. But it was such a strange word, he might have been mistaken.

He walked with the bluffs above him, one eye shut. When he closed the other, she was smiling, asleep with light on her hair. Soft fur. In a theater of stones, waltzing. His hand.

It's a peculiar urge, he woke her, this naming of things.

the name is just the beginning, she said

but of what? when we've named each thing? will the world be ours to command? will we have eden again?

climbing the bluffs, he believed perhaps he could love a city with marble halls.

breath roared through his ears the bones of his face

so then he was too warm.

he checked the pockets of his coat, to save his pipe and pistol balls matches his steaming shirt received them coldly down against his belly. his daughter's coiled braid was deep on the left, where he had always kept it, but tied with a fresh cord

his hand was standing with it

he was standing in his open hand holding it breathing while the snow sifted into it, and did not melt

love preserves us here

he took off his coat and left it, and carried the braid of hair, and walked on through the falling snow, but the world was speeding away

or in the hereafter

the coat was in a heap, far down the road in front of him

he passed it

behind the clouds, the sun's cold light and children's figures flashed and dodged, shifting in bright shadows of their shapes

He squinted. Then followed them into the glare.

The Exact Reminiscences
of Emma Ruth Ross

On april 15, 1847 we started from near Cedar Rapids Iowa. After traveling six miles we were detained by a snow storm. We made a company of 42 wagons. Elected Mr. White our Captain.

Past Missouri River was a violent storm the wind caught one of our waggons and overturned it, a man who was our driver killed beneath it. He had been with us 3 days.

Every man had to take a turn standing guard at night. For the Indians there being very numerous they were finally rewarded finding our guard napping and took a dozen or more horses some valuable mares one the Captains & also Father Mitchells.

Mr. Luelling had a wagon with a nursery of fruit trees planted in it & also a wheel to measure distances.

While in Pawnee country 40 braves came on us. Mr. K could scarcely load his gun his hand shook so. Some of his family live near here. Father picked a little twig and went to meet them. Some other men were not so fortunate caught and stripped of all & came into our view in the costume of Greek slaves.

On July Fourth, some of the men took pails to a snow field & brought snow to us.

We took a cut-off stretch and went no water all day or night and there our nice mare perished and a cow of Mr. Apperson's.

At one time one of our teams seeing a small pond ran to it and took some, it proved alkali. They died some two hours later.

Mr. K. started to swim Snake River with a horse to mark a ferry. He sank in the treacherous stream in presence of his wife and family. Some said the horse struck him with his foot.

We had five guns to guard against attack from Indians. We hauled them over the mountains & then began to trade them for Cayouse ponies. Mother said just as well for I believe they are only dangerous used as a club. Some evenings we had dancing and a gay time even though we were tired. At one time in the Grand Round valley the Indians joined also. It was a comical sight.

We visited Forts Laramie, Hall, and Whitman's mission.

We halted on the river some six weeks making flat boats the men sawed lumber with a whip saw borrowed from that mission it was Dalles Mission.

While we were there a big canoe came down & they said there was trouble up the river we should push off the quickest possible. One had been there with his Indian Wife and seen it. He said the Whitmans were dead seventeen in all.

Mothers stockings are what saved us she would not stay with them on that account I mean the Indians at Whitman's mission who stole them.

Mr. Littlejohn & some other men took the stock which came down the trail near Columbia's bank.

So we all had to hurry seven families were on the boat with us & the boat not done yet. We went a ways down the river & had to stop for wind ten days it was wind and snow we were very cold then staying on the beach.

In taking our boat over the Cascades falls it went to pieces.

On Christmas day we came in a bateau as far as Switzer's by Vancouver. We had all been in our same clothes night and day some five or six weeks. Most all of what we brought was lost or not carried the last part but a few things we did carry.

We are in Bachelor Seldon Murry cabin he is up to fight the Indians & gave us his place for now. Some of the party told us that our beautiful river was not the "Willamette" but the "William et." We have not seen most of who we knew. Names of our fellow travelers I remember of course Mr. Littlejohn Capt. White, Hall, Tupper, Tony, Tuttle, Watts, Warren, Hastings, Hill, Patton, Leabo, Wells, Richardson, Lamphere, Chatfield, Willis, Apperson, Koonse, Luelling, Olmstead, Van Allman, Wilcox, Kingery, Davis, Beagle, Knighton, Ramie, and Capt. Lot Whitcomb.

New Leaves

 ⁓⌒⌒⌒⁓

*L*UCY MITCHELL HAD GONE INSIDE one afternoon to turn the dough for Caroline, and was thinking of tea when a wren flew through the open door.

They were into the season of new leaves and warmer weather. Grass had sprung in clumps from the cleared earth, and the willows were greening, and the sun still seemed too bright and new—they were not used to it yet. Murray's cabin was dark and none too snug, half of logs. The other half, behind the chimney, was of sawn boards, and it made one large room with good windows where the children stayed. Their own bed was in the old log portion, with kitchen and table and a little door between the halves. This door generally stayed closed. But the front door stood open these days to let in the new light, and the rooms were more often empty, though she kept a fire going in the hearth.

So there she was, with her back to the fire, and the little brown wren darting through the room. It hopped and lit as she watched, and bobbed from chair back to basin. Then threw itself at the dim window, fell to the sill, and blinked. Its tiny breast ticked quick as a watch. In this one quiet hour, Lucy wished it would stay for a companion. She thought of its living in the house with them, eating crumbs. Chirping from the lamp.

We should have more animals, she thought. Though surely not enough was missing in her life now to admit even the tiniest bird. And of course, Israel had drawn up a house with very nice lines and was having it built on a small lot he'd purchased up the river in town. It would be a lovely house.

The wren had settled and taken on the shape of a small brown egg.

"Smells good."

A man stood at the open door, the young man Mr. Slavin.

"I'm getting the girls to bake these days," she said. "There is a little wren just flew in. I suppose I should help it."

"Where is it?"

"I hate to frighten it."

He stood tall in the doorway, a young dark-haired man just growing into his frame, taking on a nice proportion. He had a tall brow, and his teeth were all right. She didn't know much more than that. She had seen him twice or three times in town. Israel had surveyed his place.

She said, "The bread's not done, but I was thinking of tea."

"Well, I'd have some tea, if you were offering."

They were both watching the bird on the sill, its tiny eye glinting. It had a sliver of beak like a shoe tack. It sat on hooked spidery claws.

She said, "When we were crossing over this summer, I had a wren just like this come right into my wagon one morning. It came in as I was waking."

When she moved to make the tea, it started into flight, and they had a brief chase, she and John Slavin. The bird launched into the rafters, flew all around the front of the house without finding the door, then veered to the back and lit sideways on the chimney.

Looking up at it, she said, "Israel's away." She was a little breathless from skirting the furniture. "He's been out all week. There's a family putting him up at the Hope survey. He said he would be home tonight."

"And your girls?"

"They've gone into town and took the little ones. So it's me alone for a few hours."

"I guess that doesn't happen too often."

"No, it does not." She smiled.

The wren flew again and lit on a chair, and then on the lamp above the table, and launched again, making it swing just a little, and they lost sight of it somewhere in the woodbox or around the clutter of hats and wamusses on rough pegs by the door.

"Well, anyway," she said, and made tea and set out biscuits from the morning on a nice blue coffee plate, china, with gold stars. Israel had brought it home from town one day soon after arriving, a late Christmas gift. Because, he said, he didn't mean for her to be without her china. So that was a start, and she was getting a few more pieces. She set out a cup and saucer of nice Spode for Mr. Slavin, and served, and sat.

She looked at the backs of her hands, smooth and mottled white where they'd been burned, and thought again of the bird in her wagon.

"Did it go out, do you think?"

They thought so, and then saw it there on the windowsill. But the window was stuck, she'd never been able to open it. So they left the bird to sit while they had tea. "The girls are getting butter," she said. "I'm sorry."

But he didn't mind. So she sat and talked to him, about where he'd come from, what he had been doing since then. He'd crossed in '46, and was sick all through last winter and spring, but had made good money since and had his place now. He thought he would go down with the volunteers that summer, under Captain Ingles, to clear the Umpqua Indians. She found that he was only seventeen.

On the windowsill beside them, the bird had eased and blinked a little sleepily. It stretched and ruffled the feathers of its breast, tried a toenail with its beak. Then settled as though listening contentedly.

They talked of cattle and buildings. She had found herself growing so much more attentive to people's stories. There was something about the people here that made them easy to know and like, as though, for all their individual differences, they shared the same rueful secret. It was not so bad despite the rain. Very grand, truly, when the sun came out, and she could squint across the morning to see the great white mountain standing alone so near. With the river going by, and the forests on the hills, and the litter of industry all around: fallen trees bleaching on slopes where the sun had never shone, vines coming back in tangles. It was a fine country, or would be, different from any she had known. But if it was the promised land, it was not because of trees or climate, but because, just getting here, they'd found something new inside themselves.

Then they heard voices below on the river's slope. She leaped up, having forgotten the bread. Through the door, she saw the dog and Daniel coming up the hill, the girls behind, glossy as spring horses with this weather, their baskets full of parcels, their dresses full of spring air. Mary, in new boots, stomped up the path behind them, arms out, crying for all to wait.

Mr. Slavin stayed awhile and went his way. Israel came home late on the tall bay horse he'd bought the month before, and did not seem displeased by the usual commotion of supper, though he was tired. She remembered the bird at the end of the meal, but it must have been long gone.

She sent the children to their rooms with candles and heard them laughing as she put away the dishes, and singing as she put on more wood for the night. They had made a private world in there, hung muslin walls in various places, quarreling over territory.

> *Where will the wedding supper be?*
> *Down by the bog in a willow tree.*

She found them in nightgowns dancing over the beds.

> *What will the wedding supper be?*
> *Two green beans and a black-eyed pea.*

They flashed and laughed and dared each other, not women yet.

It would have been Caroline, of course, supplying much for Emma's reminiscences. But it was Emma's diligence—it must have taken several nights. Lucy had found the pages one day while shaking out the mattress. Six sheets of soft ivory paper, taken from something, bound with string. They had ferried off to school for the day, so she'd stood in the doorway, blushing, and read each line. But found that even children knew which things were best forgotten.

She dressed the little ones for bed and kissed them all, and shut the door behind her.

Then the room was theirs, hers and Israel's, with the log walls in the warm lamplight. She sighed, thinking that she could learn to like a log wall. It had its own interest. But there would be plastered lath and wainscot again soon.

"Did you hear we had a visitor today?" she said. "Two visitors, actually," and she was going to tell him about the bird.

But he was already asleep on the bed, chin sunk to his chest, hands balled into the pockets of the coat he'd worn at supper and forgotten to take off. Or maybe he was cold. His legs seemed slack and long, gangling as a child's. She went and pulled his boots off tenderly, realizing she had never done this. His toenails did not upset her anymore. She pulled the coverlet from the far side of the bed and lapped it over him.

She'd fallen ill one day on the journey, as they'd made their way down the Columbia banks, and been delivered of a boy. But it was much too early, so they were not to have kept him. Israel had made a little grave and had come back to see that she was warm, and kept the children from bothering her, as much as they could be, there not having been much privacy in that freezing wind, or shelter.

She sat by the fire now, while he slept, and thought of this. It was natural, to cry a little, when there was time. It was only sorrow, a necessary release.

After a while, Israel woke and washed himself for bed. She let down her hair at last. She blew out the candles, and changed, and slipped in beside him. They wore each other more easily than they once had. They fit, like old clothes of which little was expected but comfort. Because affection, she had learned, was such a civilized thing, compared to love. It exacted so much less and was therefore more enduring. And endurable.

But when she'd risen again to let out the scratching dog, she crossed her arms and sat a long while in the open doorway, with her feet on the log step, looking out across the river's shine, remembering.

REMAINS

printed Oregon Spectator *8 April 1848*

FORT NEZ PERCES 12 MARCH 1848
TO THE BOARD OF MANAGEMENT

Gentlemen,
In response to American rumours returned to me that the certain deceased lately found near our Fort be the remains of the escaped Mr. Hall, a resident of the Mission said to have perished while attempting to convey westward the tragic news of the events of 29 November, viz: I assert to all concerned that the body be not that of Mr. Hall but of James MacLaren, a Gentleman once of our employ. I furthermore assert that his death were the result of common exposure to cold and in no way caused by hostile acts related to the events of that day 29 Nov. or following. The men of my employ have continued to enjoy the respect of all the Tribes of the Columbia, and I shall lose no opportunity to defend the benefit of these relations.

> I remain, with much respect, Gentlemen
> Your most obe't hum. serv't
>
> W. McBean

PORTLAND, WASHINGTON COUNTY, O.T.

Dear Sister,
I received your letter dated May 29 '52. I have written to the family generally, but did not know until lately where you were nor what you were doing . . .

I was in debt, went to work, paid off my debts and finding Portland to be a flourishing little town, Oregon is the place for me. I took a claim of land two miles and a half from that place where I now live. I would not give it for all the land in Boon County and bind me to live on it. I have a small stock of cattle and hogs, a small barn with a small frame house, sixteen feet square with a pretty wife seventeen years and six months old the twelfth day of this month. Her name is Emma Ruth Ross, a step daughter of Judge Mitchell, a man of considerable note in this country. They were all strangers to me when I came to this country a bachelor. I kept bachelor's hall until I could do better. I am satisfied to live and die here. I would like the best in the world to see you all once more but I can never come back, I reckon, in this world. I came to a new country to make a start with the country so as to grow with it. And if I grow in point of prosperity as fast as the country improves, I will be satisfied.

I have told you all I know to tell. You must write to me and tell me all.

Farewell dear brother and sister, nothing more at present, only I remain
Your affectionate brother until death,

John A. Slavin

The sampler which I possess has been framed. It is coarsely woven linen as if a child had woven it and worked in cross-stitch are the alphabet, numerals, and "Lucy Arnold Sampler, Dec. 10 1821." I also have some Godey's lady's books, the Family Record that was framed and hung on Grandma's sitting room wall. Two or three other objects are stored away. Most of these I rescued from Grandma's woodbox one day when I came home and found she was burning them all up. I think anything of historical value should be given to the Oregon Historical Museum, especially if none of the descendants take an interest in them. So many things are lost by fire and neglect. The record is in rags, an interior decorator stole the colored illustrations from the Lady's Books.

from
Emma Prince McGrew
Granddaughter of Emma Ruth Ross Slavin

AUTHOR'S NOTE

*I*N APRIL 1847, an estimated two thousand people crossed the Missouri River and left the United States for the Oregon Territory. It was the fourth year in which parties of American families had traveled to settle in the Willamette Valley, and the first true year of "Oregon fever." Oregon (a territory that then included the present states of Idaho and Washington) had been jointly held by the United States and Britain until June 1846.

Emma Ruth's account of her crossing at age eleven forms the basis of this narrative; it is in my family's keeping, as are the two letters excerpted on the novel's final page. The oral history of my family has it that Mrs. Mitchell refused to remain with the Whitmans when her stockings were stolen shortly before November 29, and so, by luck or instinct, she saved her husband and family from the consequences of that day's events. Her daughter Emma Ruth is my ancestor.

As accurately as I could, within the artistic demands of a novel, I have recounted the peripheral histories of the Hudson's Bay Company, the 1847 Oregon emigration, the missions and missionaries in the Pacific Northwest, and the Cayuse and Nez Perce people of the Columbia region. Mengarini, Nicholas Point, John McLoughlin, John Work, William and Isabel Craig, Old James, the Spalding and Whitman families, Chief Timothy, William McBean, Nicholas Finlay, Catherine Sager (a child in the attic), and Tiloukaikt are among the many people whose true lives and accounts informed me indispensably. The character of James MacLaren was inspired by the letters and accounts of John McLean, David Thompson, David Douglas, and Richard Leigh. Although I have used recorded names and facts concerning the emigrants of the Mitchells' party, reliable information on most of them was less available. Their characters, as portrayed, range from the speculative to the entirely fictional.

ACKNOWLEDGMENTS

This book has been a journey of years through which I've accumulated countless debts. To all who helped in large ways and in small, I offer my deepest thanks. In particular, to:

My parents, Don and Mary Christensen, for their unwavering faith and support; my uncle, Alan McGrew, who, with my mother, compiled and handed down the facts, reminiscences, and letters of the Ross-Mitchell family;

Carmen O'Hara and Lowell Davis, Susan Bill and Bill Moody, and Meta and Mo Logerfo, who afforded my children countless hours of joy when I could not;

The many writers and readers whose advice and support were invaluable, including: Mara Christensen, Maya Borhani, Lorna Reese, Kai Sanburn, Kim Secunda, Heather June, Lee Cooper, and the fellow members of my local Writers' Guild.

Laurie Parker, my guide, critic, cherished friend.

To Gregg Blomberg, for his living wisdom, I dedicate the chapter entitled "Home."

I thank my agent, Kit Ward, for her enthusiam and wisdom; and thank my editor, Laura Ford—a talented friend and tireless advocate—whose surpassing courage, inspiration, and dedication has so improved my efforts.

Finally, without my children's trust and patience, and my husband's loving and inexhaustible gifts of time and faith, the book would not exist.

About the Author

Karen Fisher has worked as a wrangler, teacher, farmer, and carpenter. She lives with her husband and three children on an island in the Puget Sound.

About the Type

Jenson is one of the earliest print typefaces. After hearing of the invention of printing in 1458, Charles VII of France sent coin engraver Nicolas Jenson to study this new art. Not long after, Jenson started a new career in Venice in letter-founding and printing. In 1471, Jenson was the first to present the form and proportion of this roman font that bears his name.

More than five centuries later, Robert Slimbach, developing fonts for the Adobe Originals program, created Adobe Jenson based on Nicolas Jenson's Venetian Renaissance typeface. It is a dignified font with graceful and balanced strokes.